Praise for The Soul Mark Duology...

"In *The Soul Mark*, J. J. Fischer has created a story that is as beautiful, haunting, compelling, and heart-rending as the world it is set in. I inhaled this epic tale of adventure, treachery, and romance with its themes of justice and mercy that will resonate with readers on a soul-deep level. Highly recommend!"
~ Sara Davison, multi-award-winning author of *The Watcher* and *Driven*

"*The Soul Mark* is an exciting, character-driven journey that is sure to keep you on the edge of your seat. Fischer transports the reader straight into the world of Azazel with immersive description and world building details. This tale is an epic adventure that illustrates the many ways a heart can change—for better or worse—wrapped in a beautiful faith metaphor. I can't wait for the next book!"
~ Ashley Bustamante, author of The Color Theory trilogy

"J. J. Fischer has woven lush prose, vivid settings, and compelling characters into a tale of danger, romance, and faith. While Sela, simultaneously delicate and strong, refuses to forsake those she loves, and Caleb wrestles with the push and pull of justice and mercy, you will find yourself cheering for them as they face the evils and hidden graces in exile. *The Soul Mark* winds through a world both familiar and fantastic to capture my heart and mind. I couldn't put it down!"

~ Cathy McCrumb, author of the Children of the Consortium series

"*The Soul Mark* showcases Fischer's gift of creativity in taking familiar, well-worn truths and painting them in new, beautiful ways that inspire fresh wonder and appreciation. She writes worlds I want to live in, characters I can relate to, and themes I need to hear. Like her other books, *The Soul Mark* captivated me, moved me, and inspired me, and I highly recommend it as a must-read!"

~ Melissa J. Troutman, co-founder of *The Valley* and author of *Trust & Deception*

"In *The Soul Mark*, J. J. Fischer tells a fast-paced and gripping tale of restitution, redemption and love, all set in a fantastical and well-crafted world. Keep watching for more from this amazing author!"

~ Anna Zogg, author of the *Intergalaxia* novels

The Soul Mark Duology

Book One: *The Soul Mark*
Book Two: *Carver of Souls*

CARVER OF SOULS

OF BOOK 2

THE SOUL MARK
DUOLOGY

CARVER OF SOULS

BOOK 2

THE SOUL MARK DUOLOGY

J. J. FISCHER

For Misi, dear friend and brainstorming queen.
I could not have finished this without your help.

And for every man and woman, boy and girl
who has always felt "less."
God considered you valuable enough to die for you.
And because of Jesus, you are enough.

"For God has bound everyone over to disobedience so that he may have mercy on them all." - Romans 11:32 (NIV)

"Mercy triumphs over judgment." - James 2:13 (NIV)

Glossary of Words

Some of the following words and their associated meanings are taken from colonial or old British English. Others are of my own invention.

Ague — Recurring malaria
Ambidexter— A double dealer
Arguefy — Argue
Cheek music — Eloquent talk, but often idle in nature
Chirk — In good spirits; cheerful
Cleverly — In good health
Cramp-words — Difficult or obscure words
Crumpsy — Short tempered or irritable
Dauncy — Noticeably unwell
Eternity box — A coffin
Eye servant — A servant who only attends to their duties when watched
Feeze — Fretful excitement or alarm
Fishy — Drunk
Gallinipper — A large biting mosquito or other insect
Gapeseed — Any astonishing sight
Gut-foundered — Extremely hungry
Jeddarty-jiddarty — Entwined or tangled
King's picture frame — The gallows

Land pirates — Highwaymen; here used to refer to marauders
Lank-sleeve — A one-armed man
Limpsey — Limp and flaccid, usually just before fainting
Mutton-headed — Stupid
Pot valiant — Courage or valiance as a result of drunkenness
Polrumptious — Raucous, rude, or disruptive
Sevenday — A week
Slitherum — A dawdling, slow-moving person
Smug — Well-dressed
Solemncholy — Excessively solemn
Sullens— A bad mood, otherwise known as a fit of the sullens
Swill-belly — A heavy drinker
Unchancy — Potentially dangerous; not safe to meddle with

THE PRISON-ISLAND OF AZAZEL
W N S E
LEGEND
COASTAL PATH
FARMLAND
VOLCANIC DESERT
MILITARY OUTPOST
SETTLEMENT
Wormwood
Lobelia
Anjelica
Mt. Ecila
Uriah's hideout
Pennyroyal
Aconite
Nerium
Tansy
Belladonna
Arnica
Hanging Tree
Fort
Hellebore
Ross' House
Thaddeus' House
MAP NOT TO SCALE
COPYRIGHT J. J. FISCHER 2021

Brief Recap of Book One, The Soul Mark

After being sentenced to death for the accidental killing of a wealthy man in the Old Town, chief city of Eremia, nineteen-year-old Sela Meriweather is stripped of her "soul," branded on her palms with an X-shaped mark (the soul mark), and sentenced to lifetime exile on the prison-island, Azazel. Along with the firstborn children of the "lot," who are randomly chosen to atone for their families' sins, Sela struggles to survive in the hostile and debauched environment. During her search for her older sister Liri, who was taken in the lot six years earlier, she finds unexpected allies in Thaddeus and Briella, siblings with dark pasts who now follow the ways of the Carver of Souls (Eremia's God).

Caleb Alexander, a member of the elite "Righteous" (a priestly, Pharisee-like order), is assured of a promising future if he can endure a year on Azazel as an overseer, ensuring the guards and the "soulless" remain apart. Against all logic and reason (besides it being unlawful), and against the advice of his mentor Lord Auberon, Caleb finds himself drawn to Sela, an innocent and upright woman treated like a criminal. How can this beautiful, courageous girl be "soulless"? As Caleb struggles to understand the Carver's supposed "laws" handed down by the Righteous, he and Sela become friends.

Later, Caleb saves Sela's life and is branded (for touching one of the soulless) and stripped of his soul. Eventually, Sela and Caleb bond with (marry) each other, but they agree their relationship should remain in name only until their past misunderstandings and doubts can be laid to rest.

An ocean away from Azazel, Sela and Liri's older brother, Liron, searches for the son of the king, Prince Magnus Theodorus, who once saved Liron's life, when Liron was a child. The prince also declared he would save Sela and Liri when they were older. Prince Magnus, however, has not been seen in many years and is difficult to find.

Back on Azazel, war is brewing between the vicious land pirates, led by the feared and brutal Uriah Smith, and the soldiers under Lord Auberon's command. Sela discovers that her beloved sister has bonded with Uriah Smith and is treated cruelly. Then Caleb's brother, Tucker, arrives on the island. He is disgusted to learn of Caleb's branding and bonding to Sela, even as it is revealed that Tucker once loved Liri and is the father of two of her children. Tucker blames Sela for Caleb's downfall and strikes a bargain with Lord Auberon to separate Sela from Caleb in exchange for Caleb's restoration to his former position.

The land pirates attack the main settlement of Belladonna, murdering soldiers and burning the fort. Caleb and Sela attempt to escape with Sela's sister Liri and her children, rescuing Tucker from the pirates in the process. Before they can board a ship, however, Uriah Smith comes after them. Unbeknownst to Caleb, Sela sacrifices herself to save Liri and the children. Reinforcements arrive from the Old Town, and the land pirates retreat, with Sela as their prisoner. Caleb attempts to go after Sela, but he is knocked unconscious by his brother.

Carver of Souls opens shortly after these events.

Chapter One

The distant *boom* of cannons from the bay—probably miles away by now—signaled the arrival of Lord Janus Auberon's reinforcements and the resurrection of all Sela's hopes as she fought to regain awareness.

Her right temple throbbed, and the neighboring eye was partly swollen. When she cracked that eyelid, she possessed only half her usual field of vision. Hearing voices close by, she squeezed both eyes shut. She was lying on her side on what felt like a small mountain of scree. The rocks jutted haphazardly into her flesh, even through the men's clothes she wore. Her wrists were bound together, but not so tight as to cut off her circulation, and her ankles were free.

She forced herself to lie still. If she could escape, she might find Caleb.

Caleb. Before Uriah Smith had struck her, she had called for her bondmate and heard his answering reply. He was coming for her!

Then...nothing.

When Uriah overpowered her, she struggled and screamed Caleb's name again and again but was met only with the eerie silence of the thickening fog.

Had something happened to him?

Nay! Caleb's brother had been with him. Tucker Alexander, for all his moral deficiencies, would never let Caleb come to harm. Sela had held Uriah and his men at bay—at least until they knocked her unconscious—but what had happened afterward?

A sudden thought chilled her more than the fog lingering overhead. *What if he left without you?*

Caleb himself answered that charge—the Caleb of her past, who'd held her close the same night Liri had arrived at their cabin with her daughters. *"I'll never leave you. I promise."*

Raised voices penetrated Sela's awareness, and she shoved aside her fears to focus on the exchange of rough words.

"Ye want t' take her t' the secret trove, Cap'n Smith? She'll have t' be blindfolded."

Captain Smith? Despite her dire predicament, Sela laughed inwardly. Having been born on Azazel, Uriah had likely never set foot on a ship in his life, let alone captained one.

"Evidently, Morgan," Uriah replied, coldly polite.

Sela found herself wondering at the obvious rigor of his education, when he had been raised in a den of thieves and murderers. What kind of woman had his mother been?

"Why bother?" declared another. His words sidled up against each other as if the speaker were fishy. "The girl won't be returning to Belladonna alive."

Icy fingers crawled inside the cavity of Sela's chest and she held her breath. They meant to kill her?

"Ever the pot-valiant soldier, Price," Uriah returned, and his men snickered. "The girl's fate is mine to decide, and mine alone." His voice acquired a flinty edge. "My rules apply to this girl as much as they did to the last. Any man who touches her will find his life forfeit. You all remember what happened to Jones."

A rumble of discontented murmurs filled the gaping silence left by Uriah's pronouncement. Then the tension heightened, as if a collective noose slowly cut off the men's air.

Hot breath fanned against her cheek, shooting a bolt of electricity through her body. She hadn't even registered footsteps nearby.

"I know you're awake, Sela." Before she could move, a pair of thick hands encircled her waist and dragged her to her feet, and she found herself facing the pirate's throat. Though she was taller than most men, Uriah towered over her by several inches. He smiled, his branded cheek and twin dimples warring for prominence in a face that most women would consider exceptionally handsome.

Sela was not most women.

She jerked her chin upward, avoiding the red fox tail encircling his neck like a scarf. Tears stung her eyes at the memory of her beloved pet fox, Roux. "Where are my friends?" she snapped. "Where is Caleb?"

Uriah's smile did not waver. "You know, I asked myself much the same thing. I thought your bondmate, at least, would try to save you from me. Even though your brother-in-law and sister fled like cowards."

She squared her shoulders and steeled her spine. "You're lying. Where's Caleb?"

"What reason would I have to lie?" His mouth softened in faux sympathy. "I never saw your bondmate." He turned. "Did we, men?"

"Nay," slurred Price. He batted at a blood-sucking gallinipper that perched on his forearm, and the men laughed. At least half a dozen land pirates had gathered around. The looks they gave Sela made her want to run for the hills.

She took advantage of a distant cannon *boom* to make a quick study of her surroundings. Though darkness had almost completely fallen, she could see they had passed through the first cluster of mountains that separated Belladonna and its sheltered bay from the rest of the island. More mountainous terrain lay beyond, densely forested and shrouded in fog, along with several waterfalls, judging by the distant roar of water.

Despite the cloying humidity, she shivered. If Uriah's men took her beyond the mountains, there would be no path for Caleb to follow. Was Uriah right? Would even the Carver decline to accompany her into the wilderness at the heart of Azazel?

A groan several paces away, followed by another round of chuckles, dragged her sharply back to the present. "Ross!" she exclaimed, watching the battered man struggle into a sitting position.

His wrists were bound even more tightly than hers, judging by the purple hue of his hands. He bled from the shoulder and the side of his thigh. She stumbled toward him, only to be jerked back by a hand circling her bicep.

"You don't seem afraid, Sela." Uriah's voice came from behind her. Spinning, she found herself nearly in his arms. "Could it be that you don't yet grasp the direness of your present situation?"

"Caleb will come for me," she declared, but her voice cracked midway through the sentence. Whether from lack of confidence or scarcity of water, she did not dare to investigate further.

Uriah stepped so close to her that Roux's tail brushed against her cheek—no, it *couldn't* be Roux—and Sela's stomach churned. His hand curled around her jaw, bearing the coppery scent of blood and the acrid tang of gunpowder. He smiled at the fear she'd attempted to hide from him. "No man knows where we're going, pretty Sela, save those who ride with us."

She reared her head back and spat in his face. Then she tensed and closed her eyes, expecting a blow or a stinging slap. When she opened them again, Uriah had not even wiped her spittle from his cheek. Instead, he was studying Ross with a sober expression.

"To imagine," he murmured, "that young Thomas will become a man without the pleasant recollection of either of his parents' faces."

Though she knew his foul purpose in raising the topic, Sela resisted a tug of despair. "Ross's wounds are not mortal. Let me tend him before he loses too much blood."

The despot did not appear to have heard her. "Still, *I* succeeded without a father. So will young Thomas, should he survive his perilous sea journey."

"Nay," Sela insisted. "Let me help him. Please."

Uriah looked at her, a speculative gleam in the depths of his eyes that did nothing to dislodge the darkness that lingered within. Finally, his lips curved. Reaching for a hank of her hair, he wiped her saliva from his cheek and returned the dark locks to her shoulder. "As you wish." He extracted a dagger from his boot and sliced through her bonds.

She flexed her hands, willing feeling to replace numbness. When she turned, Uriah's hand slid to her waist. Even through the men's clothes and her stays, she felt the heat of his touch, hotter than any brand, and far more searing.

"You cannot escape the island, Sela," he whispered into her ear. "No one ever escapes Azazel. You were a fool to try it."

Jerking away from his grip, she ignored the warning and hurried over to Ross.

"I'll always come back for you," Caleb had said right before they left for the docks, where everything had gone wrong.

As she crouched beside Ross, Sela felt the looming presence of Uriah at her back, overseeing her every movement. She wondered if any man would dare to tread in the shadow of the most powerful man on Azazel.

Please, my love...come quickly.

"You're bleeding," Ross said the moment he regained consciousness. His eyes roved over Sela's face, where she leaned against the cavern wall beside him. Thunder rumbled in the distance, rendering his announcement faintly ominous.

"'Tis not *my* blood." She jerked away from the hand he extended to touch her cheek, even though doing so invited moisture from the cavern walls to drip down her back. "'Tis *yours.*"

Ross glanced down at the wounds she'd bandaged after he had fainted, and she suppressed a flicker of pride that the fabric seemed to be holding its own without any seepage—for now, at least. His gaze quickly returned to her. "Where did you get the dress?"

With one hand gliding over the scarlet satin, she waved the other to indicate the dimly lit cavern around them. It now crawled with more than a dozen land pirates in varying states of sobriety. "This is apparently one of Uriah's treasure troves, although being a former member of his gang, Ross, you likely know that already. Several of the chests are stuffed with clothing, which you can thank for your makeshift bandages. As for this dress"—her attempt at a pleasant tone soured—"Uriah suggested I abandon my men's clothing for something more...feminine."

With a smirk, Uriah had suggested she abandon more than just her men's clothing, but she would not disclose that to Ross. After one of the pirate's minions had pushed the gaudy, shamefully immodest gown at her, she'd tossed it back in his face, only to catch the warning on Uriah's face when he sent a meaningful look in Ross's direction. Seething, she grabbed the dress and sought the privacy of the deepest recesses of the shadowed cavern, surprised but grateful that none of them followed her.

However, she had understood Uriah's glance at Ross. If she tried to escape, Thomas's father was a dead man. Was that why Uriah kept him among the living? So long as Ross breathed, Sela would be a slave to the pirate's mandates.

Ross studied her carefully, appearing miffed by her unveiled reference to his former career. "I became a different man, you know. After Bess."

She eyed his bound wrists and ankles, hating that they shackled her as much as they did him. "You followed Uriah even after you bonded with Bess."

Was that shame in his eyes? "Aye, I did. I was afraid of what Smith would do to me if he knew I was an ambidexter."

Remembering his near-lynching and Bess's murder, Sela softened. "You were right to fear his retribution."

Ross glanced at the cavern's entrance, where Uriah's broad frame stood silhouetted against a darkened sky. "In the beginning, I thought that if the worst happened to me, Bess would be safe, given that Smith wanted her. I only feared for myself." His voice grew thick with emotion. "I should have known my past would catch up with us both." His gaze slid to her. "I am sorry I could not keep you from him."

She fidgeted with the lacy cuffs of the scarlet gown, grateful that Uriah had allowed her to keep her boots, instead of the jeweled slippers that had been stashed with the dress. Practicality and depravity seemed to reside in the pirate in equal measure.

"Back at the docks," Sela ventured, "did you see Caleb?"

His mouth twisted ruefully. "I heard you call out for him. I also heard Alexander answer that he was coming. But after that, I never saw him."

"Could he and Tucker have been set upon by Uriah?"

Ross shook his head. "Smith and his men fled as soon as they heard the cannons. I was conscious when they dragged me away. I would have noticed an attack on the ship."

"Caleb would never have abandoned me."

"Nay, he wouldn't." Ross frowned. "Though he may not have had a choice."

"Could Tucker—" She bit off the disturbing thought. Surely not even an acolyte of the Righteous would be so cold.

"Aye," Ross replied with chilling certainty. "He could have."

"Take Liri and go!" she had yelled at Tucker.

He'd barely hesitated before obeying. Had Tucker convinced Caleb to abandon Sela so they could save Liri and her daughters? Aye, Sela would have urged him to, should Caleb have had to choose between Sela and her sister. Perhaps Caleb had seen Sela captured and knew that confronting Uriah Smith was impossible.

But to not even *try* to save her?

Sela shook the accusation away as surely as she ignored the aching in her head. Caleb Alexander was a clever, strong, and resourceful man. Although he was no longer a member of the Righteous, he was well-respected and still had allies among the soldiers. Before the day was ended, her bondmate would come for her, Uriah or nay.

She only had to trust him, as Caleb trusted the Carver.

"You said earlier that you saw my son with Miss Briella," Ross broke into her musings. "Did he look cleverly, Sela?"

She nodded. "Briella will keep him safe."

A deep furrow appeared between Ross's dark brows. "Providing Lord Auberon's reinforcements didn't overtake their ship."

Sela could say nothing to that, so she shrugged in reply. "What's wrong with Uriah?" She frowned, observing the unmistakable tension in their captor's shoulders. "He hasn't stopped watching the sky since we sought shelter from the storm."

Ross's gaze followed her own and he lowered his voice to a whisper. "Smith is deeply superstitious. He fears being caught out in the open."

"Because of the lightning?"

He turned to her, his eyes alight with a strange glow. "Aye. Here on Azazel, lightning is said to represent the Carver's judgment."

Sela returned her attention to the pirate, who had begun to pace. "I thought he believed that the Carver wouldn't find him here on Azazel." She remembered his appraising look when she returned from donning the low-necked scarlet gown. Caged as he was, might he set upon her, even here? He had given orders that no man harm her, or Ross, so long as she cooperated.

Sela could not suppress a rising dread that every "kindness" he extended to them would soon need to be repaid in full. She recalled his words about Roux. *He'll keep me warm for the remainder of the winter. As will you, Sela.*

As if he understood the disturbing direction of her thoughts, Ross's blood-streaked hand reached out and found hers. She flinched and pulled away.

His brown eyes grew troubled. "Where Smith is taking us, no one will be able to follow. But so long as the storm rages, we are safe. Perhaps your Caleb will find us before then."

Unhappily, any respite she and Ross might have enjoyed was short-lived. Once the storm had passed, drenching the earth with an impossible amount of moisture in the space of a few short hours, they set out. Sela stumbled on the slippery mountain path as the hem of her ridiculous dress grew heavier with every passing hour. It was worse for Ross, who suffered pain in addition to his other miseries, as well as for the few pirates who'd sustained injuries in the altercation with the settlement inhabitants and were now re-entering a state of unwelcome sobriety.

Through eavesdropping, Sela learned that the pirates had conceded Belladonna to the soldiers shortly after Lord Auberon's reinforcements arrived from the Old Town, though not before they'd plundered the settlement for its treasures and made captives of dozens. The bulk of those prisoners were already headed for Uriah's hideout beyond the heart of Azazel, barely delayed by the storm that had kept Uriah, the rest of his men, and his two captives holed up in a cavern until it passed.

She had wondered what had prevented Uriah from attacking the settlement earlier in the season, given the size and strength of his small army. Now she knew. He could not abide the storms.

Two days passed without any sign of Caleb, agonizingly slow days, with nothing but long hours wading through mud and cleaning Ross's wounds to keep her from despair. The mountains gradually leveled out, the emerald green of tangled, claustrophobic jungle replaced by a vast stretch of pitted, rocky land stretching for as far as the eye could see.

"A volcanic desert," Ross said when they stopped to rest at the rim of the expanse. "Since 'tis leeward of the mountains, 'tis drier here than the rest of the island."

"You've been here before?"

"Aye."

Sela bit her lip, gazing around the wilderness of gravel, sand, volcanic ash, and the remnants of dried lava from long-ago eruptions. Was this barren desert the only thing that occupied the center of Azazel? If Caleb and the others were in pursuit, this expanse would be easier to traverse compared to the jungle-crusted slopes of the muddy mountain passes. However, the lack of shelter and vegetation also meant that Uriah and his men could easily see them approaching.

"You're not still imagining that he is coming for you, are you?"

She jumped at Uriah's voice beside her. The man moved with the stealth of a fox, but she would not compare him to her beloved Roux.

Turning, she squared her shoulders. Uriah Smith—her brother-in-law, she realized with distaste—was a coward at heart. She would not be intimidated as Liri had been. "Only a man who has never known love mocks the one who possesses it."

"Love?" He circled her, his brow creased in a combination of incredulity and mockery. "You give men far too much credit, pretty Sela. The connection between my kind and yours is a mere business of the flesh. Only a fool fancies himself in love." Some of his meaning seemed directed at the man standing behind her, and she noticed Ross's growl.

Sela lifted her chin. "Caleb is not like other men."

Uriah's gaze drifted down her frame, and he stepped closer, gripping her upper arms. When she squirmed, sudden realization dawned on his face. "Nay, 'twould appear not." He stroked her satiny sleeve. "He hasn't touched you, has he?"

When she scowled, he chuckled. "Perhaps you're right, little Sela, that your Caleb is not like other men. Perhaps he is not a man at all."

With a growl of her own, Sela lunged at Uriah, her hands reaching for the pirate's throat. But fury made her careless. The pirate twisted her around, her back against his chest and his knife at her throat.

Ross stepped forward and was instantly surrounded.

"I warned you not to be foolish." Uriah stroked her skin with the tip of the blade. "One misstep, and you lose more blood than your own."

Seeing the fear in Ross's eyes, Sela forced her muscles to relax.

Uriah tittered approvingly. He spun her around to face him, expelling a lengthy sigh while he sheathed his knife. "Better. Ah, my dear, those fine eyes see clear to a man's soul. Caleb Alexander is no fool to seek such jewels, though he unfortunately proved incapable of keeping them within his possession."

Laughter rippled throughout the watching pirates.

"Love is not possession."

Uriah nodded. "Perhaps not." Taking a length of rope from his belt, he tied Sela's wrists behind her back. When she struggled, he tightened the rope until the tips of her fingers lost their feeling. He bent close to her ear. "But I'm sure we can both agree on what constitutes a *lack* of love."

She glared at him as he retrieved a strip of black fabric from one of his pockets. "And what is that?" she demanded.

Uriah shrugged and looked around. His glance encompassed their surroundings before returning to her. "I would have thought 'twas obvious."

The fabric enveloped Sela's field of vision, and she understood. *Abandonment.*

With the absence of light, Sela had only her remaining senses to lead her. That, and the pirate whose somewhat erratic guidance threatened to cause her a wrenched ankle.

She endured barely a day of the volcanic desert, followed by a return to humidity that pressed so close it seemed to fester against her skin. Worse, the ground was slick from the recent rainfall. Judging by the weight of her gown, she guessed that the bottom eight inches, at least, were covered in mud. Her hair had long since escaped its braid to hang limply around her shoulders. The heel of one boot was missing, resulting in a limp and a fresh array of blisters.

On the morning of the fourth day, she heard the distant rush of water and the squawks of several large birds and realized they were climbing. Ross exclaimed several times when he stumbled, and a low moan of pain indicated he was struggling. Was he as tired of sleeping on the hard ground as she was? Though what awaited them next would surely be worse. She wondered if he realized that his fate was now bound to hers.

The rushing sound of a nearby waterfall swelled to a roar. The pirate steering her brought Sela to an abrupt stop, and her boots sank into sand. Uriah barked several orders to his men, unintelligible over the din. The next moment, she was lifted into the air and set down on a wooden bench that swayed to and fro. *A boat.* Someone's broad shoulders jutted into hers.

"Is that you, Sela?" Ross gripped her cold fingers behind her back.

"Aye." She squeezed his hand once then let it go, trying not to lean into him as the boat dipped with the weight of additional passengers. The next moment, the boat lurched forward, and the noise grew deafening. The waterfall's spray soaked her hair and the bodice of her gown. Then cold water rushed over her like a wave, drenching her as they glided under the bulk of the waterfall.

Ross spluttered and coughed.

A pirate chuckled. "That were refreshing, weren't it?"

"Yer lucky we didn't make ye swim," another added. A third man snorted in laughter.

The light suddenly dimmed, even through her blindfold. Were they in some kind of cavern? After several minutes of paddling, the boat bumped to a halt as if it had encountered rock, and the fragile craft bobbed while several men disembarked. Ross's protests were interrupted by several cuss words as he was manhandled out of the boat.

"Get off me!" he snarled, and she thought he twisted away from his captors. His foot connected with Sela's ankle. The boat tipped precariously.

"Careful, Ross!" Sela edged nearer the center of the bench to distribute their weight more evenly. Too late. Ross's momentum carried them both over the side of the boat and into the water.

The weight of his body forced Sela downward. He kicked out with his legs. One of his boots caught her in the abdomen, costing her the breath she had snatched before hitting the water. Winded, she fought her way back to the surface, but she had ever been an average swimmer, and the shoes and satin gown had become a dead weight. She pulled at the ropes binding her wrists, but neither they nor the blindfold would budge. Which way was up?

Was this what it felt like to drown? Already, her lungs were burning, clawing for air beneath her overly tight stays, her legs barely resisting the crushing heaviness of her gown and petticoats. She could no longer feel Ross's thrashing above her. Would the land pirates let them both die?

Caleb had saved her from her last encounter with the treachery of water. This time, though, she was on her own. Was this the reality of the branding, the utter forsakenness the priesthood and the Righteous spoke about so often? Perhaps the Carver truly saw naught beyond the soul mark, like Caleb had in the beginning.

Like he had at the end.

The very moment Sela's consciousness began to fade, strong hands gripped her shoulders and wrenched upward. Her head broke the surface and she hauled in a sharp breath so quickly that she sucked in more water and descended into a coughing fit. Unseen hands dragged her from the water and deposited her on a rocky shore to flail around like a beached seal.

Someone jerked the blindfold from her eyes and peered into her face. Sela blinked away liquid and tried to focus, seeing another gasping form not far away. *Ross.*

The smudge of color leaned over and reached for the hands tied behind her back, uttering a low cry of dismay. "She almost drowned," came a woman's voice. "Why was she bound so cruelly?" When Sela continued to splutter, the woman reached out and cut her bonds.

A shadow loomed over them. "Quit yer fussin', Elsie. She's fine now."

"*Morgan.* I should have known you were at the center of this. How old is this one? Eighteen? When my brother hears about—"

A sickening laugh from the man cut her off. It was the same pirate who'd first suggested Sela be blindfolded. "'Twas yer brother what ordered 'er captivity, Miss Elsie. This one'll be 'is personal guest."

Sela blinked a second time, and the woman's features came into focus. The first thing Sela registered was an apologetic smile, followed by youthful features that were so like Uriah's she knew she was looking at his sister.

She shrank back. *Elsie?* Was this the woman who had helped Liri escape? Near Briella's age, she was taller than Sela and square-shouldered. She possessed both the beauty and oddly aristocratic bearing of her brother. Did she also have his streak of cruelty?

"Anyhow, I'm gut-foundered. I'm off t' find me some good food an' better company." The pirate, Morgan, winked at Elsie and sauntered away.

"I'm sorry about that," Elsie said beneath her breath. She helped Sela into a sitting position. "Are you well, Miss..." Her voice trailed off, clearly fishing for a name.

Sela didn't answer. She watched two pirates drag Ross, who was still blindfolded, toward a narrow slit in the rock. Having tossed up his accounts, he seemed preoccupied with his own well-being for the present moment and made no effort to inquire after hers. Her gaze drifted past Ross and the woman and fixed on the expansive cavern.

The height of a two-story house or higher, the cavern was lit with dozens of torches, which illuminated vast walls of glittering, reddish-brown rock, the colors all but dancing on the surface of the water. Enormous stone towers reached nearly to the ceiling, look-ing as if giants had carelessly dribbled them from above, though the vast ceiling surely had no need of their support. Now that she was out of the water, Sela saw that it gleamed blue-green, much like the sea surrounding Azazel.

A natural rock jetty ran the length of the river—or pool—that disappeared from sight around a column of rock, likely leading to the waterfall from earlier. The rocky platform was large enough to hold at least two dozen men, although only Uriah's sister and a couple of pirates lingered there now. Despite her fear, Sela had never seen anything so beautiful in her life.

"What's your name, miss?"

Sela looked up and found the woman's eyes on her—curious, assessing, and yet strangely sad. "Sela Ale—Meriweather."

Perhaps it was better to forget that Caleb Alexander had ever offered her another name than the one she'd brought with her from the Old Town.

It was the woman's turn to blink. "Meriweather?"

"Aye. I believe you knew my sister?"

Elsie nodded. "Is Liri well?" Her voice dropped to the whisper Liri often used when she was afraid.

"I think so. Like you, I tried to help her escape."

Another brisk nod, which betrayed more guilt than pride. "Liri could not stay here any longer. Not with the children at risk." Her shoulders stiffened, and she glanced down at Sela's tattooed band. "Where is your bondmate, Miss Sela?"

Sela shrugged. "I don't know for certain. I think he's with Liri and his brother, Tucker."

Elsie stilled. "Tucker? Tucker Alexander?"

"You know him?"

"I know *of* him." Her pretty mouth hardened.

It appeared they both harbored ill will toward Caleb's brother.

Elsie extended her workworn hand to Sela, but at that moment, she seemed to catch sight of something behind her. Her grip faltered, and Sela heard the silky splash of oars. Elsie quickly withdrew her hand and stood. Was it only the unusual light of the cavern, or had she paled?

"Elsie," came a sugared voice as Uriah stepped ashore. "Are you greeting my guest?" He eyed Sela's sodden dress, severed bonds, and the abandoned blindfold, as well as the puddle of water in the bottom of the boat that had upended them.

The defiance wilted in Elsie Smith as surely as if she were a plucked dandelion left out in the scorching, tropical sun. Though she smiled at her brother as he approached, the corners of her mouth trembled.

"I've missed you, Elsie," Uriah said, his eyes piercing as they returned to study his sister's face. "'Twas good of you to come and greet us."

"The rest of your men arrived yesterday." She paused, clearly frightened. "I feared something had happened to you."

"We were"—Uriah's lips twitched—"unavoidably delayed."

"Uriah's sister, Elsie, is kind to me, as kind as Uriah is brutal. She and some others helped me leave while Uriah was unconscious. Though when he wakes in the morning..."

Sela rose, trying unsuccessfully to catch Elsie's attention. Had the woman suffered for helping Liri? There were no bruises or marks on Elsie's face, but that did not mean Uriah had not unleashed his anger on her, sister or nay.

"I see you have met my guest, Sela Alexander. I trust you'll make her feel welcome. Our home is her home."

"Of course, Uriah." The woman responded as readily as a trained puppy, though she lacked a dog's fervor. Her shoulders drooped.

Uriah reached for Sela's arm and steered her toward the crevice where Ross had disappeared. It turned out to be a narrow tunnel that swerved and dipped several times before they entered a second cavern, at least six times the size of the first. Bile surged into her throat.

"'Tis said they live like kings, in defiance of Eremia, and that they have a vast cave beneath a mighty waterfall, full of all their treasures..."

Esther's description of the pirates' hideout was not so far from the truth, except that Sela's friend hadn't known of the horrors lurking among the opulence. Suspended from every wall hung dozens of gibbets, each one housing skeletons in various stages of decay, the ragged edges of their clothing as garish as Sela's gown in the torchlight. The grim display presided over a cavern that appeared more like a king's hall than a hideout. An enormous throne, lined with velvet, sat at the far end, much like the ornate chair that supported the high priest back in the Old Town.

Dozens of heavy chests crowded the space, some of them over-flowing with various goods or treasures. Most boasted heavy locks, with a narrow aisle cleared between the chests so that one might approach the throne unobstructed. A sagging bookshelf along one wall of the cavern housed hundreds of dusty books, while a long table ran the length of the opposite wall, crowned with a scarlet runner and heavy gold candelabras spaced at irregular intervals.

At least fifty of Uriah's men swarmed the space—bottles or casks in hand, their weapons and clothes as ornate and garish as the cavern itself—and almost as many women. A mixture of fear and resignation occupied the mostly youthful faces, reminding her of Liri, who had lived here for six years.

Sweat slicked Sela's palms, and her heartbeat faltered. Was this the heart of Azazel? How had her sister survived such a place? And after knowing the love of a man like Caleb, how could *she*?

"Welcome to my kingdom." Uriah dragged Sela forward, beaming like a madman.

Cheers broke out among the watching men, followed by whistles and lewd comments that made Sela's ears burn.

Twisting around, she stole a glance at Elsie, who hung back, her expression blank. Seeing Sela's pointed look toward the underground river tunnel, the woman gave a slow, decisive shake of her head, followed by a sad smile.

Sela understood. There would be no escape this time.

Chapter Two

Caleb Alexander slowly retracted his fingers into a fist until his branded palm all but disappeared.

Did the Carver have mercy on men who murdered their treacherous brothers?

When the mental image of his brother, strung up by a noose and drawn and quartered, failed to satisfy him, Caleb leaned against the ship's rail. He turned his face to the wind that had finally picked up, hoping it would soothe the desperate ache in his chest.

Three days. Three entire *days* he had been unconscious, and the unspeakable headache he had woken to had rendered him inert and disoriented for at least a day more. His brother had pistol-whipped him so hard on the back of his head that the blow might have killed him. Judging by the guilt that stained Tucker's face when Caleb finally regained his senses, he knew his brother had feared the same.

Liri had tended the knot on his head, along with the bruises and scrapes on his face. Tucker, his right hand tightly bandaged, was quick to announce that he'd kept his own vigil.

His memory foggy, Caleb's attention had been seized by the trepidation on Liri's face. He sat up, stiff and sore after four days of lying in bed.

"What is it?" he asked, reaching for her hand. He searched the bed for the imprint that would indicate his bondmate slept beside him. "Are you well? Is Sela—"

Then he'd remembered. Oh, merciful Carver, he remembered everything!

Tucker, kneeling beside Caleb's bed to steady him, shrank back, and for good reason.

Caleb shot out a hand and grabbed Tucker by the throat with his ungloved hands. "I should kill you for what you've done." With a roar, he tackled his brother, pinning him against the bed. Heedless of Liri's whimpers, he planted a knee in Tucker's chest.

Tucker gasped against the fingers strangling him. He struggled as the lack of oxygen clearly began to blacken the edges of his world. "'Twas—for—your own—good."

"My *good*?" Caleb shouted. Across the room, Liri was cringing against the cabin wall. "You betrayed her! You betrayed *me*!"

"Sela—wanted—us to—escape. She fought Smith—so her sister—and you—could get away. She sacrificed—herself—for *us*."

His fingers curled around Tucker's throat, cinching tighter until his brother could no longer speak. In that moment, Caleb had understood how easy it would be to murder.

Sela, an accidental murderess, had surely never felt such blind, searing, all-consuming anger. It was like a surge of lava that swept down the side of a volcano, annihilating everything in its path and quickly hardening to black. If not for the sudden wave of dizziness that swirled through Caleb's head, which loosened his grip and sent him toppling to the floor, he might have killed his brother.

Tucker crouched over him, propping a rolled-up coat beneath his head.

Caleb fought to remain conscious. He tried to shove his brother away, but Tucker lingered.

"As for *my* actions, I did it for you," Tucker whispered as bright spots danced feverishly in Caleb's vision. "So you'd be free."

I was free.

Caleb had awakened hours later to an empty cabin. When he pulled on a clean shirt and struggled outside, he was greeted by a grim-faced Hiram Foley. Spying his brother standing at the rail,

Caleb pushed past the former captain of the *Deliverance*, only to have his arm seized in a grip as strong as a constrictor snake's.

"*Think*, Alexander," murmured the grizzled man. "Brother or nay, he's one of the Righteous. If you kill him, you'll answer to Lord Auberon. It will likely cost you your life."

"I don't care," Caleb growled. "He's a blackguard and a wretch. His cowardice has sent Sela to her death."

"That may be, but if your bondmate still lives, you're no good to her dead. Why don't you use that fine mind of yours for something besides plotting revenge? Don't you know where we are? We could use another pair of hands, once your head has settled down."

Foley's words penetrated the haze in Caleb's brain. "What do you mean, *where we are?*"

The sloop's captain had told him everything that had happened since he lost consciousness, beginning with their departure from Belladonna.

Soon after departing, Tucker had drawn his flintlock pistol and ordered Foley and his men to make for the nearest mainland port. Foley and the other sailors would have fought back, but for the fact that Tucker had tossed their cache of weapons over the side. Grudgingly, they'd handed over the rest. Shortly after that, the ship had run into a storm and been driven south of Azazel. Worse, there had been no sightings of Thaddeus's ship.

"We are days of good wind away from Azazel by now," Foley had concluded with a bitter twist of his mouth. "And there's no wind to be had."

He was right. The sails had hung limp for a full three days, until their time at sea stretched to almost a sevenday. Unable to trust himself with the sight of his wretched brother, Caleb kept to his tiny cabin in the single-masted sloop.

Tucker wisely stayed away.

Deprived of vengeance, Caleb spent his time tearing the beds of his fingernails to shreds. How could he feel so desperate to return to the one place he had been so happy to leave behind?

On the seventh day, the wind had returned.

After helping with the sails, Caleb now stood at the rail, harboring murderous thoughts and willing Azazel's coastline to materialize from the unending, dazzling blue. His jaw boasted a sevenday's growth of beard that rendered him a vastly different—and far more unchancy—man.

That morning, he'd caught a glimpse of his reflection and hastily scraped his tangled hair back into its customary queue. He wondered at the wild man who had replaced the white-coated, spotlessly groomed second-in-command to Lord Auberon. The acolyte-lieutenant whose biggest worries until now had related to the ofttimes indeterminate extracts from the Book of Souls.

Carver, are you here?

Not just his heart, but his very soul ached. After everything Sela had endured—after everything that had kept them apart all these months—how could the Carver allow this? Was it not enough that Liri had been the slave of the wicked Uriah Smith for six years?

Caleb had no doubt that Smith had captured Sela to taunt her, the bondmate who had run from him. To taunt Caleb too, who loved Sela more than he'd loved anything the Carver had given him.

She's been gone a sevenday as Smith's captive.

Caleb cringed. He knew what fate awaited her. Aye, he knew, and it had kept him from his sleep since he'd regained consciousness. The barest contemplation of what she must be suffering made his fingers itch for Tucker's throat all over again, though he had never before thought himself a violent man. He recalled the circlet of bruises above Tucker's collar that signaled the business of Caleb's vengeance was yet unfinished. Beginning to shake, he returned to his cabin.

The sound of a woman's soft weeping from within prompted him to close the door gently behind him, rather than slamming it as he wished to. Liri sat perched on the edge of the bed he'd left unmade, her eyes rubbed red and raw, and her cheeks streaked with tears.

Caleb fought the urge to turn and run. He had no use for her tears. He had enough of his own.

"I came to apologize, Caleb."

Reluctantly, he sat down beside her, the thin mattress dipping beneath his weight. Instead of looking at him, Liri bowed her head and plunged restless hands into her blond hair. This habit no doubt was responsible for the snarls that surrounded her pale face.

"I should have fought harder." She planted a clenched fist in the mattress beside her, as if to stabilize herself. "I should have scratched out his eyes and torn out his hair. I should have slit his throat in the middle of the night."

Did Liri speak of Uriah or Tucker? Caleb imagined—and hoped—she meant both. "You had your children to think of."

She scrunched her eyes closed but looked helpless to prevent the rolling descent of another tear. "The girls have barely left our cabin all these days, not even when the sun returned. Anwen is old enough to understand what happened. But even little Sela knows—" She broke off and looked at him, absorbing his rigid posture and clenched jaw. "I am sorry. I have kept her confined, knowing she would remind you..." She paused.

...of your bondmate, Caleb finished silently.

Liri's younger daughter was a perfect replica of Sela, down to the girl's stunning violet eyes and raven-black hair. Of course she would remind him of what he'd lost.

He turned away. "Please don't sequester them for my sake. I will manage." His branded hands curled into fists. "In a few days, we'll be back on Azazel. I won't rest until Sela is found."

"I know you won't." Liri's tears dripped onto the collar of her faded dress. "I'll help you in any way I can, since 'twas my fault she was taken."

Unable to prevent the growl that rose in his throat, he twisted to face her. "None of this is your fault, Liri."

"You say that, but I know better. Barely five months after our Binding, Uriah discovered that our twins were not his own. Though I insisted they were born prematurely, he had only to look at them to know the truth. I had already discovered his crueler side, but this changed things between us even more. He became darker, more tormented. Uriah swore revenge for what he saw as my betrayal. If he knew 'twas Tucker who fathered Anwen and little Liron..." She shrugged helplessly. "He surely knows already. And Sela is his way of taking vengeance."

Caleb shook his head. "If he wanted to punish you, he wouldn't have let you and Tucker go free, along with his own daughter." He swallowed, unable to say his niece's name. *Sela.*

"Don't try to absolve me, Caleb. 'Twas only because of Sela's interference that he let us go free. And afterward? I carry the blame for that, as well. I saw Tucker preparing to strike you. I didn't scream loud enough to warn you. If I had, you would have known his intentions. And Sela would still be—" Liri broke off and scrubbed at a fleck of dirt on her dress. "Once you were unconscious, I couldn't move. 'Twas like I was frozen to the ground. By the time I freed myself from the paralysis, 'twas too late. Nothing I said or did convinced Tucker to go after her."

When Caleb made no reply, she gnawed at her lip.

"I could have done something, you know. I could have sabotaged the ship so we were forced to turn around. I could have stolen or made myself a weapon. Sela would have done that. But I was so afraid. For years, I survived by doing nothing that would attract Uriah's attention. Then the one time Sela needed me to act to save her, I did nothing." She dissolved into tears.

Caleb felt Liri's failures as his own. Traitorous brother or nay, what kind of man foolishly turned his back on his enemy as he had done? Or unwittingly gave his bondmate into his enemy's keeping?

"Perhaps Azazel will be the making of him." Caleb had said those words to Sela right before Tucker had delivered her to the devil himself.

Though Caleb blamed the Carver in part, he reserved the bulk of the blame for himself. Since arriving on Azazel, Sela had faced every challenge with courage and determination, however reckless her decisions were at times. At first glance, she had known what sort of man Tucker was, while Caleb insisted there was a clear avenue for his brother's redemption.

I have been so blind!

At the first sign of trouble, Caleb had proven to be what he truly was—a naïve, good-for-nothing, disappointment of a man. He'd failed to protect the woman whose well-being had been entrusted to him. Now, he could not bring himself to comfort his sister-in-law, who was drowning in her guilt.

If you give Sela back to me, Carver, I swear I'll never let her out of my sight again.

Liri's soft cries were his only answer.

"The fault is mine, and mine alone," Caleb spoke at last. He rested his elbows on his knees, adopting Liri's nervous habit of thrusting fingers through hair that was hopelessly tangled and caked with salt. Where was the scholar who had never once wavered from his path? "We will find her, Liri. I promise."

She faced him, and Caleb fought a wave of despair at the emptiness behind her tears. "I chose a life with Uriah, Caleb. I based our union on lies, so I have only myself to blame for six years of misery. But Sela was taken against her will, an innocent. I know what he'll do to her to spite us both. What kind of woman could survive all that and remain the sister I knew? The bondmate you loved? Aye, you might retrieve her body. But I fear for her soul."

Before he could reply, Liri scrambled to her feet and fled the cabin.

Coward as he was, Caleb could not bear to go after her. *Do you truly see all, Carver? Is this Your will, or have You turned a blind eye to our pain?*

When no response was forthcoming, Caleb closed his eyes and gave in to his grief.

"You must not show him fear," Elsie said once the two women were alone. "Uriah delights in it. Feeds off it. The Carver knows, he needs it more than air."

Clasping her arms across her chest, Sela shivered in the tiny room that served as Elsie's bedroom. Unlike the rest of the tunnels and caverns she'd seen, it was clean and well-kept. What made this woman linger here when she was so clearly cut from a different cloth than her brother?

While Uriah and his men drank to his victories—never mind that they had been forced to retreat after the reinforcements arrived from the Old Town—Elsie ushered Sela to her bedroom, where she gave her dry underclothes in exchange for her sodden ones. She exclaimed over the welts from the rope that had cut into Sela's wrists, and she inspected the bruises on her face.

Muttering something unintelligible, Elsie stepped around Sela to tighten the laces on her stays. "You're not like your sister. There's fire in you." Elsie shook her head. "You must not let him see it, Miss Sela. Otherwise, he'll make you suffer more."

Sela raised her chin. "I'm not afraid of him."

"Nay?" Elsie's gray eyes darkened to the hue of an approaching storm. "Then you don't know him as well as you should."

When Sela huffed, Elsie disappeared into a small closet and returned with a jade-green gown draped over her arms. "You're the woman who shot him, aren't you?"

A flicker of pride stirred in her belly. "Aye, I am." She lifted her arms and let Elsie pull the gown over her head. When it settled around her waist, Sela eyed the plunging neckline and frowned. "I can't wear this. 'Tis indecent."

"Believe me, 'tis this, or something far worse." Elsie began to do up the buttons.

Remembering Caleb's unexpected gift of a white gown on the day of their Binding, and suffering a twinge of regret that her future with him might be lost forever, Sela tugged the neckline higher. "Your brother deserved worse than a shoulder wound for everything he did to my sister and her children. And also for what he did to the Bryants."

"Aye, he did," was the softly spoken reply. Fine lines fanned across Elsie's temples. "I ever told Liri that she should leave him. But she wouldn't escape without the girls."

"Why didn't you leave when Liri did?"

A sigh escaped Elsie's lips, laced with equal parts of hope and regret. "Because there is good I can do, yet. Innocent souls such as yourself are in need of tending. And because"—tears pearled on her tanned cheeks—"Uriah was not always this way."

"I don't understand. You're practically his slave. What kind of man treats his sister in such a way?"

Finishing the buttoning, Elsie sought the stability of a chair and sank into it breathlessly, tugging at the collar of her high-necked gown. "The kind of man who butchered his own family."

Sela reached for her own chair. "His *family*? *Your* family?"

Elsie nodded. "You have no doubt heard of our father."

"He was a marauder too." *And a former friend of Thaddeus*, she added mentally. Although Elsie Smith seemed kind, Sela would not betray this confidence.

"Aye, and a worse man never lived." Elsie loosened the buttons at her throat and fanned herself with her hand. "He captured our mother, a child of the lot, not two months after she arrived on Azazel. She was a fine woman, a lady of some standing back in the Old Town, although she never told us much about that life. It hurt too much to speak of it, I would think."

That explained why Uriah and Elsie appeared well-educated, though Sela would not attribute refinement to a man like Uriah.

"Our parents' union bore three children besides Uriah and me, all of them as brutal as our father. Uriah followed after our older brothers, although he had a special bond with our mother, which I never quite understood. She even gave him her coin, the one from the lot. To this day, he wears it around his neck. As penance, I would think."

"Penance?"

"Aye." Elsie's shoulders sagged. "Years before your sister arrived on Azazel, Uriah fell in love with a woman from one of the settlements. She wanted him as much as he wanted her, which came as no surprise to me. He has ever possessed the ability to use charm to conceal his madness. Our father believed that women were intended to be a man's plunder, not his pride. Fearful of this woman's influence over my brother, Father had her killed in an ambush on her settlement. For a long time, my brother deeply mourned her loss. When he discovered 'twas our father who ordered her execution, and that his brothers carried it out, Uriah lost his tenuous grip on his sanity."

Elsie shuddered. "I remember the day in greater detail than this brand that marks my palm. Uriah had always idolized our father and our brothers. When he found out the truth, he went mad with grief. He shot our father dead on the spot. My eldest brother found himself the unfortunate recipient of Uriah's skill with a sword, a craft they had spent years together refining. When they saw what he'd become, our other two brothers ran from him. But Uriah—"

Elsie scrunched her eyes closed. "He hunted them down. When he found them, he swore he'd slaughter them like dogs. My mother entered the room at the last moment and attempted to shield them. She was killed in the process."

"And he enslaved you, his own sister."

Elsie turned her face to the wall. "He would have killed me too, but for the regret he felt over accidentally murdering our mother. Later, he realized I had not known of our father's plan, so he allowed me to stay as a housekeeper and cook. At first, I stayed because I had nowhere else to go. Afterward, I remained because I hoped there was a chance he might turn from his ways."

"How long have you been here?"

Her mouth tipped ruefully. "Too long. You would think me a fool if you knew how many years, Miss Sela. When your sister arrived, I hoped her beauty and gentle innocence would keep Uriah's cruelty in check. But her goodness only provoked him to greater madness. When he found out your sister's twins were not his, I was afraid he would kill her. Instead, he set his mind on how he might destroy her completely. I was surprised she stayed, especially with the"—Elsie colored—"other women. In hindsight, I realize she felt guilty. And she was terribly afraid for her children."

Elsie reached out and seized Sela's hand. "Like my mother, I fear you will suffer for your sister's sake. That is why you must never show him your fear, nor your fire. He will only crave more of both. There is no rhyme or reason to his lunacy."

Sela shrugged aside the warning. "Is he cruel to you?"

Elsie froze, just as she had done when Uriah appeared in the river cave. "I think I hear him coming." She jerked to her feet and pulled Sela away from the door.

"Wait." Sela tugged on her hand, and Elsie released her. Was the woman so fearful that she imagined any approaching footsteps signaled the imminent arrival of her brother? "Why does your brother have three brands? The two on his palms, and the one on his cheek?"

Just then, the door flew open. Elsie lost so many shades of color that Sela lurched forward to prevent her from fainting.

A deep voice from the doorway halted Sela's steps. "Perhaps you should ask me yourself." Uriah snapped his fingers, and the well-trained Elsie stumbled past him and left the room.

So much for not showing fear. Elsie looked terrified.

Sela forced her breathing to steady and turned around. The coin Elsie had told her about dangled in the open space of Uriah's partially unbuttoned shirt. The brand on his cheek showed pale against the flush of whatever spirit reddened his face. He strolled forward, and Sela smelled his breath. *Rum.*

"You are a very curious girl, Sela." He noted her study of his mother's coin then began a study of his own that, despite her bravado, made her blush. "I am in a particularly good mood, so I will answer your question."

He extended his hands, palms up. "I acquired the first brand by virtue of being born on Azazel and surviving the second lot. The second brand on joining my father's gang, since twin brands are something of a trophy among those of my kind."

He eyed her clenched hands and lifted his right hand to caress his cheek. "This third brand came after I murdered my father and brothers. No doubt you already ferreted out the why of *that* story."

"Why were you not executed?" Sela remembered poor Ira, the branded healer aboard the *Deliverance,* who had died for far less.

He dropped his hand and summoned a thin smile. "Lord Auberon's predecessor was not so mutton-headed as to execute the man who kept his pockets lined with gold. Even so, his insolence cost him his life in the end. As it earned me this scar."

So the rumors that the Old Town's administrators were in league with the land pirates were true. "But Lord Auberon's predecessor returned to the Old Town alive."

His smile widened. "Aye, though he died of a sudden heart problem shortly after arriving. 'Tis astonishing how suddenly such attacks can come on."

Sela stepped back, bumping into a small table. An ornate ceramic urn teetered atop a circle of yellowed, crocheted lace. She reached out to steady it with both hands.

Uriah Smith's influence extended as far as the Old Town itself? No wonder Liri had considered it impossible to leave him. Sela, though, was not her sister. Neither was she the same girl who had left home all those months ago, been arrested, and then been left for dead on Azazel, knees knocking and voice trembling.

Uriah came closer. His hand reached for her throat. "I hear you have a fine voice. Won't you sing for my men?"

"I think we both know the answer to that question."

Something dangerous flashed in Uriah's eyes, and his fingers curled around her neck.

Sela reached behind her and felt the smooth surface of the urn. *Perfect.* Carefully, she maneuvered it against her dominant hand, not breaking eye contact with Uriah.

"Courage is but a wavering flame, Sela, unpredictable and indecisive. You would do better to yield to me."

The moment he pulled her toward him, she was ready with her makeshift weapon and sidestepped his embrace. The sound of the pottery shattering atop his head was both satisfying and horrifying. She gaped at the bloody shards just before he sagged against her. Wrenching herself free of his weakened hold, she fled the room.

She had been a fool not to memorize the twists and turns of the tunnel, for she was quickly lost. The tight stays constricted her breathing. Worse, she was barefoot. Elsie had removed her shoes and stockings.

Seeing torchlight ahead, Sela surged forward. She stopped briefly to grab a pair of flintlock pistols someone had left lying in the rubbish-strewn corridor. Was that light from the river cavern? If she could only reach the water, she could swim the short passage to daylight. Better yet, maybe she could acquire a boat.

She burst into a cavern and skidded to a halt. This place looked strange. Several faces stopped to stare at her over the rims of their drinks, their conversations ending as abruptly as her wild run. Another dining hall of some kind, or a sitting room? Her heart gave an exultant leap when she spotted a familiar face. She cocked one of the pistols, hoping it was primed and loaded, for she had no time to do it herself.

"Ross!" She weaved her way to his side, past several men and women, and warily watched the pirates. Ross's wrists and ankles were unshackled, and he wore fresh clothes. She lowered her voice. "Come on, let's go. Do you know the way out of here?"

He nodded, then swallowed. "What are you doing? You shouldn't be—"

"Uriah is unconscious. Come on, there's no time." Why had the other pirates not attacked them? She shoved the second pistol at him. "We must escape."

He eyed the pistol as if it were a snake. "Sela—"

"If you won't come with me, I'll leave you here. I don't owe you anything." She winced at the threat and her callous tone. What was she becoming?

The sound of a gun cocking spun her around. Her breath hitched and shallowed.

"Don't let me keep you from your drinks, ladies and gents." Uriah aimed his double-barreled flintlock at her chest. Blood trickled down the side of his face. "I'm merely unconscious."

The men laughed, and the women glanced away.

Sela raised her pistol. "Come closer, and I'll shoot you." She forced her voice to remain steady. "Again."

A snort sounded from the corner, then hastily turned into a cough.

Uriah's eyes narrowed. "Do your worst, my dear."

Could she do it? Could she shoot a man in cold blood? Her finger slid to the trigger. This man had hurt Liri and her daughters. He had murdered his own family. Shot Ross and his bondmate. Killed and maimed Roux.

Aye, she could shoot him.

She squeezed the trigger. To her shock, the click was not followed by a resounding *bang*. Had it misfired? She dropped the gun and reached for the weapon she'd given Ross. After it failed to discharge, she backed up beside Ross.

Uriah's eyes gleamed black. "Who do you think left the pistols for you to find, Sela?"

She watched with unveiled satisfaction while the blood tracked down one side of his ashen face. "Did you leave the urn for me to find too?"

His lips firmed into a thin line. "*Enough.*" He aimed the gun at her head.

"Do your worst, Uriah."

"My worst?" He gave a slow, snakelike smile and moved his arm to the left.

Aiming at Ross.

"Nay!" She pushed herself in front of Ross and asked him, "Why did you not run when we had the chance?"

When he didn't answer, she glanced at his face. Looking stricken, he stared at Uriah. Clearly, he was as terrified as Elsie of the pirate.

Uriah's voice filled the room. "Choose, Sela. The death of your friend—the father of a young son—or yield to me."

Was it too much to hope that Uriah's aim would be thrown off by the blow she'd given him? Seeing that the arm holding his dragon-mouthed weapon never wavered, she reluctantly acknowledged that it *was* too much to hope.

"This fortress is impenetrable and heavily guarded. Even if you by chance kill me, you will never escape my men. Men who will be only too willing to avenge my death."

As if in silent agreement, several men put down their foamy beverages and edged closer.

"'Tis as he says," Ross whispered. "Surrender, Sela. 'Tis hopeless."

That's it? No fierce commands from Ross to let *him* face Uriah like a man? No show of bravery, however pathetic or misguided? What kind of father showed such a pitiful example to his son?

His *son*. It was for Thomas that Sela could not risk Ross's life. Weak-kneed and lily-livered as Ross was, little Thomas needed a father.

Her mind flew back to Cadence and the Old Town. Instead of Uriah Smith, the evil Joss Brigham stood before her. Once again, there was nothing she could do.

Where are You, Carver? Do You care nothing for us?

She dropped her remaining pistol and held up her hands to Uriah. She would save Ross's life, even if he abandoned her.

As the Carver has abandoned me.

"You're a coward." She spat and stepped away from Ross. "If Caleb were here, he would throttle you."

But Caleb wasn't here. *He's abandoned me too.*

She approached Uriah, wondering why she suddenly felt so cold. The weather never grew this cold on Azazel. She clutched her arms, starting as she registered the sheen of satin. It stifled her more than the seven feet of water she'd nearly drowned in.

Smiling, Uriah pocketed his weapon and took her arm. As the men snickered, Sela twisted to look at Ross. He sat slumped against the cavern wall, gazing at the pistols at his feet. Had he known the pistols were not loaded? Was that why he looked at them so longingly, as if it were his dearest wish to put a lead ball into his brain?

Were Sela properly armed, she might have been tempted to oblige him.

Uriah spun Sela around, pulling her from the room. Although long-legged, she couldn't match his stride while he dragged her down unfamiliar tunnels that bled moisture all over the slippery floor. Twice, she nearly fell, and twice, he wrenched her to her feet.

"Let me go, you brute." She scrabbled at his hold on her wrist.

Reaching a door, Uriah set his shoulder against it. The door flew open, and he tossed her inside. Stumbling into a large bedchamber three times the size of Elsie's, Sela whirled to face her captor. Her chest heaved. "Caleb will kill you if you touch me."

"The former white fist?" Uriah mocked.

For the first time, Sela got an up-close look at the madness Liri and Elsie had described. It swirled vividly in his eyes.

"The last time I saw your bondmate, he was sprawled on his face with a mouthful of jetty. Should he survive his fall without becoming permanently mutton-headed, I doubt he'll have the courage or the capability to reclaim his property."

Her stomach knotted. Caleb had been hurt? "You said you never saw him."

"Aye, I did say that." He shut the door and began circling her. "You should know better than to believe me."

A tear slid down Sela's cheek. If Uriah was telling the truth, Caleb had not abandoned her. He had been struck unconscious, but by whom? Was Tucker capable of such violence?

However, it had been days since her capture, and Caleb had not come for her. Was he permanently injured, as Uriah claimed, or even—

No, she would not speak that word. She scrubbed furiously at her cheeks. This was the feminine frailty Elsie urged her not to show, and here she stood, with tears streaming unchecked down her face. Declaring that she loved Caleb Alexander without reservation, even though she might have lost him forever.

Uriah mopped his face, and his sleeve came away bright red. Ignoring the bloody streaks, he strode toward her.

Sela retreated until she felt the solid wood of an armoire at her back. She was trapped, and Uriah knew it.

The mad grin stretched across his face, and he reached for a lock of her hair. "And now, pretty Sela, I will make you sing."

Chapter Three

"No, no, *no!*"

Caleb jerked upright, his body streaming with sweat. His hands fisted in the damp sheets beside him. "'Twas only a dream," he muttered, but his heart still beat impossibly fast. His gut clenched remembering the vivid images that crowded his dreamworld. Given the nightmare he now lived, the images were not so far-fetched that he could reassure himself as to the nature of reality.

He threw the covers back and swung his feet over the side of the bed. The tiny cabin was pitch black, but he could not bear to sleep a moment longer. Passing a hand over his stubbled jaw, he grabbed his shirt from the back of a chair and headed outside.

The sliver of pale moonlight indicated that it was near midnight. The deck lay empty, except for the dark shape of a man taking the watch.

Nay, not only the watchman. Caleb flattened his body against the shadowed side of the cabin and listened to the murmur of voices coming from the main deck.

"I don't understand, Alexander—"

"That's *Lieutenant-Commander* Alexander to you, Foley," Tucker cut in.

"Lieutenant-Commander, then. I respectfully disagree with the change in heading. We are only a few days away from Azazel. Your brother wishes to return to the island to rescue Miss Sela. If he discovers that you plan to take Miss Liri and the children to the mainland first, he will be—"

"Do I need to remind you, Foley, that you are now a wanted man? Should you return to Azazel, you risk recapture, as do the rest of your men. I thought you wanted to return to the Old Town for your family."

Foley hesitated. "Aye, I do. But sir, you also wish to go back to Azazel, do you not?"

"Aye, with Caleb, once Liri and our daughter are safe." Tucker's tone soured. "Smith's brat too, though it may be better to return the girl to the island, lest Smith come after us for his progeny."

Caleb had heard enough. Straightening, he left the shadows and approached the two men.

Foley paled but stood his ground, while Tucker retreated like the coward he was.

Grabbing his brother's collar, Caleb pinned him against the nearest hard surface he could find—the door to the captain's cabin. He planted his other fist against the solid wood, wishing it had landed several inches to his right, in the middle of Tucker's perfect nose. However, if he shed even one drop of his brother's blood, there was no telling how much more would be enough for him.

"Haven't you had your fill of lies?" he demanded.

Tucker's voice turned sullen. "Caleb, you know Sela would not want us to endanger her sister's life. By returning to Azazel with Liri and the children, we would be doing exactly that. I was simply reminding Foley of the magnitude of the risk."

"No one would be in danger. We will drop anchor a fair distance from the island and row ashore."

"What if we stumble across one of the Old Town's warships?" Tucker pressed.

"Then we will face them like men, instead of the cowards you would have us become." Caleb glared at Foley. "Return us to our previous heading," he growled.

The man scurried off to do his bidding.

Caleb narrowed his eyes at his brother. "Have you told Liri of your glorious plan to abandon her sister to Smith? Or did you lie about that too?"

Tucker's eyes sparked. "She hasn't spoken to me."

"Not surprising, given your plans to deprive her of her daughter as well as her sister."

"I would never harm a single hair on Liri's head." Tucker shoved at Caleb's chest until he released him.

Caleb furrowed his brow. *Why isn't Tucker wearing his gloves?*

With a petulant twist of his mouth, Tucker chewed his lower lip. "Liri should have been mine to begin with."

"You fathered two of her children. You already took what didn't belong to you and lied about it. How many more will suffer for your selfishness?"

"Liri is free now. She doesn't belong to Smith anymore."

"Because you traded Sela in her place." Caleb felt for his pistol, only to remember that Tucker had removed it, along with his sword, while he lay unconscious. "Liri is still bonded to Smith. Do you imagine he will forget that so easily?"

Tucker's mouth curved. "By the way he looked at Sela, I can only hope."

With a howl that would surely wake the entire ship, Caleb tackled his brother, bringing them both to the deck. Heedless for his own safety, he channeled his pain and rage into his fists, unleashing a side of himself that he had not known existed.

Evidently, Tucker had not known of it, either. After landing several ineffectual punches to Caleb's chest and arms, Tucker shrank into a ball beneath his brother, presenting as small a target as possible and shielding his face with his hands.

"Caleb!"

A woman was calling his name. The similarity of her musical voice to his bondmate's recalled Caleb from his mindless fury. He raised his head. Liri stood with her arms crossed over her chest, tears streaming down her face. He was dimly aware that his hands were bleeding.

"Don't kill him, Caleb. The Carver knows he deserves to die for what he did to Sela. But if you kill him, you will never forgive yourself. You are a better man than he is, and you must not forget it. Please, Caleb, don't forget it."

Her chanting of his Carver-given name, along with the mention of the Carver Himself, shattered the veneer of invincibility that had fanned Caleb's anger into full flame and left him floundering in its ashy wake. He blinked, seeing half a dozen men standing behind Liri, Foley among them. Liri's daughters clung to her skirt, with fear etched on their pale faces. Had she brought them above deck intentionally? What did they think of him?

He focused on little Sela, her round, violet eyes so large in the moonlight that they mirrored everything around her. Hair as black as obsidian, now cut to a short bob, framed her sweet features. Her hair was so fiercely straight that it would be impossible to curl.

Withdrawing from Tucker, Caleb closed his eyes. No matter what his brother had done, the Carver did not sanction murder. How easily he had forgotten it—forgotten himself. When he opened his eyes, two sailors were helping his bruised, bloodied brother pry himself from the deck. Caleb stood and moved past Liri, but his sister-in-law gripped his hand with surprising firmness.

"She will need you, Caleb. Not your anger, but your quiet strength."

He shaded his hand with his eyes, though the moonlight was hardly blinding. "I have no strength to speak of. Not anymore."

Not since the Carver had deserted him.

Liri glanced at her youngest daughter, then back up at him. "Then for Sela's sake, you must find it. Or you will both be lost in the wilderness."

Liri always liked to imagine that in the beginning, the Carver had painted the world He'd fashioned with a vast array of colors. Thousands, if not hundreds of thousands, of colors. He reserved the most stirring hues for grass and sky and ocean, and the more extravagant ones for the creatures that roamed them.

People had colors too—colors that could change as time went on. Liri's mother was the palest blue, for she had been morose in the days approaching the coming-of-age lot. Her mother's color had once been gold. Vibrant, honey-gold, like the sun pooling below the window of Liri's childhood bedroom with the first light of morning. Her father's was brown, an earthy, dependable brown, like the worn, leather harness of a working horse. Despite the shade of her unusual eyes, Sela's color was red, a wild, passionate red that had colored her movements from childhood until early womanhood.

The older Liri grew, the more the world turned to *shades* of color, rather than the bold hues that had dominated the first eighteen years of her life. She watched as carrot orange faded to a listless melon, canary yellow to a pale lemon, and emerald green to a hue like whipped seafoam.

Then there was the black, in shades Liri had not known existed—ink and sable and pitch.

When Sela unexpectedly arrived on Azazel, Liri saw that her red had deepened to something older and more mature, like port wine. She was not the same girl Liri had left behind in the Old Town, though her eyes still begged Liri to fight her fate.

What Sela did not know was that Liri's color had also changed. Years ago, she had faded to gray, like a garment washed too many times and left to bleach in the sun. She had allowed the future she'd dreamed about to slip away forever.

Submerged in a world of grays and blacks, Liri had forgotten what it was like to behold such vivid, startling colors. Sela had been nearly blinding in her light, as had Caleb. It came as no surprise that Sela's red would be drawn to Caleb's deepest blue, though in the light of Tucker's betrayal, the memory of them together was painful.

For Tucker's color had once been deep blue, as well.

Now, his color increasingly neared the black. The mud miring his soul appeared the same as that which surrounded Uriah's...and her own.

"Sela loves you," Caleb had told her. *"She would always sacrifice herself for you. Even at the cost of her very life."*

Aye, red was the color of a blood sacrifice, a sacrifice she would never forget.

While her daughters slept, Liri watched the sun rise in willful defiance of the shadows, in shades of gold that roused memories of the heavenly chorus she'd heard in years past. She closed her eyes and listened. She'd long ago learned that few people were like her, hearing the sounds in colors and the colors in sounds, though the angelic notes of the sunrise had always been too loud to pretend she could not hear them. Only later on Azazel, with the waterfall's roar drowning the memories of her past life, had her attempts to forget the colors been successful.

"I hoped to find you here."

Liri did not need to open her eyes to recognize Tucker. His voice sounded hopeful, expectant, and full of barely restrained longing.

She glanced up at him, observing the vivid patches of color blooming over his tanned features, the purple-blue hue matching the bruises that wreathed his throat. Blood seeped from his busted lip. She could still hear the pounding fists that had struck him.

He leaned heavily on the ship's railing.

"I don't wish to speak to you, Tucker."

"I'm Anwen's father," he retorted with the same arrogance she'd once found so appealing. "How long will you keep the truth from our daughter? She is old enough to know."

"Caleb was right. How can you speak of truth after so many lies?"

He reached for her hand, but when she saw his glove, she pulled away. She raised her palm, exposing the two things she knew he wished not to see—the soul mark and the tattooed band encircling her pale finger.

His jaw clenched. "Why did you not accept my help? I sent word to Azazel, and money. 'Twould have provided for you and our children." He ground his teeth. "Instead, you chose a life with Uriah Smith. Do you fall in and out of love so easily?"

"As easily as you do." Liri moved to leave, but he snagged her hand. Through the leather, she felt him squeeze her cold fingers.

"When I came to see you after the ceremony, I apologized for what must have seemed like abandonment. I swore I'd provide for you. What else did you want from me, Liri?"

"Something you were clearly not able to give." She tugged on her hand, and he released her. "You have no right to judge me for Uriah." Her gaze swept his bloodstained cream coat with disdain. "Your standing before the Carver is no less uncertain than mine."

His pale eyes narrowed. "I did what I did for you, and for Caleb."

"By the look of your bruises, I think your brother appreciates your actions no more than I do."

"He will thank me once he is—" He glanced at her.

"Once he is *what*?"

"Reinstalled in his rightful place."

She stared at him. "You mean to have him restored as one of the Righteous? Tucker, Lord Auberon will never—"

"'Twas *his* idea."

"Should he set my sister aside permanently, I'd wager." Her lips flattened into a thin line. "Tell your brother your plans at your peril. But I would thank you to never again mention them to me." She pushed away from the railing. "As for Anwen, you are not to—"

"Ship sighted! She's off our stern and gaining on us!"

At the shout from the crosstrees above, the deck suddenly became awash with people. Standing on her tiptoes, Liri struggled to see beyond the crowd to the ship in pursuit. Tucker strode past her and joined Foley and Caleb.

Caleb glanced at his brother darkly.

Was it an Eremian warship? Or worse, one of the mainland countries' warships? How would they survive a fight at sea?

"Since you tossed our weapons overboard, I hope you have a pair of cannons stowed among your belongings." Caleb scowled at Tucker.

He glared back. "I didn't toss *all* the weapons overboard. I'm not mutton-headed. They're under the mattress in my cabin."

Foley nodded at one of his men, who departed to retrieve the weapons.

Caleb peered up at the mast. "Can you identify the ship?" he bellowed to the man in the crosstrees.

"Nay, sir. She's not flying her colors. We must wait until she's a little closer."

A little closer, and they would be within range of her guns.

When the sailor returned with an armload of muskets and pistols, Liri watched the tension stiffen the shoulders of the Alexander brothers. How could they be so alike and yet so different?

With all the yelling, Liri's daughters would likely have awoken. She turned to go below, but Tucker's voice drew her back.

"'Tis an Eremian merchant ship," he announced, and the men relaxed. Only Caleb remained on alert.

"She's sailing close in our wake," said one of the men. "Perhaps she wishes to hail us."

"Nay, she's overtaking us," replied Caleb. "She must be headed for Azazel."

Something inexplicable drew Liri to the railing. She watched the ship sail past them, a twin-masted craft that made quick work of the waves. It appeared almost to glide over the surface of the water. A schooner? A dozen or so sailors stood at the rails looking back at them, including a tall man holding the hand of a dark-haired boy.

A shout rang out from the opposing ship. The tall man was calling across the water. A brisk wind snatched up his words, and Liri stepped closer, hugging herself for warmth.

Tucker turned to face her, looking pale.

"Liri!"

She stared across the blue expanse, wondering how a stranger knew her name. What had made Tucker blanch? Did the merchant ship have guns, after all? It was easy, she knew, to sail under false colors.

Like Uriah, and like Tucker.

"Liri!" The shout came again. She was dimly aware that the man had let go of the boy's hand and was jumping up and down in his excitement, waving at them. "*Liri!*"

She took in the man's dark hair, as black as Sela's. The ship was too far away to see his face, but she saw that the boy's hair was the same color.

"Liri." Tucker gripped the rail, his knuckles turning white. "'Tis—"

It can't be…but it is. She sucked in a breath. Her brother, Liron, was hailing her.

And somehow, he had found her son.

The two ships slowed and came alongside each other, allowing the merchant ship's passengers to board the smaller sloop. Caleb stood back and watched with an odd twinge in his chest at the reunion of those who had long been parted from each other.

If anything proved the Carver's hand still moved in orchestrated ways, it was this. A meeting between vessels in a vast expanse of water could hardly be put down to mere chance.

The reunion of the older twins came first. Liri collapsed into her brother's arms and wept against his shoulder. Liri and Sela's brother, Liron, seemed not to mind that his sister was branded. This young man was a far cry from the marine Caleb had expected. He was dressed in faded civilian clothes and sported scruffy black hair, which looked as if he had hacked it off himself. Had he deserted the king's navy, as he had promised Sela he would?

It appeared so.

Supporting his sister with enviable composure for a wanted man, Liron turned and gestured to the boy behind him. His identity was obvious, even without the coin hanging from a leather cord around his neck. Liron said something low in his sister's ear, words Caleb could not discern.

"You found my son!" Liri threw her arms around the boy, whose stolid demeanor soon dissolved into tears. In the same way that little Sela resembled her namesake, the younger Liron resembled his, down to the forest green of his darkly lashed eyes, although he had very little meat on his bones.

Caleb looked at his brother, realizing the boy was not only Caleb's nephew, but also Tucker's son. Tucker dropped to his knees beside Liri, embracing the child as soon as she let him go.

"I'm your father," he said to the dazed boy, while the elder Liron's eyes darkened in understanding.

Caleb studied the younger Liron. He would be tall when he grew, like his father and uncles, and despite his thin body, he looked to have a sturdy build. Though the color of his eyes was Liri and Liron's, their shape was Tucker's, as were the strong cheekbones and jaw. The light sprinkling of freckles matched the pattern of spots that had once sprawled across a boyish Tucker's nose.

"Mama?"

Caleb turned, and the rest followed his gaze. Holding her little sister's hand, Anwen glanced uncertainly between the adults.

Liri left her son in Tucker's keeping and hurried to Anwen's side, murmuring words of reassurance. She guided the girls over to the others, explaining as she went. "Do you remember how your mama lost your brother years ago? Well, my darlings, he has been found! Anwen and Liron, you are twins to each other, just as I am your uncle's twin."

The twins eyed each other shyly from either side of their mother, bonded by blood yet divided by the lot. The twinge in Caleb's chest became an unbearable ache. Sela should be here to witness this tender reunion. For her sake, he committed everything to memory, from the vein that pulsed in the elder Liron's neck when he gripped Tucker's outstretched hand, to the tremble in the boy's lower lip as he was introduced to the family from which he never should have been parted. For the boy's sake, Caleb was glad he had allowed Tucker to live.

The bewilderment on Anwen's face showed she was just learning that Tucker was her father.

"You must be Caleb."

He turned to see Liron standing beside him, his bare hand extended.

Caleb held up his branded palms. "A caution, my friend."

Liron laughed. "Don't tell me you believe in such foolishness." He extended his hand farther, his expression encouraging.

Immediately warming to the man, Caleb took his hand. The firm grip and the calluses indicated that Liron had worked with his hands far longer than Caleb had. The former marine would be older by only a year—Tucker's age—but his face was weatherworn from years at sea. Though his smile was friendly, and his wind-blown haircut betrayed a certain carelessness of manner, his eyes were assessing.

Liron scratched his chin. "No doubt the doubling up of names is confusing."

"A little. In good time, we'll have to work out what to call you. For now, Liron Senior and Liron Junior will suffice."

Liron chuckled, but as his gaze moved to Tucker, he scowled. "Aye, Caleb, though I have an inkling of what word I would use to refer to your fool brother."

Caleb swallowed. Sela was right. She was more twin to this man than her sister Liri. "There's more to his treachery than meets the eye." His shoulders slumped, costing him the inch of height he possessed over the other man. He met Liron's startling green eyes and explained, "You see, I am not only Tucker Alexander's brother. I am also your brother-in-law through the Binding. Your younger sister Sela is my bondmate."

Liron stared at him, one coal-black eyebrow suspended aloft. "You are bonded to Sela? When did this happen?"

"Barely three months ago. I came to Azazel as one of the Righteous, second-in-command to Lord Auberon. Several months ago, I was stripped of my position and branded." He lifted his hands to expose the twin brands. Liron's expression softened with sympathy.

Of course, Caleb had more to tell Sela's brother, but that would come later.

Liron's gaze swept him with new understanding. "'Twas a willing match? An agreeable match? For both of you?"

"I would have entered into no other arrangement, nor would Sela." Despite himself, Caleb smiled. "And you should know that even the fox approved."

Liron laughed, though he quickly returned to his quiet, contemplative state. "You love my sister, Caleb Alexander. I see it in your face."

"Aye, I do." Caleb's voice softened to a whisper. "With everything I am and everything I was."

Liron frowned. "I don't understand. If you are here, then where is Sela?"

Across the deck, Tucker stiffened. His eyes darted between Liron and Caleb. Liron was well-armed. A pistol and a sword hung from his baldric holster, along with a selection of knives. The hand Caleb had shaken indicated above-average strength. Liron had taught Sela to fight.

No wonder Tucker feared retribution.

"Caleb?" Liron's eyes searched his face, then moved to Tucker's. Seeing the bruises, and glancing down at Caleb's scraped knuckles, he paled. "You?"

Caleb nodded.

Liron swallowed. "Is Sela dead?"

"Nay, she lives. She's on Azazel, a captive of the land pirate, Uriah Smith." Liron would now know the extent of Caleb's failure to protect the woman he loved.

Liron's hands twitched. "Tucker?"

Tucker watched his brother from across the deck. His eyes pleaded, clearly unaware that this very look would betray him to Liron.

Does he expect me to shield him?

Nay, it was time for his brother to face his reckoning.

"Aye, Liron. 'Twas Tucker's doing."

Chapter Four

After the fire came ash, and this ash suffocated, much like the animals and plants in the volcanic desert of Azazel must have suffocated so long ago. It blanketed Sela's days with grim, weary sameness until all parts of her old life had been snuffed out. Only the memory of fire's comforting warmth—the barest recollection of her life with Caleb—kept her from complete despair.

When the knock came at the door to her nearly bare room, Sela stiffened. In the sevenday she'd been a prisoner of the caverns under the waterfall, she had learned to be wary of approaching footsteps and no longer scorned Elsie for her fear. Still, Uriah never knocked before entering a room. Why would a man ask permission to enter a place he believed he owned?

She stood and brushed the dust from the skirt of her dress. Was Uriah's sister returning at last?

Elsie bustled into the room. "Sela." The pity in her voice was unmistakable. She gently took hold of Sela's upper arms. Somehow mindful of the bruises beneath her dress, Elsie steered her to the chair she'd spurned in favor of the floor. "Have you eaten today?"

Sela shook her head.

Elsie scowled. "I could strangle him with my bare hands for what he's done to you."

But you won't. Sela forced a smile. "Believe me, Elsie, I've already tried."

Twice, when she believed her captor was sleeping, she'd attempted to smother him, but he awoke and inflicted greater punishment. After that, she'd learned it was of little use to fight back. Uriah feared nothing save lightning, which would not save her here, deep underground.

Not even Liron's training helped when Uriah had a legion of soldiers at his command. She would have to try something far more insidious, like poison.

"Oh, my dear." Elsie stroked Sela's disheveled hair. "Would that I could spare you everything."

"Don't you cook his food? Couldn't you put something in it?"

She shook her head. "Not since I did so to help your sister escape. Uriah is wary of me these days. He has a man watching me constantly. I am searched every time I enter this room." She patted Sela's hair.

Sela flinched. Elsie's kindness following Uriah's brutality was a contradiction impossible to stomach. "What of tonight?"

"After a bath and some food, I am to bring you to him."

"If you would only slip me a knife, Elsie, I could—"

"Nay, Sela, I will not endanger your life, or Uriah's. Despite all he's done, he is still my brother." Her voice softened. "Perhaps your Caleb will come for you."

Sela had discovered, a sevenday ago now, that it was better to let that particular fire burn low. It was better not to hope. Hope only increased the burden of her torment, while weary acceptance made it somehow bearable.

Numbness settled over her like a heavy pall. "If Caleb still lives."

Sela scrubbed the dust and filth from her body until her skin felt raw. She wished she could linger in the tub of briskly cooling water forever, but Elsie was waiting with a new gown and clean undergarments.

A fresh kind of torture.

After dressing Sela, Elsie brought her to Uriah's chamber, the sight of which turned Sela's stomach every time she saw it. This time, the raucous sound of rum-edged laughter emanated from within. Uriah had company?

When she and Elsie entered the room, Uriah sent her a lingering smile. His arm lay draped around a woman with blond hair and a curvaceous figure. Her posture toward the pirate appeared oddly willing.

Relief swept over Sela. Was she to be given a respite? Despite her fear of Uriah, her gaze shot past him to the man standing just behind the pirate.

"*Ross.*"

All this time, she had thought of Ross as Uriah's prisoner, crammed into some Carver-forsaken hole without light or food. Yet, here he was, looking hale and hearty, and more chirk than she'd ever seen him. Fishy too, judging by the brimming mug in his hand.

"Sela," Ross greeted her amiably, taking a swig of the ale. "Why so solemncholy?" He eyed the sapphire-blue dress Elsie had stuffed her into. "You look beautiful, as always."

"But you were..." She looked at Uriah, who smirked. Seeing the cruelty in his eyes, her voice wobbled and faded away.

"Ah, little Sela, your soft heart will be your undoing," Uriah said. "Bryant is an ambidexter, a man two steps ahead of his own fate. He will always change sides in a bid to escape the noose."

She stared at Ross. "Is this true?"

He shrugged. "I'm not so swell-headed as to consider myself some kind of martyr."

"Enough cheek music, Bryant." Uriah grinned at Elsie. "I'm preoccupied tonight. Send Sela to the dining hall, with my compliments."

Terror flooded Sela. She had not imagined that life in Uriah's possession could get worse, but to be at the mercy of Uriah's men? Ross's betrayal was nothing in light of this new horror.

"Please, Uriah, nay." She knew begging would get her nowhere, but desperation drove her words. "You cannot mean to—"

"Give her to *me*." Ross set aside his drink and ambled forward.

Uriah raised an eyebrow, clearly tiring of the conversation. "To you? An ambidexter? Why should I reward *you*, Bryant?"

"You robbed me of Bess." Ross's arm curled around Sela's waist. "Consider this reparation." Gone was the terrified man from before. Emboldened by drink, he held Uriah's gaze in a subtle challenge.

Uriah looked at the blond woman, clearly impatient for them all to leave. "You and your cramp-words, Bryant. Very well. You may have your *reparation*." The pirate flicked his hand, and Ross grasped Sela's arm and steered her out of the room.

Elsie had disappeared.

The moment the door closed and they were alone in the hallway, Sela elbowed Ross hard in the ribs and slipped from his grasp. Winded by her tight stays and hampered by her slippers, she made it a few yards before he caught up with her.

When he drew close, Sela tried to knee him in the groin but missed. Avoiding her flailing hands, Ross grabbed Sela and tossed her over his good shoulder, pinning her legs with one hand while fending off attacks from her broken fingernails with the other.

"Stop struggling, Sela. I won't harm you."

"Traitor!" She yanked on a section of his hair.

Ross yelped and adjusted her so that his head was safely beyond her reach.

By the time another door closed behind them, a welcome energy had returned to Sela, and a fire smoldered in her belly. No man would touch her again.

Ross surprised her. He set her on her feet and stepped away. Then he held up his hands, appearing oddly sober for a man who had stumbled around in his drunkenness only minutes before. "'Tis me, Sela. I swear I mean you no harm."

"'Tis *you*? You're an ambidexter and a wretch. You deserve to have your—"

"Though I'd dearly love to hear you describe my punishment in vivid detail, there's no time. You have to escape while you still can."

She went deathly still. "Escape?"

"Aye. *Escape*." He came a little closer. His gaze swept her, and his look turned sober when he noticed the bruises marking her face, neck, collarbone, and arms. "I wish it could have been arranged sooner, but Smith didn't give an opening until now."

The fight went out of Sela, and she sank onto a chair. "You're taunting me, Ross. Please, I cannot bear it." Mortified, she watched her tears drip onto her dress, easily repelled by the satin.

"Nay. I am the same Ross Bryant whom you visited and helped so many times without fear. Thomas's father. Though I admit I was angered that you chose Caleb Alexander over me, I would never take you against your will."

She took in his clean clothes and the pistol at his waist. "But you're one of *them*. One of Uriah's men."

He shook his head. "I have been the Carver's man for some years now. Though I was not always good to your kind, Sela, 'tis a long time since I behaved as one of Smith's ilk. I asked for you tonight not only so I might spare you the horrors of their company, but also that you might quit this place permanently. I mean to free you."

"Did Elsie—"

"Nay, she knows naught. I didn't know if I could trust her." He leaned back against the wall. "You must stay tonight with me, though I swear on my son's life I will not touch you. By the early hours of the morning, Smith's men have usually drunk themselves into a stupor. There is a storm coming this way, which will break before dawn. The Carver willing, if you escape into the storm, Smith will not readily follow you. 'Tis my hope you'll make it back to Belladonna before they set out after you. There, you can seek sanctuary from the settlement men and women."

"You're not coming with me?"

He gestured to his leg and shoulder. "In case you've forgotten, Smith recently shot me...twice. If I go with you, I'll only slow you down." He shook his head. "'Tis better if I stay here for now."

She considered the breadth of his shoulders. "Uriah will never believe I overpowered you."

"I'm a better actor than you give me credit for. I'll pretend you escaped while I slept."

With a wry smile, he made for the bed and set about wreaking havoc among the sheets and pillows.

Her face heating, Sela turned away, but she had more questions for him. What had he done to convince Uriah that he was one of them? It was obvious that he had gained the man's trust, despite having betrayed him in the past.

She shivered. Perhaps Ross only pretended to help her so she would let down her guard.

When she turned, he was watching her. "When you return to Belladonna, would you see if there's any news of my Thomas?" Such a striking vulnerability ignited in his face that all her objections vanished, and she believed he was a man transformed.

"Aye. I will."

He came closer, his mouth twisting. "I am truly sorry I could not save you sooner. Short of getting myself killed, I could have done nothing to stop Smith from taking you. Forgive me."

She remembered that when Tucker retreated on the jetty, Ross had attempted to defend her. Surely, he knew his attempt was hopeless. "I forgive you. And I thank you." She winced at the scratches on his face. "I'm sorry I didn't believe you at first."

"You were right to doubt me."

"At the jetty, Tucker ran. You stayed."

The shoulders, which before had seemed broad enough to bear the weight of his cares, now sagged. "Smith used me against you. That you endured all for my sake is a debt I can never repay, Sela Alexander. Perhaps one day, I will."

His use of her bonded name, when he'd barely acknowledged it before, convinced Sela of Ross's new resolve. "You were once a man who took what he wanted," Sela said, discerning the pull of the desire of his flesh against the man the Carver was fashioning him to be. "Do you only hesitate for fear of Caleb?"

Ross smiled. "Nay, though your Caleb's skill with a knife is formidable. Smith would do well to fear his retribution. Nay, Sela. I only fear the Carver. I have learned that such fear is the wellspring of every truly wise thought and action."

"Then you believe He watches us? Even here on Azazel?" If this were true, where had the Carver been the past sevenday, when she suffered Uriah's torment?

The smile moved to Ross's eyes, replacing the anguish she had observed moments before. "Not only watches us. I believe He cares."

An hour before dawn, Ross slipped inside the chamber. He held a finger to his lips as he closed the door behind him. "All but two of Smith's men were too deep in their cups to be roused, and those two are taken care of."

Sela rose from the bed. She'd had no more than an hour's restless sleep while Ross watched the door. A headache sank sharp stakes into her skull. "Did you kill them?"

He gave a light laugh. "Nay. The powder I slipped into their waterskins last night did the trick."

"Uriah will suspect you."

"I expect greater suspicion will be cast on Smith's sister, since she has worked such trickery before."

"Elsie?" She moved to push past him. "Nay, Ross, I cannot put her in danger."

He caught her wrist and turned her around. "You think too well of the woman who has handed you over to Smith each night on a silver platter."

"She *helped* me. As she helped Liri."

"She all but ran from the room when I claimed you last night."

Was it true? Could Elsie be in Uriah's employ? Nay, the woman had shown Sela naught but kindness since she'd arrived. "I will not believe the worst of her."

"Hope for the best, but plan for the worst." He handed her his pistol. "'Tis primed and loaded. Be careful, Sela. Smith does not submerge himself in his cups as deeply as some. He may still be awake."

"I'll be careful."

He glanced behind her to the tousled bed. "Be sure to tell your bondmate that I was a gentleman during the night you spent with me, lest I find myself at the mercy of his sizable fists."

She blushed. "I will."

At the sight of her color, his mirth dissolved. "The Carver keep you, Sela." He lifted her hand to his lips and kissed it.

Thinking of Caleb, she registered naught but a temporary warmth at his gesture. "And you, Ross. Thank you for the clothes." She fingered the breeches, shirt, and coat he'd given her. They were too big, as were the men's boots, whose toes she'd stuffed with spare stockings, but they would keep her warm on the cold nights.

"You look better in the gown, but I understand your preference." His head tilted to one side, and he listened. "I hear thunder. You'd better go. Do you remember the directions I gave you?"

Sela nodded, gave Ross a brief smile, and slipped out the door.

Lurid as they were, she was thankful for the torches that lit the tunnels. Clutching the pistol, she threaded her way across the cavern where she'd first seen Ross, keeping to the shadows and willing her boots to make no sound.

Several men lay sprawled across tables or had made their beds on the floor. They stank of sweat, tallow, and rum. None stirred, not even the hefty fellow in the chair near the exit. He snored as if he were competing for a coveted title.

Clink! Sela froze.

Turning slowly, she watched a cup rattle across a table and drop to the floor. The sand greedily drank up the amber liquid.

When none of the men woke, Sela heaved a sigh. *Safe.*

She tiptoed her way out of the cavern and turned left, as Ross had instructed, into a tunnel. It dripped with moisture, forming a series of tiny, dribbled towers on either side of the passage.

To keep her fear at bay, Sela tried to focus on something other than the dark, dank tunnel. Uriah had told her that Azazel had been inhabited long before people from the Old Town discovered it. The first occupants found and enlarged this network of caverns. They were accessible only through an underground river that exited near the base of the mountain, beneath the second river and its concealing waterfall.

The original inhabitants had long since died out. Whether by the sword, or famine, or disease, Uriah did not know. When his father stumbled upon the "cave of wonders," as he termed it, he knew he'd found a home for the treasures he plundered from the Old Town.

During part of the year, when the monsoonal rains came, the cave was inaccessible, due to the sheer volume of water that shielded the entrance. The pirates kept vast amounts of supplies within for such occasions.

The story faded from her mind, and Sela's anxiety returned. She tightened her grip on the pistol, sweat slicking her palms. She hoped Ross would not be harmed for his part in helping her escape, nor Elsie. Perhaps the two could escape together once Ross's wounds were fully healed.

She passed through two more caverns, empty of occupants, and then entered the vast hall she had seen her first day under the mountain. Shivering, she avoided looking at the gibbets suspended overhead, picking her way between a trio of pirates who seemed to have fallen asleep mid-conversation. One propped his head up with a ring-encrusted hand. The fine yellow lace of his sleeve appeared a bilious contrast to the flecks of vomit in his beard.

She shuddered and kept going.

Reaching the end of the cavern, she spied the two guards Ross had sedated. They lay slumped against the wall. She sent up a quick prayer of thanks to the Carver.

Sela all but bounded into the tunnel, feeling like a caged bird unexpectedly turned free. The river cavern was unlit, but enough light remained to see the small boat tied to an outcrop of rock, a pair of oars lying in the stern. The water glowed faintly beyond, reminding her of Caleb's eyes.

"Sela!"

Sela jumped, whirled, and raised the pistol.

She saw no one, but the loud *thumps* that indicated footsteps echoed from the tunnel. She had only a few seconds before whoever it was burst into the river cavern and discovered her. If her pursuer was Uriah, he could easily overpower her.

Sela's heart raced. If she fired first, she would have the advantage, although she might wake the others. However, if the man discovered her and used his weapon before she could, she was dead. Or a slave.

And this time, Ross could not save her.

Holding the gun with both hands, she forced her shaking hands to still. Dark shapes loomed from every shadowed corner.

"Sela!"

The river cavern magnified the sound of her name until it bounced off the walls, mocking and degrading her, taunting her with its closeness. The tone sounded full and imposing. There was only one man with a voice like that, the man who would haunt her dreams for the rest of her life.

Just then, a tall form emerged from the narrow slit, and though her vision blurred, she thought she discerned broad shoulders and a muscular build. The figure strode forward, revealing a mane of unbound dark hair.

Uriah.

I won't be a slave again.

She sighted her target and squeezed the trigger. The gun's report was deafening in the vast space, although dampened somewhat by the roar of the distant waterfall, swollen from recent rains. Still, it sounded loud enough to rouse the dead.

The figure slumped to the ground, and Sela let out the breath she'd kept captive. A bloody streak marked the wall where Uriah had slid down.

Sela spun and made for the boat. She could not stop to see if he was dead. Any minute the pirates would—

"Sela?"

Her heart froze at the failing, questioning voice. She turned. *Nay, Carver, it cannot be!*

Against her will, Sela hurried over to the crumpled figure and dropped to her knees. "*Elsie?*" She sat motionless beside the outline that she had been sure was the source of all her nightmares. Ross's pistol fell from her grip.

Elsie gasped and nodded. Her fingers scrabbled at a bloody eruption from the left side of her chest.

Sela grabbed the woman's hand and held it. She had only to recall Liron's lessons to know that this wound was mortal. How had she hit that target at such a range, and in the near dark? "Elsie," she whispered. She found her other hand and reunited it with the bloodied mess of the first. "I thought you were your brother."

"Aye, we...look...alike." It didn't help that Elsie was wearing men's clothes.

Sela thought herself beyond tears, but they slipped freely down her face and dripped onto the woman's bloody chest. "Elsie, I am sorry. So sorry. I didn't know it was you."

Fear lanced Elsie's eyes, then the taut lines around her mouth relaxed. She caught her breath and slowly let it out. "Now, we will both be free." She squeezed Sela's hand. "Go, my friend. I will tell Uriah that your Caleb came for you."

Sela shook her head. "I cannot leave you, Elsie."

"You must, or my brother will find you here. *Go!* I don't wish you to watch me die."

"Nay, I—"

Elsie pushed Sela away with surprising force, sending her scuttling across the rocky ground. Elsie sank against the cavern wall, clearly exhausted by the effort. Her smile turned wan but pure.

Had Elsie found the absolution that Sela still craved?

Blinded by tears, Sela swiped them away then dragged herself to her feet. She stumbled to the boat, leaving Ross's pistol behind. Releasing the boat from its mooring, she jumped into it, holding the sides until it stopped rocking. She grabbed the oars and slipped them into the oarlocks.

Raised voices spilled into the river cavern, edging closer. Their approaching torches splashed light across the rock walls, throwing Elsie into sharp relief. The woman lifted a bloodied hand in a grim gesture of farewell.

Sela choked down a sob. In her imagination, she still heard the ill-fated gunshot that would soon rob Elsie of her life. Past bled into future, the unearthly beauty of this place shattered by the violent intrusion of sound, now degrading into nothingness. Wrenching her eyes away, Sela plunged the oars into the water and made for the waterfall that would sweep her away.

Somewhere *far* away, where she might one day forget the life she had stolen from the Carver in exchange for her own.

Chapter Five

"Give me one good reason why I shouldn't shoot him."

Liron surprised Caleb with his reaction on learning of Tucker's role in Sela's capture. The man became rigidly calm, his only tell the vein that throbbed in his neck. "Liri"—he did not break his stare at Tucker—"'tis cold up here. Perhaps your son might want a coat."

Though the boy's arms were indeed exposed to the chilly breeze, Liri no doubt grasped her brother's true intentions. "Liron, I—"

Caleb shot her a look he hoped was both grim and reassuring. *Liron will not kill Tucker on my watch.* However, neither would Tucker escape her brother's wrath.

Swallowing, Liri nodded and reached for her son's hand.

As soon as Liri and her children were safely below deck, Liron repeated his demand, eyes glittering. If looks alone could butcher a man, Tucker would have been keelhauled.

The onlookers wisely scattered to perform their various tasks, leaving Caleb and Foley standing between Liron and Tucker. Caleb's brother seemed to have recovered his composure and stood with his arms folded, the tilt of his chin defiant, his gloved fingers only inches from his pistol.

"Two such reasons just went below deck, Liron," Caleb said. He wished he could grind his Carver-given conscience to dust beneath the heel of his boot. "Knave and scoundrel as Tucker is, he is father to our niece and nephew. And he was once your friend, as I understand it."

Liron stepped closer, his eyes blazing hotter than a forest fire. "I don't have to *kill* him. There's still a bit of white on his face. I could color in the blank spaces you so generously left for me."

"On that count, Liron, be my guest."

Tucker scowled. "I am not unarmed."

Liron expelled a laugh of reckless abandon, his eyes grazing Tucker's cream sleeve. "You are one of the Righteous, are you not? Whatever your training, you cannot match a man of the sea. Then again, I wonder if I should limit myself to physical retribution. Does this Lord Auberon know about your son and daughter? The Righteous, as I understand it, are not permitted to father illegitimate children."

Tucker paled. "Were it not for the lot, I would have bonded with her."

"I would have sooner had your head for defiling my sister." Liron's lip curled. "No doubt your illustrious contacts removed your coin from the chest the day of the coming-of-age ceremony. You're exactly the kind of man who excels at keeping his own head above water."

Tucker growled. "Like you, I would have substituted myself for Liri if it were possible."

"As you substituted yourself for Sela?"

"I told Caleb," Tucker snarled, "that 'twas Sela's choice to stay behind."

"You seduced one of my sisters and left another to die. Why should I believe you?"

"Don't you know your own sister, Meriweather? The girl is ever the custodian of impossible causes."

"Aye," Liron shot back, "and never selective over whose hide she saves. This time, 'twould seem, to her own detriment."

"I said impossible, not *noble*. She is a reckless, irresponsible girl. 'Twas Sela who killed my cousin, after all."

Liron backed up a pace. "Josiah Brigham was your *cousin*?" His gaze flicked to Caleb, who stood with his fists clenched. He nodded. "Then you know of his vile character. You know what he tried to do to her."

"I know 'twas Sela who recklessly and needlessly destroyed Joss's life." Tucker's mouth turned sullen. "Just as she destroyed Caleb's."

"Do *not* involve me in this," Caleb snapped, stepping to Liron's side.

"Why not? Were it not for Sela, you would still be one of the Righteous, would you not?"

The question dangled in midair. Liron twisted to look at Caleb. Pain rippled across his tanned features. "Is it true?"

"Aye," Caleb slowly ground out, "and nay."

It was true that Sela would have died if he had not intervened. However, the decision to confess his actions to Lord Auberon—trusting in the man's mercy—had been his own. Until then, he had not known of the elder's true nature.

Caleb faced Liron. "I broke the law to save your sister's life. I would do it again if I had to. Even before I saved Sela, I loved her."

The hard set of Liron's jaw softened, and he returned his gaze to Tucker. "Look no further than your brother's example for the man you should have been, Alexander."

"You can bluster and chide me all you like, Meriweather, but I could only save one of your sisters. I chose Liri—and her children."

"Nay," replied Liron wearily, "you only chose yourself." He looked at Caleb. "I would hear the full story from you, but first, there is a decision to make." He glanced around the ship. "I assume you are returning to Azazel?"

Caleb nodded. "With all haste."

"Then come with us. The schooner will reach the island in two days. This sloop will barely make it in three."

"Alexander," ventured Foley.

Both brothers turned, but the former captain addressed Caleb. "If you aren't needing this ship after all, I would return to the Old Town to seek my family's well-being, and their forgiveness."

Unease shuttered Tucker's expression. "What of Liri? Our son and daughter?"

Caleb scowled at his omission of Uriah and Liri's daughter, but before he could speak, Liri interjected from behind them. "I'm coming to Azazel." She planted her hands on her hips, and something unspoken passed between her and her twin.

"'Tis not safe—"

"Nay, Tucker," Caleb interrupted him. "But 'tis right."

"You're not a father," Tucker spat back.

"Nor are you," Liri said, surprising them with the cold strength of the look she directed at Tucker. She hitched her shoulders higher, as if her courage had been bolstered by the presence of her twin. "A father knows the true value of sacrifice."

For the briefest of moments, something like shame sparked in Tucker's eyes, but it was quickly doused by anger.

Before Tucker could say something inexcusable, Caleb turned to Foley. "Return with our blessing, Captain. We wish you well and thank you for the troubles you've endured on our behalf."

Sadness flickered in Foley's grizzled visage, perhaps at the daunting task that lay ahead of him. At Caleb's words, he nodded and melted away.

Caleb turned to Liron, whose arm was now threaded around his sister's shoulders. "I'll come with you, of course. I'm going after Sela as soon as we drop anchor."

"Consider my sword and pistol at your service," Liron replied with a smile that didn't reach his eyes. He clutched his sister closer.

"Your ship, Meriweather," said Tucker. "To whom is it loyal?"

Liron's gaze slid down him with disdain. "Not to the Righteous, nor to their smugly dressed eye servants, who only attend to their duties while under close observation."

He turned his back on Tucker and addressed Liri and Caleb. "The captain does not oppose Lord Auberon, exactly, but he has agreed to enter the bay of Belladonna under cover of nightfall. He is accustomed to transporting forbidden cargo and bribing the soldiers for their silence. He will not likely object to more passengers, should there be gold involved."

"I have the necessary funds," Caleb replied, "though your captain may find Belladonna a somewhat different place to when he glimpsed it last. We do not know what manner of rule or order exists there now." His stomach clenched. What if Smith's men had overrun Lord Auberon's reinforcements? Would it be any better for Sela if the soldiers *had* regained control?

Liron looked thoughtful. "It seems there is much you have to tell me, Caleb."

"Aye, there is."

"You're all fools," Tucker scoffed. He tried—unsuccessfully—to catch Liri's eye. "But since I have little desire to return to the Old Town, I may as well come with you."

Something glinted in his eye—something that, for now, he seemed eager to keep to himself. Caleb resolved to watch his brother closely. Unable to manage a civil retort, he headed for his cabin to gather his few possessions.

Liron's voice stopped him. "There's one more thing you should know." A feverish excitement brimmed in his words.

"Speak, Meriweather."

Liron did not respond to the sneer in Tucker's voice. "Prince Magnus Theodorus is alive," he said. "And he's on his way to Azazel."

The waterfall was cold and fast-flowing, but bearable. Sela escaped the deluge with nothing more than a drenching, shooting out into a heavily overcast dawn.

The merging of the underground river with the river from above spurred her small boat to impossible speeds, rendering the oars ineffectual. She gripped the sides of the craft and watched a small beach along the riverbank disappear into the gloom. How much rain had fallen during the past sevenday to whip the river into such madness?

A gunshot sounded from far away, above and behind her. She crouched low in the boat. Were Uriah and his men already in pursuit? As if in answer, lightning cracked against the side of the mountain like a whip, and thunder snarled overheard. The heavens opened, soaking her hair and clothes. Water puddled in the bottom of the boat.

Was Ross right that Uriah would not follow her into the storm? She hoped it was true. As the river bore her farther away, and naught but silence pursued her, Sela's breathing evened. Slowly, she straightened, adjusting her boots so that they no longer tested the depth of the growing pool inside her vessel.

Lightning and thunder continued to fracture the gray dawn. Searing pain lanced her upper right arm. She cried out and buckled. Kneeling in the puddle, she looked back.

A man holding a smoking musket stood on a black-sanded beach upriver. Uriah? He was so far away that she hardly knew how he had made the shot, and he made no attempt to come after her.

The pool of water turned bloody from the rivulets streaming down her arm, but the sound of another deluge dead ahead stole her attention. She chanced a look over the rim of the boat and sucked in a breath. No time to grab the oars.

She wished she'd known about this second waterfall.

"Carver, help!"

Sucked forward by the strength of the current, the boat slid over the falls, heedless of the terrified woman within. Flung from the craft, Sela registered a second of weightlessness before she plunged back into water, far colder now that she was fully immersed. Pain swirled up her right shoulder, rousing memories of another wound and near-drowning.

She lashed out with both arms, trying to keep her head above the raging, frothy current. How far had she fallen? Five yards? Ten? Her leg struck a sharp rock, and she bit back a gasp. The current seized the opportunity to drag her under again.

Once again, she called out to the Carver, this time in her mind. Her lungs were clogged with water. Would she survive Uriah Smith, only to drown?

When her head burst to the surface again, she dragged in another breath and looked around. The boat floated beside her in an upright position, though the force of the waterfall should have upended it. Sela was not in possession of the strength to heave herself into the boat, especially with her wounded arm, so she reached out and grabbed the side with her left arm. She hung on while the current sped her past rocks sharp enough to slice her in half.

Numbness crept up her legs. Her right arm burned as if the entire length had been branded. Splinters slid like tiny daggers into the fingers of her left hand, loosening her hold on the boat. Rain pelted down, a trifling force compared to the torrent now sweeping her along. Lightning lashed so close she felt the growl of thunder in her bones.

Carver, I can't hang on much longer.

Abruptly, the river widened and slowed, the bulk of its current emptying into a large, fern-lined pool. When her ankle struck a sandbar, Sela clawed for a foothold. She lost her grip on the boat, which continued drifting downstream. For a moment, she teetered, nearly sucked along after it. Then, finding her footing, she wrenched herself from the river's grasp and headed for a narrow beach with the same distinctive black sand of the one upstream.

Exhausted, she lay against the sand, not caring that the sky continued to splutter. She was *alive.* The rushing river tugged on her boots, which trailed in the water. Too late, she realized she should have kicked them off in order to better stay afloat. But they would serve her well on the journey ahead.

Remembering her wound, Sela struggled to a sitting position and examined her arm. Had the man on the beach intended to kill her, or only wound her? The lead ball had grazed her just above her right elbow, gouging out a chunk of flesh. The wound did not seem deep, but it was bleeding profusely.

Gritting her teeth against the pain, and biting back a moan, she tore a strip from her shirt and bound the wound. It was awkward, but she finally managed it with the help of her teeth and good hand. Superstitious or not, Uriah might send his men after her, even if he declined to pursue her himself.

Spying a shallow gash on her left ankle, Sela used another strip to stem the bleeding before clambering to her feet. She was cold, tired, injured, and shaking.

But she was free.

Looking around, she tried to get her bearings. Ross had instructed her to head directly east down the mountain, then to follow the river to the ocean. Once there, she could find the coastal road that led to either Pennyroyal or Nerium.

He could not have known she would be injured, or that Uriah's men would discover her missing so quickly. Would it not be better to head inland, a route the pirates did not expect? She glanced down at her arm, already feeling light-headed from the loss of blood. How long could she last before she passed out?

She considered chasing after the boat, but she had no wish to spend more time on the water. Besides, the oars had disappeared. Seeing the grooves she had left in the sand, she hastily set about smoothing them then retreated into the shallows. She knew enough about tracking to realize that any depressions she left would announce her movements to anyone hunting her, especially if she left prints in the mud.

I will need to be very careful.

She mentally bid the boat goodbye. Perhaps its downstream course would throw Uriah's men off her trail.

Spying an enormous tree, whose branches lingered on the surface of the water, she made for it and reached for the lowest limb. Her wounds protested, but she hauled herself up and over the branch using her good arm.

Once out of the water and squatting on the branch, Sela cautiously traversed the limb to a higher, sturdier support, one that brought her above solid ground. She moved toward the tree's center. Inching her way across the surface of the trunk, her foot found another branch. It shot outward, into the thickly forested wood. Near the fingertips of the limb, she squatted again and dropped into a pile of leaf litter.

Thunder rumbled ominously, but it sounded far away. Sela glanced behind her. Thanks to the tree, she had traversed at least a dozen yards without leaving tracks from the water's edge. Though an expert tracker would likely laugh at her attempt, it would have to do.

She angled her face down the mountain. Now, she only needed to last until she could find shelter. At least she would not run out of water.

If you are truly there, Carver, please help me find Caleb.

To ask for more would be too daring, especially from one who had twice taken life from the hand of the Carver to save herself.

She hoped Caleb was on better terms with his divine caretaker of late.

Liron had been right. The merchant ship was a swift and elegant craft. It devoured the nautical miles until Caleb sighted a smudge of jagged land just before the sun dropped below the horizon on the first full day. Gray clouds descended with the tenacity of the clinging fogs of the Old Town.

Despite the ship's speed, the bands encircling Caleb's chest had tightened. Every day was another day Sela might be suffering.

There was little room aboard the merchant ship, and only Liri had been given a cabin. Liron insisted on sleeping at her door, while Caleb and Tucker were given hammocks in the hold with the other men.

While Tucker made himself scarce, Caleb worked alongside Liron, marveling at the man's knowledge of the ropes and canvas that were so foreign to him.

"You're a hard worker, Alexander," Liron said as he descended the crosstrees to where Caleb was securing a rope. Approval flickered in his eyes at the calluses on Caleb's hands. "Certainly, no soft-pawed scholar."

"I was once." He wondered how he could explain the value of the Carver's work. "There's no shame in either trade. Every profession has its calluses, though they are not always visible."

Liron frowned, but he eventually nodded his shaggy head. Rather than contain his hair in a queue like most men, he left it loose. It matched the wildness—and somewhat reckless nature—of the man, although he protected his sister and her children with unswerving devotion.

"What are *your* calluses, Caleb?" Liron glanced down at Caleb's palms. "Besides the obvious."

Caleb finished his task and straightened, rolling the tension from his aching shoulders. "Do you speak of the Carver's work, or of the loss of my bondmate?"

The mirth vanished as quickly as if someone had doused a candle. "Whatever troubles you the most."

Shadows cobwebbed the railings as night veiled the ship. The sails bulged, glutted with wind from the impending storm. A torch flared to life nearby, exposing the worried lines about Liron's mouth.

Caleb shivered. "Of the loss of Sela, I cannot speak. I am terrified that by the time we return, she will either be crushed in spirit...or dead."

"Or spoiled?" Liron's question had a hard edge. "You were once one of the Righteous, described to me by several sources as a most celebrated and talented acolyte."

Caleb returned his pointed look. "Whatever Sela's state when we return, I will not sever our bond."

"Under the rules of the Binding, you have every right to put her aside if she is tarnished."

"So says the Righteous, but the Carver instructs men differently."

"Does He now?"

"Aye," Caleb retorted. "The Carver says that the Binding is for life. No matter what happens, the bond between man, woman, and Carver is not easily rent."

Liron stepped closer, rubbing his gloveless palms together. "Even if Sela carries another man's child?" The telltale vein throbbed in his neck.

Caleb swallowed but did not look away. "Even so."

Liron broke his gaze and spun, seeking the railing. "You are an uncommon man, Caleb. Are you sure you don't want me to kill Tucker for you?"

Though his tone was light, Caleb knew Liron spoke sincerely. He shook his head. "I would not have his blood staining either of our consciences."

"Because you fear Lord Auberon?"

"Because I fear the Carver." Although of late, the Carver appeared not to mind whatever Caleb did.

Liron offered an uneven smile. "And this forms the calluses of which you spoke."

Sighing, Caleb joined him at the railing. "Every man or women who studies the Book of Souls and comprehends its true meaning bears the burden of understanding their own guilt, as well as grappling with the inevitable cost of their sins. Of those, some choose either to ignore the problem at hand, becoming hardened or blinded to their own evil, or to seek absolution in sacrifices that can never truly remove the stain of human selfishness."

"You're referring to the lot."

"Aye, the lot."

Liron glanced around as if looking for Liri, then lowered his voice. "And what of the soul mark?"

"A mere brand cannot rob a man or woman of what only the Carver can bestow," Caleb replied with certainty. "Nor can it grant absolution to others."

The other man huffed. "On that, at least, we agree."

"Do you not believe in the Carver?"

Liron shifted uneasily. "'Tis difficult to place my trust in anyone who could oversee so much suffering and yet do nothing to rectify it. It seems rather"—his lips quirked—"callous."

"Aye, I understand your doubts." Caleb knew that Sela shared these doubts, as well. He leaned on the railing, peering out over the inky water. "I can't stop wondering why the Carver allowed Liri to be taken. And now Sela. It seems like glaring evidence of divine ineptitude. Yet, I must confess there is no failing greater than my own."

Liron drew himself up. "From all you've told me of Liri's defection from Smith and Sela's capture, no one could hold you to blame, Caleb."

"Then you weren't listening well enough." He scraped his fingers through his thick hair. He could not forget the memories of all the mornings he'd awoken to midnight-black tresses splashed across his chest, a vivid contrast to the red fur curled in a tidy ball at their feet. He recalled the smoothness of Sela's cheek against his shoulder. The enticing hills and valleys of flesh that he had ever longed to explore, once she trusted him and consented to know him in return.

He clenched his fist, and the memories and sweet anticipation crumbled into dust, along with the rest of his dreams. "I'm not seeking reassurance, Liron. I should never have left her with Tucker."

Liron watched him with a bruised, almost wistful smile. "'Tis not the first time Sela waited for a protector to emerge through the fog, and he did not come."

Though he'd heard much of the account before, Caleb listened as Liron recounted the events of the day Sela had killed Joss. He spoke with the air of a criminal confessing to a priest, his shoulders dejected, his eyes downcast.

Far more forthcoming with details than the sister whose hair color he shared, Liron told of Sela and Cadence being forced to brave the long walk home from the seminary alone. Of Sela's wild fear as she searched out her mentor. Of her seeming agreement to decide matters with her family upon the morning, only to leave before they awoke to give herself over to their local priest, unable to subject her sister to a life spent concealing a lie.

Caleb's chest filled to brimming. If he had loved Sela before, he found it tempting to worship her now. Her decision to save Liri was the natural extension of a life lived without fear for herself.

A great pity, then, that she'd bonded with a coward.

"Our two families are impossibly intertwined, are they not?"

Caleb glanced at his brother-in-law, realizing he had yet to respond to Liron's account. The beds of his nails were as ragged as Caleb's.

"I consider it a worthy acquaintance," Caleb replied. "From every angle."

"Likewise."

Thinking of Tucker, Caleb doubted Liron's approval extended beyond himself.

"I'm surprised I never knew you back in the Old Town, Caleb."

"I entered the halls of the Righteous when I was only a boy, barely sixteen. I finished my final year of schooling with the priests. After that, I was welcomed by the elders into their ranks. I was with them for nearly six years before I came to Azazel."

"You were at Liri's ceremony?"

"Aye, for Tucker's sake." Caleb's throat clenched at the memory. "'Twas there I met Sela for the first time, though I didn't know her name then."

She had been very young, the four-year gap between them all the more stark since she was still a girl, and he was nearly a man. Rejoicing over Tucker's absolution, he had reached out to stop the girl from falling as she passed him, overwrought at the loss of her sister. He remembered the flash of violet fire that had startled him—and entranced him.

With his own dreams so close to being fulfilled, he had quickly forgotten about her.

Liron heaved a sigh. "All this and more, Prince Magnus may yet put to rights. He is likely already on Azazel."

Caleb frowned. "I have heard your tale, and of the prince's promise after he saved you as a child, but I still do not understand why such a man would come to Azazel."

He had heard stories of Prince Magnus's rare and noble character, but the man had been missing for years. It seemed of little consequence to the Old Town, since neither Lord Auberon nor the other elders of the Righteous ever spoke of him, nor did any of his royal advisors depend on his counsel. Driven by a childhood memory that could easily be the product of wishful thinking, Liron risked everything chasing after a man who could have him branded or even killed.

By the look of his corded throat, Liron knew the dangers. Without answering, he turned to face the sea, furrowing his brow when he glimpsed what Caleb had noticed only moments before. Flashes near the horizon lit up the sky like a distant sea battle. In place of cannon and musket fire, however, the elements warred.

"I'm going below deck to make sure Liri and the children are safe. Find yourself some rope, Alexander, to tether yourself to the mast. The sailors will need every limb you can spare them."

"At last light, Azazel was close," Caleb said. "We may yet reach it safely."

"Not that close." Liron's voice turned grim. "That storm will strike before midnight."

Chapter Six

As night fell, Sela conceded that she was lost. Wary of staying too close to the river, where Uriah's men might be hunting her tracks, she had kept her distance, forcing her way through thick jungle that pressed close enough to serve as a compression bandage for her wounds. Only, she had gone so far that the snakelike twists and turns of the river had vanished from sight. Now, several distant waterfalls, urged to life by the torrential rain, made it impossible to use her ears to find it again.

She frowned. Something was wrong with her head. She felt as if it were encased in cotton, and her balance was so thrown that she had twice bumped into trees. She cried out when her foot hooked around a tree root and she went sprawling. Her palms encountered tangled vines, wet earth, and leaf litter. She hauled herself up onto a raised root, rationalizing that it might serve her ascent as well as it had served her descent, then brushed off her clothes.

She pressed a hand to her forehead and hissed. It was warm—far too warm to be the result of exertion. Was that why the jungle had begun to shimmer as if she viewed a mirage? It was too soon for her arm wound to become infected, yet her skin felt hot and waxy, and her stomach roiled, making her nauseous. It had barely tolerated the handfuls of water she'd snatched along the way, though she continued to sweat profusely.

Birds warbled above her head, several exotic varieties that she had never seen in the Old Town. Had the Eremian exiles to Azazel ever tried to learn their names? She suppressed a shiver. According to Uriah, the green interior of Azazel teemed with wild boars and poisonous snakes. Were there mountain lions as well? So far, the jungle seemed almost benign.

It might well tell a different story come nightfall.

Sela jerked to her feet. The world lurched and blistered, but as soon as it righted itself, she pressed onward, refusing to look at her arm. It had stopped bleeding, at least for the moment, and she could do little for it if it had become infected.

Darkness fell, another stifling blanket over the lingering humidity. Although the skies had cleared, no moon rose. Her entire body ached. Realizing she could go no farther, she gingerly climbed into the arms of a sprawling tree like the one that had assisted her escape from the river and rested her head against the rough trunk.

She would rest for an hour, maybe two. Then she would continue. Her eyelids weighted.

Sela jolted awake and immediately chastised herself. Light gilded the edge of the horizon, announcing the dawn. Had she slept the whole night? Her stomach growled, reminding her that she'd had nothing to eat or drink except river water since early yesterday morning.

She chanced a look at her arm, pleased to see that the fresh strip of fabric she'd used on it the evening before was unbloodied. Her forehead felt clammy, but not unusually warm. *Good.* Perhaps it had only been a slight fever, borne of her dunking in the river.

Cursing her stiff muscles, she slid down from the tree and looked around. This jungle's sameness would be the death of her. How would she find the river when nothing appeared distinctive? With a huff, she set off, feeling new blisters rub against the heels of her ill-fitting boots. For an instant, she wished she'd lost them in the river. Then she looked at the ground and shuddered. No, in spite of the blisters, she was better off wearing boots.

In the early morning stillness, Sela heard the rush of water nearby. She altered her path, guessing that she was nearly at the base of the mountain. With luck, she would be at Pennyroyal or Nerium by nightfall.

When she burst through a thick screen of trees, her heart sank. This was not the river she'd been hunting, only a small stream welling up from an underground spring. The birds overhead fluttered their wings and cawed. Did she imagine it, or were they mocking her? Luckily for the birds, nausea had replaced hunger, or she might have grabbed pebbles from the stream and tried her hand at knocking the onlookers from their perch.

With a heavy heart, she trudged onward. Hours passed. Did she go in circles? She no longer walked downhill. Surely, the river was not far. She pressed on into the fading afternoon, ignoring a growing desperation. Much later, the trees thinned and then vanished altogether.

Sela stopped short at the view that opened before her. She stared out at a rocky wasteland and knew she'd wandered far from her intended path. Somehow, instead of angling north, she'd come too far east, stumbling onto the volcanic desert.

She licked her dry lips. She had drunk her fill from the stream, but the jungle dehydrated a person quickly, and she had lost her waterskin yesterday at the second waterfall.

Sela closed her eyes and tried to recall the map of Azazel. Caleb had shown her the map a month ago, when he first told her about Anjelica, the settlement on the other side of the island.

It would take less than a day to cross the expanse she had first traversed with Ross, Uriah, and his men. The mountains that separated the desert from Belladonna rose on the other side. It had taken them two days to cross those peaks.

Sela thought harder. The group had moved slowly because of Ross's injuries and Uriah's fear of storms. If she made it across the desert, she could find water—and possibly food—on the other side. She had taken note of the mountain trail and of Uriah's caves along the way, with their stockpiles of food and other provisions.

Perhaps she could make it back to Belladonna on her own. Her spirits rose.

Turning a slow circle, she tried to gather her muddied thoughts. Should she find the other settlements, she had no guarantee that anyone would help her. The people might even return her to Uriah.

She swallowed. *Nay, better to return to Belladonna.* There, she might encounter Caleb or one of their friends.

After tending to her blisters, Sela headed east. Oddly enough, she was no longer hungry. Perhaps the pangs would not bother her overmuch after going awhile longer without food. She remembered something similar during several lean winters back in the Old Town, when her stomach had learned to be satisfied with less.

She quickened her pace, feeling exposed. In the jungle, she had been surrounded by life and movement, but in the desert, there was nothing. Deep furrows ran the length of the expanse, the scars widening to small canyons in places, where they had cracked and blistered in the sun. Patches of scrub looked shriveled and burnt, as if they had no way of absorbing the rains that swept across this forsaken place. Empty as it was, this desert stifled her more than the jungle ever had.

As she walked, Sela became aware that she was no longer alone.

No human or animal stalked her. Nay, her thoughts summoned the specters of Elsie, Uriah, and the others from the gathering shadows. The faster she walked, the more quickly the phantoms pursued her, so close that she felt they might tap her on the shoulder if she turned.

Her arm throbbed, and her blistered feet protested the brisk march. She slowed, watching the sun dribble down between two distant mountains.

Sela blinked a sheen of moisture from her eyes. She had come far, through the tangled jungle and across the scabbed, blistered expanse. But was it far enough to outrun Uriah Smith, and the memory of accidentally killing Joss Brigham, and the look in Elsie's eyes when she had realized she was dying? The recollection of their faces spurred Sela into a near jog.

When she stumbled, tendrils of heat curled up her neck. She lifted her hand to her cheek and found it hot. Her arm wound was not inflamed, and it was far too early to be dying of thirst.

What is wrong with me? She dragged herself up and pushed on.

A few minutes later, her foot found a stray fissure. She lurched forward and was sent sprawling headlong onto the unforgiving ground, only just catching herself on an outcrop of rock before it cracked open her head. Wincing, she curled into a tight ball. Fatigue threaded through her body, along with a dull ache that rendered it painful to move. Her throat felt thick, as if she'd swallowed sand.

"Caleb," she gasped. She tried to remember the deep blue of his eyes as the color drained from the world around her. The setting sun left behind a barren wasteland of jagged shapes and outlines, too shadowy to discern if they were friend or foe.

"*Caleb.*" Her fingers curled, struggling to remember the sensation of her bondmate's hair gliding across her palms, and the warmth of his hands holding hers. Or the fire that kindled in his eyes when she'd confessed she wanted to bond with him in truth.

A soul-crushing grief swept through Sela, driving away the numbness that had been her companion for a sevenday. Uriah had stolen all of that away. What should have been Caleb's had been plundered by the enemy.

Aye, she had fought and struggled and screamed in the beginning, as the bruises marking her skin testified. Bruises, though, would mean nothing to a man who valued purity above all else. Who *was* purity itself.

There was more than one stain which marked the soul.

Tears dripped down her face, dampening the rock. Was it folly to return the shell of her body to a man who had once hesitated to touch her branded skin? Worse…what if she carried Uriah's child? Sela would never expect her bondmate to be a father to the offspring of his enemy. Not Caleb, who had given up everything for her—family, fortune, and his place among the Righteous.

Not Caleb, who had never even been with a woman.

"How could You do this to us, Carver?" she whispered to the sky. Her throat was too dry to rage as she wanted. Her voice would crack if she raised it above a whisper. "Do You delight in tormenting us?"

Her gut ached, and she clutched her belly. It felt as hollow as the river cavern where she'd murdered Elsie. She'd been tortured by the thought of remaining Uriah's prisoner, and fearful enough not to care if she shot him dead.

Perhaps this is my punishment for Joss, and for Elsie—that the Carver has forsaken me.

She gazed at her branded palms, now almost invisible in the creeping darkness. If ever she had felt truly soulless, it was now. And Caleb? Because of her, he'd been dragged into the pit. If she had not sparked his interest, had never met him, Caleb would have returned to the Old Town, to glory and acclaim. He would never have questioned the Carver or doubted the Righteous.

He would never have to decide what to do with a woman ruined.

She looked up. The night sky spread above her like a smothering cloak. She spotted the Soul Stars, the constellation Caleb had pointed out during their voyage aboard the *Deliverance*.

"'Twas by following those stars that our people first guided themselves to Azazel. Eventually, they became a symbol of exile for those of the lot. And later, a symbol of judgment for those doubly branded. Though one might say 'twas also a sign of mercy."

Sela choked down a sob. How cruel that the miseries of thousands were forever enshrined in the celestial tapestry. The stars mocked the very mark the soulless bore on their hands, which kept them from all they loved. The soul mark was not only part of Azazel, or even Eremia, but also woven into the fabric of the world itself.

Was this proof that the lot was the Carver's will? That despite what Caleb hoped, mercy could *never* triumph over judgment?

Hearing a rustle behind her, Sela spun. Only the shadows greeted her, unfurling and drifting like columns of smoke, mingling with a gathering fog. She propped herself up on her elbows. Her head throbbed, and weakness stole through every limb.

What is wrong with me? She had to move, had to reach the edge of the desert. If not, she'd become prey for some wild animal, or worse, Uriah.

The thought of Uriah drove Sela up on her knees, and then to her feet. The world blackened and peeled like the edge of a parchment held to a flame. She moaned. Her wounded arm felt plunged into fire. The brands on her palms burned afresh. A bat flapped its leathery wings overhead.

Tight bands of fear constricted her ribs. "Carver of Souls," she whimpered, "if You care as Ross and Caleb believe You do, show me. If 'tis Your will that I die out here, then please let me die quickly."

Her legs had the dexterity of wooden blocks, but she pushed on, following the Soul Stars. Their heavenly course now directed her earthly one. Each step screamed that her blisters had birthed blister colonies of their own. The touch of her skin grew scorching. At the same time, her body became wracked with uncontrollable shivers. She hunched over, clutching her sides.

Reaching the boundary of the desert, she found a sand-covered rocky plateau and began lowering herself to the ground. She intended to rest for only a moment, but her legs gave way and she crumpled. She was dimly aware that her bandage had come loose. Blood dribbled down her arm in rivulets, soaking into the sand. Was it her imagination, or did it sizzle on contact?

Hearing a stir of movement, she started, but she could not lift her head. Her groan emerged as a faint croak. Sprawled flat on her back, she stared up at the Soul Stars. They were beautiful, draped in glittering mantles of cold elegance. Now and then they winked, as gossamer clouds drifted below them like bridal trains, arrayed with lacy splendor at their feet.

Perhaps this is a good way to die.

Her parents and Cadence wouldn't hear of her end, but since they didn't receive any news from Azazel, they would know no more grief than if she had lived to be an old woman, bearing Caleb's children and eventually holding their grandchildren. Teodoir would sit in his favorite armchair, the springs pushing up through the upholstery like knives, his sharp mind worrying the fate of his most rebellious pupil like a dog with a bone.

But he too would pass beyond the veil, as would Sela's parents, and eventually her siblings. Even Lord Auberon would journey into the eternal realm and face his judgment before the Carver.

As they beheld all manner of changeless sorrows, how could the stars not purvey indifference? Perhaps—as in the jungle—human sorrow, viewed from the same angle hour after hour, blurred into weary sameness.

Time slipped away. Ice crept into Sela's veins, and her pulse faltered.

If only I could have seen Caleb one last time.

If the souls of the branded truly ceased to exist at the moment of death—save those that floundered for a time in torment as recompense for earthly sins—then she would not see Caleb ever again. A grave loss. Sela doubted any woman could feel for a man what she felt for her bondmate, though such love was no less mortal than anything else humankind encountered.

She sighed. It was only a dream.

While Caleb lived, I almost believed You loved, Carver.

The thought trailed off into nothingness as the shadows nudged closer. Her eyelids fluttered and she dozed.

A hissing noise neared her ear. She flinched awake. Something scraped against her arm. Smooth, dry scales brushed against her fingertips. The flick of a serpentine tail flashed in the gray darkness.

No! Help! But she couldn't move. She couldn't speak.

Then light fell around her, and the snake slithered into the shadows. The figure of a man emerged from the gloom, as bright as if he walked in the glow of the sun. How was this possible? Night had closed in around her.

Sela could not see the man's face. Was he holding a lantern in front of him?

"Caleb?" she ventured.

The figure knelt beside her. Though he shone too brightly for her to discern his face, she knew it was not her bondmate.

"Don't be afraid." His voice sounded deeper than any man Sela knew. Warm fingers, workworn and callused, gripped her hand, which was slippery with blood. "This is not the end, Sela." He addressed her like a father to his daughter. A brother to his sister.

"How do you know my name?" she whispered, but the light faded. The man vanished too, though she still felt the warmth of his hold.

Seconds passed, and then she heard distant shouts.

"There, where the light was! I see her!" The voice of a man, different from the first man, and excited rather than reassuring. He was gaining on her position. "Over here! Quickly, now!"

"Do you see her? Oh, there she is!"

Sela tried to struggle upright. She expected Uriah to materialize from the gloom, but her body had gone limp and unresponsive.

A lantern swung into her field of vision, a feeble recollection of the glory of the earlier one. Light splashed on the eager faces of a woman, a man, and a boy.

Strangely familiar faces.

"Sela!" Briella rushed forward and lifted Sela's lolling head into her lap. Her fingers stroked the hair back from Sela's burning face. "Can you hear me?"

"She's nearly unconscious," Thaddeus said.

"Keep the lantern out of her eyes, Jax. 'Tis blinding her," Briella ordered. "'Tis just as Noemia's dream said, Thaddeus." Her voice sounded like a faint echo of her usual self, but held wonderment.

"What's wrong with her?" Jax retracted his lantern.

Callused fingers probed Sela's arm, then gently pressed against her forehead. "The wound is not infected. Unless she's injured elsewhere, it appears she might be seasoning."

Seasoning, also called the ague. Sela faintly recalled what she knew about this illness. Many endured a period of fever after arriving on Azazel. It often proved fatal for some, and resulted in lifelong weakness for others. After all these months on the island, she thought herself immune from the affliction.

Thaddeus muttered something that sounded like a prayer, then said, "She's very weak. We must get her back to Belladonna or she'll die. Jax, would you bring the horses?"

Footsteps retreated, and someone held a waterskin to her lips. She drank eagerly, suddenly registering her thirst.

"Caleb," she murmured. Her eyes opened. A faint glow surrounded the concerned faces of the brother and sister hovering over her. "Was there someone else?" she asked. "Where did the man with the light go?"

Thaddeus appeared puzzled. "There's none else here besides us."

The world lurched, and Sela was lifted over a shoulder. Why did her limbs feel as if they were made of lead? Yet, Thaddeus carried her as easily as he had the day she sprained her ankle.

"Hold on, Sela. We'll get you home soon."

She dangled helplessly over Thaddeus's shoulder and clung to the words of the first man, who had known both her fear and her name.

This is not the end.

When Sela opened her eyes, her first thought was that she was back on the mountain. The sky was gray and overcast, and thunder growled faintly in the distance. A burst of light illuminated her old room at Thaddeus's house. Two women sat in twin chairs beside her bed. Both worked at needlepoint, though the younger appeared distracted.

The older woman stirred first.

"Sela," Noemia said, raising sightless eyes to the bed. "You're awake."

How had she known?

Briella straightened. Faint creases smoothed from her brow. She set aside her needlepoint and approached the bed. "How do you feel, Sela?"

"Like every muscle in my body was on fire, and the flames only recently doused."

Briella laughed and helped Sela into a sitting position, stuffing a pillow behind her back. Someone had washed her hair while she was unconscious. It hung in a soft braid over her shoulder, tied off with a green ribbon.

Beneath her chemise, tight bandages wrapped her arm and lower leg, though the pain from both wounds had nearly disappeared. A dull ache permeated every inch of her body, as if she'd run up a mountain and tumbled back down, collecting every stone and hollow on the way. "I don't understand. How are you here? I thought for sure you'd left Azazel."

Noemia, dressed in a muted gown, bent to her work.

Briella's face angled away, her pallor matching the sky beyond the half-drawn curtains. "We did leave, Sela, thinking you right behind us. Captain Ward anchored close to Azazel for as long as he could, in the hope that you would follow. But when we sighted the warships from the Old Town, he had no choice but to depart."

Sela nodded.

"We sailed away from Azazel on the trajectory that Captain Ward and Captain Foley had agreed on. Three days into the journey, when you still had not joined us, we began to grow uneasy. That night, Thaddeus had a dream. The Carver told him to return to Azazel. We were needed there."

Briella gnawed at a lip that had evidently endured several days' worth of worry. "I don't know how my brother persuaded Captain Ward, but he agreed to return to Azazel, hoping to see what had befallen his friend. We anchored in the bay and rowed ashore under the cover of night. Belladonna and the fort had been damaged in the attack by Uriah Smith, but the soldiers had managed to restore some semblance of order in the six days we were gone."

"What of Lord Auberon?" Goosebumps popped up on Sela's arms beneath the covers.

Noemia flinched.

"He lives." Briella shot a sideways glance at Noemia. "He must have hidden himself away during the worst of the attack."

"Like a coward."

"Nevertheless, he was quick to reassert his authority. The settlement men and women who were uninjured in the attack were ordered to help rebuild the fort." Briella grimaced. "Many of their homes lie in ruins, and 'tis only a few months until the monsoonal rains begin in earnest. We have sheltered as many as we can, but Thaddeus and Jax and the others labor from sunup until sundown."

Sela watched Briella's face furrow. "Shouldn't you be resting?"

"I am well," the other woman replied. "I rest when I am able."

"What of Tempe? And Thomas?" Sela swallowed, remembering Ross's request to ensure his son was taken care of.

"Aye, they are well, praise the Carver. As is your friend Esther." Briella fidgeted with the branded hands in her lap.

Sela remembered the desert, the snake, and the figure of light. She had to ask... "Thank you, Briella, and for rescuing me too. But how did you find me?"

"When we arrived on the island, Noemia had a dream," Briella replied.

Noemia plunged her needle into the stretched fabric with a steady, comforting rhythm. Why would not Noemia tell of the dream herself? She seemed oddly quiet.

Briella went on, "Some of the settlement men and women saw Uriah Smith carrying a woman with long, black hair away from Belladonna, toward the mountains. There were reports of an injured, dark-haired man also taken captive. We thought it might be you and Caleb."

"Me, aye." Sela's voice was thick. "But 'twas Ross, not Caleb. Have you not seen Caleb?"

Slowly, Briella shook her head. "We've had no sign of Caleb, his brother, or your sister and her children."

"No sign at all?" Sela felt as if she lay at the bottom of the mountain, winded and gasping for breath.

"Nay. I am sorry." Briella brushed a strand of pale-blond hair from her face. "What of Ross?"

Briella's use of Ross's Carver-given name, rather than his usual title of Mister Bryant or Mister Ross, piqued Sela's curiosity. "He pretended to rejoin Uriah's band so I could escape, but he was still alive when I left."

When I left. A muscle tugged at Briella's mouth.

"He was injured," Sela added gently. "Otherwise he would have escaped, too." She glanced at Noemia. "You said there was a dream?"

"Aye." Briella once again spoke for the older woman. "Noemia dreamt that you were on the boundary of the desert on the other side of the mountains. She saw the entire thing, down to the stream near where you lay. It was dark when we arrived, and we could see no farther than the reach of our lanterns."

She shook her head. "I don't know how it happened, but we saw a bright flash of light—brighter than any moon or star, and like a bolt of lightning. We followed it and found you, nearly unconscious, just as the light vanished."

Despite the weakness in every muscle, Sela bolted upright. "Did you see him, then? The man who spoke to me?"

"The man?" Briella frowned. "There was no man besides Thaddeus. And Jax, who considers himself near fully grown." Her mouth quirked.

"'Twas not Thaddeus or Jax." Sela described the figure of light who had reassured her before the others appeared.

"Nay," Briella said at last. "We were alone in the desert."

"Never alone," murmured Noemia, speaking for the first time. She looked up. Her eyes were unseeing, but they were filled with a strange warmth. "The Carver holds all of us in His hands." With a sad smile, she squeezed Sela's hands and quietly left the room.

"Forgive her reticence," Briella murmured. "Noemia has been out of sorts of late. Weighed down with much grief. Thaddeus and I are not sure what ails her."

Feeling deflated rather than encouraged by Noemia's words, Sela wrenched her thoughts away from Caleb and back to the figure of light. "Almost everything she once loved is lost, stolen away. How could she not be lost also?"

Briella leaned forward and took her hands, as if she understood that Sela spoke not only of Noemia. "Everything, Sela?"

Searching her face, Briella's eyes begged her to insist otherwise. But by her expression, she had already seen the bruises on Sela's body. She must know what had been stolen from Sela.

"Everything," Sela replied. The word sounded like the final nail in the coffin of all her hopes. Aye, it was for good reason that coffins were termed *eternity boxes*.

"You've endured a harrowing voyage to Azazel, Sela. Several brushes with death. And now the seasoning. There is no 'sooner you cannot weather. Not with the Carver looking out for you. And Caleb too."

But the sag of Briella's shoulders betrayed her doubt. For all she knew, Caleb could be dead. Without him at her side, would the Carver even care what happened to Sela? She fingered the tattoo on her ring finger, the mark that bound her to a man who might even now have abandoned her, along with his God.

"How long have I been asleep?" she asked suddenly.

Briella shifted. "Sela, I don't think—"

"Please, Briella. I want to know."

Briella's restless fingers twirled a lock of her hair. "We returned to Belladonna a sevenday ago. 'Tis only a day more than that since we found you on the rim."

"Eight days? I don't understand—"

"'Tis not so long. You are young and strong, and you endured the seasoning better than most. You are weak now, but in another sevenday, you will have regained your full strength."

Sela turned away as tears dissolved the hope she'd entertained. Carver-fearing as she was, Briella could not understand.

It was time to face what Sela feared most, what she had known in the desert just before the light appeared.

Wherever he had gone, Caleb was not coming back.

Chapter Seven

Janus Auberon picked his way along the pockmarked street, wishing his horse's hooves and not his own boots were being soiled by the clinging mud. His open-topped carriage had been the first casualty of looters. They came across his possessions, along with the horse—whose legs and flank had been cruelly slashed—leaving Janus no choice but to put the beast down.

It was fortunate that his most prized belongings, including a chest that contained a treasure far more valuable than gold, were safe. The Carver's doing, to be sure.

When Janus first emerged from his hiding place—an underground bunker deep beneath the fort, one of the more useful aspects of his predecessor's legacy—he'd been pleased to learn that the land pirates, in their zeal to plunder the armory and treasury, had not seen the wisdom of burning down the fort in its entirety. Foolish, given it now housed the reinforcements that would ferret them out from their mountain stronghold and bring them to their knees, but Janus could hardly ascribe the happenings to luck.

On the contrary, 'twas more proof that the Carver was with him. The reinforcements from the Old Town had arrived just in time.

It was unfortunate that many of the settlement women had been seized—along with the rest of the treasures—and more than a hundred people were dead, including a dozen pirates. However, Janus found comfort in the thought that the children of the lot would no longer suffer needlessly. Their existence had been snuffed out, as it were, by the very same breath that had first given humankind life. The breath of the Carver Himself.

As for the doubly branded?

Janus kicked aside an empty cask and skirted the body of a nightwalker sprawled face down in the mud. Her branded hands splayed out, as if she reached for something just out of her grasp.

Aye, the doubly branded only reaped what they had sown.

"Lieutenant Griffin," he called to the man across the street from him.

The lieutenant picked his way over the muddy ground to Lord Auberon, pinching the bridge of his nose. "Yes, sir?"

"I want the rest of these bodies buried or burned by the end of the day."

"Burned, my lord?"

"They are beginning to decompose. That will spread disease."

Lieutenant Griffin nodded and hurried away to disseminate his orders.

Janus looked around. Belladonna had been restored to him for nearly two sevendays, but many bodies still lay where they had fallen. Some among the living traversed the streets as he did now. Unlike them, he was not searching for survivors.

A hopeless endeavor, he mused, eyeing the lifeless form of the nightwalker. From the corner of his eye, he spied a flicker of movement. To his right, an old woman leaned on the arm of a boy not yet a man. His features appeared mottled. Dark-brown skin warred with patches of pinky-white. By the look of his hands, the disease was not contained to his face.

Janus grimaced. It was not every day that one of the Righteous beheld a child cursed.

The woman on his arm exclaimed, and Janus discerned the flash of a gaudy, yellow gown. Her dark, gray-streaked hair was bundled untidily into a fat chignon, as if she'd attempted the feat without the assistance of a mirror. By the way she lifted her skirts and muttered, she'd become mired in the mud.

"Mistress Noemia," the boy said. "Here, let me help you." He leaned down and tugged at her boot, while she used him for balance. With his assistance, the woman came free of the quagmire and straightened, dropping her hem. She peered across the street, seeming to look directly at Janus.

Janus sucked in a breath. The woman's features, paired with her unusual name, declared her identity. When he'd returned to Azazel, he knew *she* might be here, though he had wondered if she had passed beyond the veil. It had, after all, been many years since he had seen her last.

Janus felt an unfamiliar squeeze of his chest at her gaze. Did she recognize him? Something about her stare felt wrong. When she took the boy's arm, maneuvering a slender cane with her other hand, he understood.

She was blind.

Intent on his mission, the boy failed to notice the attention he'd drawn. He continued past Janus, as did the woman. Janus watched her pass by several settlement women, touching their shoulders and hands—even faces—when they stopped to declare their identities.

So, she is kind.

Janus felt another inward squeeze but brushed it away. Aye, she might be kind. But he—Lord Auberon—could never know her.

"My lord?"

He turned and inwardly groaned at the sight of the lieutenant hovering at his elbow. "What is it, Griffin?"

"Some of the settlement men are saying—" Griffin's resolve wilted and his gaze slid to the ground. "They are asking for the soldiers' help to rebuild their houses, my lord. Many were destroyed in the flames."

Janus waved an impatient hand. "Do they not understand the danger? First, we must rebuild the fort. The men will then be returned to their families to build structures to their heart's content."

The lieutenant bobbed his head. "Aye, my lord."

When the man scampered away, Janus sighed. These soldiers were boorish and crude compared to the initiates of the Righteous. He had probably worn the Carver out by now with petitions to return Tucker Alexander to his side.

He frowned. The promising young man was nowhere to be found. None of the soldiers remembered seeing the acolyte beyond the beginning of the attack, either.

Tiring of the settlement, Janus returned to the fort. The musty, damp odor of his office greeted him as soon as he opened the door, along with something far more pungent. He closed the door and sniffed.

Tobacco.

The man standing behind his desk turned at Janus's entry. He grinned, removed the clay pipe's stem from his mouth, and upended it on the edge of the desk, spilling the spent, compacted leaves.

"I see that you are a man of action, my lord." Uriah Smith eyed the mud staining Janus's boots. "I must say, I appreciate that quality in a bureaucrat."

Janus seethed. "On my command, fifty soldiers could descend on this office to arrest you."

In answer, Smith tapped the holster at his hip. "No doubt you've heard of my unparalleled aim, *my lord*, and would rather live a long life than bleed out on this dusty floor. Besides, I think you want to hear what I've come to say."

"Speak quickly, then, Mister Smith. I have no desire to exchange pleasantries with a murderer." He crossed his arms and remained standing.

"*Captain* Smith, my lord."

"A captain is a man in command of a ship, Mister Smith."

"Aye." Uriah's mouth curved. "I am in command of more ships than you can possibly imagine." He claimed the commander's chair.

Janus frowned. "I understand that you were once in league with my predecessor, at least before he disgraced himself. After your vile actions this past fortnight, you cannot hope to entertain such an alliance with me."

"Have you not wondered at the ease with which my men took the fort?" Smith reached for the pipe, tapping the empty wooden bowl against his branded palm. "And yet, you seem so sure of the loyalty of the men in your employ."

"My reinforcements are fresh recruits from the Old Town, Mister Smith. You do not command their loyalty."

"Do I not?" Something glinted in Smith's feral eyes. "When you first arrived, my lord, I warned you that my reach extends far beyond Azazel."

"I did not respond to your threats then, and I will not respond to them now. You are a branded man and a criminal. You will never leave this island."

"I don't need to." Smith leaned back in the chair. "Have you never wondered what happened to your predecessor? I understand he died rather suddenly on returning to the Old Town."

When Janus said nothing, Smith expelled a tobacco-laden sigh and traced the intricate carving on the pipe stem. "You know, my lord, I don't even smoke. Most of the time, I dislike the stuff. But in the right company I will bear with it, to put my friends at ease." Smith eyed Janus's white coat and gloves. "Your predecessor understood the necessity of compromise."

"You have yet to convey its *necessity*, Smith."

The land pirate smirked. "I own the contents of your treasury and armory, my lord. Through ideology or terror, I command the loyalty of many in the settlements. More still on the settlement farms. Reinforcements or nay, if I were to attack Belladonna again—or any of the settlements—you would be hard-pressed to repel me. Not with your fort in such disarray, and your men so dependent on us for food."

"*Disarray?*"

"I hardly broke down the doors to gain entrance to this room, my lord."

Janus's eyes narrowed. "My men outnumber yours at least two to one."

Smith remained silent, but a smile danced on his lips, teasing him with what they both knew. Janus's men would be no good to him if they all starved.

"What are you offering, Smith?"

The pirate planted his hands on either side of the chair's armrests. "Peace, my lord. Your king will look kindly on an administration with little conflict or bloodshed, will he not? Not to mention you would gain the approval of your order."

"The Righteous care not for earthly conflict."

"Nay, my lord. You are only here to preserve souls. To keep the Pure from associating with the tainted. Am I correct?"

Janus gave a tight nod.

"To that end, I can help you. I will keep my men away from the fort—and from the unbranded—giving you free run of *your* Azazel." He paused. "Providing you allow me free run of mine."

"What of the branded captives your men took prisoner?"

"You do not care for their pawned souls, do you, Lord Auberon?" He lifted a branded palm, his eyebrow raised in mockery. "You cannot possibly care for mine."

Janus scowled. "You are a wretch and a scoundrel."

"Aye, and I despise the Righteous." Uriah smiled. "But we can live with each other, can we not? It seems a mutually beneficial arrangement."

"'Twould benefit you far more than I, Smith, since more reinforcements are a single order away."

"An order that would see you—and your beloved Carver—made a laughingstock back in the Old Town, my lord. They will say that you cannot control your acolytes—or should I say *acolyte*—let alone a mob of soulless cowards."

"You speak of Caleb Alexander."

"Aye, I speak of Alexander. My brother-in-law, as fate would have it."

"Brother-in-law?" Unused to being in the dark, Janus wanted nothing more than to throttle the pirate. Were Smith not in possession of a flintlock and an array of wicked-looking knives, he might have attempted it.

"Aye. Caleb Alexander has recently bonded with the pretty Sela, my bondmate's younger sister. In his haste to leave Azazel, Alexander left Sela behind. She and I recently spent an enjoyable sevenday together." He smiled, leaving no doubt as to his meaning.

Janus shrugged. He felt no more pity for Sela than he'd felt for the dead nightwalker. "Where is Caleb now?"

"Consider my information the beginning of a promising alliance, my lord. A gift, you might say." He studied his fingernails. "The Alexander brothers left Azazel together, along with Sela's sister Liri and our children. The brothers had a disagreement before they departed. Perhaps the younger coerced the elder to leave."

"'Tis likely."

"Regardless, Caleb Alexander considers himself deeply in love with his bondmate and will not abandon her for long. When the brothers return, you will have Tucker Alexander, your protégé, back. And...once Caleb determines his bondmate is no longer untried—"

"Untried?" Hadn't they been bonded?

"Aye, my lord. *Untried*. Another thing you may eventually thank me for. Once he discovers she is spoiled, Caleb Alexander will have no choice but to put her aside."

"'Tis more likely he'll come after you."

Smith tapped his holster. "If he does, I will be waiting for him." He smiled. "Should the conditions be right, Caleb may yet return to his brother's side...and to yours."

Janus stroked his chin, considering.

With a decisive nod, Smith got to his feet, executed a mocking bow, and glided past him.

Janus swiveled. "You would leave before I give you my verdict?"

The pirate smirked. "You have given it, my lord. I see it in your eyes."

"Do not presume to know my mind," Janus snapped. "Very well, *Captain*. I agree to leave your men in peace, provided you do the same for mine. But there are terms we must discuss. Specific details of this arrangement."

"Another day, perhaps." Smith reached for the door handle. "I need a drink. And since I've established that you keep no liquor in your desk drawers, I must hunt for it elsewhere."

"Will you go after Sela Alexander again?"

Smith stilled, and his dark eyes gleamed. Then he shook his head. "I got what I wanted."

"You would let the woman who shot you remain among the living?"

Something gnawed at Smith's mouth, eating away the composure he'd previously displayed. "'Twould be a pity to destroy such beauty." His look turned pointed. "Besides, so long as Sela lives, Caleb will be clay in your hands." He pushed his pipe into Janus's gloved palm and slipped from the room.

Janus looked down, studying the clay pipe. It would not take much force to break it. Was it possible, though, to bend the carved façade to his will? He closed his fist over the pipe and crossed to the threshold of the open door. "Captain Foster!"

Seconds later, a man emerged from the shadows of another building, his red coat askew. Beads of sweat broke out on his forehead at his commander's dark expression. "My lord?"

"Summon the officers—all of them. And bring me every last guard who was on duty a half hour ago!"

The breeze fanned Sela's face, trying to stir her back to life. It might as well have saved its breath.

Sitting on the sand with Briella, who held a sleeping Thomas, Sela watched Tempe. The child ran up and down the tiny beach. Had she ever played with such abandon? Aye, she must have, at least before Liri had been taken.

"She misses her little friend." Briella rearranged her shawl so that it sheltered Ross's son from the sand the breeze was whipping up. "She asks each day when Anwen will return to us." When Sela didn't answer, Briella sent her a concerned look. "I am sorry. I should not have mentioned it."

"'Tis no matter." Sela tamped down the hollow feeling in her stomach. That was one small mercy, at least. She was not with child. Her monthly cycle had resumed shortly after she'd regained consciousness.

Her relief was short-lived. Three more days had passed without any sign of the others. She wavered between bittersweet hope and gut-wrenching emptiness, unable to accept that Liri or Caleb had abandoned her. Something must have happened to them.

Briella's hand reached out and found hers. "I would spare you this grief if I could."

Glancing up, Sela saw not only sorrow but also guilt in the other woman's face. *Guilt?* "You could have done nothing to save me from Uriah."

Briella watched Tempe, who was now building a sand castle, with shells for the windows and a moat of glistening emerald seaweed. "I thought the past would remain in the past. I did not believe he would come for you, as Thaddeus and Caleb believed he would. Yet he did, to spite your sister. For that, I am partially responsible. For 'twas I who first drove a wedge between Uriah and Liri."

Sela frowned. "I don't understand."

"Do you not see it?" Briella let go of Sela's hand and pointed to her daughter. "Our fates are more tightly interwoven than you know."

Squinting, Sela studied Tempe. She saw the blond hair and blue eyes, much like Briella's. She looked closer. The little girl's laughing face showed twin dimples in her cheeks.

Sela caught her breath. "It can't be."

"Aye, Temperance is Uriah's daughter, though he has never acknowledged her as such."

"Then you too were taken prisoner. Oh, Briella, I did not know."

"Nay, Sela. Do not misunderstand me, even in your kindness. I was *not* his prisoner." Her eyes held a shimmering sadness. "I was his bondlessmate, even while he was bonded to your sister."

Sela gaped, speechless.

Thomas murmured in his sleep.

Briella rocked the child in her arms and went on. "I regret that part of my life more than you know, and I have paid for it"—her eyes lifted heavenward—"the Carver knows, I have paid dearly. Uriah was with me when Liri's twins were born, twins he'd discovered were not his. A year later, near the time of my own daughter's birth, he was with me again. That was the day the soldiers tore

Liri's son from her arms. Because of *me*, little Liron was stolen from her."

Liri's words replayed in Sela's head.

"My son was taken in the lot more than four years ago and returned to Eremia. Had Uriah been there when he was stolen by the guards, he would have torn them all to pieces. As 'twas, he was elsewhere, with another woman."

Sela suddenly understood the tension between Liri and Briella, although both women always behaved courteously. It explained why they had never become friends, even as their daughters befriended each other, or why Sela had never once seen them speak together beyond a few polite words.

"Liri was right to blame me for the loss of her son," Briella continued, "but she never raised a hand or even spoke a harsh word against me. Soon afterward, Uriah set me aside. With a child on the way, I had nowhere to turn. So, I knocked on my brother's door, even though I'd spurned his help many times before. He took me in and gave me a home, clean clothes, and warm food. Noemia helped bring my daughter into the world, not even repulsed by my profession. 'Twas through their love that I first knew the Carver, though 'twould be some time before I knew Him in truth. Upon the full discovery of His mercy, I changed my daughter's name."

"You called her Temperance."

"Aye, as a mark of my new life. A pledge that I would never return to what I'd left behind, not even if I was near death."

Sela watched Tempe play, shuddering to think of the girl's parentage. Was the child aware she was the daughter of one of the vilest men who ever lived? "Uriah has not come for her?"

"He cares naught for his girl children. Were Tempe a boy, for certain he would feel differently."

A new thought occurred to Sela. "When I first arrived on Azazel and was searching for my sister, you knew who she was. Who *I* was."

"Aye," Briella replied softly. "While you are different women, you have the look of your sister. I knew you, and I knew you searched for her."

Her eyelids shuttered. "At first, I remained silent. I knew going after Uriah was impossible. Now, after everything that's happened, I would rather you know the truth from me than hear it elsewhere. No doubt you think poorly of me upon learning these revelations."

Briella was a great deal like Thaddeus, honest to the bitter end. Swallowing the lump in her throat, Sela shuffled closer and slipped an arm around the woman's waist. "I do not condemn you, not for any of it."

Briella's expression turned hopeful, but then her shoulders sagged. "You haven't asked me why I am dauncy."

Sela thought of Teodoir. "I'm guessing you'll share when you're ready."

Tears misted Briella's eyes as she watched Tempe dribble wet sand onto the topmost turret of her castle. "You know, my father used to say that." She hugged Thomas closer. "A few sevendays after Tempe was born, I grew restless. I could not bear living on my brother's charity, so"—she sucked in a breath—"I returned to the only living I'd known, leaving Tempe in Noemia's care."

Sela's gut clenched, understanding what she was going to say.

"I lasted only a sevenday before I returned, begging Thaddeus to take me in again. He did, but 'twas not long, a mere sevenday later, before I realized..." Her voice thickened. "Years of doing what I *did*, and a sevenday unraveled the future I might have had. Perhaps even a single encounter."

Sela gripped her hand. "Briella—"

"I am dying, Sela. I don't know how long I have. There are times when I think it will be many years, and other times when I believe it will be mere months. Of late, I've been better. Stronger. But my illness is cunning. I feel well one day and am bedridden the next, as you have seen."

"Does Thaddeus know? Or Noemia?"

"Aye. They have both known since the beginning. Though he would have taken you in regardless, Thaddeus hoped you might be a mother to Tempe when I am gone. She knows nothing of my wasting illness."

"I don't understand why the Carver does not intervene. 'Tis unfair. 'Tis wrong."

"Perhaps," Briella replied, "though 'tis not undeserved. I knew the risks, and I returned to that life in spite of them. Do not fear for me. There is good, even in this."

"How can there be good?" Sela choked down a sob. "You say you are *dying*."

"'Twas at the end of myself when I first found the Carver, Sela. Even when I was exiled from the Old Town and doubly branded because of my trade, I knew they had not robbed me of my soul. If they had, then why did I feel the shattered pieces of mine within me? But 'twas many years later, after I realized I was dying, that I knew real despair. From that, and from far worse, I have been rescued. Even if I die, I know I will live."

At that moment, Thomas awoke, and Briella brushed away her tears to tend him.

Tempe came running. "Mama, Mama! Won't you come see my castle?"

"Of course, my darling."

Standing with her, Sela reached out for Thomas. Briella held him close against her. "Don't fret. He will fall asleep soon enough."

Sela understood. If Briella could have no part of Ross—a man she clearly admired—then she would devote herself to the tender care of his son. Why had Sela not seen it before?

A man's voice sounded from behind her, and she jumped.

Thaddeus came forward. "I'm sorry I startled you." He gazed at his sister, who was inspecting Tempe's castle with admirable enthusiasm for a woman who knew she was dying. Then he looked at Sela, whose cheeks were still striped with tears. "She told you?"

"Aye, she told me everything."

Thaddeus looked weary, muddied and slumped with fatigue from a long day laboring at the fort. He cradled his useless arm against his chest as always. Not for the first time, Sela wondered how he'd acquired the injury.

"You must know that I would have given you shelter regardless of whose sister you were."

"Briella said as much." Sela lifted her eyes to his. "Thank you for saving me, Thaddeus. My second day on Azazel, and again in the desert. You didn't have to come after me."

The Remenant had risked everything for her.

"'Twas the Carver's will, and my pleasure." He watched his sister, and a companionable silence stretched between Sela and Thaddeus.

She remembered Briella's reference to her father. He had a similar saying to Teodoir. Something shifted into focus for Sela. "Who was your father?"

Thaddeus turned to face her. "And now, I must offer my own confession."

Sela frowned, puzzled. "I don't understand."

He smiled ruefully. "I have known who you are, Sela, almost since the beginning."

"Aye, Briella knew me as Liri's sister."

"Nay." He shook his head. "Though you have lived in my house all these months, you have likely not heard my last name. In the settlements, I am merely Thaddeus. My full name is Thaddeus Gaskell. I believe you know my father?"

"Teodoir?" Stunned by this revelation, she gaped at him. "Your father is *Teodoir* Gaskell?"

"Aye. I am his eldest son."

Her gaze swept him with new insight. He had his father's height, though Teodoir was not so broad. Had he been so in his youth? Meribah, Teodoir's bondmate, had also been a strong woman.

"I see your questions, Sela. Why not voice them?"

"You knew who I was?"

"My father gave you a letter, did he not?"

"'Twas destroyed on the crossing from the Old Town before I could read it." Never had she so regretted the spoiling of a missive.

"Teodoir was never a man to invest in a single venture. He wrote to me too, though I did not receive his letter until a sevenday after you sought shelter and employment from us. He testified to your innocence and asked me to be your guardian." He smiled. "By that time, I already considered myself in such a light."

"Then he's been in contact with you? All these years?" Teodoir's eldest son had been a child of the lot. Teodoir rarely spoke of his children, except to fondly recall a childhood habit, or to muse over a worn toy they had delighted in.

"Aye, Father wrote to me from the beginning of my exile. I fell into poor company and a life of disrepute soon after arriving on Azazel, so 'twas many years before he received a reply." His eyes shone warm and bright. "He forgave me for the hefty silence, for which I am grateful. For a long time now, his letters have offered advice and instruction, as if I were his esteemed and beloved son and not a branded criminal."

He offered another smile. "He spoke well of you, Sela."

She pondered this. "Then, his letter to me contained instructions to find you?"

"Aye, I believe so."

"Thaddeus *Gaskell*."

"Aye, the name has humble origins. It means 'shelter for goats.'" He laughed. "There is no significance to such a name, of course, unless you wish to cause yourself offense by considering yourself kin to such an animal."

Shelter. "'Tis an apt name." She wet her lips. "Does your father know about Briella?"

His smile disappeared. "Aye, he knows. He sends what medicines he can from the Old Town in an attempt to prolong her life. He also offers up a multitude of prayers to the Carver. But so far, 'tis to no avail."

"Your father does not condemn her?"

"How can he? His own bondmate was once such a woman."

Meribah? Teodoir's now-deceased bondmate? Sela recalled the faded green dress Teodoir had given her after she'd killed Joss Brigham. She knew even less of Teodoir's bondmate than she knew of his children. She crinkled her forehead as she remembered. Meribah's favorite fragrance was rosewater, she saw great beauty in small things, and Teodoir had loved her deeply. He'd suffered greatly after her death.

"Aye," Thaddeus was saying. "Our mother was a nightwalker before our father rescued her. She lived the rest of her life, short as 'twas, to please him. She was a remarkable and Carver-fearing woman, but she never recovered after learning her daughter had followed in her footsteps. 'Tis another source of my sister's guilt that our mother succumbed so easily to the river fever."

"Teodoir gave up the priesthood to bond with your mother?" Sela asked.

"Aye. Neither the priesthood nor the Righteous could accept his Binding to a former nightwalker. So, he left it all behind."

How much Teodoir had lost to pursue the woman he loved! *Like Caleb*, she thought. Did Teodoir still grieve for his previous life? The respect, admiration, and even wealth he might have enjoyed? The love of a pure woman, unsullied by other men?

Briella approached just then, holding Thomas in her arms. A windswept Tempe trailed behind. Thaddeus stooped to let the little girl climb onto his shoulders. He showed no revulsion or distaste in the way he responded to her.

Aye, he is a man like his father.

Briella, Thaddeus, and the children started up the hill toward the house. Sela lingered behind, spying something floating in the surf. She recognized the glutted object as it was tossed to and fro across the sand, its every movement at the mercy of the outgoing tide.

A glove, perhaps belonging to one of the guards.

She picked it up and studied the ruined white leather. The interior was clogged with sand and stank of rotted seaweed.

Memories assailed her. Roux, running along this same beach with Caleb's glove as her bondmate reclined in the sand beside her. The feel of the leather against her cheek when Caleb kissed her on the clifftop near the outpost. The arc of his strong arm as he tossed the hated artifact of his past life into the sea.

Yet, it had so easily returned to haunt her.

Her hand curled into a fist, and she gritted her teeth. Drawing back her arm, she hurled the glove with every ounce of her failing strength into the tide. It disappeared beneath the foam of the receding water.

If only it would stay.

Chapter Eight

"Your hands, brother. They look as if you've stripped them of their flesh. Are you trying to rid yourself of the brands?"

Caleb glanced up and scowled at Tucker, who strolled along the beach as if they hadn't been marooned for more than a sevenday. True to Liron's word, the storm had struck the ship around midnight, and struck hard. The hull sprang numerous leaks, and one of the schooner's masts had been reduced to shards and splinters. The captain had been forced to divert to a nearby island for repairs, or risk sinking before they reached Azazel.

If possible, Caleb would have leaped overboard and started swimming. He was almost certain Liri and the elder Liron would have swum along with him, if it did not mean leaving the children behind.

Tucker lowered himself to the sand beside Caleb, grimacing as he observed the raw, bloody flesh across both of Caleb's palms. "What did you do to yourself?"

Caleb clenched his fists, wincing at the pain. He'd helped cut and install a new mast—a task Tucker shirked in favor of lighter duties more easily accomplished without the removal of one's gloves. Caleb had also continued to work alongside Liron, driving himself to feverish lengths to speed up their progress.

As always, his hands bore the brunt of his zeal.

"You dare approach me, Tucker?"

"I've concluded that if you truly wished me dead, the deed would have been accomplished already, injuries or nay." He watched Caleb wind strips of fresh linen around his palms. "Besides, I know you fear the Carver too much to risk such an offense."

The Carver was another source of Caleb's frustration, another bond that seemed to be slipping away from him. He wished he'd thought to bring the extracts from the Book of Souls along, but in his haste to leave Azazel, he'd forgotten them. Next to Sela, they were his most treasured possessions. He sorely missed the comfort of the Carver's words, even though he'd committed many passages to memory.

"The Carver is not against seeking justice," Caleb said through gritted teeth.

"Aye, though He usually prefers to dispense it Himself."

"For someone who claims to know the Carver, you are ignorant of the heart of His teaching."

"And what is that?"

"That the essence of the law is mercy."

Tucker fingered the coin around his neck, visible now that his shirt was partially unbuttoned. "Letting the sins of the many go unpunished?"

"To your great benefit," Caleb observed dryly. He watched Liri walk along the beach beside her brother, her three children splashing in the surf. The young ones seemed glad of the damage done to the ship. This tiny island offered a welcome freedom.

Only Sela's siblings and Caleb chafed at the delay.

"I have spent almost seven years of my life dedicating myself to the Carver's decrees," Tucker defended himself. "Pursuing a life of purity. Surely that counts for something."

Had Caleb not said as much to Sela once? He crossed his arms. "Your sleeve only remains crisp and white because the blood of your wrongs covers another's sleeve. But the Carver sees all."

Tucker's expression soured. "She has influenced you."

"*She?*"

"Sela."

"Nay. I entertained these thoughts long before I left the Old Town."

Tucker studied his brother as if his intense perusal would uncover green skin or horrifically distorted features. "You have changed."

"Have I? Or have you only stayed the same?"

Tucker sniffed. "'Tis as I feared, though I never expected you to succumb to such an affliction. Azazel has corrupted you. *She* has corrupted you."

"Azazel opened my eyes, Tucker. Being tethered to Lord Auberon forced me to see the truth. There is no power in the lot, nor in the soul mark. The branded and the unbranded stand before the Carver as one, and...they stand equally condemned."

"*Heresy!*" Tucker hissed. "Misguided as you are, surely you are no friend of murderers and nightwalkers! Do you not see that you were meant for a life set apart? 'Tis not wrong to pursue such a life, and 'tis the lot which makes it possible."

Caleb stared at his brother. In that moment he saw him not just for who he truly was, but as if Tucker held up a mirror to himself. Was this how Caleb had appeared to Sela? Self-righteous, narrow-minded, and hypocritical? No wonder he had driven her away so many times. The soul that Tucker considered so untainted—so pure—was glutted with filth.

Tucker could not see that it was Liri's blood—*Sela's* blood—that dripped from his hands.

"He deserves to die for what he did to Sela."

Aye, Tucker did deserve to die. They both did.

Caleb didn't answer.

Tucker gave an exasperated sigh and scrambled upright, showering Caleb with sand. Liri and Liron were coming his way, but Tucker avoided them and instead headed for the son he adored.

At first, the younger Liron had regarded his father as cautiously as the elder did, but his need for approval was strong. Tucker proved himself devoted, showering Liron with attention and affection. The boy had lived almost his entire life alone. Even Tucker would seem a good father.

After uttering something to Liri, the elder Liron broke away and crossed the sand to Caleb. "You should tend those hands, my friend."

"You sound like Tucker." Caleb raised his palms. "I've bound them with linen."

"*Properly* tend them." Liron now sounded like Caleb's mother. "With rum and salve." He glanced at his sister. "Liri will gladly assist you."

When Caleb gave in and nodded, Liron eased onto the sand beside him. "The repairs are nearly finished. We'll be ready to depart come first light. By sundown tomorrow, we'll be in view of Azazel."

The sky had darkened, and the Soul Stars flickered overhead. How many nights had Caleb stared at them, listening as they urged him to return to Azazel? Yet, the prison-island seemed the one place he could never reach.

"So near and yet so far," Liron echoed his grim thoughts. "We will find her, Caleb. Tomorrow, we will begin our search."

Caleb did not tell his brother-in-law that he'd been tormented by dreams in which Uriah, tiring of Sela, had killed her. In his mind, he had seen her die five nights in a row—bled out into the sand or drowned in inches of water. He refused to voice the fear he knew Liron shared.

By tomorrow, I fear it will be too late.

Sela climbed the bay's southern headland. She marveled at the way the dying light glanced against the westward-facing cliffs, lancing the tips of the waves. Far below, the water churned in a cauldron of jagged rocks, swirling and sucking against the coastline. Each wave seemed to bear a little more of it away to deposit elsewhere.

For once, she was glad to be alone. It had been no easy task to lose her retinue of guardians, particularly Jax, who followed her like a self-appointed knight-protector of old, his jaw set and his eyes alert. She loved the members of the Remenant. Each had sworn their fealty in their own way, but the guilt in their eyes was too heavy to bear. All carried a piece of responsibility for her captivity, but unnecessarily so.

It had been her choice, in order to save Liri and her children, and later to save Ross. Traumatized as she was, Sela would have made the decision a second time. Her only deliberation concerned what to do now with the remaining, broken pieces of her life.

When she gained the summit, she took a moment to catch her breath. Here on this clifftop with Caleb, safety had descended on her like a comforting blanket. Here, she finally admitted her love for him. On this headland, the future had seemed secure, if not perfectly clear.

Passing the ruined outpost and the grassy patch where Caleb had kissed her, she made for the edge of the cliff. The closer she neared the edge, the more the wind swelled. Forceful gusts buffeted her, though earlier, the day had seemed calm.

Gripping her skirt, Sela peered down. The cliff dropped away, showing a ledge a little way below, just wide enough for a single foothold.

Shivering, she drew back a step.

Far below, other rocks jutted up from the swelling, frothy water. Were they sharp enough to break her body apart? Inky darkness inched toward the horizon, reclaiming the space the sun had warmed with a cold more contagious than river fever. It stole through every limb, reminding Sela that she had yet to fully recover from the seasoning.

The darkness conjured up memories that she now believed belonged to another life.

"Caleb, what you have lost—"

"I consider nothing against what I have gained. The Carver is still with me, and with you. And He has mercifully given us each other. We need only to be thankful."

If Caleb still lived, what would he say now? How did he know the Carver was with them? Was not presence a sign of great love? And was not abandonment the hallmark of its opposite?

If that were true, and Caleb was alive but had chosen to leave Azazel without her, then he had never truly loved her. Had he not claimed to have fallen in love with her during the sea journey on the *Deliverance*? Men surely did not impart their affection so readily.

If Caleb was dead, however, then Sela wanted no part of living.

The wind howled around her, reminding Sela of Roux, her beloved pet fox.

Another loss she dared not contemplate.

In the loneliness of the clifftop, more memories swirled, summoning others she had forbidden herself to recall—her mother, her father, Cadence, Teodoir. Why had she come here? The past only existed to taunt her.

Sela moved closer to the edge again. It would be easy—too easy—to lean forward. She would not even have to jump. The fall would be over in seconds, and the voices that haunted her would be silenced forever.

Even if Caleb comes back, he will not have you.

Nay, she shot back. *That's not true.*

The voice persisted, the polished words bearing a seductive, almost serpentine charm.

Don't you remember how in the beginning, Caleb Alexander feared to even touch you? So much so that he proposed bonding in name only? What will the good lieutenant do when he learns you were robbed of your innocence?

"He loves me!" she declared, but the wind sucked the words away as soon as they were voiced, rendering them hollow. Cross breezes tugged loose hair from her braid, scattering the black strands around her face.

He was one of the Pure, Sela, the serpentine voice said. *S-s-such a man would never love a woman defiled.*

She glanced back at the southern outpost. She'd once thought it beautiful and glorious in its crumbling ruin. Now, as the light receded behind the mountains, casting shadows across the grassy headland like long knives, she glimpsed what she'd failed to notice before. The stones were cracked and choked with weeds. The sagging roof had caved in and was covered in moss. Muddy puddles from recent rains lingered around the ruins, like festering sores amongst the verdant green.

Across the bay, the northern outpost gleamed like a polished gem, rivalling the wink of the white house far below. She could not ignore the jarring comparison. Caleb was a strong, stalwart structure next to her crumbling ruin. If she remained on Azazel, might she become the cause of his destruction, as Tucker believed?

Haven't you taken enough from him?

She looked over her shoulder. Sunlight pierced the stone outpost behind her, but it was faltering.

Caleb would grieve for me if I were lost.

She rubbed her thumbs over her aching temples. He would grieve, aye. But what if he also felt relief? Relief that he would not have to try and love her back to life, as he'd once tried to revive her with his breath.

Sela. One of the soulless. A woman damaged beyond repair.

Fatigue threaded its way through her body. She closed her eyes.

Give him a way out, S-Sela. It would be the s-s-selfless thing to do. The brave thing.

The smooth voice struck a chord. Sela was nothing if not brave. She opened her eyes and gasped. How close she'd come to the edge! The water pounded below in a soothing, comforting rhythm, a hypnotizing cadence.

She had been brave many times before. Why, then, could she not shake her fear of death? Nothing existed beyond the veil. The Carver cared naught for the soulless, whatever Ross or Caleb believed. There was only this clifftop, and the wind urging her to lean into its cold embrace. Icy fingernails scrabbled at her, urging her to cease her deliberations and surrender.

To live is easy. The charming voice spoke into her mind, eroding her resolve. *To die is the hard thing. This is your chance to give Caleb back his life.*

Just as suddenly, a new voice sprang forth, as if out of nowhere. At first, it seemed no more than an echo, but the words gained strength until the voice spoke louder—and more boldly—than the serpentine voice.

I will never leave you nor forsake you.

Caleb? She turned but saw no one. Perhaps it wasn't a voice. Perhaps she was remembering the words she'd read over Caleb's shoulder from the Book of Souls. At the time, the words had seemed more jeddarty-jiddarty than the jungle of Azazel. Did she only reach for the voice now because she was desperate for comfort?

"Who are you?" she shouted. She fended off a wave of despair that would have tumbled her over the cliff like chaff.

I AM.

No mere extract had answered her. She teetered on the edge, suddenly aware that the wind had risen. The sole of her boot scraped against stone, scattering loose rocks over the edge of the cliff and downward into shadow.

And she suddenly knew who had spoken.

"Everything changed the day that Liri was taken, Carver of Souls. *I* changed."

I AM the same yesterday, today, and forever.

"Why did You not save her?" she choked out. "Why did You not save *me*? You know what the truth will do to Caleb. He is a slave to Your every whim. Surely, You would not destroy Your most devoted servant."

Before the voice could reply, Sela continued, this time in growing anger. "What kind of God lets those He loves die? How can You be any better than me?" She remembered Elsie, who had died in exchange for Sela's freedom. Guilt nearly swallowed her whole.

I AM love.

She sank to her knees. "I thought Caleb loved me. I thought *You* loved me. But I am all alone in this wilderness."

For truly, Azazel was a place that existed not only on a map, but also in her heart. Her heart, an expanse more barren than any desert.

I AM close to the broken-hearted.

Sela frowned, remembering that line from Caleb's extracts.

"I am *beyond* broken," she whispered. "I have no other reason to go on." She leaned forward.

This is not the end.

The figure of light in the desert came to mind. She reared backward and struggled to her feet just as a burst of wind rushed past her, driving her forward again.

Teetering on the edge, her boots scrabbled for purchase on the rocky clifftop, but they encountered only loose gravel. She felt herself plunging downward. Her arms shot out, grabbing for a hold, but she only sensed them scrape against stone.

Shafts of light suddenly shone through the gaps in the ruined house, and a figure silhouetted itself against the glorious display. Her angel of light?

It was too late. She was slipping—

But nay. One of her boots found the ledge a little way down the cliff. Her body slammed against the rocks. She winced. A moan escaped her lips.

Her fingers gripped a tuft of grass growing from a crack. How long could the shallow-rooted plant hold her before shearing from the cliff face? Her heart thundered, and her stomach lurched. Where was that serpentine voice now, when she was so desperately clinging to life?

All was silent.

The silhouetted figure loomed above her. Then a man crouched at the edge of the cliff. He dropped onto his stomach and extended both hands to her. His position seemed almost as precarious as hers.

Caleb?

Nay, this man would be twenty years the elder of her bondmate. He was brown-skinned, with a dark beard hugging his rugged face. The hands he offered were bare but unbranded.

Nay, not Caleb.

"Reach out your hand and I'll grab you." His voice was deep and oddly reassuring. Why did it seem like she had heard it before?

She stared up at him, hope and desperation warring for predominance.

"Reach for me, Sela! There is not much time."

How did he know her name? She eyed his unmarked palms, feeling the tuft of grass giving way. "You don't want to touch me, sir."

"I know what I'm doing," he replied gently.

"You could be killed." Did he not know the punishment for touching one considered unclean?

His eyes, along with the extension of his hands, declared his answer remained unchanged. "I would save you, Sela, but you have to allow it."

As the tuft yielded its hold on the rock face, Sela knew she did not wish to die. Reaching up, she caught his hand, which immediately closed around hers. The tuft gave way, and her boot slipped from the ledge.

For a moment, Sela dangled in midair, tethered only by the man's firm grip. Grabbing both arms by her wrists, he hauled her up and over the cliff face. She gasped and caught her breath, flipping over like a fish on solid ground.

The man slowly straightened, and she saw that he was tall—around Caleb's height—but nowhere near as broad. How did he possess the strength to lift her dead weight up and over the edge? Sela was no slender reed, and this man seemed more scholar than warrior. However, the hands he had extended to her looked workworn and deeply callused, and his grip had been strong.

"Who are you?" she asked in wonderment.

His smile suffused his plain features with warmth, and she thought of her Remenant friends. He made no attempt to wipe his dusty hands against his clean tunic. She searched for the flicker in his eyes or the twist of his lips that would betray his disgust, but Sela saw naught but warm, steady, and unchanging regard.

"I am Magnus Theodorus," he said at last. "And I have come to set all to rights."

Chapter Nine

"Thaddeus and the others will be overjoyed to see you, my lord." Sela stepped to one side so Prince Magnus could enter the house ahead of her. "We had no idea you were coming to Azazel."

He nodded but said nothing.

Sela wondered, yet again, why the prince had declined to be escorted to the fort. Would he not want to meet with Lord Auberon or one of the officers directly? Instead, he'd asked to be taken to the place where she lived.

Sela hid a smile. Briella would have a feeze when she learned they were entertaining royalty.

A prince. A *prince* had come to Azazel—*the* prince, for the king had only one son, one child. Not only that, but he had saved Sela from certain death.

Stepping into the sitting room, she spied Thaddeus near the hearth, looking haggard and preoccupied. He turned a slow circle, but his eyes gave no flicker of recognition when he saw the prince. No wonder. The prince was dressed in the clothes of a commoner and appeared unremarkable, despite his unmarked palms.

"Thaddeus," Sela said, coming forward, "this is Pr—"

"Magnus," the man interjected. "I am newly arrived on Azazel and looking for shelter and work. Might I prevail upon your hospitality?"

"Aye," replied Thaddeus. He appeared as tongue-tied as Sela had been during the long walk from the headland back to the house. The prince had remained largely silent and did not elaborate on his astonishing announcement of why he'd come to Azazel.

To Sela, his presence was oddly comforting. He had answered her questions with the same warmth he'd demonstrated on the clifftop.

Nevertheless, why was he looking for work? No man of the prince's stature and pedigree need work for a living.

And to seek work among the branded? Unheard of!

"You are welcome, my friend," Thaddeus said, "for however long you wish to stay."

"Thank you." The prince joined Thaddeus at the fire, and the two men began to converse in quiet tones.

Why did Prince Magnus not introduce himself by his royal title or his Carver-given last name? Perhaps he was used to travelling incognito and had no wish to attract a crowd—or a mob. Yet, the man carried neither trunk nor retinue. Even a commoner would have brought along a sack or bag of some kind, but the prince had only the clothes on his back.

Sela backed away from the room, nearly bumping into Noemia, who was watching the man with sightless eyes. "I'm sorry." Sela reached for the woman's arm to steady them both.

Noemia's mouth quirked. "One would think the blind old woman the clumsy one. You have a visitor, Sela?"

"Aye, a man called Magnus."

"'Twould seem he's not merely a man."

Sela stared at her. "You knew the prince would come?"

"I hoped," Noemia replied in a voice just above a whisper. The words were heavy with longing.

"I don't understand," Sela began, words she uttered with increasing frequency of late. "Why would the prince of Eremia come to Azazel, of all places? And after all these years?"

Noemia leaned close, as if she sensed the salt in Sela's hair or the dust she'd not yet brushed from her dress. Did she know how close Sela had come to not returning this evening? "He did not tell you why?"

Aye, he had, *to set all to rights*, but despite his royal birth and status as one of the Pure, Prince Magnus had no real power against the priesthood—or the Righteous. As far as Sela could tell, he brought no army to stand against Lord Auberon or Uriah Smith. He did not even carry a sword or a flintlock. What did the prince hope to achieve?

"He said he would put all to rights," Sela replied at last. "But I do not think the prince knows how wretched Azazel has become. He is royalty, after all. How can he understand the way we live? Even if he could, how could he ever convince his father, the king, to act on our behalf?"

Noemia turned her gaze back to the prince with something that exceeded ordinary human sight. "He found *you*, did he not? In the dark of the night?"

Did Noemia refer to the desert, or to the clifftop where Sela had contemplated ending her life? Not for the first time, she wondered at the woman's near-prophetic gifting. "Aye, he did."

"Then have no fear, Sela. For he will surely find the rest."

At the first light of dawn, Caleb rowed ashore with Liron, suppressing the pain in his hands as he strained at the oars. Dismal winds had slowed their remaining journey, and the captain, exasperated by Caleb's repeated questioning, had told him once and for all that he could coax no more speed from the sails.

Caleb had not wanted to leave Liri and her children in Tucker's keeping, but his brother had sworn to watch over them until Caleb or Liron returned. At that offer, Caleb had scoffed and wanted to toss Tucker overboard.

Liri had eventually persuaded Caleb to leave her behind, with a gently reassuring smile that belied the urgency in her eyes. "Please, Caleb. There's no time to waste. Every moment matters, and I would rather you find Sela than linger here."

With a glance at Sela's little namesake, who watched him wide-eyed from within her mother's skirts, he finally nodded.

This day, I will find her.

The muscles in Caleb's shoulders knotted and throbbed, but he pressed on.

Liron watched him from the prow. "If ever I doubted your regard for my sister, my friend, I cannot doubt it now."

Preoccupied with his task, Caleb grunted.

"You don't regret your insistence to take the oars?"

"Nay," Caleb replied, though the pain seared him more than any brand.

As the boat glided toward shore, he observed his brother-in-law's first reaction to Azazel—the widening of his eyes when he spied the impaled skulls through the fog, and the furrowing of his brow while he discerned the cemetery and hanging tree beyond. Both these landmarks boasted more victims since the last time Caleb had seen them.

"How could my sisters survive such a place?" Liron whispered.

"You haven't seen the worst of it yet," Caleb returned with a sardonic smile. "The best parts are still to come."

"The best?" Liron's ghostly gaze swung to him.

Caleb recalled that this man had twice attempted to offer himself in his sister's place. Sela's brother was as brave as she was.

Caleb ran his tongue over dry lips. "I would have spared them all of it, if I could."

"I know, Alexander."

They came ashore on the southern arm of the beach in a tiny, sheltered cove not far from the cabin Caleb shared with Sela. By the look of the colors flying over the fort, the soldiers had regained control of Belladonna. After securing the boat, Caleb drew his primed and loaded flintlock, pleased when Liron did the same. Creeping toward the cabin, Caleb drew the edges of his borrowed greatcoat more tightly around him.

Except for deep furrows and muddy puddles from the recent rains, Azazel looked much the same. The cabin lay untouched, though upon entering, Caleb half-hoped to find Sela curled up in their bed, Roux on her feet as morning light turned the fox's fur to molten red. What had become of the animal?

He had not expected to find his bondmate there, but a pang of disappointment stabbed his heart when he surveyed the empty bedroom. He strode into the main room.

Liron faced him, arms folded across his chest. "What now, Alexander?"

"We make haste to Belladonna. The Carver willing, we'll find a lead there for us to follow."

Dawn was not an hour that usually saw Belladonna rife with activity and purpose, but this morning proved to be an exception. The main street swarmed with people. Farmers with loaded wagons churned through slippery mud that tarnished every boot and coated every hem. Crates of squawking chickens and makeshift corrals of grunting pigs filled the streets. Men piled lumber on the high side of the road, the freshly sawn planks smelling of sawdust and industry. Other wagons carted away shadowy figures that resembled corpses.

Caleb shuddered.

Charred ashes remained of several buildings, including the tavern from which he and Sela had rescued Esther. Several nightwalkers moved among the crowd, many favoring sensible cotton or wool over their usual satins. Their powdered faces, however, betrayed their occupation.

The stench of stagnant water, animal excrement, and something else—something far worse—assailed his nostrils. By the way Liron held his sleeve against the lower half of his face, he suffered even more than Caleb.

"I thought I was glad to leave the Old Town." Liron moved out of the way of a wagon bearing half a dozen empty barrels.

"The air is fresher beyond the settlements," Caleb replied. *But not by much.*

Everywhere men settled on Azazel, the island bore the tarnish of their influence. The other settlements fared little better than Belladonna. Hellebore, at least, was worse.

"There are hundreds of people here. How are we to find Sela?"

Caleb pointed. "That way lies the fort, and beyond it, Thaddeus's house." He had told Liron about the Carver-fearing man who'd taken in Sela, not even withholding his sordid history. It was far better, he'd reasoned, for Liron to come to terms with the man's past before it was thrust upon him, likely by Thaddeus himself. "I don't know if any of the others will have returned, but we must question everyone we meet."

Liron nodded.

Just then, a commotion drew Caleb's attention. Motioning Liron to follow, he went along with the crowd, peering over the heads of the onlookers.

Two wagons had collided in the din. The wheels of the second wagon interlocked with the first, and both sat in several inches of mud. Black-coated guards circled the wagons, scowling. One man clutched the bridle of a horse who snorted and tossed its head, nostrils flaring as if he too could not bear the stench.

Nearby, a red-coated officer wearing the gold trim of a captain jabbed a gloved finger into a shorter man's chest. "You drove your wagon into mine deliberately, did you not? You soulless have no respect for your betters."

The settlement man's mouth tipped sullenly. "I did not run into ye, sir. Perhaps if yer men were lookin'—"

"Silence!" The captain's nose reddened. "You're one of Smith's men, aren't you? Trying to slow down the rebuilding of the fort? Should Lord Auberon hear of this..."

Caleb ignored the remainder of the officer's threat. *Lord Auberon is alive?*

Beside him, Liron tensed. Caleb could tell he was nursing his own private flagon of hatred for the man who had stolen his two sisters.

The wagon owner must not have remained silent, for the captain grew livid. "I said *silence*, man, or you will find yourself standing at the gallows come sundown."

The man's chin jutted forward. "Better t' die a free man than t' live as a slave."

Dread coiled in Caleb's stomach.

"That's some mighty fine cheek music," replied the officer. "I will grant you your wish." He retrieved his pistol from the holster, cocked it, and pulled the trigger.

The gun fired. Smoke curled upward.

And the dead man fell backward into the mud.

The watching crowd dissolved into chaos, settlement men shouting and shoving at the soldiers.

Caleb felt Liron react along with them. It took all his strength to hold his friend still. "Nay, Meriweather." He planted a hand against Liron's chest and pushed him backward, away from the rioting crowd. "You cannot intervene."

"I would thank you not to tell me what I can or cannot—"

"Would you put Sela in further jeopardy?"

At this, the glazed look disappeared from Liron's eyes. He shook off Caleb's hand with a mutinous scowl. "I'm no fool, Alexander. There is a line between brazen recklessness and open cowardice."

"Aye, and right now you stand clearly to one side of it." Caleb frowned. "The *reckless* side."

"I thought the Righteous sought to intervene in matters of life and death."

"Matters of life and death, aye, but that is a senseless mob, with no thought other than vengeance." He indicated the crowd. They were attacking the soldiers with whatever rough tools or implements they gripped in their hands.

"I am no longer one of the Righteous." Caleb eyed Liron's clenched fists. "And you, my friend, are wanted for desertion. 'Tis best you not draw unnecessary attention to yourself."

Screams pierced the air, but Liron moved away, clearly heeding Caleb's warning.

Caleb turned to follow, stopping when someone seized his arm. He twisted around. A woman was about to be trampled underfoot. He reached out to catch her, grabbing her around her slender waist.

She regained her feet with his help. He discerned pale cheeks beneath an ebony-black fringe of hair. His heart jolted and he searched her face. *Sela?*

No, not his bondmate. Disappointment trickled through him, and he sighed.

The woman, however, mistook his scrutiny for interest. She smiled prettily up at him, her hand clinging to his forearm.

"I am sorry, miss. I mistook you for someone else. Are you well?"

At her wordless nod, he withdrew his arm and spun to follow Liron, who had disappeared into the writhing crowd, apparently no longer in need of Caleb's directions.

And then saw her.

Sela!

She stood not ten yards away, whole and unharmed, her spine ramrod straight in the violet gown he remembered—the one she'd planned to wear the day of their Binding, until it was replaced with the white dress.

Everything about sweet Sela was permanently tattooed onto his brain, the same way their bond was etched onto his finger. Her black hair hung in a tight braid over her shoulder, tied off with a green ribbon.

Her violet eyes travelled up him, sparking with recognition when her gaze connected with his. Her lips parted.

Caleb's heartbeat raced, heat igniting in his chest. He was dimly aware that shouts and gunfire splintered the air. Smoke from the soldiers' muskets stung his nostrils.

The woman he'd saved touched his arm. "Sir, I wonder if you might..."

The rest of her offer fell on deaf ears. Caleb stepped away and closed the distance between him and his bondmate. "Sela," he breathed.

Her gaze flicked to his left, staring at someone or something behind him. Sela's mouth firmed, and her eyes shimmered with tears.

"Sela!" He reached for her. Relief pulsed through every nerve like lightning. Caleb expected his bondmate to fall into his arms and sob against his chest.

Instead, she ran.

She did not want to know.

Sela had no wish to uncover why Caleb had appeared in the middle of a riot, looking as healthy and strong as the last time she'd seen him. Nor did she have any desire to learn the identity of the beautiful woman he had been so zealous to save from the mob. Her bondmate's hands had lingered around the slender waist as he stared down into the pretty eyes.

She could not bear to witness this connection, especially when the woman came after him and brushed her bare hand against his arm with sickening familiarity.

I don't care who she is, she raged. Her boots pounded across the dirt, and her breath punched the morning air in staccato bursts.

"Sela! Wait!"

No! She walked faster. The Carver willing, Caleb would be detained by the mob or the soldiers. Then she would be free to nurse the shards of her broken heart in peace.

Clearing the bulk of the settlement, Sela reached the beach, hoping to lose herself among the shrubbery. *Hurry. Hide!*

She'd just set foot on the sand, though, when heavy boots crunched behind her. Strong hands seized her shoulders and spun her around.

Sela resisted, clearly stronger than Caleb expected. His embrace turned into a tackle, and they fell together to the sand. "Sela," he said, crouching over her. "I'm sorry. I didn't mean to knock you over."

"Get off me."

He frowned. "I don't understand."

Sela shoved at his chest, but he didn't budge. Caleb appeared frozen, the weight of his body pinning her to the ground. "*Off.*"

Pain flickered in his expression. He lifted a hand to her cheek. "Why did you run from me?"

At his question, anger flashed behind Sela's eyes. "You were otherwise engaged. Quite pleasantly, it seemed." Tears trembled along the rims of her eyelids.

She's jealous? Of the woman he'd prevented from falling? He could not even remember her face. "She was a nightwalker."

Her sudden slap stunned him. Face stinging, he rubbed his cheek. "What was that for?"

"Employ that fine mind of yours to work it out for yourself."

He blew out a frustrated sigh. "A small child could be running into your arms, Sela, and you'd search for a snake in the trees."

Caleb easily caught her next swing at his face. "I thought for a moment that woman was *you*, Sela. Did you not see the color of her hair?"

"I saw that she was beautiful."

"Aye, as are *you*."

Sela's eyes narrowed, but her mouth softened.

Caleb's heart resumed its hammering. He lowered his head to kiss her. He'd found her, and so easily!

Sela flinched at his touch.

He frowned and drew back, giving her more room. "Did you think I abandoned you?"

In part, he *had* abandoned her. She had every right to be furious with him. He had sworn to protect her, and he had failed her in every way a man could fail his bondmate.

Sela didn't answer.

Caleb reached for her other hand. "I did not leave you willingly, my love. I swear it."

"He speaks the truth," Liron said from behind him. Where had he come from?

Sela's eyes widened. "*Liron*!" She squealed and pushed at Caleb. "Let me up!"

Caleb rolled aside, and Sela sprang to her feet. She ran into her brother's embrace. The joy of their reunion felt far more stinging than the recent slap. Caleb had hoped for such a greeting.

"This can't be!" Sela drew back, glancing between her brother and Caleb, who had risen to his feet. "You were in the king's navy, Liron, headed for the mainland. How did you—"

"There will be time enough for questions later." Liron gripped her elbows. "Are you well, Sela? Are you safe?"

The fire seemed to seep out of her. She faltered, looking as if she would collapse if not for her brother's support. "I am safe." She looked at Caleb with an expression he could not identify. Fear? Grief? Whatever it was, it was undeniably raw. "Thaddeus and the others returned to Azazel," she went on. "They found me on the rim of the desert and brought me back to Belladonna."

In a desperate attempt to contain his emotions, Caleb turned away. So, the others had been there for Sela, when *he* had failed her. His fists clenched. If Tucker were on the island right now, he would deposit his white-coated brother into the midst of the rioters. They could tear the flesh from his bones like a murder of crows—an apt name for the collective grouping of carrion birds.

You say forgiveness is the true mark of the righteous, Carver, but how can I ever forgive him?

His chest heavy with grief and anger, he returned his attention to Sela. She was watching him intently. If he had doubted the strength of her affection before, he did not doubt it now. There was no masking the love in her eyes. Why, then, did she seem so ill at ease? So estranged from him?

Once again, she sought her brother's arms—not Caleb's—for stability. "The soldiers will come soon to quell the riot. We should return to Thaddeus's house before they arrive."

To punctuate her warning, a gunshot sounded in the distance.

Caleb registered the sound of pounding hooves from the direction of the fort. "Come on." He crossed the sand to Sela's side. When she held out her hand, he took it and squeezed.

In return, he felt an answering tremble. Dread rippled through him.

Carver, what has happened to her?

Hope deferred makes the heart sick, Caleb's Book of Souls boldly declared, *but a promise fulfilled is a tree of life.*

Why, then, did Sela feel as if the world was a bedsheet that had been violently jerked out from under her?

She'd rejoiced to see her brother, having believed she would never see him again. Liron spoke little of how he had come to Azazel, but she saw the changes in him. A year had transformed the boyishly valiant soldier into a man. His firm, angular jaw and his bearing projected strength and confidence, although his eyes still sparkled with mischief, as they always had.

Caleb, on the other hand—

Liron let go of Sela's arm. "I must retrieve Liri and her children."

She glanced up hopefully. "She is with you?"

"On a merchant ship in the bay." He exchanged a dark look with Caleb. "Along with...others."

Caleb's face turned rigid. "You have my permission to tie Tucker to the heaviest anchor and drop him into the deepest part of the bay."

Feeling his hand close around hers, and the strips of linen banding his palms, Sela wondered at the dangerous look in his eyes. What had Tucker done to make Caleb despise his brother so? At worst, he was guilty only of fleeing like a coward.

Yet, Liron clearly shared this hatred of the elder Alexander. "Don't tempt me." He gazed at Sela, and his voice softened. "Go with Caleb. I will find you, I promise." He turned and headed back to the ship.

Sela flinched at her brother's instructions.

Caleb's hand tightened around hers. "Come on. Can you run?"

She nodded and they set off, his hand never once leaving hers. Skirting the soldiers that marched from the fort, Caleb led her toward the white house, not even breathless when he climbed the hill with long strides. Still weak, Sela lagged behind, tugging on his hand.

His face filled with concern at her ragged breathing. "Sela?" Hands encircling her waist, he drew her close.

"'Tis...the...seasoning," she managed between breaths. "I am not yet...fully recovered."

Caleb's eyes swept over her in alarm.

Sela sighed in relief that the sleeves and bodice of her dress hid most of her bruises.

However, his eyes narrowed when he saw the marks that *were* visible, now faded to a sickly yellow-green. His blue eyes darkened, pupils sharper than any reef. "Sela—"

"As Liron said, there will time enough for questions later," she replied, anxious to forestall the inevitable as long as she could. For now, she could not bear it if he turned away from her. "We must get to the house."

After a long moment, he gave a brisk nod. Then he bent and swept her into his arms.

"Caleb..." she protested weakly.

"Put your arms around my neck."

Her heart was suddenly awash with foolish desires, and she complied. Caleb continued his march up the hill. She leaned her head against his shoulder, acutely remembering—though it had only been a few sevendays ago—the way he had held her in the night, as securely as he held her now. The steady *thump-thump* of his heartbeat was more reassuring than the crash of the surf on her favorite beach.

Aye, Sela Alexander. You are *a fool.*

When they reached the base of the white house's stairs, he set her down on the bottom step. They stood at eye level, his hands still at her waist. She did not step away, and he made no indication of wanting her to. So, she remained. Her eyes traced every feature of her bondmate's handsome face.

This time, she saw what she'd missed before. The shadows beneath his eyes spoke of many sevendays without sufficient rest. Worry grooves carved his mouth, which had formerly been given to laughter. Fatigue rested like an invisible weight upon his broad shoulders.

He leaned closer and flicked her braid aside. "You know, green was once my favorite color."

"Once?"

"Surely you remember 'tis violet now."

A sob rose in Sela's throat, and he pulled her against him. She pressed her face into his shirt. He smelled of the sea, the acrid tang of gunpowder, and tempered steel. Easing back, she touched his face, noting that he had not bothered to restrain his hair in a queue. "I've never seen you looking so wild, Caleb Alexander."

A commotion sounded from within the house, feet clomping down the stairs.

"I want to hear everything," he said softly. He glanced at the door. "Once we're alone."

Everything? Sela remembered how he'd turned away when she spoke of being rescued from the rim and wondered how she could bear to confess the rest. She swallowed and looked at her feet.

The door flew open. "Mister Caleb!" Tempe launched herself from the top step, and he was forced to let Sela go to catch the little girl. "You're back!"

Chapter Ten

S ela watched through a haze as the fragments of her life were quietly stitched back together. No one broached the topic of what had caused the rending. Tempe chattered on about flowers and lessons before vanishing up the stairs once again.

Overjoyed at Caleb's return, the members of the Remenant welcomed him warmly. He didn't flinch when Noemia took his hands and squeezed them. A quick glance at Caleb confirmed what he thought of the stitching, that despite the happy reunions, light still poked through the seams.

"I want to hear everything."

Sela must avoid Caleb as long as she could, and forestall his questions. She could not endure another sundering from him.

When Thaddeus returned from the settlement with Prince Magnus, Caleb showed no recognition of the king's son but greeted him as he would an equal. To Sela's surprise, the prince tolerated this lapse in formality. He wore the same casual garments he had worn the day of his arrival. Covered with dirt like Thaddeus, both men looked as if they had spent the day rebuilding the fort.

Sela had yet to understand why the prince kept his identity concealed, and why he sought the company of murderers and nightwalkers rather than the Righteous. Since she owed him her life, perhaps even twice over, she would trust his reasons.

When night fell, Caleb wanted to return to their cabin, but Thaddeus shook his head. "There's still trouble down in the settlement, my friend. Stay up here tonight and go down tomorrow. I imagine Sela's brother and sister have been delayed coming ashore because of the riot. They will know to find you here."

Sela quietly rejoiced for his intervention, and for Caleb's grudging acceptance. Though she hated herself for it, she wished for one selfish moment that Briella was dauncy. Then Sela might excuse herself to look after Tempe and Thomas, thus delaying the questions that were sure to follow, when she and Caleb were alone. After she began another of her myriad tasks, however, Briella urged her to her room.

"Go, Sela. There's nothing else for you to do except seek your rest."

Some of the devastation in Sela's heart must have spilled onto her face, for Briella's features softened. She took Sela's hand. "There's no hiding the past, my dear. Caleb must manage it in his own way."

A tear slipped down her cheek. "And if he turns from me?"

"'Twas not your fault what was done to you." Briella's eyes sparked. "If Caleb turns from you, rest assured that Thaddeus will have his head. Or *I* will."

This seemed hardly a comfort, since Sela rather liked Caleb's head. She nodded, abandoned the laundry she was folding, and slipped into her room.

Sela found Caleb standing next to the window, gazing out at the moon-streaked grass. His hand rested lightly on the pane. How many times had she watched him in the garden from this vantage point? The last time he'd been in this room, she had pledged herself to him, body and soul.

She was no longer certain as to what had become of either.

When she stood beside him, he slipped his arm around her waist. She reached for one of his bandaged palms. "Your *hands*, Caleb—"

"—will heal, as always."

"And what of wounds that won't heal?"

Silence stretched between them at her soft question. With a low sigh, he pulled her into his arms. "I promised you I'd never leave you," he whispered against her hair, "and yet I left you alone on that jetty."

"You did so unwillingly."

"Aye."

After a long moment, he began to speak. He told her of the moment he'd realized that she and Tucker had strayed from their position. The gunshots. How Tucker had reappeared, dragging Liri and her children. How Caleb had come after Sela, only to be attacked by Tucker from behind. And of the blow that had felled him, leaving him helplessly watching through the fog as Uriah bore her away and he slowly lost consciousness.

His hands tightened around her back as she slipped her fingers into his thick hair. She felt the knot at the base of his skull that had rendered him unconscious for days. He stilled at her touch, and his eyes closed as she gently probed the wound.

Did her touch cause him pain?

Then he continued in the same weary voice, explaining how he'd nearly killed Tucker. "I would have prevailed on the last attempt if not for Liri's intervention," he murmured. He spoke of their unexpected, impossible meeting with Liron—and Liri's son—in the middle of the ocean.

Sela felt a quiver of joy for Liri, who had been so long divided from her twin brother and her son. It dissolved when Caleb told of the two storms that had driven them off course, the second forcing them to a nearby island for repairs. As her mind computed the days, Sela realized it was the same storm that had allowed her to escape from Uriah.

When Caleb finished his retelling, he leaned his forehead against hers. "As you can see, 'tis not a lengthy tale. Besides the usual tasks of a novice sailor, I did little else besides sleep, eat, and watch the horizon."

She traced the lines at his eyes. "I see little evidence of sleep."

"Every dream has been full of you," he admitted. A simmering darkness returned to his gaze. "You warned me that Tucker was not to be trusted. I should have believed you. I should never have left you alone."

"You had no choice." She remembered Tucker's injured hand, which had prevented him from helping the sailors. "And you had no inkling he would resort to such violence."

"Nay. Because I was blind."

What could she say to absolve him, when she could not even absolve herself? "You kept your promise, did you not? You came back for me."

"Aye." He traced the lace edge of her bodice over her shoulder until his thumb glided lightly across the bruise marking her collarbone. "But I was too late." He held her gaze with infinite compassion. "Wasn't I?"

Sela bowed her head. She tried to pull away, but he held her—tenderly, she thought—as her vision blurred with tears. Her head found the space between his arm and his shoulder. Though she believed he would withdraw once he knew the truth, he rubbed her back while she wept.

"Naught will change my love for you, Sela." His hand moved to caress her hair. "I am not a priest that you must confess to me. You do not have to share anything until you are ready."

At the mention of the priesthood, Sela's tears became a flood, more raging than the river that had taken her from the mountain. "You don't know what you're saying."

"Aye, I think I do."

He bent and lifted her into his arms. As he carried her to the bed, she fought a surge of panic. Clearly seeing her anguish, he placed her on the mattress and sat beside her, taking her hand in both of his.

"I would hear it all, but only when you are ready."

Aye, she was ready, but he did not know how much they would lose in the retelling.

She told him everything. Of her capture, of Uriah and his fear of thunderstorms, of Ross and his injuries, of the debauched secret hideout under the mountain, and how she'd given in to Uriah to save Ross's life.

When she had finally ceased to fight the pirate, he had tired of her within a sevenday. The chase exhilarated him, but he'd quickly turned bored by the reality of possession.

Caleb said nothing.

Sela did not look to see if the tension in his face matched that which resided in his fingers. Instead, she told of Ross's asking for her, and how he'd helped her escape. When she spoke of killing Elsie in Uriah's place, a tear slipped down her face. A long moment elapsed before she could speak again.

In a soft monotone, she related her flight from the river cavern, her gunshot wound and growing sickness, and her journey across the desert. She ended her tale with a cursory mention of the snake and the figure of light, and then her discovery by Thaddeus, Briella, and Jax.

Sela did not tell him about the clifftop, and how Magnus had pulled her to safety. Caleb need not know how close she'd come to giving in to despair.

Moonlight trickled through the window and splashed to the floor. Sela wished Caleb would speak, and yet she feared his reply—his anger. Finally, she looked up.

Caleb's head was bowed, and his eyes closed. Tears hovered on the edges of his dark lashes. She quelled her surprise. Sela had rarely seen a man cry, and never had she seen one cry over a woman.

And yet, what did she expect, unleashing such devastation on him?

As if he felt her watching him, his eyes flickered open. He made no attempt to brush away his tears. He opened his mouth, only to close it again. By the look in his eyes, his heart was breaking.

For her, or for himself?

"I am so sorry, Sela."

"'Tis not your fault."

He frowned, clearly unconvinced. When he spoke, his voice held conviction. "Nor yours, my love."

My love?

She took her hand from his and knotted her fingers together. "I might have fought harder."

"Nay."

You may as well get it over with. Don't be a coward. She stood and faced him. "I would not think less of you if you pursued the Unbinding."

Horror flashed across his face. He surged to his feet. "*Nay!*" His fierce denial startled her. "'Tis not an option."

"You were one of the Pure. And I..." Her voice trailed away.

He drew her close. "'Tis not even a thought in my mind."

Caleb was stunned and could not possibly know his own mind, Sela mused. He couldn't comprehend what they had lost. Nothing would ever be the same between them. "He robbed me, Caleb. He robbed me of the one thing I had left to give you."

He reached out and skimmed the tears from her cheeks with a newly callused thumb. "Nay. Smith cannot steal what is impossible for him to possess."

"I don't understand."

"Your heart. Do I not possess it?" He stared at her, as if daring her to insist she wasn't in love with him.

Don't you see that you deserve more than I can give you? She rushed on, desperate to make him understand. "Aren't you going to ask if I'm with child?"

She expected him to blanch, but he gazed at her levelly. "I'm guessing you'll share when you're ready."

"Caleb—"

"If there is a child, it will be mine, Sela. As *you* are mine."

She watched him as he said it and knew he meant every word.

He reached for her tattooed hand with his own, caressing the band etched in ink. "I gave you my word. I am not a man who gives it lightly."

Sela closed her eyes. "There is no child." Then she thought of Briella. "But what of the other consequences of an unblessed bond?" What if the seasoning she'd endured was something else entirely? She opened her eyes, hoping to open his, for surely, he loved her blindly.

Caleb swallowed, but judging by his expression, he'd already thought of it. "One day at a time, Sela. Whatever happens, I will *never* give you up. I swear it on my life."

She forced down her doubt, wanting to believe the sincerity in his eyes. When she extricated herself from his hold and reached for her nightgown, he spun away and left her to change. His boots receded softly down the stairs.

Expecting that he had gone elsewhere to vent his true feelings, Sela was surprised when he returned ten minutes later, his hair wet and his body shaking with cold. She averted her eyes while he exchanged his wet clothes for dry ones, briefly toweling his hair.

"Did you go down to the beach?"

He didn't answer her question, but instead nodded at the armchair next to the window. "I'll sleep there for now. When we return to the cabin—" He offered her a smile, no less warm for the sadness in his eyes. "One day at a time."

After she slid into bed, he leaned down and kissed her cheek, blew out the lantern, and settled into the armchair. Sela marveled at the way the moonlight transformed his features to molten silver, though his face was already more handsome to her than any man she'd ever known. What kind of man promised to love a woman in ruins? And why, after all that had happened to them, did she desperately want him to?

She laid her head on the pillow, though she knew sleep would not come easily. To her surprise, she must have dozed off, for near the middle of the night she awoke to rain drumming on the roof. Thunder rumbled in the distance. *A storm!* The fear that had been her close companion since her captivity leached out of her like a lanced boil. She smiled.

Uriah would not come for her tonight.

Swinging her legs over the side of the bed, Sela walked on bare feet to Caleb's side. Flashes of lightning cut a jagged path across the floorboards and illuminated her way.

He turned at her approach and smiled, a little of the old Caleb flickering in his eyes. Had he not yet slept? "Are you cold?" He extended his blanket to her.

She shook her head.

"Do you want to watch the storm with me?" His behavior was almost shy, like Tempe when she offered a flower to Jax or Caleb.

She returned his smile and nodded.

Caleb wriggled to one side of the enormous armchair, patting the space beside him. When she crawled beneath the blanket, he tucked her against his side, arranging her legs over his lap and wrapping his arm around her. She watched the display through the window as the storm approached, feeling the steady thud of her bondmate's heartbeat, so at odds with the stormy rhythm overhead.

"Why did you go down to the beach earlier?" she asked.

Caleb tensed, then drew her closer. "The Carver forgive me," he whispered against her hair, "but I would kill him now without a second thought. In truth, I have killed him a thousand times in my mind tonight, since I blew out the light."

"Smith or Tucker?"

"Both." His heartbeat quickened. "They could never suffer enough to satisfy me." He closed his eyes. Was Caleb praying? By the time he opened them, the tension in his body had eased. He gazed down at her, his love obvious.

"You're a fool, Caleb," she murmured. *How can he still want me?*

He chuckled. "Aye, so I've been called, and not only by you."

"Perhaps you should learn to listen better." She snuggled closer to him.

Caleb sucked in deep breaths, each one taking at least five seconds to expel. Whether anger or desire sought to master him, she did not know.

"Aye, Sela. You and I both."

"I've never seen you look so wild, Caleb Alexander."

It was for the best, Caleb mused, that Sela had not seen him at the beach, down on his knees and retching like a swill-belly at the contemplation of what had happened to her. He was grateful that people could not peer into the minds of others, for if Sela had seen into his, she might have feared for him.

As it was, his calm exterior had given her much-needed reassurance. She remained in his arms while he stared out at the storm, enjoying the way it unleashed its wrath with such abandon.

After the storm passed, he lifted her and returned her to the bed. She sighed and shifted, sliding her arms around his neck. Through the nightgown, he felt the bandages encircling her upper arm.

"Please, Caleb," she mumbled against his ear, "stay with me."

When he set her down, she clung to him, so he slid into bed beside her, letting her sleep against his side. Thinking of her admonition that he should listen better, and his own cryptic reply, he recalled the way she'd courageously defended her sisters and Ross, at such cost to herself. Shame pinched him when he wished she'd been more of a coward.

Caleb finally found his own rest closer to morning. When he woke at first light, she lay curled on her side, with him behind her, his arm around her waist.

Fearing she might fret if she woke to find him in her bed, Caleb gently extricated his arm and slipped out of bed. He dressed quickly, taking his weapons from the chair where he'd left them. He would purchase a musket today, in addition to his pistol.

Padding down the stairs, he found Thaddeus's guest, Magnus, sitting beside the ashen remains of the previous night's fire. At first, the man had aroused no great curiosity in Caleb. Thaddeus often sheltered outcasts and misfits, and physically, Magnus fit that description. Today, though, Caleb found himself drawn across the sitting room to the hearth.

"I bid you good morning, sir." He reached out to shake his hand.

"And to you, friend," Magnus replied, extending his hand.

Caleb hesitated. Neither of the man's palms were branded. He raised his own hands, displaying the marks that declared him an exile.

Magnus smiled and stretched out his hand farther.

"Do you consider yourself a friend to the soulless, sir?" Should any of the Righteous or the guards see him, Magnus would be arrested and flogged, perhaps even branded.

"Aye, Caleb. I do."

Caleb wondered at the ease with which the man used his Carver-given name. They had only been introduced the night before. "You do not fear the Righteous then?"

Magnus's smile broadened. "My only thought is of the Carver, my friend. And in Him, there is no fear."

His interest piqued, and driven by an inexplicable force, Caleb shook the man's hand. Magnus's grip was firm, though Caleb noted his left shoulder looked slightly misaligned, as if it had once been broken or dislocated and healed poorly. "You speak as one who has studied the Book of Souls. Were you one of the Righteous? The priesthood, perhaps?"

"After a fashion," Magnus replied cryptically.

"I never knew you in the Old Town."

"I have been there, but rarely. On the occasions I visited, I found that few of those who'd once called me friend still knew me."

"How did you come to be on Azazel?"

"There is much work for me here." Magnus glanced behind Caleb.

Caleb turned to see Thaddeus. His eyes were sharp and alert. Did Magnus know in whose house he sought shelter? Did Thaddeus know his guest's true purpose for being on the island?

When Caleb turned to face the hearth, Magnus was gone.

Thaddeus came forward, his eyes lined with sorrow—and guilt. "I am glad to see you well, Caleb."

His throat felt pinched. "'Twas you who rescued Sela from the desert. You have my heartfelt thanks."

"You have no doubt heard her tale. 'Twas not my hand that delivered her, but the Carver's."

Caleb suppressed a flicker of doubt. If that were true, why had the Carver not rescued Sela sooner?

Thaddeus watched him carefully. "She has suffered a great deal. When we brought her here, I feared she would not survive the seasoning, let alone a gunshot wound."

"She was shot in the arm. Why? By all accounts, Smith does not miss."

"A warning, I think." Thaddeus rubbed the short beard shading his chin. "Yet, he has not come after her."

"He may still try." Caleb gritted his teeth. "That would explain why he did not kill her."

Thaddeus's gaze flickered to the belt bearing Caleb's weapons, including his sword. "Do you intend to go after him?"

"'Tis my right as her bondmate, and the only way Sela will ever feel safe again on Azazel."

"I would think her greater need is that you stay by her side."

Caleb's stomach clenched. He had no wish to leave Sela—not when they had been so cruelly parted and only recently reunited—but after what Smith had done, how could Caleb not exact his vengeance?

"Do you go on her account, Caleb, or on your own?" Thaddeus's tone held compassion, incongruous with such a rough man.

"Smith doesn't deserve to live."

Thaddeus glanced at his palms. "Nay. Nor do I."

Caleb abruptly remembered that this man had once been second to Smith's father. What foul memories of that life still brewed in his mind?

"Does not vengeance belong to the Carver, my son?"

Caleb winced. How could the Carver possibly understand how he felt? He writhed inwardly, imagining the terror his innocent Sela had experienced at the hands of a cruel and sadistic man. He guessed that she had not confessed the half of it.

Unable to refute Thaddeus's statement, Caleb took a different approach. "Ross Bryant is still Smith's prisoner. Would you let the man rot?"

Thaddeus sighed. "I know. But should you storm Smith's hideout, even with help, you would be easily overwhelmed. With their vantage point, we could never take the land pirates unawares."

"Then you would bid me do nothing." Caleb planted a hand against the wall near the carved mantlepiece. Oh, how he wished he could hurl something across the room! Never in his life had he felt such all-consuming rage. It was a mercy he had managed to conceal it from Sela, and now from Thaddeus.

Yet, it seemed that the older man's keen gaze saw what Caleb believed he kept hidden.

"Not *nothing*, Caleb. Wait for the Carver's guidance. Pray. Love the woman you were given to cherish. She needs you alive far more than she needs Uriah Smith dead."

The fire in Caleb returned to smoldering at the old man's words. He looked across the room and saw Magnus in the foyer, head bowed as if in thought or prayer. Had the stranger heard Caleb's conversation with Thaddeus? What if he was a friend to Lord Auberon? The Remenant, as Sela called them, were oftentimes far too trusting.

As Caleb had once been, before his brother betrayed him.

"Very well," he agreed at last. Inwardly, though, dark thoughts plotted mutiny. "For now, I will stay." *And I will do all in my power to protect the woman I have failed so completely.*

Out of nowhere, a new thought struck him. Sela's pet fox. Roux had gone missing the day Smith attacked Belladonna, and they had left Azazel without him.

He turned to Thaddeus, frowning. "Have you seen Roux?"

Chapter Eleven

The sun rose swiftly, and Tucker uttered a curse. He needed to get off this boat before Liri's brother returned and slit his throat or threw him overboard.

Or both.

Sailors scurried across the deck of the merchant ship, readying it for its legitimate entrance into the harbor. Tucker gripped his flintlock pistol and stared out at the smudged outline of Belladonna. Caleb and Liron had gone there at first light, heedless of their safety. They'd shown no thought for the woman and children who remained below deck.

His children. Were Caleb a father, he might understand Tucker's decision to save Liri and their daughter instead of rescuing a woman who could fend for herself.

Scowling at the thought of Sela bearing Caleb a child, he turned to see Liri standing behind him. She held her sister's namesake, who slept against her shoulder.

"Where are the twins?" he asked.

Tucker disliked that his son bore the name of a man who hated him, but the boy had quickly become the delight of his life. He was yet unbranded, which meant young Liron had a future ahead of him among the soul-bearing. Under Tucker's tutelage and guardianship, the boy might yet make something of himself.

"They are below deck. The cook is giving them breakfast." Liri hugged her daughter tighter. "I came to speak to you...of the future."

He studied her. "I'm surprised your brother insisted you return to Azazel."

"Do not speak to me of my brother's actions," she snapped with uncharacteristic acid, "when your own are so despicable."

"I have only your safety in mind, Liri. You must think of our children."

"I never cease thinking of them."

"If Smith learns you've returned to Azazel, he may come after you." Tucker eyed the child in her arms. "After his daughter."

"Uriah cares naught for girl children. Nor did he mourn the one we lost."

"Liron? But you said he knew Liron was not his—"

"I speak of another little one." Tears pearled beneath Liri's eyelids. "One I was not able to meet."

Sorrow pierced Tucker, along with the jealousy he could never completely extinguish. He didn't know Liri had been expecting, nor that she'd lost the child. "When?"

"Just before you arrived on Azazel."

"I am sorry."

"So says your mouth, Tucker, but I see the envy in your eyes."

He flinched. Liri was startlingly perceptive. Her sister's capture had clearly awakened something in her, something Tucker had not known she possessed. "And what of you? Smith may yet claim you as his bondmate."

Her lips wobbled. "My brother will protect me. Sela too, once she is found."

Remembering the possessive gleam in Smith's eyes when he gazed at Sela, Tucker wondered if she was still alive. Men like Smith cared little for the women they used and discarded. The thought triggered a squeeze of pain in his gut, one that had been growing more acute of late.

It was for Caleb and Liri that Sela had sacrificed herself. Sela would no doubt thank Tucker for preventing Caleb from hurtling after her. His mind had only to convince his heart of this fact.

He swept all thoughts of Sela away. "We must speak of Azazel, Liri. Our son is yet unbranded. Perhaps I could take him—"

"Nay." Liri paled and backed up a step. "You will not part him from me again."

"Again? 'Twas not I who parted you from the boy the first time. You must think rationally, Liri. I cannot live on Azazel forever." Eventually, he would need to return to the Old Town, or else rouse suspicions regarding why he lingered so long on the island.

She bit her lip. "What of the Righteous? If you claim him as your son, you will be expelled from the order."

He recoiled at the statement. "I can provide for him as my ward. A foundling I discovered while on Azazel. None need know the truth."

"*Liron* knows the truth."

"The boy must learn to keep a secret."

Liri's pale brows drew together. "He is only five years old, Tucker. You cannot force him to live a lie."

He stepped closer. "Would you have me live without my son?"

"Perhaps 'twould acquaint you with the pain of loss."

"Is that what this is about?" Tucker peered down at her. "You want me to suffer as you have suffered?" He swore softly, using a word the Righteous forbade.

Another mark against his name. "I know the pain of loss as well as you, since I have loved you from our youth. Did you not think it agony to watch as you were parted from me? Since that day, I have not touched another wom—"

He broke off, feeling an odd sense of shame at the admission. Liri had gone on with her life, while his own dreams and desires remained stunted. "Your pain is no greater than my own," he went on. "I had to endure knowing you were likely the bondmate of another man. That I'd lost you forever."

Tears misted Liri's eyes. She'd never been able to keep anything from him, and the truth of her feelings was visible now.

"You still love me," he pressed. "Do you not?"

Aye, she did, but by the look in her eyes, her admission was a shallow victory, one that would bring both of them naught but heartbreak. For the reward could never be claimed.

At his strident tone, the child in Liri's arms awakened. Tucker gritted his teeth as Liri hurried to reassure the little girl. *Sela*, ever the division between them, and in more ways than one. Liri set her down on her feet.

The child scampered away, and Liri faced him. Her eyes flickered over the white coat he'd so painstakingly tried to restore to its original brilliance before meeting Lord Auberon. "As always, Tucker," she said softly, "there is more standing between us than the lot, or Uriah Smith, or even Sela. The greatest shadow over us is the shadow you yourself cast. While you live a lie, you will never know contentment."

She glided past him in pursuit of the little girl, who was chattering eagerly to the sailors. Then she paused to speak into his ear. Tears dampened her voice. "Your brother understood that, as did my sister. 'Tis the reason Caleb gave up his life for Sela, and the reason she gave up her life for him. There is no great love without great sacrifice. Until you understand that, Tucker Alexander, I can never offer you my heart."

Janus Auberon studied the young man standing before him and smiled to himself. His favored acolyte had returned unscathed. Though for certain, he wrestled with a weighty care that had not bothered him before the attack on Belladonna. Did Tucker Alexander possess the same weaknesses as his brother?

Regardless of Tucker's personal failings, Janus was glad for the acolyte's competency in more general matters. The tempers of the other officers, as recent events had proven, only brought unrest and riots. Perhaps Janus had been too quick to dismiss Caleb Alexander.

"I am pleased you have come back." Janus propped his elbows atop the desk and steepled his fingers. "I prayed some ill had not befallen you, my son."

Tucker smiled. "'Twas not my decision to leave Azazel, my lord. If the pirates had not overcome the fort, and had you not gone missing, I would have stayed to defend what I could. I am pleased the reinforcements arrived before the renegades could destroy Belladonna completely."

"You were mindful of preserving your purity, and for that, I commend you."

Did the young man grimace? "I'm afraid I will need to undergo the purification ceremony, my lord. The ships on which I travelled bore the soulless. There was no separation to speak of between soul-bearing and soul-marked."

"'Tis a shame, but no matter. You have my approval to conduct the ceremony."

Tucker bowed his thanks and moved to depart, but Janus stilled him with a raised hand. With his other hand, he caressed the coins in the open chest atop his desk. Hidden in time, the pirates had not discovered this treasure.

"Your brother has also returned, my son?"

"Aye, my lord." Tucker's mouth worked, as if he tasted ash. He had not torn his gaze from the chest. "Caleb hopes to find his bondmate."

"I understand that Sela has returned to Belladonna."

Tucker stepped forward, betraying his interest. "Smith let her go?"

"She escaped." Janus tapped his chin thoughtfully. "Nevertheless, Smith has decided to let her live."

Was it Janus's imagination, or did relief smooth the creases on Tucker's forehead?

It was quickly replaced by puzzlement. "How do you know this, my lord?"

"I spoke with Smith a few days ago." Janus indicated the chair opposite his desk. "Sit, my son, and I will acquaint you with some things you should know."

"Oh, Sela." Liri buried her face in Sela's shoulder. "I missed you more than words can express."

Sela hugged her sister back, unable to keep her gaze from straying to the others who had returned, including her brother, Liron. He had brought Liri and her children ashore under the cover of early morning. Joy had swept through Sela on meeting Liri's son who, encouraged by Anwen and little Sela, soon befriended Tempe. The four children quickly escaped to the garden.

Briella, holding Thomas, welcomed Liri as warmly as she had Sela. This time, though, Sela noticed the tension between the women. Liron was introduced to Thaddeus and the others. He didn't bother to put on his gloves to shake their hands, if he even owned gloves in the first place.

Caleb stood back, leaning against the wall. His eyes never left Sela, as if he feared she would disappear in a puff of smoke. Disappointment had squeezed her when she woke this morning to find him gone, remembering her plea during the night and his agreement to remain at her side.

Heading downstairs, she had panicked at the thought that he had left the house. When she found him in the kitchen helping Noemia and Tempe make bread dough, his hair carefully groomed and clubbed at the nape of his neck, Sela had leaned against the door frame and heaved a sigh of relief. She'd watched him elicit giggles from the little girl with a rapid succession of jokes.

If Caleb knew Tempe was Uriah's daughter, would he be so kind? She thought he would.

Tearing her gaze from him, Sela looked at her sister. "Where's Tucker?"

Liri drew back, her eyes red-rimmed. "He returned to the fort."

"You will stay here?"

"Aye, Sela," Liron answered for their sister. "We'd be pleased if you stayed with us."

"What of you, Liron?" Sela frowned. "You're wanted for desertion. Should any of the soldiers find you—"

"There's little chance they'd recognize me. The soldiers from Consuela had no idea I left for Azazel."

"Tucker knows your identity."

Caleb stepped to Liron's side. "I told Tucker that if he betrayed Liron to Lord Auberon, I would reveal his own secret. Purity is the Righteous' most sacred mandate. If it became known that Tucker fathered a child—*children*—outside of the Binding, the penalty is certain. The Righteous would remove him from our—from the order."

A cold fist squeezed Sela's gut. Whatever Caleb said, the slip betrayed some of his thoughts. Despite his anger, did he miss Tucker? Did he miss his old life? In loving her, he'd exchanged gold coins for ashes. In time, might he grow to resent her?

Liron glanced between Sela and Caleb. "You should remain here under our protection, Alexander. Should your brother not prove as reticent as you imagine, it may be better to consolidate our forces."

"Nay." Caleb shook his head. "Smith likely knows Sela is here. Soon, he will hear of Liri's whereabouts. We must relocate to another place."

"What if we left the island again?" Liri asked.

Liron frowned. "'Tis not possible at present. The merchant ship we sailed on is headed back to Consuela. Captain Foley, as you know, was sailing for the Old Town."

"What about Captain Ward's ship?" Hopefulness blossomed across Liri's delicate features.

"Ward has also returned to the Old Town," Thaddeus said, joining them. "Since our return, I've spent almost every day down at the settlement. The fort is nearly rebuilt. Lord Auberon's reinforcements have it well-guarded, and 'tis rumored he has sent for more soldiers. Belladonna is on a tight leash, and the coves and beaches are closely watched."

"Caleb, Liron, and Liri came ashore easily," Sela put in.

Caleb frowned. "Lord Auberon does not fear new *arrivals*, only deserters. Those who come here cannot leave. The merchant ship will be searched before it departs, along with every other craft." He glanced at Liri. "Tucker was right to fear that you'd be trapped here."

"I regret nothing," Liri replied softly.

Thaddeus stroked his chin. "Lord Auberon is sending patrols all over the island, Caleb. The word is they are detaining innocents for their own amusement." His expression conveyed his true meaning, and Sela shivered. "I fear that Anjelica—or any of the settlements—are not as safe as they once were."

Liron slipped an arm around Sela's shoulders and pulled her close. "How are we to fend off both soldiers and pirates?"

Footsteps sounded in the foyer, and Liron turned. His arm around Sela slackened, and he gasped. "My lord!"

A lengthy pause ensued as Magnus entered the room.

"Prince Magnus Theodorus," Liron ventured, sinking into a bow. "I had hoped to find you here." His eyes were alight.

The others, save Sela, looked at Liron and then at Magnus and his well-worn, commoners' clothes. His gloveless hands. As far as Sela knew, the prince had not undergone the purification ceremony after saving her at the clifftop. Did he, like Liron, have no regard for the laws of the Righteous? Perhaps royalty could do as they liked.

"*Prince* Magnus?" Caleb echoed. "*The* Prince Magnus?"

Caleb stared at the man he'd previously considered unremarkable, unable to see past the rough-spun fabric of his shirt and the grizzled beard masking the lower half of his face. The prince wore no gloves, and his shirtsleeves were more earthy brown than creamy white. Dirt lined the creases in his palms, and his boots were tarnished and muddied. If he stood beside Lord Auberon, the elder of the Righteous would most likely wrinkle his nose at the mingled smells of sweat, leather, and earth.

Yet, Liron called him a prince. He was not simply one of the priesthood or a member of the Righteous.

His name surpassed them all.

Caleb focused on his brother-in-law. Perhaps this Magnus was an imposter, stirring up false hope among those who had no other comfort. "Liron, do you know this man?"

"Aye," Liron replied with wonderment. "'Tis the man who saved my life as a child."

Liron approached him, and Magnus extended his hand. Liron took it without hesitation.

Caleb envied his brother-in-law's ease. Ah, the freedom of an unbranded man!

"Well met, Liron Meriweather," Magnus greeted him. "You were only a boy when I saw you last."

"Your shoulder, my lord?" Liron asked with concern.

"'Twas a worthy exchange," Magnus replied.

For reasons unknown to Caleb, Sela sucked in a breath and looked away.

A grave sadness settled over Liron's features.

Neither Sela nor Thaddeus looked surprised at the revelation of the prince's identity. Did they doubt Magnus's claims, as well?

Caleb bowed. "Why did you conceal your true lineage, my lord?" For now, at least, he would play along with the charade.

Magnus looked at him seriously, as if he saw through Caleb's pretense. "Everything I told you was true, my son. 'Tis my father's work which has brought me to Azazel."

"The king?" Caleb frowned. Why would the prince of Eremia use a term of endearment like *my son* on a mere subject? "Then you mean to speak with Lord Auberon?"

"Nay," the prince replied. "Janus Auberon must not know of my presence here. Not yet."

"But the soldiers...Smith and his band..." Caleb's words trailed off.

Did the so-called prince not understand the gravity of their situation? Should Magnus intervene, Sela and Liri would finally be safe from Smith. In the peace that followed, Sela might begin to heal.

"'Tis not the right time." Magnus's eyes betrayed a compassion rarely seen among royalty, though Caleb's frustration remained. The man seemed as good-hearted as he was rumored to be, but what use was one man against the power wielded by Janus Auberon and Uriah Smith?

The prince had been missing for years, presumed dead by many after war broke out between Eremia and the mainland countries. Without his entourage or the proof of his birthright, or even a set of elegant clothes, Magnus might easily be discredited by his opponents.

If the man was truly the prince, he must realize that coming alone to Azazel would be ineffective. This meant there was a good chance that this Magnus *was* an imposter. Liron seemed to know him, but Liron had only been a boy when he met the prince. People changed in twenty years, and a child did not always see true. Caleb would caution his brother-in-law to be careful.

Thankfully, Thaddeus interjected just then, "The day ages while we deliberate. Caleb, might we persuade you to stay another night?"

Would it be foolish to strike out alone? Caleb glanced between Liron and Magnus. Too many secrets resided in this house. Whatever intrigues surrounded the prince, Caleb had no wish for Sela to be part of them. Also, if they remained under Thaddeus's roof, she would only be more vulnerable.

Though Caleb regretted that she would be parted from her family, Sela would be safer with him. He would make sure she saw her siblings as often as he could arrange it.

"Nay," he said at last, "we must carve our own path." Perhaps returning to the place where they'd enjoyed a fleeting happiness would mend the breach between them.

Thaddeus nodded his understanding.

As the others clustered around the prince to ask more questions, Liron appeared at Caleb's side. "Don't be a fool, Alexander. If Smith comes—"

"I will be ready." Caleb glared at him. "You are not the only man who has trained in the art of war, Meriweather."

"You are even more stubborn than Sela," Liron hissed. "Very well, then. Make your own way, but I'm coming with you."

"Nay."

"You cannot take every watch, Caleb. Not if you don't want to be dead on your feet by the end of a sevenday."

"*Nay*, Liron. Your twin sister—"

"Is coming too." Liri threaded her arm through her twin's. "I will not let any of us be parted again."

"I would never keep Sela from you," Caleb assured her.

"I will not lose her," Liri said emphatically. "Not again."

Caleb glanced at Sela, who stood pressed against the door frame as if she could meld herself to it, and relented. "Aye," he agreed. He glanced between the twins, who gazed back at him with something like pity. "Though I fear she is more lost to us now than before we arrived on the island."

Liron gripped his shoulder. "It will be set to rights, my friend. It must."

As Caleb rode with Sela to the cabin on a horse borrowed from Thaddeus—the rest of her family to follow on the morrow, since Anwen had caught a cold—he wondered at the truth of his brother-in-law's words. Before her traumatic experience, his bondmate had been passionate and energetic. Now, she had fallen into a listless melancholy from which nothing, not even the affections of her nieces and nephew, seemed to retrieve her.

Had it been only this morning that Sela begged him to remain with her? Now, she appeared cold and distant, holding herself stiffly apart from him, as if she wished to be elsewhere.

Arriving at the cabin, Caleb dismounted. He reached for his bondmate, only to find her already sliding from the saddle. He caught her and noticed, not for the first time, how thin she had become. The fine bones of her face stood out in greater prominence, though nothing could rob her of her loveliness. Was it the seasoning or the trauma of her captivity that had stolen the flesh from her frame?

Sela squirmed beneath his scrutiny. When he set her on the ground, she ducked under his arm and fled inside the cabin. Perhaps she was angry at him for bringing her out here, away from those who'd saved her in the desert. Perhaps she wanted to stay another night with her family. If so, why had she not said something?

After stabling the horse, Caleb entered the cabin and found her at the kitchen window, staring outside. Her vantage point gave a good view of the stable. Had she been watching him?

She didn't turn when he approached, and when he placed a hand on her lower back, she started, as if she hadn't registered his entry. "I am sorry," he said hoarsely, "for Roux."

She twisted to face him, pain inscribed in every feature. "You know?"

"Thaddeus told me."

"I knew Roux would not have abandoned me." Her shoulders sagged. "Uriah's men must have captured him in the garden."

Was the fox's capture the rustling they'd heard in the bushes, just before the cannons began firing? If so, then why had the pirates not attacked right then? He and Sela were alone, armed only with Caleb's flintlock.

Yet, Smith had waited until the docks to capture Sela.

Did she really believe Caleb had abandoned her? He took her in his arms, but she tensed. Though he urged himself to be patient, his temper, shortened by lack of rest and an excess of worry, flared to life. He bit his lip before he said something he would regret and let her go.

Why does she hold me at arm's length, Carver? Yesterday, she clung to me.

At the thought of the Carver, Caleb remembered his extracts. His anger died. The Carver would have answers for him, as well as a way to restore his bondmate to the vivacious woman she'd been.

Seek and ye shall find, the priests and elders always said.

Aye, a remedy existed. He only had to search for it.

Night fell, bringing with it another storm. Caleb locked and barred the door, having spent the remainder of the day fortifying the cabin with spare lumber and nails. Thankfully, the cabin's previous owner—an unbranded officer—had been mindful of security. He'd lived among those who would not care to privilege his welfare, and the structure was solid.

Caleb admitted to himself that when Liron finally arrived, he would be glad of a second musket and another man to take the watch. It did irk him, though, to rely on Sela's brother for *anything*.

In the bedroom, he found Sela already asleep atop the bed covers, not even undressed. He contemplated waking her and assisting her into her nightgown, then thought better of it. It would only make her wary of his intentions.

Maneuvering her beneath the blankets, he drew the covers over her, blew out the lantern, propped his loaded musket against the wall, and settled himself into a chair. The straight-back chair felt decidedly less comfortable than the armchair at Thaddeus's house, but Caleb was too exhausted to be choosy. He intended to doze, but the pattering of raindrops on the roof lulled him to sleep.

He woke with a start. Something was wrong.

Thunder clapped overhead. Hail needled the roof like splintered glass. Caleb glanced at the bed. An explosion of light illuminated the empty imprint where Sela had lain.

"Sela!" Jolting to his feet, Caleb grabbed the musket. Where was she? How had she slipped past him? He was a light sleeper, but apparently not tonight.

Perhaps she had sought a drink of water. Nay! The front door hung wide open. A chill breeze gusted in, rattling the unlit lantern sitting on the small kitchen table.

Caleb's heart seized. He rushed onto the porch and stopped short.

Sela stood not ten yards from the base of the steps. Her hair trailed in limp locks around her shoulders as she tilted her face to the sky. She didn't flinch as the hail struck her skin and pooled at her feet like snow.

"Sela!" Setting the musket aside, he bounded down the steps. He spun her around, noticing that she was soaked through. "What are you doing?" Hail stung his face. He tugged on her arm. "Come inside before you're injured."

When she didn't respond, he lifted her into his arms. She didn't resist as he carried her into the cabin. Water dripped from her sodden clothes.

"*Never* do that again." Worry turned his voice strident. He crushed her wet body against his. "I feared Smith took you from me."

"Nay, Caleb," she spoke as if to a child. "We are safe. Uriah is afraid of storms."

Was that why she had been so calm the night before? And now? At least she was speaking to him again.

He set her down on the bed, then went back to lock and bolt the front door. Whatever Smith's fears, he did not trust them to keep him away. When Caleb returned to the bedroom, Sela was shivering violently.

He shucked his coat and draped it around her shoulders. "You must get out of these wet clothes, Sela."

She nodded numbly, stood, and set aside his coat. Her shaking hands worked feebly at the hooks on her gown. When her attempt proved unsuccessful, Caleb gently turned her around and unhooked them for her, acutely remembering how he'd done the same the night he first heard her sing.

The night she'd agreed to be his.

The night his whole world had caught on fire, shortly thereafter dissolving into ash.

He helped her remove the soaked dress and petticoats, then circled her to work on the laces of her stays, training his mind on anything but the task at hand. By the time she stood before him in her chemise, he felt flames of color licking up his neck like a thousand greedy tongues.

Dragging the quilt from the bed, he tucked it around her. Thankfully, her limbs had thawed enough for her to drag the wet chemise over her head while he kept the quilt in place. He forced his eyes to abstain from lingering on the bare skin of her shoulders. She needed his steadiness, not his ardor.

Sela lowered her arms, and he glimpsed the bandage near her elbow—still dry—and the bruises marking her skin from wrist to collarbone. At the sight, all emotions evaporated, save fury. He swallowed and formed fists, then glimpsed the vulnerable look in her eyes.

Carver of Souls, forgive my wrath, but I would cut Smith into a million tiny pieces for what he's done to her.

He crossed to the armoire, where her dresses hung, and retrieved her nightgown. Laying it on the bed, he backed out of the room.

Right now, he could use a dunking in a torrential storm.

When he returned, Sela was sitting on the bed, with her knees drawn up under her nightgown. Oddly, she also wore his coat. "Discard it." He nodded at the blanket instead. "It'll be nearly drenched."

"So is your shirt."

She was right. He strode over to the armoire, retrieved a dry shirt, and peeled off his wet one. Pulling the warm fabric over his head, he turned to find her staring at him.

A flicker of masculine pride bubbled up inside him at the knowledge that she found him attractive. A second later, another observation soured his pleasure. Uriah Smith possessed uncommon good looks. Did Caleb remind her of the man who'd used her?

He sat beside her. "I feared the worst."

A blank look slid over her features. "There was no danger."

"I woke to find you *gone*, Sela."

Again, she appeared impassive.

Frustration rose. Sharp words sprang from the hurting place deep inside, the one place he had worked so hard to conceal. "I thought your brother trained you to be a fighter. Will you not even fight for *us*?"

She bowed her head. Her jaw clenched, as if she too worked to hold something at bay. "Perhaps there is nothing left to fight for."

"What does *that* mean?" He reached for her hand, remembering how she'd fought Molly many months ago back on the ship, and Smith, and even him. "You're giving up?"

She pulled away, but not before he saw a flicker in her eyes—a spark of violet flame. He captured her hand in his. "I know you can fight," he said, satisfied when her head jerked up.

"Aye, I can fight."

"You just don't want to."

Her eyes came alive at the recollection of their past conversation, when she had accused him of the same. The vulnerability returned, along with the fire. "Nay, Caleb. I want to fight. But this is not your war."

He raised his tattooed hand. "I beg to differ."

"I heard you before. Purity is the most sacred mandate of the Righteous. Unlike your brother, 'tis a mandate you honored."

"Which is greater, Sela? The man or the mandate? The law, or the God who spoke it into being? The Carver knows you are not at fault. 'Tis only Him I seek to please." He thought of Magnus, who had denied being afraid of the Righteous. Who had declared he sought only the Carver's favor.

"The man I once knew would not so readily shirk the Righteous' precepts."

He held up both hands, exposing the brands. "Such laws belong to another life."

"So says your mind—and the Carver bless you for it—but your heart wants differently." Her eyes challenged him.

Caleb paused. She spoke the truth. He did at times long for his old life, but not in the way she meant. Didn't Sela realize that she was a part of him now? "Should I have to choose again, I would do everything the same. Except leave you alone with my treacherous, soul-rotted brother."

"The first time you laid eyes on me, 'twas the death of you." Sela edged closer. "If I had never known you, you would have returned to the Old Town by now, to a far better life than the one you have here with me."

"'Tis futile to talk of *what ifs*. If I had remained at the outpost, I would have been captured, along with Beck. I might have been executed, as he was." He watched her eyes soften, feeling a squeeze of pain at the memory of his dead friend.

Another mark against Uriah Smith.

"Love is not a feeling, that you might be in danger of being set aside every time we disagree or fight. If the Carver's love were as such, He would have struck us down long ago. Nay, Sela. Love is a choice. A choice we must make each and every day."

"And what if you chose wrong?" Her voice trembled. "I am no longer the prize you once believed I was. I am not the same woman. What if neither of us are strong enough to love each other perfectly?"

His power is perfected in weakness. The Book of Souls.

Caleb gazed back at her solemnly. "That is where the Carver comes in. Lucky for us, He plugs every leaking hole."

The wall she'd erected between them crumbled a little. She moved closer, until she was kneeling on the bed beside him, her damp hair arrayed around her pale face like a mourning shroud. "I am full of leaking holes that I know naught how to fix," she admitted. "Each day, another leak springs."

Caleb wrapped his hands around her smaller ones. "Then we will find them and fix them together." He brushed a tear from her cheek. "I'm not afraid of a little moisture."

She gazed at the puddle of wet clothes on the floor, then eyed the lightning that continued to flash outside. "I wanted to feel something again," she whispered in explanation of her nocturnal wanderings. "It seems like an eternity since I truly felt anything."

She looked into his eyes. Her hands traced the lines of his face as if she were blind like Noemia, gently fingering the damp tendrils that had come loose from his queue.

The pain in his gut was overturned by longing. He closed his eyes, relishing her hesitant touch and bidding himself to be content with only that.

"Caleb?"

He opened his eyes to find his feelings mirrored in her expression.

Cradling his face, she kissed him.

He moaned inwardly and gave into his passion. She tasted of salt and peppermint and the sweet anticipation that had first tortured him aboard the *Deliverance.* He pulled her against him. At her yielding, he was briefly lost.

It would be easy—so easy—to succumb to his desires. It would hardly be selfish, since she clearly loved him in return. He believed their bond was Carver-given, but what of his timing? He slid his hands down her back and remembered the tears in his bondmate's eyes.

No, she was not yet ready. The wall between them was not fully disassembled.

He broke off the kiss and pulled her into his arms. "You are beautiful, my love. And as I promised before, I promise again, to make you mine when you are ready...and not before." He lightly pressed his mouth against hers.

Sela's arms came around his waist. The tension eased from her, and Caleb knew he'd made the right decision. Still, as he ruminated with increasing frequency of late, he wished he was rather less virtuous a man.

As she snuggled against him, her elbow slipped and caught him in the ribs.

"Ouch." He rearranged her body so she sat on his lap. "When I said I wanted you to fight for us, I did not mean *now*."

A little of the old Sela returned to her face, and she grinned. "Beggars cannot be choosers, Caleb. I either fight my way or not at all."

"I wouldn't have it any other way."

Chapter Twelve

"We commit your soul to the Carver's keeping, my friend."

Caleb bent down, scooped up a handful of dark, loamy earth, and scattered it across the fresh expanse of Lieutenant Beckett Arkwright's grave. Though Beck's high position among the inhabitants of Azazel had cost him his life, in death it had earned him an engraved stone, along with the other officers and soldiers who'd been killed in Uriah's raid. Many of the settlement men and women who'd been brutalized and murdered were not half as fortunate. Twenty yards to their left, dozens of bodies lay in an unmarked mass grave.

Caleb brushed the dirt from his hands and slipped his arm around Sela's waist. She leaned into his warmth, craving his strength in the absence of her own. "I did not know him well," he murmured, "but I hope he has found his rest."

Sela understood the sorrow her bondmate did not voice. According to some of the Righteous, if a man or woman was branded—even by mistake—and died unabsolved, they would suffer torment in the afterlife. The absolution afforded by the lot only stretched so far. Earthly vindication was a tenuous thing.

She felt for his hand as Caleb continued, "Why Beck died and Tucker lived, I do not know." His dark eyelashes swept low over his deep-blue eyes as he studied the upturned earth.

"Once upon a time," Sela reflected, "you would have explained it as the Carver's will." Did he remember his words at Liri's coming-of-age ceremony?

"Aye," Caleb replied, as if through a mouthful of sand, "and so it is. Though at times there is little comfort in the fact. For all his wrongdoing, and Tucker's white coat, Beck was the better man."

What caused one person to turn to the left and another to the right?

Briella had left behind her life of darkness, while Esther returned to it with all the enthusiasm of a man craving the stiff drink that tortured his waking hours. Sela had discovered this truth when she'd seen her friend on the arm of a man one night, when Caleb and Liron escorted her home from Thaddeus's house. Belladonna had swiftly gone back to its debauched ways, all the more fiercely for the losses the town had suffered.

When confronted, Briella admitted that she had kept the truth from Sela, not wanting to cause her friend any further grief. "Esther and I spoke often aboard Captain Ward's ship. When we returned to Azazel, Thaddeus offered Esther a place with us. She agreed to stay, and even seemed content for a time. However, one night she simply left. Thaddeus and Jax found her at the newly rebuilt tavern. They confronted Murphy's replacement, but Esther refused to go with them."

Briella had grimaced at her retelling, and Sela knew she was remembering her own past. "She knows we are here for her, Sela. There is naught else we can do."

Caleb enclosed her hand in his, and Sela returned to the present, though she sensed her bondmate's mind lingered elsewhere. Something had come over him the night he'd found her standing in the hailstorm. She sensed a renewed determination. It sparked in his eyes and coiled every muscle, as if he prepared for war.

Most nights, Caleb buried himself in his scrolls, coming to bed well after midnight. His sleep, she knew, was restless. What he searched for, she never asked, though she sensed he wanted answers.

Answers to what? How one might go about the task of restoring a fragmented, tainted woman? If so, Caleb searched in vain.

Yet, even before her captivity, he had been tormented. His fall from grace necessitated answers, a fact that was all the more apparent when he stood at Beck's grave. He was likely contemplating the unfinished business of his own soul. It was not merely the scholar who hungered for absolution. It was also the man.

Sela's strength ebbed and flowed in concert with Caleb's. All at once, he was simultaneously close and distant. She relished his frequent touches and embraces, knowing his awareness of them was diminishing.

When he came to bed, Sela felt his mind miles away, and her fortitude was too weak to follow him. Not for the first time, she was jealous of his closeness with the Carver. Whatever comfort he received from his endless searching, she eagerly devoured, but more often than not, she fed on his despair.

With one last look at the grave, Caleb turned away, steering her with him. She watched his profile, hating the troubled look in his eyes. Firm conviction had once resided there, but he seemed to shake off his lingering anxiety.

"'Tis getting late. I should not spoil our day off by dwelling on our losses."

Caleb and Liron had originally planned to take turns guarding Sela, Liri, and her children, while the rest of the men worked with Thaddeus on the farms that had escaped destruction. Liri, however, insisted on returning to Thaddeus's house during the day so that her children could be schooled together with Tempe, as Briella cared for Thomas. Both women were anxious to reestablish a sense of normalcy.

Sela had no desire to be parted from Caleb, not even to help teach the children. Liri could manage. So, Caleb had allowed her to come with him to the various fields where he and Liron worked six days out of seven.

Sela suspected that Caleb shielded her from the lion's share of the work, and he frequently ordered her to rest. However, she found the physical labor a welcome distraction, fruitless as it felt with the annihilation of crops only one 'sooner away.

With Caleb, Liron, Thaddeus, and Jax present, no one troubled her. She remained at Caleb's side, developing calluses that matched his. This arrangement eased her concern as much as she knew it eased his.

For even now, Uriah Smith might come for me.

In the midst of her thoughts, her boot toe found a tiny crevasse in the ground.

Caleb caught her before she faltered. "Are you all right?" He watched her carefully, seeming to realize that more than the uneven ground had stumbled her. He led her off the path into a grove of palm trees and brush that shielded them from onlookers. "Are you weary?"

Aye, she was, but not in a way he would understand. She had endured the loss of her family, the pawning of her soul, and the treacherous voyage from the Old Town. All of that Caleb too had borne, and he had fallen from a greater height than she. Something had died within her during her captivity, though, something she feared would always be lost. She had begun to believe that not even Caleb could find it again.

Was it her soul? Perhaps that was the true curse of Azazel—to be always thirsty and looking for water to quench it, and finding naught but wilderness.

In the growing dark, Caleb's fingers traced her face. "Sela? You're working too hard. I should have—"

"Nay, Caleb." She reached up to smooth the worried lines from his mouth. "I am fine."

"'Tis the seasoning, then?"

"'Tis Uriah." She wanted to be honest, but she hated the anger that enlivened Caleb's features, as if the emotion lurked just behind a curtain, waiting for his call.

"You would be safe with Liron while I—"

"—hunt Uriah down?" She shook her head. "What became of the Carver's justice?"

His hands tightened around her waist. "Perhaps 'tis for men like me to dispense."

"Follow that road to its end, and you will join up with Lord Auberon."

He pressed her close. "And what of your nightmares?"

"My nightmares?"

"Aye, I know whose face haunts your dreams. Why not be rid of him forever?"

Her chest constricted. "What if it costs your life?"

He frowned. "I'm no pot-valiant soldier, Sela. I can handle myself."

"And...if it costs your soul?"

"You believe I am still in possession of one?"

"If any man could lay claim to such a state, 'twould be you."

The anger leached out of him, and he leaned his forehead against hers. "The Book of Souls says that a spirit of forgiveness is the true mark of a righteous man." He expelled a guttural sigh. "'Tis robust proof that no man who has been wronged can ever lay claim to righteousness, for only hatred and murder reside in my heart."

This was another way she stood between him and the Carver. Yet, he tenderly brushed the strands of hair back from her face. "Sela—"

A dog barked nearby. Footfalls came from the path they'd abandoned.

At the sight of activity beyond the grove, Caleb stiffened. He pulled Sela against his chest, placing one hand over her mouth. His other hand moved to the flintlock at his waist. He drew the two of them into the shadows.

Four men stood in the clearing. Two wore white coats, and a third man wore red.

But it was the fourth man who made the bottom of Sela's stomach fall out like a trapdoor.

"On foot, are we?" Uriah Smith chuckled. "'Twould seem a shipment of fresh horses from the Old Town cannot come quickly enough."

"Are you to blame for the delay, *Captain* Smith?" Lord Auberon growled. "If I discover you've been tampering—"

"Tampering?" Uriah threw up his arms in a declaration of innocence. "My lord, you have me all wrong."

Caleb urged Sela farther back into the brush, but she shook her head and peeked through the leaves to watch the exchange. Standing between Lord Auberon and a red-coated captain she did not recognize, Tucker Alexander wore a similar scowl. "Answer the question, Smith."

Uriah stepped to the left in an elegant grapevine, circling the others like a carrion bird circled his prey. "'Tis not *my* doing, Lieutenant Commander." His eyes narrowed. "I do not readily forget past agreements."

Tucker gulped, but Lord Auberon continued, "We had a deal, Captain. You pace your strip of Azazel, and I'll take charge of mine."

Caleb's hand over her mouth suppressed Sela's cry. Lord Auberon and Uriah Smith had formed an agreement? Caleb stiffened, showing Sela that she was not the only one enraged by the revelation.

"Aye, we had a deal, my lord. Why then do I hear tell of your patrols harrying men and women all over the island?"

"Surely, you care not for the island's inhabitants, Captain."

Uriah gave a lazy smile. "Now, you understand me."

"Then why your...*concern*?"

"Your patrols threaten the safety and stability of *my* settlements. Until the balance of power is restored, my lord, normal trade to the island cannot resume."

The red-coated captain stepped forward. "Why, you insolent—"

Lord Auberon raised a hand, and the captain broke off. His attention remained on Uriah. "I will not be blackmailed or threatened, Smith." His voice held a warning.

"My lord, certain items cannot be brought onto Azazel while your soldiers retain control of all the coves, docks, and coastal paths. You must loosen your stranglehold. You might find that Azazel flourishes all the better in its newfound freedom."

"Discipline is the established habit of the successful, Captain. Something I do not expect you to understand." Lord Auberon's posture did not slacken. "You will have your freedom, though I warn you not to trifle with me further. If I see you in these parts, my men will hunt you down like a beast."

"They would need horses to accomplish such a feat." The pirate grinned.

Lord Auberon turned away, the red-coated captain with him. After a brief, inaudible exchange with Lord Auberon, Tucker remained behind. He faced Uriah.

Sela looked down. Caleb's flintlock rested in his free hand, primed and loaded. He removed his hand from Sela's mouth and nudged her behind him. Then he raised the gun, aiming for Uriah's heart.

"Nay, Caleb!" she whispered, grabbing his arm. "Do not!"

"'Tis a clear shot." He detached himself from her grip. "A gift from the Carver Himself."

"And what of your beliefs?"

"My beliefs?" His eyebrows shot up. "Did you not fire a gun, believing it was Uriah?"

Aye, but it cost me what was left of my soul. "You're a man of mercy, not vengeance."

His eyes sparked blue fire. "I am neither, Sela. I am a man of justice."

Grasping his sleeve, Sela tugged him deeper into the copse of trees. "If you kill Uriah, 'twill destroy you."

"Nay, I will free Liri. And I'll free you." Caleb swept her to one side and crept back to their original position. He raised the flintlock, but his arm remained motionless. His finger rested on the trigger.

"'Tis not every day a man comes face to face with his enemy," Uriah was saying. "Though I did not know you as such when I faced you last."

Tucker's fingers hovered over his flintlock. "You said nothing to Lord Auberon of Liri. Why not?"

Uriah chuckled. "'Tis wise for a man to understand the knife point on which he balances, Lieutenant Commander. Aye, one revelation from my lips, and you would be no better off than I. But you know that, don't you, Alexander?"

Tucker's lip curled. "You hurt Liri. And her sister. More than a hundred people are dead because of you."

"You fathered two children with a woman you could never call your own," Uriah shot back. "By the Old Town's reckoning, both deeds are enough to earn a man the soul mark."

"Then it appears we have the makings of a deal, Smith. Never come near Belladonna again, and I won't report Lord Auberon to his superiors in the Old Town for consorting with rebels."

"You would never betray your elder, boy. You don't have it in you."

"Try me," Tucker replied with surprising resolve. "And if I go down, I *will* take you with me."

Caleb's arm wavered when Uriah's charming smile soured. "All this for a woman, Tucker Alexander? The only question is, which one?" When Tucker didn't reply, he stepped closer. "After what you did to the love of your dear brother's life, surely you cannot hope to reconcile with him?"

Tucker tilted his chin but said nothing.

"Neither woman is worth your efforts, Alexander." He gave a sly smile. "Believe me, I've had both of them."

Steel surged along Caleb's arm. He raised his flintlock.

Sela snatched at his sleeve in a last-ditch attempt to persuade her bondmate not to fire. She would not let him suffer the guilt she nursed for Elsie. They struggled, but his strength prevailed. He freed himself from her grip and lifted the gun to fire.

But Tucker was faster.

Sheltered in the grove of trees, Caleb felt Sela's agitation like a wave. After everything she'd been through at Smith's hands, why did she beg mercy for a man who openly mocked and taunted her? Sela was the fiery one, not Caleb. Sela, who had twice fired on the pirate, the first time injuring his shoulder, and the next time killing his sister.

As her bondmate, Caleb had the right to exact vengeance on her behalf. Did he not?

Caleb pushed her away and raised his gun, but his brother got off the first shot. Tucker's aim had evidently been affected by his rage, for the lead ball missed the pirate by several inches.

As if realizing he had no time to reload, Tucker stumbled toward the trees. His broad form blocked Caleb's clear shot at Smith. Instead of pursuing Tucker, or discharging his own weapon, the pirate chuckled and headed the other way, melting into the gloom.

Coward! Caleb seethed inwardly, resolving to go after Smith himself.

Just then, Tucker reached the hidden grove and plowed directly into Sela.

She gasped and fell backward, taking the brunt of Tucker's weight as he knocked her to the ground. His pistol went flying. Planting his gloved hands on either side of her shoulders, he rose to a sitting position. His legs straddled her green skirt.

"Sela?" Tucker's voice was etched with disbelief. "What are you—"

"Get off her," Caleb snarled. He lunged forward, dragging his brother away from Sela and tossing him aside. Tucker appeared too stunned to resist. Caleb helped his bondmate to her feet. "Are you all right?"

She nodded, clearly winded.

Caleb returned his attention to Tucker with a glare. "Done hurting my bondmate, Tuck?"

"I didn't see her."

"Nay," he retorted. "You wouldn't." He scowled at the flintlock, which lay on the ground. "You not only missed, but you blocked my own shot."

Tucker raised an eyebrow. "How long were you watching us?"

Long enough to shoot, he admitted silently. *Why did I listen to Sela? Why did I hesitate?*

Smith was far away by now. Caleb's sole chance at easy vengeance had been snatched from his hands. "Long enough to understand how seriously the Righteous take their custodianship of Azazel these days."

Tucker scowled. "'Twas not my idea to consort with Smith."

"Yet, you readily went along with it. That pristine sleeve of yours grows ever fouler, brother."

Tucker spun away. "I have work to do."

"Aye, though 'tis certainly not the Carver's."

Tucker stilled and slowly turned to face him. "All this from a man who nearly shot another in the back?"

"Would you have done differently?"

"Nay."

At Tucker's admission, Caleb realized the error of his inquiry. *Is this what I have become, Carver? No better than my brother?*

Tucker finally looked at Sela.

Caleb followed his brother's glance and saw what his brother took in. Sela's sevenday captivity had wrought disturbing, lasting changes. Her too-slender body, the fading bruises and scrapes on her skin, and her pallor that declared her still under the sway of the seasoning...and the change that was most obvious, the loss of her "fire."

Before her ordeal, Sela had known no fear. Now, she was ruled by it. Caleb knew it, and Tucker surely knew it too.

Tucker stepped toward her, and she flinched. Did regret ease the dislike from his face? His expression softened, and his gloved hands relaxed. "You should know something, Sela. Smith told Lord Auberon that he will not come for you again."

Without another word, he picked up his pistol and walked away, leaving them standing in the gathering darkness.

Caleb reached for Sela, and she melted into him. Although he wanted to pursue Smith, he could not leave her alone. Not with Tucker nearby. "Are you truly well? That was quite a fall."

"I'm getting used to being knocked over by Alexanders," she replied with a hint of her old self. It vanished as she peered into his face. "Would you have killed him, Caleb?"

"Smith?" The pent-up breath eased from his chest, though not in relief. "Aye, I would have killed him." He holstered his gun. "With luck, though, Smith will keep his distance from Belladonna from now on. If he so much as steps on our soil again, I swear I'll not miss as Tucker did."

Once upon a time, he would have only sworn such oaths while about the Carver's business. Fear shadowed Sela's eyes, and he felt driven to reassure her. What had she felt when she saw her tormentor? Not for the first time, he bid his anger burn low, replacing it with the gentleness she needed.

He must have been successful, for she sought his arms. "Hold me?"

His response felt wooden, removed from the sweet, breathless anticipation of the earlier days of their romance. Inside, though, the fire she'd imparted to him burned the brighter, and he yielded to it all the fuel it wanted.

Every single part of him he could spare for the burning.

The streets of Belladonna were teeming with life when Sela and Caleb returned. He tightened his grip on Sela's hand. With so many taken prisoner by Uriah's men, there was a shortage of women in the settlement. Caleb was all too aware of the looks they gave Sela.

The men who gazed too long received Caleb's glare or a motion toward the hilt of his sword. That was enough to set most of them on their way.

Several fiddles grated against the taut atmosphere, fraying the nerves of the restless townspeople that hurried about their business. Passing the blacksmith's forge, Caleb spied Liron leaning against the wall of the wheelmaker's crowded shop and steered Sela in his direction. As they drew closer, he discerned a knot of twenty or thirty people. They gathered around a man who spoke with the sonorous tones of a priest.

Magnus.

Preoccupied with Sela's welfare, Caleb had barely conversed with the man since learning of his supposed identity. Magnus said that his father had bid him come to Azazel. Yet, he had done naught since his arrival but work in the fields alongside the other settlement men, acquiring calluses in exchange for his meals and board. Not even Thaddeus treated him like royalty.

Caleb reached Liron's side and nodded. His brother-in-law had proven himself a true friend since coming to Azazel. He was not only a devoted brother to his sisters, but also a loving uncle to his nieces and nephew. How long could Liron stay on Azazel before the soldiers discovered him? Caleb did not want to imagine what his capture would do to Sela and Liri.

"Caleb." Liron grasped his hand and smiled at his sister. "Sela."

Caleb returned the greeting, but the would-be prince captured his attention. Magnus Theodorus stood before a table cluttered with tools, though his hands were empty. Had he been assisting the wheelwright? Those gathered around him looked riveted by whatever Magnus said.

Caleb left Sela with Liron and edged closer.

Several women stood among the crowd—nightwalkers, by the looks of their gowns—including the dark-haired woman Caleb rescued the day he'd returned to Azazel. Lord Auberon would have recoiled and ordered his soldiers to drive the nightwalkers away, but the prince made no objection to their presence. They listened as intently as the settlement men.

The prince's words sped in a blur through Caleb's tired brain. Why would a royal son of lofty birth, purity, and unbranded innocence come to a place such as Azazel? Why would he associate with those others considered soulless and unclean? It would not do to create unnecessary enemies of the Righteous and the priesthood.

Caleb eyed the man's hands. He was certainly no stranger to hard work. Evidently, he'd spent the years of his youth learning the trade of a master craftsman.

"Mister Magnus, sir." A short man with expansive shoulders spoke up as soon as the prince ceased speaking. "Belladonna be plundered from outside an' from within, an' ye speak of *love*?"

All eyes turned to Magnus as the question rippled through the crowd, earning nods of agreement from those whose haunted faces had been hollowed out by both hunger and hatred. The Old Town...the soldiers...Smith's marauders...

The soulless of Azazel had no shortage of enemies.

"Aye," said the prince, his dark eyes steady. "'Tis the fulfillment of the Carver's law to tend to others as one would want to be tended."

"You can't mean the soldiers. Or Smith's men."

This came from a battered-looking woman in a wine-red dress, who stood apart from the others. She seemed nearer the beginning of her life than its end, and her thin face was flushed with fever. Her collarbones protruded from her décolletage like bony elbows. The wasting disease?

"The Old Town tore us from our families and sent us here to suffer," the nightwalker blurted. "They care naught if we live or die."

Magnus gazed at the woman with compassion so evident in his bearded face that something shifted in Caleb's chest. "Aye, I know. Repay someone exactly what they deserve, my daughter, and the cycle of violence will never end. Your attempt to avenge your sorrows will only multiply them. But excuse the wrong done to you, count the offense as naught, and the cycle will be broken. For to forgive is the true mark of the Righteous. Just as the Carver shows kindness and mercy to the unkind and merciless, so His children must also."

Caleb exhaled sharply. Several blasphemies dwelt within the prince's admonition, and none so stunning as his intimation that the soulless might be considered children of the Carver. No wonder the prince had no relationship with the Righteous or the priesthood. They had likely thrown him out of their seminaries.

Excuse the wrong? Count the offense as naught? Caleb thought of Uriah Smith and Tucker Alexander, and everything they'd done to Sela. To himself.

He spun away, heading for Liron. "Come on." Caleb reached for Sela's arm. "Let's go."

"Wait, Caleb." Liron stepped between them and grasped his shoulder. "You didn't hear it all."

"I heard enough. The *prince* has lost his mind after his long years of exile."

"He told a story—"

"I have no time for stories, Meriweather. Nor do you."

Liron seized his arm and turned him around. "Look, Alexander. Before you judge, *look*."

Reluctantly, Caleb allowed his body to turn in the prince's direction. The crowd had begun to disperse, some tense and angry as he was. Others looked strangely buoyant. As he watched, Prince Magnus crossed the small workshop to the nightwalker's side and spoke softly to her. He reached for her hand and pressed something into it. A vial?

"Doesn't he know that—"

"Hush, Alexander. He knows."

The woman took the prince's hand, and a change seemed to work in her. She stood taller, though she still looked drawn and wan. A smile stretched across her lips, and tears slipped from her eyes. Forgetting herself, she took Magnus's hand in both of hers.

A prince would never let such a woman touch him, Caleb scoffed silently.

Sela gasped.

Caleb chided himself for forgetting her presence. "What is in the vial?" he murmured to Liron.

"Medicine," replied Liron. "Rather powerful medicine. From the king's private supply, the prince says, though I didn't think he brought anything with him. He has been busy these past few days."

Caleb eyed the prince's misshapen shoulder. "Then why does he not heal himself of his affliction?"

A wounded healer? An impossible paradox.

Sela covered her mouth, as if aghast at his question.

Caleb wondered at her reaction. She had known the prince's identity ahead of the others. Now, she gazed at Magnus with a mixture of awe and fear. What business lay between her and the prince?

Liron shrugged. "I asked him the same. He said his purpose would reveal itself in time."

"If Lord Auberon hears of this, Magnus will find himself at the mercy of the soldiers. They will want to know where he got the medicine and will accuse him of robbery if he cannot explain."

"Aye, Caleb. I warned him to be careful."

Was this where Liron spent his free time? Following the prince around like a puppy, listening to his preposterous ideas about absolving one's enemies? Perhaps Magnus had few enemies. After all, he was yet to meet Uriah Smith. Or Lord Auberon.

If he did, he would understand why forgiveness was impossible.

"I want to speak to him," said Sela.

"We must be getting back," Caleb objected. He had no wish for Sela to be caught up in this business between Magnus and the rest of Azazel. It could only turn ugly. Inevitably, there would be some kind of showdown between the prince and Eremia's appointed representatives, most likely before the monsoonal rains arrived.

"You go on. I'll escort her home." Liron's gaze was still trained on Magnus. He patted his sword hilt. "She's safe with me, Alexander. You have my word."

If not for the pleading in Sela's eyes, Caleb might have refused her request and Liron's quick assurances. Even so, he was uneasy. "Smith is about. And it's unwise to linger here after nightfall."

Liron stood taller. "Liri and the children are finishing up at the grocers. Why don't you go retrieve them? Then we'll all walk back together."

At last, Caleb gave a heavy nod. "Very well."

He turned to go, but his attention remained for several moments on his bondmate. Sela searched for absolution, just as he did, but she would do better to look for it in the pages of the Book of Souls, rather than in the shifting power struggles between Eremia and Azazel.

After all, everything she'd suffered to date must surely prove to her the dangers of placing trust in any man, no matter how noble his intentions.

And that included himself.

Chapter Thirteen

As soon as the nightwalker left the prince's side, Sela was ready to take her place. The crowd had noticed the vial in the woman's hand, and they clustered around her. One man offered money for the medicine.

The prince turned to Sela. He wore the same homespun clothes, heavy with dust after a long day's labor. His face looked weary—not like a royal's at all. "Sela." Magnus's voice betrayed uncommon kindness. "'Tis good to see you here."

Seeing his injury, Sela wondered how the prince had been able to haul her weight up and over the cliff edge. His injury was no less severe than Thaddeus's. Had he damaged his shoulder further by reaching for her? "My lord." She bowed her head.

"'Tis only Magnus," he replied, reminding her of Thaddeus.

"*Only* Magnus?"

"For now, my daughter. Though you may thereafter call me by that name, even when I am known by other names."

She frowned, remembering what Magnus had said about forgiveness. Caleb's rigid disdain and recoiling, when she'd only known gentleness and openness from her bondmate before. What was happening to him? "How did you know I was in trouble that day on the cliff?"

He gave her a gentle smile that matched the one he'd given her on the clifftop. "Did you believe you were alone?"

I will never leave you nor forsake you.

The voice she'd heard. Had the Carver sent Prince Magnus to rescue her?

"You aren't at all what I would expect of a prince," she said at last. "If the people of Azazel knew the king's son was here—"

"They will know," he replied, with a solemncholy air. "But not all will see."

"You told me on the clifftop that you have come to put all to rights." She thought of Liri...Caleb...herself. Did the prince have medicine for what troubled her? Perhaps it only mended physical ailments. "Have you come to free us?"

Again, the gentle smile. "Aye, to free all who are held captive. Not all cages are made of bars, though. And not all chains are of a blacksmith's making."

"'Tis true." Sela braced herself against the craftsman's worktable. "I know it well."

Magnus laid his callused hand over hers, a gesture forbidden by every law of their land. Yet, the prince showed no trepidation. "Your bondmate was here before, Sela. Where did he go?"

How could she explain Caleb's pain, or her own? A prince, even one as kind as Magnus, would hardly care for a commoner's affairs. *Yet, Magnus was gentle toward the nightwalker.* "He has a great love for the Carver," she said. "That is why he takes everything so hard." It was not really an answer.

"Don't be afraid, Sela. If he truly loves the Carver, he will eventually discover the truth." He smiled. "Caleb has yet to discover that the Carver is present not only during times of blessing, but also in times of trials."

If that were true, she would do well to learn the lesson herself. "You know his name?"

"We met before he knew who I was."

Sela sensed that his response carried more meaning than the one she grasped. "While he was one of the Pure?"

"There are none who are Pure, Sela."

"Not even the Righteous?"

"Not even the Righteous."

In a few words, Magnus shattered every foundation upon which the elders and the priesthood—and Eremia itself—stood. "Then the lot cannot absolve us. It cannot save."

"'Tis the lot that first made man aware of his wrongdoing and offered a way out of the mire. Though, 'tis not the lot that you know now. However, a blind man cannot help another to see. For such, I have come."

"Then my sister's sacrifice was for naught." Sela stared up at him, willing him to disagree, begging him to say she'd misheard or misunderstood him.

"I have not forgotten your sister." He held her gaze. "Nor your brother. Nor you, Sela. I will not waste your pain."

His promise to Liron. Was that all that bound him? A reckless, youthful oath to a small child? Yet, somehow, Magnus had *known* that Liri and Sela would one day be captives on Azazel. That they would be in need of rescue.

She withdrew her hand. "More than the lot stands between me and the Carver, Prince Magnus. You don't know everything I've done. You don't know it all."

If he could glimpse the extent of her failings—the deaths of Joss Brigham and Molly, her failure to rescue Esther, her murder of Elsie—the prince would distance himself from her, as he ought. Perhaps, she should do it for him, just as she'd tried to do for Caleb's sake.

"I am nothing like my bondmate, my lord. If you only knew..." Her words trailed away.

Magnus reached out and clasped her hand. "When Caleb Alexander realizes the Carver loves him just as he is, without any-thing—or any*one*—to recommend him, he will possess the heart to love you truly, my daughter. No matter what he's done, or what's been done to him, or where he's been, or where he will be in the future. No matter anything he will ever do. And you, Sela. You must realize that the Carver bears a great and unconditional love not only for Caleb, but also for you."

"How can such a thing be?" she whispered. "How can you call me 'daughter'? No man can truly forgive who has lived a sevenday on Azazel."

Show mercy to the merciless, Magnus had said.

Father Monroe and Father Larkin would blanch at such heresy. This sentiment repelled the branded and the unbranded alike—those who thought themselves safe from the lot, and those who believed themselves condemned.

What of punishment? What of justice? Even the kindly Father Monroe had sent Sela into exile without a second glance.

"Aye, no man can show mercy, not unless he first drinks of the Carver's mercy for himself."

"From what source, my lord? There is naught at the heart of Azazel but wilderness." With a pang, Sela remembered lying in the desert, her body wracked with the seasoning. The hissing, serpentine voice still haunted her, taunting her with reminders of her guilt. Her uncleanness. All the ways she was unworthy of Caleb Alexander—and of the Carver. "'Tis a snake-infested wilderness, suited for naught but abandonment."

"Aye, 'tis snake-infested," Prince Magnus agreed. "But you are not alone in this fight. Indeed, you need not fight at all. Wait a little while longer, and I will crush the vipers of this island beneath my boot."

Sela's mouth dropped open. "How do you... How *can* you—" She broke off, at a loss for words.

The figure of light appeared in her memory, the one who had saved her. Once by scattering the snake that would have finished her, and then by leading the others to her with his otherworldly lantern of light.

Thaddeus, Briella, and Jax. *My Remenant.*

Was this the same man Liron had sworn would one day grant her pardon?

"Aye, my daughter," Prince Magnus said, in the deep voice she recognized at long last. "'Twas I who was with you in the desert that night."

At midnight, rain once again drummed the cabin roof. The sound should have eased Sela's tension, but she was all too aware of the empty space beside her. Rising from the bed, she pulled on a dressing gown and slipped from the room.

A lone lantern scattered light over the table and onto a vast array of parchments, some single pages or fragments, and others bundled into sheaves. Caleb slept atop the nearest pile, his head supported by one bent arm, his unbound, chestnut hair tumbling past his ear and over the collar of his partially unbuttoned shirt. One ink-stained hand curled against a sheaf of parchments like a dragon guarding his treasure.

Sela sighed. Every moment Caleb was not working or sharing watches with Liron, he pored over his extracts. What did he hope to find, when he had searched a hundred times before?

With Liron in residence, Caleb had returned to his long runs across the island's beaches. Sela no longer accompanied him, unable to keep up with his frenzied pace, and also wary of the sea, whose waters had several times nearly proved her undoing.

She reached out to touch Caleb's shoulder just as the door opened.

"Don't wake him." Liron stepped inside, closing the door behind him. He cradled a musket, and his wet, black hair stuck out from his head at impossible angles.

He set the weapon aside and came closer. "If ever a man deserved his rest, 'tis Caleb." He nodded at the bedroom, where Liri and her children slept. "Is the boy asleep?"

"Aye, at last."

The younger Liron had experienced difficulty adjusting to life on the island. His face often showed his fear that he might be separated from his mother a second time. He clearly missed his father, but Caleb and Liron had forbidden Tucker to visit. The boy's night terrors finally eased when Liron promised to sleep directly outside the younger Liron's room.

Sela dropped a blanket around Caleb's shoulders and glanced at her brother. He was studying Caleb, who sprawled across the parchment-littered table. "He works himself too hard," he observed.

"Aye, you both do."

Liron glanced down at his unbranded palm. "Caleb cannot be both scholar and farmer. One day, he will have to choose."

She frowned. "Caleb can never return to the Righteous."

Her brother hesitated, biting his lip. Was he keeping something from her? "Should anything happen to me, I know he will look after you, Sela. He loves you more than his own life."

A squeeze of pain flashed through her. Aye, Caleb had not set her aside, as she feared he would. But whatever bond had once existed between them was surely lost, or at least greatly diminished. Every day, he retreated more deeply into himself.

She forced herself to dwell on other matters. "Are you going to return to the Old Town?"

"Nay, not as a wanted man." Liron smoothed down his hair, shoving back his fringe. "Until recently, I thought of returning for our family in secret, as Hiram Foley planned to do for his."

"Until recently?"

"Until I saw Azazel." His shoulders sagged. "I cannot bring Cadence here, or our parents. Not even Teodoir, for all that his family is here already. 'Twould be wrong to expose them to such a life."

"And Etta?" she probed gently, thinking of the girl her brother had been courting before Sela left the Old Town.

He raised his head. "Before I left, I asked her to bond with me."

"She agreed?"

"Aye, though she will not likely have me now."

"Oh, Liron." Sela grieved that she'd cost him his choice. "You should never have come to—"

"I do not regret it, Sela." He opened his arms, and she drew close. "You and Liri are my family too. Our parents have Cadence. They would want the three of us to all be together."

Sela returned his hug. "Then you intend to stay on Azazel?"

"Aye, for as long as I can."

"Meriweather, your watch is over." Jerking awake, Caleb rose, the blanket slipping from his shoulders. He stretched then halted at the sight of his bondmate. He retrieved the blanket and passed it to Sela. "You should be in bed."

She took the blanket. "I thought to keep you company during your watch." She waited for him to forbid it.

To Sela's surprise, Caleb nodded. He shoved his stiff limbs into the arms of his greatcoat, took the musket from where it leaned against the wall, and moved past his brother-in-law. "Sleep well, Liron."

"Aye."

Sela wrapped the blanket around her shoulders and accompanied Caleb to the porch. She waited until he had shut the door and settled himself into a shadowed section before she sat beside him. With heavy clouds masking the moon's light, she could just see the outline of his body.

Determined to preserve the stubborn silence he'd maintained since they'd returned home from hearing Magnus, she was surprised when he spoke first.

"You woke to find me missing?"

"Nay, Caleb. I never slept."

He reached for her, and she scooted into his embrace. Wrapping one arm around his waist and leaning against his warm chest, she settled the blanket over them both. Except for the musket beside Caleb, Sela might have imagined their midnight discussion to be nothing more than a romantic escapade. "What have you discovered of the Carver?"

Sela felt tension return to his body. He sighed, as if attempting to expel it. His arm slid around her back, and he tugged her closer. "I thought I knew every one of the Carver's words. But somehow, my Sela, I missed it. I could not see the ocean for the waves."

Thrilled at his affectionate address of her, she waited for him to continue.

"We have one chance," he murmured into her hair, "and only one. The lot was a divine agreement between our ancestors and the Carver. It was established and written into law by the sacrifice of innocent blood—an innocent willing to be branded on behalf of the guilty. Only by innocent blood can the lot be undone. Should such a person—one of the Pure—offer himself, the curse of the soul mark would come to an end. And all that lingers within shadows would be abolished, as well."

He paused, then went on. "But that's not everything."

"What else?"

"The innocent party must be of royal blood." He turned his hand palm up, exposing one of his brands.

Sela's heart fluttered with the hint of excitement. She slid her cold fingers over his warmer ones. "Prince Magnus."

Caleb stiffened. "Nay, Sela. Magnus is no prince."

"He is the firstborn son of the king."

"Magnus has naught but the clothes on his back to support his claims. Even then, they paint him as a commoner."

"Liron knew him as a boy."

Caleb grunted, as if disputing that a mere boy could prove a reliable witness. "With what weapon do you expect Magnus to overcome Uriah Smith? Or Janus Auberon?"

Sela was no scholar, nor did she possess his mind, or his faith. However, she could not forget the lantern-carrying figure that had found her in the desert, and the hand that had pulled her up and over the cliff.

She shivered. Magnus was a man of nobility and integrity. A true king's son. "What of the truth, Caleb?"

"When Caleb Alexander realizes the Carver loves him just as he is, without anything—or anyone—to recommend him, he will finally possess the heart to love you truly, my daughter."

Was this the cage the prince had spoken of? It seemed to Sela that Caleb's heart and soul were as fettered as hers. Shadows of his illustrious past tugged at him constantly. Perhaps Liron was right. Caleb could not be scholar and farmer forever. One day, he would have to choose between her and the life he'd left behind.

She shuddered at the thought that her bondmate might decide to walk away from her, after all.

"Are you cold?" Caleb pulled her closer. "The Carver of Souls is the only source of truth, Sela. The prince must be an imposter. Where is his medallion, the proof of his status?"

"You heard his words. You saw the medicine he gave to that woman. He must have been sent by the king. And if so, why? There is nothing on Azazel that would tempt a prince. Will he not one day own it all?"

Caleb grew silent, and Sela felt his unease. Over the past few sevendays, they'd somehow exchanged places. Now, she was the trusting one, and he the skeptic.

She was hollower than a sea cave, and he full of righteous fire.

She desired peace, and he wanted controversy.

"The prince told me he would set all to rights, Caleb."

"I would have set all to rights *today*."

So, this was the truth of it. He had not forgiven Sela for preventing him from shooting Uriah. She was still stunned that she had objected in the first place. But after Elsie—after the clifftop—her bloodlust had evaporated. Aye, she was afraid of Uriah. However, she no longer wished him dead.

What had happened? Was there something wrong with her?

"I would not have you become a murderer." She withdrew, trying to discern his face. "The guilt, Caleb. 'Tis a burden impossible for anyone to bear."

He pulled her into his lap, and Sela knew his anger had dispelled. He tucked her head into his shoulder and pressed a kiss on her hairline.

Silence stretched between them, until she was fearful to break their uneasy truce. For once, his mind encamped near hers. His hair smelled of salt and damp earth.

"I overheard some of your conversation with Liron," he said at last. "If 'tis possible, one day I will take you far from Azazel."

"Over the sea?"

"To the mainland, if we can find a ship to bear us hence."

"'Tis so far, Caleb."

He stroked her hair. "I know you fear the water."

She stilled.

"Did you think I would not notice, my love?"

Aye, she feared to walk beside the ocean or cross even the shallowest of rivers. She bristled at his powers of observation, then softened at the care in his voice. It would seem that not everything had passed Caleb by.

"We will overcome it, I promise. Together."

She warmed to his certainty. "Perhaps Azazel may yet be turned to peace. Liron still hopes in the prince."

Caleb hugged her closer. When he spoke, emotion throbbed in his voice. "I fear he hopes in vain."

Another sevenday passed, and Liron waited for Magnus in the wheelwright's shop. He could hardly see him amidst the crush of people. The wheelwright was a close friend of Thaddeus. He'd been intrigued by the prince's ideas—even though Magnus had not yet revealed his true lineage—and opened his shop to the prince.

The people listened, but mostly, they came for the prince's medicines.

Show mercy to the merciless, Magnus said.

The words were naught but laughable to those who'd spent time among the branded, especially on Azazel. However, no one who heard the words from the prince's lips laughed. Even without princely clothes or a crown, the soulless sensed something different about Magnus. What man could quote from the Book of Souls as if it were branded on his brain?

Not even Caleb, with all his study, possessed the prince's understanding.

Magnus shared what he called "messages from the king," messages that either attracted or repelled new hearers. The prince had no interest in parroting the empty platitudes the priests or the Righteous circulated.

Nay, Magnus's ideas were harder to stomach. Yet, his words settled in Liron as if they had been formed to fill the empty places inside of him.

The judgment of a man's or woman's soul belonged to the Carver of Souls, so Magnus proclaimed. No man, branded or unbranded, could determine the eternal fate of another.

Not only that, but the prince openly denounced the debauchery that had cracked and rotted much of the heartwood of Azazel. He urged his listeners to turn away from their lives of soullessness. The king would come, he said, and there would be a reckoning.

When he heard these messages, Liron always looked around fearfully, waiting for the black-coated soldiers to descend upon the prince and drag him to Lord Auberon. Magnus, for his part, ignored Liron's pleas to be more careful.

If anything, the prince became bolder.

Liron frowned. Did the man not fear for his earthly body, if he truly had no care for his immortal soul? Why did he not unveil his true identity? If he did, even Lord Auberon would be forced to cower at Magnus's feet.

When the prince finished speaking, most of the crowd dispersed. Liron made his way to Magnus's side. "May I speak with you, my lord?" Liron kept his voice low, cautious of the others who lingered nearby.

Magnus turned and gave Liron a weary smile. "You may always speak with me."

Liron recalled the hours he'd spent waiting for the king that long-ago day, when Sela and Cadence were attacked. His advisors had finally announced that the king was ill. "An audience with your father, the king, is not so easy to secure of late."

"Nay," Magnus replied. "So it has been for many years on Azazel as well. And for such, I have come."

Liron leaned against the workbench, where he'd listened in on Sela's conversation with the prince. They'd spoken of a clifftop, and Liron realized that Sela and Magnus had met before. Later, he'd searched her out. After much questioning, she'd reluctantly recounted the circumstances of their meeting.

Liron had clenched his fists and fought the urge to hunt down Tucker Alexander and Uriah Smith. He wanted to murder them with his bare hands. If not for the prince, his sister would have plummeted to her death.

"Sela told me what you did for her," Liron said. "My lord, I cannot thank you enough. If she had been alone..."

Magnus inclined his regal head. "You are both welcome, my son."

"But your shoulder, the injury you sustained when you saved me as a child."

"You are full of much fear, Liron. 'Twas a gift, freely given."

"A gift, Prince Magnus?"

The prince smiled and used his hand to scrape wood shavings into a small pile. "The Carver's grace is not a length of iron, my son, that it can be bent or manipulated into a more pleasing form. 'Tis not coin to be earned or traded. Nor is it wood, that it may be shaved off by a craftsman's plane or whittled away to naught, according to a man's deeds."

"The Righteous would execute you if they heard such a statement," Liron replied. "They consider themselves paragons of virtue and pride themselves on being the sole instructors in the business of absolution."

He thought of his brother-in-law. In some ways, Caleb still hung on to the life he'd left behind. Liron saw how it tortured Sela.

"The Righteous have built their lives on the blood and sacrifices of others," Magnus said, "but 'twill not save them in the end."

Liron looked around, searching for prying eyes or overly zealous ears.

At that moment, a patrol drew near. The leader of half-a-dozen guards headed for the group of men and women who clustered around Magnus. Liron shrank back into the shadows of the workshop, fearing one of them would recognize him.

"Did you not hear Lord Auberon's orders?" the leader demanded. "There is to be a curfew at dusk. All those who defy the mandate shall be taken to the fort and flogged."

Liron raised an eyebrow, cognizant of the taverns, which loudly plied their sordid trades less than a hundred yards beyond. The white fists frequented these establishments as often as the settlement men. As such, they were ever selective in their enforcement of Lord Auberon's "curfew," which could just as easily conclude in the early hours of the morning as at dusk, depending on their inclinations. It came as no surprise to Liron that the taverns had been the first buildings to be rebuilt after Smith's attack, after the fort.

He stepped forward, but Magnus held up his hand. "Peace, my son."

"Captain," said another of the soldiers, likely a deputy, "it looks like the soulless are cavorting with the soul-bearing."

The captain scowled and addressed Magnus. "Are you soul-bearing, man?"

"I am."

"Then where are your gloves?"

The prince said naught.

If the captain only knew to whom he speaks.

Behind the captain, a soldier shifted. Liron recognized him at once. This man had sought out the prince the sevenday before for a pain in his bones that would not ease. Would he speak up in defense of the one who'd given him life-altering medicine formulated by the king's own healers?

The soldier opened his mouth, then closed it.

Apparently not.

The captain's face reddened. "Soulless and soul-bearing are to have *no* contact, unless proper precautions are taken. 'Tis the order of the Righteous."

"What of the king?" Liron growled. He couldn't stop himself from coming to Magnus's aid.

"Peace, my son," the prince repeated. He rested a hand against Liron's chest. "'Tis not the time."

"Why not heal himself of his affliction?"

Caleb's question from many days' past. Liron would add this mystery to the others that surrounded the prince. Why did he not reveal himself? Did he truly fear Lord Auberon? Or Uriah Smith?

"The king's will and Lord Auberon's will are one," replied the captain. "And I'll thank you not to question either, boy, unless you want to find yourself swinging from the gallows come sunrise."

Liron choked back a laugh. He was no boy, and the captain was naught but a few years older than himself.

Clearly sensing Liron's mirth, the captain drew himself up. "The lot of you, get to your homes. Consider this your final warning. If I catch *any* of you loitering here again after dusk..." His threat trailed off. He spun, barked something at his men, and headed in the direction of the taverns, obviously more of a mind for entertainment than punishment.

Liron grimaced, remembering Sela's friend, Esther. Would she be compelled to amuse such a man?

As soon as the patrol disappeared from sight and the rest of the crowd had scattered, a man stepped out of the gathering gloom. "I fear you invite trouble with your speeches, my lord," said Thaddeus. He cradled his bad arm like a child.

The young man with the patchwork face, Jax, stood beside him. He gazed at Magnus with undisguised reverence. The prince was one of the few who was kind to him.

Liron had taken an instant liking to Thaddeus on arriving on Azazel, and his respect grew on learning he was Teodoir's eldest son. Thaddeus displayed his father's easy manner, and the long pauses he entertained before speaking his mind were all Teodoir's.

Magnus appeared unruffled. "'Tis not their approval I seek, Thaddeus."

"Still," said Thaddeus, "you should be careful."

Liron agreed. He was glad to have an ally in his bid to preserve the prince's unbranded status.

He and Thaddeus took their leave and returned together to the white house. Liron offered his farewells and made for Caleb and Sela's cabin, ignoring the bold look of a painted woman, who glided across his path. He heaved a sigh of relief when he cleared Belladonna.

A short distance from the road, his brother-in-law sat on the porch steps, with his elbows propped behind him on the highest step. He looked almost casual, save for the soul ache that had taken up permanent residence in his eyes.

Liron hurried up and sank onto the steps beside Caleb, hearing a succession of squeals from inside the cabin. Anwen, by the sounds of it, was playing a game of chase with her twin and younger sister.

"'Tis no wonder you escaped out here, my friend," Liron said amiably, "what with all that racket. 'Tis enough to drive any scholar mad."

Caleb smiled. "They are only children. I thought to enjoy the sunshine while it lasted."

Liron nodded, entertaining the idle thought that his brother-in-law possessed all of Magnus's weariness, but none of his peace. "Not long till the monsoonal rains, I hear."

They would talk of the weather all day if Caleb allowed it, but Liron had absorbed some of Magnus's courage. He hoped to mend the tie between his sister and her bondmate. That they loved each other fiercely was obvious to any man with eyes in his head, but the splinter between them had somehow grown into a wedge.

Why, Liron did not understand. They were rarely angry or petulant with each other. However, after Sela confessed the full extent of the despair that had driven her to the clifftop, Liron had probed further.

"Does Caleb know?"

She'd glanced up, frightened. "Nay, Liron. If he knew, 'twould break him to pieces."

"Truth has a way of asserting itself, Sela. You cannot keep this from him. Besides, he should know for how much he has to be grateful to Magnus."

Was this the wedge that widened the distance between his sister and her bondmate? If so, there was naught to do but pluck it out himself.

Now, sitting at ease on the porch steps, he glanced at Caleb. Liron had often been accused of impulsivity—even recklessness. This time, his worst fault would be appropriately channeled. His meddling might restore to Sela the bondmate she loved.

"Liron?" Caleb asked, apparently sensing something of his turmoil.

Liron turned to him and grasped his courage with both hands. After this, Sela might never speak to him again. "There's something you should know."

Chapter Fourteen

Be calm, Caleb. An unsteady hand cannot write smoothly. The admonition of one of his favorite teachers, never more closely heeded than now.

In his temporary madness, Caleb had forgotten his coat, but his rage was warmth enough as his horse climbed the hilly path to the clifftop and he was buffeted by the trade winds. After Liron's revelation, Caleb had paused long enough to write a shaky letter, saddle his horse, and ride into Belladonna. He gave only a hasty word of explanation to Sela and Liri that he needed to visit Thaddeus. He would be home in time for dinner.

After he'd killed his brother.

It had been easy to find a white-fisted soldier to deliver his missive to Tucker, and Caleb had no doubt that his brother would come. In the meantime, he had only to wait.

Reaching the top of the cliff, he dismounted and tethered the horse to a crumbling stone pillar—one of the more solid structures that remained of the outpost—and settled upon a large rock. The wind's fingertips jabbed at his exposed throat and vee of chest like an awl. His lungs constricted painfully at the punctures.

What had driven Sela to this place? Had she believed he was dead, or that he'd deliberately left her behind? He could not blame her despair on the seasoning, as Liron had.

Sela had stood at this precipice and contemplated ending her life. She must have decided to jump, since Magnus had caught her and hauled her over the cliff edge. In the wake of his anguish, Caleb hardly felt gratitude for the man's intervention.

I should have been here. He jerked to his feet and began to pace. *I failed her.*

He did not have much time to expend in mental self-flagellation, for the object of his fury approached, picking his way over the cliff and leading his horse. Tucker wore his white coat, the hated gloves that had given the soldiers the nickname *white fists*, and an expression of hopeful regret. His copper hair, wavier than Caleb's, winked in the failing light. The flash of a coin at his exposed throat sparked Caleb's anger afresh.

Tucker is the failure, not I. Tucker will pay the price.

Although Caleb's mentor had intended the instruction for a vastly different lesson, he commanded his body to stay calm.

Tucker tethered his horse beside Caleb's and approached uncertainly. "'Tis unwise for us to meet in public."

"Because of Auberon's curfew?"

"Those who break it are flogged and beaten. I have seen it."

Caleb shrugged, though he still felt the bite of Lord Auberon's whip on his back. That, and the shame of tumbling so far from his lofty precipice. More had been lost that day than blood and pride. "I don't fear the Righteous."

Tucker stepped closer, looking eager. "Caleb, even now that life is not lost to you. Lord Auberon said—"

"Lord Auberon?"

"Aye, he regrets his hasty punishment. 'Twas much too harsh for the magnitude of the crime."

"There was no crime, Tucker." He recalled the moment he'd blown air into his bondmate's lifeless mouth. "I saved Sela's life."

'Twas the Carver who saved her, came the swift reminder, but Caleb continued, "As I told Liron, I would do it again."

Tucker grimaced and folded his arms across this chest. "You know, I always believed you immune from temptation."

"Temptation?" Caleb bit his lip to keep from swearing. "Feeling as you do for Liri, will you deny any knowledge of love?"

"Is it love?" His brother's stare was hard, unyielding. "Sela is an uncommonly beautiful woman—"

"'Tis *love*," Caleb replied firmly. "Men do not give up everything—do not die—for the sake of lust."

Tucker's face caved inward, his eyes full of anguish. "Because of her, you *will* die, Caleb. Do you remember naught of the fate of an unabsolved soul? But even now, Lord Auberon has promised—"

"Promised what?"

"Should you return to us, he will be merciful."

Caleb raised his palms and his eyebrows in unison.

Tucker swallowed. "There are ways of concealing the soul mark. Disfigurement using certain chemicals, for one. There are several whose punishment has been successfully retracted."

"What of the Carver?"

"The Carver?" Tucker repeated blankly.

"You think His judgment is so easily retracted? According to the whims of His supposed servants?"

"Caleb, I admit that I do not understand your anger. I am offering you—"

"What do I care for what you offer, when it was you who nearly took my life?"

Tucker's gaze slid sideways, as if he searched for the bump on Caleb's skull that had long since disappeared. "I regret that I hurt you."

"Not me, Tucker. Because of you, Sela was nearly lost. A part of me would have died with her."

"You exaggerate. She would not have died by Smith's hand."

"Nay, but she nearly died by her own."

Tucker straightened. "Her own?"

"I summoned you here for your reckoning, brother. Perhaps you might forget my absolution and spare a thought for yours."

Caleb raised his pistol, primed and loaded for this moment.

Tucker paled. "You would kill me? Your own brother? For what reason?"

"Because you are a coward. It should have been you who tried to save Liri—six years ago, and again, sevendays ago—not Sela. Had you been a man, Sela might not have stood at this clifftop and decided to end her life."

Tucker took a step back. "What do you mean?"

"Drowning in her despair, Sela threw herself from the cliff edge behind me. Thankfully, she was saved by a"—he could not betray Magnus's identity, even if Caleb thought him an imposter—"passing stranger."

Tears pushed at his eyelids, but Caleb refused to release them. "She almost died"—he cocked the pistol—"because of *you*."

His brother's lips drifted apart. "I didn't know." He turned away. "I never intended to kill her."

"Like I said, Tucker. 'Tis time to face your reckoning."

Tucker's head came up. "You would render your niece and nephew fatherless?"

"They have family aplenty."

"My son is unbranded. I am his only chance for a good life."

"Again, the words of a coward. Why should a boy have such a man for a father?"

Forgiveness is the true mark of the Righteous.

The words tore into him, but Caleb refused to let them take root. Once Tucker was dead, Sela would be avenged. Then Caleb would go after Smith, or die in the attempt. Perhaps he would even take down Lord Auberon.

His lips curved into a maniacal grin at the thought.

"This love you profess has driven you to madness, Caleb." Tucker edged closer, holding up his hands. "Put down the pistol and I will fix this, I promise."

"'Tis not for any man to fix," came a breathless voice from behind them.

The brothers turned to see Sela standing there, panting, as if she'd run all the way up the hill. Her hair was unfettered, as dark as the night that crept up on them, and her slim shoulders heaved.

She looked deathly pale as she focused on Caleb. "I overheard you speaking with Liron."

"Sela, go back to the cabin." Caleb gave her the barest of glances, not wanting to take his attention from Tucker.

She shook her head. Before he could react, she placed herself in front of Tucker as a shield. She stood close enough that his treacherous brother could reach out and pin her to his chest. But neither she nor Tucker moved.

Caleb took a step forward. "Sela, move aside! This is not your business."

"I overheard enough to know you would murder Tucker because of me. Therefore, 'tis exactly my business."

"'Tis not murder, but justice."

"You may be the scholar, Caleb, but I am no fool. I see no justice in your eyes."

He shifted sideways and growled at Tucker. "Would you again cower behind a woman, brother?"

Tucker flinched and moved, but Sela kept pace with him.

"You would protect a man who left you for dead, Sela?"

"I only protect you from the consequences of your actions, Caleb." She stared at him, begging with her eyes. "This is not the future you want. Believe me."

Just then, the fire in her gaze went out, and her eyes rolled back in her head. Tucker caught her as she fainted, his gloved hands propping her upright as they sank to the ground together in mingled white and scarlet. Tucker tilted her head back and pressed his fingers to the artery at her throat.

Caleb lowered his gun and ran for her. "Fool!" He shoved Tucker away and reached for Sela. "You will never feel her pulse through the gloves."

He took her in his arms and cradled her body against his, letting her head fall against his shoulder. Inky strands of hair whipped across his cheek. He felt for her pulse, reassured when it beat strongly against his fingers. Her skin was cold to the touch, and no wonder. She'd run after him without even a shawl. He rubbed her pebbled skin, wishing he'd thought to bring his coat.

"Here." Tucker shucked his white coat. "Take mine."

Caleb hesitated, eyeing the creamy material with distaste.

"Do you want her to freeze?"

Decided, he snatched the exquisite coat from Tucker's hands with a brisk nod and wrapped it around her. As she lay limp against him, he traced the pale ridge of her cheekbone, feeling the barest puff of breath on his face.

When he looked up, Tucker was staring at him. "You truly love her, then," he whispered.

"Of course I love her," Caleb snapped. "Did you not once declare me to know my own mind?"

That was true, except in matters relating to the Carver. However, Tucker had no need to know the extent of his conflict...his doubts.

"I envy you that," Tucker said and stood.

"This isn't finished," Caleb warned, conscious of the flintlock that lay abandoned beside him. He need only let go of Sela to reach for it.

"Nay," his brother replied. "You have my coat. I have no doubt you will return it to me." Tucker looked down at Caleb's bond-mate. "Sela?"

She didn't stir.

Tucker bit his lip then glanced at Caleb. "I will see you soon, brother." He returned to his horse, mounted, and rode away.

Tucker had no sooner started down the hill than another rider approached. Liron, by the shape of him. He said naught to Tucker, passing him by like a ship in the night. He stopped where Caleb had tethered his horse and dismounted. Tying his horse, Liron watched Caleb from a distance but did not draw near. He likely knew better than to interfere—at least more than he had done already.

"Caleb?" Sela came awake, looking up at him with such love that it displaced his fury—and his fear. Her hair tickled the edge of his collar, turning his upper arm into a glossy raven's wing. She gazed past him to the clifftop. "I did not jump. 'Twas the wind that drove me over the edge before the prince saved me."

"You despaired because I did not come for you."

"Aye," she replied, and his heart sank, "and nay. I despaired because I believed a lie—more than one lie, really. 'Twas the Carver—'twas Magnus—who showed me otherwise."

He understood her meaning. In her mind, she was convinced that he too believed a lie. She thought that coming after him would be enough to save him from himself, as she'd been saved by Magnus.

As if a passing prince of Eremia could pluck his sorry self from the metaphorical precipice from which he dangled. As if he would collapse in relief on the cliff edge, gasping for breath and spluttering his thanks.

She was wrong. He wasn't staring down a cliff.

He was lost in the wilderness.

The colors of the sunset were thin and streaky, like fabric stretched too tight on a weaver's loom, when Liri heard a knock on the door.

She stiffened. Who could it be? Liron had run off to retrieve Sela, who had gone after Caleb. Liri was alone in the house with three small children. Only a barred door stood between her and the outside. She had no idea how to fire the musket.

What if it was Uriah?

Grabbing the lantern, she left the children playing and crossed to the window, hissing as she recognized the visitor. She crossed to the door, unbarred it, and dragged it open.

Lanternlight splashed across Tucker's taut face. Despite the evening chill, he was devoid of a coat.

She used her body to bar the doorway. "Have you come to see Liron?"

"Liron and Anwen? Nay, Liri. I came to see you."

He seemed...different. The children had not yet noticed the visitor, so she pulled her shawl around her shoulders and stepped onto the porch, closing the door behind her. "Why have you come? Our son is barely settled, and here you are, wanting to disturb him again."

His shoulders slumped. "'Twas not my aim." He stretched a coatless arm toward her and closed a gloved hand around her forearm. Something more than the brisk wind reddened his cheeks. "I have missed seeing you every day."

Her cheeks hot, Liri pulled her arm from his grasp. "I meant what I said. I will not open my heart to you again."

"Nay, you misunderstand me." He backed up a step. "I came to say"—he expelled a heavy sigh—"what I hoped my letter would say in far more polished words. I am sorry, Liri. For everything."

The heart she'd thought to deny him entrance flickered, as if a tiny flame had been lit therein. "I do not need polished words. Only heartfelt ones."

Tucker nodded. "You have them." His eyelids shuttered. "I wish I could redo the past. If I could, I would have taken your place that day. Or I would have followed you into exile."

"Do you even know what you say, Tucker?"

He met her gaze. The pain there—the loneliness—nearly drove Liri into his arms. "Aye, I know."

Her eyes filled with tears. "I am sorry, but I cannot believe you."

Because of Tucker, Uriah had stolen Sela—not only her body, but also the light from her eyes. If Tucker had done as his heart bade, Liri would never have met Uriah. If she had not surrendered her virtue back in the Old Town, she would not have been forced into a convenient but unhappy Binding with Uriah.

Regardless, Liri shared the throne of guilt with Tucker, a reluctant queen to his kingship of shame. She had shared his bed as willingly as she'd shared Uriah's. Her guilt stung her. Sela—sweet, beautiful, *innocent* Sela—would never have met Uriah if not for Liri's choices.

Tucker angled his head away from her and then nodded, clearly accepting that she would not forgive him. "I cannot stay. Sela comes with Caleb and Liron. She fainted."

Sela fainted? There was something else, something he did not say. Where was his coat? Why had Tucker come here alone?

She watched him melt into the darkness. Shadows pooled around the sections of porch not touched by her lantern. Colors thinned and dissolved into a cinereous hue. She dimly registered hoofbeats striking the compacted earth like a blacksmith's hammer. A moment later, Liron and Caleb rode into sight, Sela sitting across Caleb's saddlebow.

Dismounting and handing his reins to Liron, Caleb reached up for Sela, who slid into his arms. He carried her up the porch steps and into the cabin, pausing only long enough for Liri to open the door.

She glimpsed the coat wrapped around her sister's body.

Tucker's coat.

For all his dislike of Sela, what had made him give her such a precious thing?

Liron tethered the horses and came up the steps a minute later.

"What happened?" Liri whispered. "Tucker came by and gave me forewarning of Sela's condition, but he departed quickly."

"Aye." Liron frowned at the mention of Tucker. "Perhaps 'tis for the best."

"Because Caleb loathes his brother?"

"Nay." Liron's face was etched with regret. "Because Caleb just tried to kill him."

Chapter Fifteen

One thing was becoming starkly apparent. Tucker Alexander was slipping away from him. Janus turned to face his desk and squeezed his eyes closed. Both gestures were unwise, given the bulk and reputed aim of the heavily armed pirate who stood behind him. He turned around.

"Did you find your shipment of horses in good order, my lord?" Uriah grinned roguishly at Tucker, who glanced away with a frown.

Janus scowled. "'Tis not for idle chatter that you were summoned here, Captain Smith." For once, he was glad he wore the military garb of a religious officer rather than his more familiar cassock and shoulder cape. He would rather the sacred clothing not be sullied by the presence of this pirate.

"I await your instructions, my lord."

Tucker crossed his arms and leaned into the shadows, as if he wished to retreat into their dark embrace. Janus wrinkled his forehead. Something seemed different about the young man since his return to Azazel, even after undergoing the purification ceremony.

Where was the young man's zeal, his passion for the cause? Janus would have to have him followed.

He returned his attention to Smith. "It would seem we have once again attained some measure of order and peace on Azazel."

Janus had sent for more soldiers, but he would not share that with Smith, who would just as easily share his table as dig his grave. "In the meantime, there is an opportunity for the branded to prove their worth."

"Worth, my lord?" Smith chuckled.

The pirate's perceptiveness did him credit. He likely felt the edge of Janus's hatred as keenly as he felt his own knife blade. On one thing only they had reached an agreement. It mattered little what the branded did with their debauched lives.

Janus offered the pirate a cold smile. "Of sorts." He circled his desk and sank into his chair, swiping distastefully at a layer of dust on the armrest. He made a mental note to interrogate the man who called this *cleaning*. Such filth would likely settle under his fingernails and eventually enter his bloodstream.

"What do you have in mind, my lord?"

"Your men, Captain. How many are under your command?"

"Just over a hundred."

A conservative figure at best, and an outright lie at worst. Smith would never leave his cave of wonders guarded by so few.

"Good." Janus sniffed. One could have a lung seizure with the amount of dust that lingered in the room.

He briskly outlined his plan. Smith's men would serve as branded overseers in the same way that Eremian ships employed branded healers for the sake of the prisoners. This would temporarily bolster the ranks of Janus's soldiers, whose numbers were increasingly insufficient to quell the growing restlessness from Azazel's populace. A restlessness that had swelled with the arrival of that posturing, pretentious revolutionary, who called himself Magnus.

Janus smothered a smile. His idea was ingenious. The officers would learn the weaknesses of Smith's men, all the while planting false weaknesses regarding their own soldiers. When Janus's reinforcements arrived, he would crush the pirates ruthlessly.

Once and for all. Then he would never have to negotiate with branded men again.

Janus had watched Tucker Alexander nearly gag on hearing the plan, although the young man seemed to stomach its wisdom. After all, if Azazel became overrun by soulless hags and demons, might not some of the demons be called upon to guard the others? Perhaps not all of them would need to be executed in the end.

Only the ones loyal to Smith.

"My lord," Tucker had said shortly before Smith arrived, "won't the settlement men and women rebel all the more under the rule of Smith's pirates? After their losses when Belladonna was ransacked—"

"If there are uprisings, they will be quelled," Janus had returned swiftly. "Remember our endgame, my son. Think no more of the soulless. They are beneath your notice."

Looking at him now, the young man appeared a little green. "Go get some fresh air," Janus ordered with a dismissive flick of his hand.

Tucker escaped the room with a grateful smile.

Pah, Janus thought. *Perhaps Caleb is the stronger brother, after all.*

With his acolyte out of the room, Janus looked at Smith. "You agree, then?"

"I will drink to it." Smith glanced slyly at the door. "What ails your skittish second?"

"Perhaps something disagreed with his stomach."

"Or his heart." Smith propped a shoulder against the wall and grinned. "Are you sure 'tis not a woman?"

"Are you sharing knowledge, Captain, or merely plumbing the depths of mine?"

"Miss Sela has a sister. A very pretty sister."

"Your bondmate." Janus was no fool. Smith concealed agendas like other men stowed weapons. If he was not careful, one of Smith's knives would end up between Janus's ribs.

"Your second and my bondmate were friends as children. 'Twould not be the first time two brothers fell in love with two sisters."

Was this possible? Janus's spies would, of course, ferret out the truth. In the meantime, he would call Smith's bluff.

He leaned back in his chair, crossed his arms, and leveled a hard look at the pirate. "Speaking of the Meriweather sisters, I thought of having both women arrested and executed. I'm sure one could uncover a suitable crime without much effort."

The tiniest of frowns creased Smith's forehead—indiscernible to any but a man who was hyperattentive to such cues. Then he chuckled. "'Twould be a terrible waste of beauty, my lord. Have you not seen the women? They are roses among mud."

Janus scowled. "As we have established before, I care naught for the soulless. I care even less for beauty."

Smith waited, saying nothing.

"They will live," Janus conceded. "For now."

Smith spun on his heel, hiding his reaction, and Janus *knew*. One of the women, at least, mattered to him. Why? Without the rich nourishment of a vibrant soul, a conscience quickly faded. So it was for all the branded.

When he turned again, Smith was once again master of himself. Cruelty flickered in his dark eyes. "So, my lord. When do we begin?"

Having exchanged his flawless coat for dark robes and a hood, Janus stood at the edge of the shadowed alley and watched the brightly dressed woman cross the street on the arm of her helper. Three times he had stood here in the early dusk and watched her, but she never saw him. Perhaps it was because he had originally sprouted from the wood of this place that he could so easily blend into its shadows.

The thought chilled him, and he continued studying the woman.

It had taken many years for Janus to understand that Azazel made its mark in ways beyond the obvious. Even a pure soul could be tainted by association with it—even one redeemed—regardless of whether or not one bore its stain.

He remembered nothing of his first year of life, but he had felt the presence of Azazel as he grew into boyhood. He lived under the smothering shadow of this older brother, a brother who exulted in taunting his parents. Ever it tugged at him, and for his troublesome brother's sins, Janus paid the price.

"One of the restored," the elder had declared him as a young boy, newly come to the hallowed halls of the priesthood.

"Soulless runt," he was to everyone else. *"You should be grateful."*

No task was deemed below the priesthood's Azazelian-born slave. Cleaning the ashes from the fireplaces, scrubbing the cobbled path to the seminary gate, or mucking out the stables. Even, on occasion, unclogging the sewers.

All the chores the other acolytes shunned were sent his way, accompanied by that hated word, *grateful*. Janus, constantly filthy, and with his shoe soles rubbed raw, bowed his head and obeyed, resolving that one day, he would wear clothes so spotlessly white that all who beheld them would be forced to shade their eyes.

By the strength of his will, his vision became a reality. Though his new peers never forgot his parentage, they learned not to mention it. The former outcast became a man of formidable power.

Janus discovered inside himself a natural ruthlessness, perhaps nourished by his early years of indentured service, a willingness to do what others would—or could—not do. Because of *him*, the weeds among the Righteous and the priesthood were plucked out and bundled up to be burned. No task, however mediocre, was beneath his notice. This time, though, everything would be accomplished without sullying his sleeve.

Janus had forgotten all memories of his previous life until he visited Azazel for the first time as a young elder of the Righteous—the youngest ever elected. He knew *her* instantly. Her features were imprinted on him as deeply as his parentage.

He was grateful, then, that the Carver had seen enough greatness in him to pluck him from among the thorns. Still, he had not been able to refrain from watching her the next time he visited, or the visit after that. Something about her mesmerized him.

Janus blinked and found himself back in the present. The blind woman leaned heavily on the arm of a younger woman, whom he recognized as Sela Meriweather—Sela *Alexander*. His former protégé's bondmate was indeed a striking woman, though Janus had never much cared for the charms of her sex.

He scowled. For Caleb to return to him, he would have to destroy her. Her, and this new *imposter* from the mainland, who led the people astray with his pretty lies about the king's will.

Janus returned his attention to the older woman. Then, shaking himself, he plunged into the growing crowd. Aye, he was grateful. Grateful he was not like *her*. That he had been carved from altogether different wood.

For there were many names Janus Auberon might call Noemia of Azazel.

Soulless.

Child of the lot.

Mother.

Sela clutched Noemia's arm, mindful that it was nearing curfew. She needed to escort the older woman to the white house and return to the cabin.

Walking several paces behind them, Liron wore a grim expression. Only in her brother's company did Caleb allow Sela to go about the settlement, and Liron took his guardian duties seriously. He took them even more seriously since the fainting episode on the clifftop. Sela's hasty assurances that it had been no more than a lingering weakness from the seasoning were not enough to convince either man of her ability to look after herself.

The street was crowded with others finalizing their own business before the day's end, and as Sela guided Noemia through the press, someone bumped her arm. Before she could right herself, another jostled her from behind. She lurched forward, colliding with a man about her height.

A pair of black-gloved hands shoved her away. Still holding Noemia's arm, Sela stumbled backward, catching a glimpse of the face beneath the man's hood. Even in the gloom, she recognized him. "Lord Auberon, I'm sorry," she apologized. "I did not see you."

Noemia's arm stiffened. Her body turned rigid.

"Have a care where you're going, girl," Janus retorted with none of his usual calm and swept past her. The edge of his cloak snapped against her gown.

Sela stared after him. What was the elder of the Righteous doing in Belladonna near dusk, cloaked in disguise?

"Are you all right?" Liron appeared at her elbow. When Sela nodded, he glared at the cloaked figure. "I heard you say his name. Is that Caleb's lizard-hearted mentor?"

"Aye, that's him." She turned to Noemia. "Best we get you home—" She broke off as a tear glided down the woman's soft cheek. "Noemia? Are you well?" She had been out of sorts lately, most likely a belated adjustment to her blindness.

Noemia sniffed and nodded, though she allowed the tear to remain on course. "I had hoped that one day he might be restored to me."

"What do you mean?"

Then she stared at Noemia and recognized the resemblance, just as she had finally *seen* Tempe and noticed the little girl's likeness to her own father, Uriah.

Her breath left her lungs in a rush. "Lord Auberon is your son."

Liron swore softly under his breath.

Noemia nodded. "I would say that he is much changed, except that I never really knew him."

Noemia had lost all three of her children in the second lot. None had celebrated a second birthday on Azazel. Was Lord Auberon truly one of Noemia's lost children? How could such a wonderful woman birth such a loathsome son?

"Does he know?" Sela whispered.

"Aye," Noemia replied. "He knows. Though I doubt he knows about his siblings. Before I lost my sight, I oftentimes saw him watching me, though he always hastened away before I could approach him. I have never heard his voice until now."

Her son's first words had been cold, as cold as the man himself. Lizard-hearted, indeed.

"He was not always Janus, you know. Janus is his middle name. Oh, but he was a beautiful child."

"He is a handsome man," Sela agreed through gritted teeth. As fine-looking a specimen as Uriah Smith, and with just as black a soul.

"Aye," Noemia mused. "One day, I pray he will return to me."

Sela sent up a silent plea of her own, but of a vastly different bent. Noemia had not seen the expression in Lord Auberon's eyes. They held hatred of the woman he had never called mother. That he resented his Azazelian parentage was clear. Was that why he persecuted the branded so bitterly?

Let her heart not be broken, Carver, when she understands he will not be turned.

"I have Jax," Noemia said at long last, squeezing Sela's arm. "And Tempe, and Briella and Thaddeus, and you. 'Tis more than enough love to fill my barren heart."

On their way back to the white house, Sela eyed the setting sun. She wanted to speak more with Magnus—Magnus, who alone might restore Caleb to her—but Noemia's shopping errands had taken too long. They would have to hurry back, or else miss the curfew.

As they passed the jacaranda tree, Sela was surprised to see Thaddeus standing beneath it, looking lost in thought. Then he seemed to find himself and turned to watch their approach.

"Thaddeus," Sela hailed him. "Might I have a word?"

"Perhaps Liron could help me the rest of the way," Noemia suggested.

Liron smiled and took Noemia's arm. "Of course."

Noemia leaned over and kissed Sela's cheek. "Thank you for your company, dear."

When they disappeared inside the house, Sela turned to face Thaddeus, who was still looking after Noemia. He set one foot in front of the other, accompanying her up the rest of the hill. "She seems rattled," he said after a long moment.

"'Tis what I wanted to mention to you. We came face to face with Lord Auberon in the settlement." Sela got straight to the point. "You knew he was her son?"

"Aye, I knew." He shifted his injured arm. "And for that, at least, I was once glad not to have killed him."

The door banged open, and Liron came back down the steps. He hurried to catch up and indicated Thaddeus's useless arm. His brow furrowed. "'Twas Auberon who gave you that injury, wasn't it?"

"Liron!" Sela warned.

"Nay," Thaddeus interjected, holding up his good hand. "He guesses correctly. Except 'twas not by Auberon's hand that I was injured, though he gave the order."

"I am so sorry, Thaddeus." No wonder Noemia was rattled. Thaddeus wasn't her child by blood, but in her mind, one of her sons had hurt the other—and badly.

He nodded, his face creased in remembered pain. "You should both be getting home."

They gave their farewells. "Did Lord Auberon see you?" Sela whispered to Liron when they were again on their way. "Back at the settlement?"

Only now, in light of Thaddeus's ordeal, did she realize the danger. If the highest-ranking officer on Azazel learned who her brother was, he would not hesitate to arrest Liron for desertion.

"I stayed in the shadows," he replied. "Have no fear, little sister."

Magnus Theodorus had medicines from the Old Town. Twice, Caleb almost renounced his pride and considered taking Sela to the would-be prince. Ever since the seasoning, his bondmate had been weak and not herself, though she insisted on working in the fields with him and her brother. They gave her the lighter share of the work where they could, but Caleb knew she was never more than a few steps away from complete exhaustion.

Nor, he had to admit, was he.

The daily labor in the sticky heat plus the nightly watches had taken their toll. Desperately tired, he no longer hovered so closely over his extracts. Sensing the mood of the four adults, Liri's children were more subdued than usual.

What little sleep Caleb snatched turned into visions of Tucker, Lord Auberon, Uriah Smith...and Sela. He dreamed of the clifftop, where she had prevented him from taking his brother's life. Had it been Sela's intervention, or the Carver's? It was so long since he'd heard the Carver's gentle reassurances or felt the guiding touch of His hand.

Had Caleb only imagined them?

He woke one night to find Sela writhing beside him like a sea snake, her body tangled in the sheets. He reached for her, but she twisted away. Sweat dampened the front of her nightgown. "Sela," he murmured. He had no wish to wake Liri and her children. "Sela!"

He gripped her shoulders, but instead of calming, she fought him, full of the fire that she lacked on waking. Her right fist struck his jaw, and he winced. Even in sleep, she packed a powerful punch. He used his body weight to pin her.

Her eyes shot open, and raw fear swirled in them like a maelstrom. Her body arched. She flung her fists at him. He caught her wrists before she scratched out his eyes. "Sela, it's me, Caleb. There's nothing to fear."

A jet of air escaped her lips, as if she'd suddenly been winded, and he felt the tension leave her body. "Caleb," she sighed. "I thought you were—"

"Uriah," he finished for her. Pain twisted his gut.

She reached up and traced the hair over his ear. "I am sorry." The moonlight shining through the window must have caught his face, for her fingers slid to his jaw. "Did I hurt you?"

Moved by the affection in her voice, he smiled. "You have a formidable arm, my love."

"So Liron always said."

"He trained you well."

The light died. "'Twould seem not well enough."

He shifted away from her, hoping she could not see his expression. She likely felt his anger, though, for she laid her hand on his lower back as he sat up. Comforting *him*, after all the nightmares she'd endured...was still enduring.

"Prince Magnus says the evil will not go unanswered," she whispered. She crawled to sit beside him on the edge of the bed. "Justice will be served."

"What authority has the prince on such matters?" Caleb questioned bitterly.

"He is the king's representative—the *Carver's* representative."

"And yet, Magnus refuses to reveal himself. Perhaps because he knows Lord Auberon would expose him as a fraud."

Sela withdrew slightly, and Caleb regretted his harsh manner.

"None would expect a prince of Eremia to be dressed in such humble garb," she argued. "Perhaps he waits for his entourage."

"Then you believe him?"

She hesitated.

"This Magnus comes from the mainland countries, Sela. Liron says he met dozens of Magnuses while he searched for a way to free you and your sister. Why would the king send a man from the mainland? You must admit 'tis suspect."

If Magnus was truly the prince, he was the last man anyone would expect to go to Azazel. Lord Auberon was the highest-ranking official to venture here to date. The king's officers had been more than enough for the island-prison since its inception. What other business might a royal—the sole heir to Eremia—have in such a forsaken place?

Magnus was risky company. His revolutionary ideas about mercy, guilt, and justice had begun to draw the attention of the soldiers and officers. Lord Auberon was no doubt watching Magnus closely. The man was a threat to the continued peace of Janus's realm. His words undermined the very foundations of the Righteous.

Sela drew in a long, slow breath. "All I know is that his medicine heals."

Did it? He'd not healed Sela, or Thaddeus. Or even himself.

When Caleb pointed that out, Sela shook her head. "There's more. He seems to...to know things. As if he's in contact with the Carver. The clifftop, Caleb. How did the prince know I was there?"

"There are many angles from which one might view the cliffs. He might have seen you were in trouble and of a mind to—" He bit off the unpleasant speculation. *To do yourself harm*, he thought.

"If he'd seen me from a distance, he would have been too late." She took his hand. "Did I ever tell you of the night Thaddeus and the others found me?"

When he shook his head, Sela wove an outlandish story—lying on the rim of the desert, deep in the throes of the seasoning, a deadly snake slithering close to her body while she was helpless and unable to move. A lantern of light and the deep-voiced man who carried it, scattering the snake. If she were not a woman who prized the truth, he might have scoffed and turned away.

"You said yourself, Sela, that you were ill. Even near death. Might you have dreamed it?"

"Nay, I did not dream it. Thaddeus and the others saw the light. But when they reached me, the light—and Magnus—were gone."

"Magnus?"

"He later confirmed 'twas him that night. And his voice...it was unmistakably the prince."

"Or the man who calls himself the prince."

"You're reaching the point, Caleb, where it requires greater effort to disprove the story than to believe it." She pressed his palm, reminding him of the scorching brand. "Liron would never lie about what he saw. 'Twas the prince who saved his life eighteen years ago. And 'twas the prince who saved me that night in the desert, and again on the clifftop."

When I could not. He forced down the answering bile. Was that the truth of it? Was he jealous that Magnus had twice saved the woman Caleb had sworn to protect? Bitterness rose, and he could not restrain his tongue. "What of Smith? Where was Magnus when you were stolen away to be used and discarded?"

Even before the tears sprang to her eyes, Caleb repented of his words.

She slipped off the bed and stood.

"Sela, wait." He rose to beg her forgiveness, but a shout rang out from the other side of their bedroom door. Was it his watch already? Or had Sela's siblings heard their argument?

Sela scrambled into her dressing gown, and Caleb pulled on his boots. He followed her into the main room, where Liron was training his flintlock on a dark-haired man holding what looked like a squirming bundle of rags.

"I thought you might want to shoot this one yourself," Liron said.

Caleb reached his side. Liri, also in her dressing gown, bent over the lantern. It flared to life, revealing the identity of the newcomer.

Behind Caleb, Sela gasped. "*Ross.*"

Chapter Sixteen

Sela bounded past a speechless Caleb. Heedless of her bedclothes, she threw her arms around Ross's grimy neck.

Caleb's gut squeezed. Did she care so much for the man? Ross had ultimately saved her from Uriah Smith. Ross helped her escape, while he remained to bear the brunt of Smith's wrath. Ross, who would have become Sela's bondmate if Caleb had returned to—

A yelp cut into Caleb's musings. Sela jumped back, releasing Ross. She gaped at the squirming rags in his arms. "W-what?"

Ross smiled. He set the bundle down on the floor and unwound the dirty cloths.

Twin pairs of dainty, black-tipped paws emerged, followed by a red-and-white coat, pointed ears, and a mouth stretched wide in a vulpine grin.

Sela gasped. "Roux!" Bursting into tears, she sank to her knees.

The fox gave a delighted squeal and threw himself into her arms, licking her face and the tears that streamed from her eyes.

"We are fugitives from Smith's reign of terror," Ross remarked by way of explanation.

Sela buried her face in Roux's fur.

Liron lowered his flintlock. "You're Ross Bryant?"

"Aye." Ross's expression grew serious. "You must be Sela's brother."

"Aye. I'm Liron. And how did you come to be freed from Smith's tyranny?" Ice coated his voice. "Sela said you joined his band of pirates."

Caleb regarded his brother-in-law with new appreciation. Liron did not welcome new acquaintances readily.

"Aye," Ross said. "When Sela escaped, Smith figured out the truth of my allegiances. Thankfully, he was too distracted by Elsie's death to kill me straightaway. Nevertheless, it was some sevendays before I was able to escape."

"How?" Liron probed.

"A man named Vex helped me." Ross's eyes shadowed. "Unfortunately, 'twas to his own detriment, since he lost his life in the process."

"I know that name," Liri put in. "Vex was a friend to me."

"Why did Smith not kill you in revenge?" Liron asked.

Caleb wanted to hug his brother-in-law for his interrogation.

"Likely, Uriah thought to use me as leverage if he recaptured Sela. I believe he kept the fox alive for the same reason." He shrugged. "He must have acquired another fox's tail to taunt her with."

Just then, Anwen appeared at the bedroom door in her nightgown. Her eyes brightened at the sight of Roux, but Liri quickly ushered the child away.

A divine finger prodded Caleb's conscience. Sela appeared overjoyed at her reunion with Roux. He stepped forward to offer Ross his hand. "You have my thanks for all you did for Sela."

But for naught else. He felt Sela's gaze boring into him.

Ross grasped his hand and shook it. Caleb's jealousy was mirrored in the other man's eyes, as if neither of them had found what they sought, even though the matter of possession had been settled in Sela choosing Caleb as her bondmate.

Beaming, Sela gained her feet. The fox lay curled in her arms, placid and content, with his head resting against her neck. "When first we met, Roux was my enemy," she remarked. "He'd been trying to steal my family's chickens. 'Twas some time before I learned to call him friend. But friend he became."

Show mercy to your enemies, Magnus said.

'Tis easy for him, Caleb thought, *for he has very few of them.*

Sela smiled at Ross. "Thank you for bringing Roux home to us."

"To us." Caleb wanted to believe she included him in her family. She spoke generously for one who had been betrayed so often. Ross had been a turncoat before, and Caleb knew better than to trust a man whose alliances shifted as easily as palm trees in a breeze.

His arm curled around Sela's waist, and his pride was gratified when she leaned into him, away from Ross. The fox nuzzled her neck with his whiskered jaw, then licked Caleb's cheek.

Caleb watched Ross...who watched Sela...who watched the fox.

Liron, standing behind them, gave Caleb a look that told him he understood the dangers of unleashing a fox in a henhouse.

A fox who, unlike Roux, was no true friend in disguise.

The morning brings new mercies, Sela thought. She felt oddly free as she tugged at a weed in the small garden she'd helped plant behind their cabin. Briella worked nearby, while young Thomas sat in the dirt beside her, mashing his hands in a mud pie Tempe had brought him earlier. The other children had worn a track around the cabin chasing Roux. The fox seemed unaffected by his long captivity. It certainly hadn't dimmed his energy.

Thomas's presence was another mercy. With the upheaval caused by Uriah's attack, the soldiers seemed to have forgotten that the child had passed his first birthday. So far, they had not come for him as part of the second lot.

Earlier, Sela had watched Ross's reunion with Thomas with a tender smile. Did the man notice how fine a mother Briella was? How well Thomas played with Tempe and the other children?

In the sweet-scented sunshine, it was easy for Sela to forget that Briella was dying. That she would die without seeing her father again. And that Caleb—who'd once seemed content despite his own losses—was each day more lost to Sela.

And she knew not how to get him back.

Sela turned from observing Ross and Briella and found Caleb watching her closely, his expression unreadable, and his jaw announcing his tension. Did he think about *their* children, wondering if he would ever hold his own son or daughter in his arms?

It was long past time for Sela and Caleb to leave the past behind and look to their future. Though she would never forget the memories of Uriah, she wanted to make new ones with Caleb. She wanted his light to banish Uriah's darkness.

The more time Sela spent with Magnus, the stronger she grew.

Briella raised her head and peered at Sela from beneath the brim of her wide hat. "You seem different, Sela. As different as Thaddeus."

"Thaddeus?"

"For as long as I've known him, my brother has been morose. Yesterday, he came home singing. Not humming, Sela, but *singing*! I asked him what he'd done to poor Thaddeus Gaskell."

"Perhaps 'tis a lady we must thank."

Briella batted a fly away from her nose. "I admit I'd hoped he might find a woman, one whose cheerful ways would complement his melancholy. But nay, I believe 'tis Magnus. Thaddeus has been different ever since the prince arrived. He has hope now, that the king will not forget us forever. That the Carver has not abandoned us."

Although neither Thaddeus nor Briella had been healed of their ailments—she didn't know why—they had each taken to the prince as if he were balm for their wounds. Liron and Jax also hung on his every word, and the children loved to play games with him. Even Noemia's spirits lifted in Magnus's presence.

One change was clear. Thaddeus no longer looked at Briella with guilt in his eyes, as if he punished himself for her suffering.

Sela sighed. If only Magnus would do the same for Caleb. Yet, as Thaddeus freed himself from his cocoon of self-doubt and shame, Caleb burrowed deeper into his, hoarding his suffering like a dragon his gold. He lived and breathed guilt and anger like he breathed air. An almost righteous indignation that reminded her of the man he had once been.

"The prince attracts too much attention," Briella said, breaking into Sela's thoughts. "I wish he would reveal himself to Lord Auberon."

Sela recalled the hate-filled face of Azazel's leader when he'd gazed upon his mother. She thought of the rough-looking men Lord Auberon employed as guards and spies, men rumored to belong to Uriah Smith. "Even if Magnus did reveal himself, Lord Auberon would not accept his claim. The prince is openly critical of the Righteous, is he not?"

"Aye," Briella agreed. "'Tis true Lord Auberon would make a powerful enemy. I fear the prince does not understand the power of the sleeping dragon he prods."

Lord Auberon had not faced his challenger, but his officers and soldiers denounced Magnus as an imposter from the mainland, a rebel, a friend of the unbranded, a madman, and even a man possessed. Not for the first time, Sela wondered why Magnus did not simply declare himself the king's heir and produce the heir's medallion as proof.

Caleb was right. This was hardly how a prince went about things.

If Magnus declared himself and brought his entourage to Azazel, the truth would be revealed. Caleb would believe. Questions swirled inside Sela's head. Why did Magnus remain silent? Why had he come alone? No one would doubt who he was with a fleet of warships at his back.

The sun slid behind a cloud, and some of the beauty of the day vanished. Roux's bark indicated the children had caught up with him, and Sela heard Liri's light footsteps on the porch.

A sun-browned hand covered her own. Sela looked up to find Briella smiling sadly. "The prince says we should not worry about tomorrow, Sela."

Doubt stirred to life, like dust motes from the rug Liri was beating against the side of the cabin. *'Tis fine for him to say,* she wanted to reply, *since he is a prince.*

But in his current disguise, Magnus lived every day with the danger of being dragged before Lord Auberon, flogged, and branded as a criminal. He'd spent his youth and middle years among the mainland countries, working as a craftsman. Whatever his child-hood, the prince knew something of suffering.

"Do you never fear, Briella, that one day it might all be for naught?" Sela asked.

The pressure of Briella's hand lifted. She reached out for Thomas, cradling the muddy boy against the clean bodice of her dress. His flailing arms left dirty streaks across her cheeks. She looked tired, but not dauncy.

"Aye, I fear," she murmured, pressing a kiss to the boy's head. "But fear has been my companion for a lifetime. I will no longer be ruled by it."

Caleb strode through the cane field, wary of snakes as the sun slid lower on the horizon. He was more than ready to be home with Sela. Her siblings, clearly mindful of the now-yawning distance between him and his bondmate, had arranged to spend a few nights with Thaddeus's household.

Liron insisted that any danger had passed. He looked weary after many nights of watching for intruders. The only potential conflict threatened Magnus. For once, Caleb was grateful someone else had drawn the attention of Azazel's leader.

Leaving the cane field and entering a grove of trees, Caleb became aware that he was not alone. Steel-sharp alertness ran the length of every limb.

Caleb drew his flintlock, assumed a defensive posture, and made his way through the grove. When he cleared the last tree, he found Uriah Smith waiting for him. He appeared oddly relaxed, holding his weapon the way one might a mug of ale. To Caleb's surprise, he wore no sword.

"Caleb Alexander," the land pirate greeted him with a wide smile. "I heard you were making enquiries about my whereabouts. I thought to assist you directly."

Caleb drew up short. He *had* been probing for information, but delicately, not wanting Smith or Sela to get wind of his actions. It appeared Smith had more spies than Caleb had first believed.

"As to *your* whereabouts," Smith continued, "well, 'tis not hard to track a man who walks the earth like he owns it."

Caleb kept the flintlock steady, mentally rehearsing the location of the knife in his boot, and wishing he'd brought along his sword. Liron would have made a good ally, or even Ross, for no doubt Smith had men hidden in the trees.

He frowned. *Not Ross.* Thaddeus, then, or Jax.

"I came alone," Smith assured him. "There is unfinished business between us, is there not?"

"Aye," Caleb replied carefully. "On that only, we agree."

"I admit that I expected to be dueling with your brother, not you. 'Twas, after all, Tucker Alexander who stole my bondmate."

"And you stole mine."

"Aye, Caleb, but perhaps your anger is misplaced. 'Twas not I who betrayed Sela, but Ross Bryant. And they *you*." He raised a quizzical eyebrow. "Did neither of them tell you of the night they spent together? I heard Ross returned the sevenday before last."

Smith chuckled, entertaining a private joke. "By the looks of the room the next morning, 'twas a most enjoyable night."

Caleb's heart set to pounding. All lies, he was certain of it. However, a tiny sliver of doubt wormed beneath his skin like a splinter. Nay, Sela would never betray him in that way. She had sworn that Ross had never touched her.

But what if she cared for him? When he'd returned, she embraced him as warmly as she embraced her brother.

"I see my warning has taken root." Smith shifted his weight from right to left boot. "Now, we must face each other, man to man." He raised his weapon.

Caleb's arm tensed, and his finger curled around the trigger.

Smith sighed. "Though I *do* wonder if 'tis truly a *man* I face. After all, your bondmate was—how shall I put this—*untried* when she came to me."

Fury seared Caleb's brain. He growled and lifted the weapon. "You...you—" He fired.

The next few moments exploded in a dizzy blur of images and sounds.

His pistol would have marked the pirate's heart if Uriah had not lurched sideways at the last minute. The returning shot from Smith's pistol would have killed Caleb, if he'd not done the same. Instead, the ball skimmed the outside of his arm.

Smith raised his arm to fire again but tripped over a tree root. The pistol flew from his hand.

Tossing aside his own weapon, Caleb lunged, catching the pirate around the middle just as Uriah regained his balance. Both fell to the ground.

Caleb got in a punch to Smith's abdomen before the pirate rolled, throwing him off and kneeing him in the stomach for good measure. Wincing, Caleb recovered and dove for him again. The pirate, though about Caleb's height, was broader in the chest and thick with muscle.

Caleb soon realized his folly in taking the offensive and staggered back. He heaved in a breath. That second blow to his chest had winded him.

"Good." Smith nodded. "*Very* good, for a scholar and Lord Auberon's former lapdog." He closed in.

It was the end of the day, and Caleb was unspeakably weary, but Smith's taunts enlivened his aching muscles. Blocking the pirate's blow, Caleb darted to the side and landed a well-placed fist against the man's ribs. Smith barked his pain.

Caleb scuttled away with a grim smile. Aye, Smith was strong, but Caleb was quick.

Smith paused, breathing hard. He eyed Caleb with new respect.

Caleb knew the pirate would soon size up the distance between the magnificent, double-barreled flintlock he'd lost his grip on, which could fire one more time.

This time, Smith would not miss.

After several more exchanges of blows, Caleb failed to discern any weaknesses in the man's fighting style. He had one chance, and settled on a vulnerability that might prove the pirate's undoing.

Caleb let his guard down, pretending fatigue. Smith grinned and moved in closer, slowly circling his opponent to the place where he'd lost his flintlock.

The pirate was down a knife, which Caleb had barely dodged earlier by rolling. A bloody scrape over his shoulder testified to the fact. Hoping the pirate had no more weapons, Caleb stayed on the move, more evasive than he had been in the beginning, letting his fear become the bait Smith craved.

"I will give you this," Smith said. "You put up more of a fight than she did."

Anger heated his chest, making him clumsy. He struck out, but Smith blocked his punch. Caleb feigned a stumble backward, landing in the dust on his backside. Smith gave Caleb a confident smile and reached for his flintlock.

In one swift motion, Caleb grasped his boot knife and threw it. The blade sank to its hilt in Smith's chest.

Caleb rose and kicked the flintlock away from the pirate's hand. It had been a good throw, one of his best. Almost perfect, in fact, giving Caleb several minutes to watch his enemy die.

Smith fell onto his back, gasping for breath. Caleb crouched beside him, wary of the surrounding jungle, but no man rushed to Smith's aid.

Perhaps the pirate truly had come alone.

"You are devastating with a gun," Caleb admitted as blood bloomed beneath the pirate's coat. "But not so good with a knife."

"Trickery," Smith spluttered. "Deception."

"You said it yourself, Smith. I'm a scholar, not a soldier."

The pirate scowled. With considerable effort, he forced his lips into another smile. "Does the *scholar* know where his woman is right now?"

Caleb's chest clenched, then he relaxed. Likely, the words were naught but a dying man's final jibe, an attempt to keep him trapped in the jaws of fear. The wound was undoubtedly a mortal one, and Smith would die in minutes. However, if Smith's men were attacking the cabin, every minute counted.

He could not wait. "Enjoy Hel."

Caleb turned on his heel and ran back to Sela faster than he'd ever run in his life.

Sela heard Caleb long before she saw him. His boots pounded the dust with the fervor of a stampede. He hurtled up the steps, his clothes dusty, with twin streaks of blood seeping through his shirtsleeves. Another scrape showed on his shoulder, and yet another on the opposite bicep.

Liron, who'd remained with his sister until Caleb returned home, met him on the porch. The door hung wide open behind him. "What happened to *you*? You look as if you tangled with a boar."

"Aye, I did," Caleb replied. "His tusks will gore us no more." He pushed past Liron before he could reply and entered the cabin, his eyes roving, searching. When his gaze settled on his bondmate, his taut shoulders relaxed. Coming over, he pressed her tightly against him.

"Caleb?" she ventured. He held her so firmly that she could scarcely take a breath. Why did he look so disheveled? "Are you well?"

"Aye," he said, though there was a hardness to his eyes she'd never seen before. "All is well."

"Caleb," Liron called.

He turned, and his shoulders lifted, as if he was presenting a front.

"Do you need..." Liron's voice trailed away and his gaze swept Sela. He looked at her, clearly fearful of leaving her alone.

"Thank you for staying with Sela, Liron. There's nothing to fear. You can go. I'll see you tomorrow."

Caleb's voice sounded like it belonged to a different man, but Liron seemed assured when Caleb's arm slid over Sela's shoulders. "I'd best get going, then."

Roux trotted at his heels, anxiously awaiting the walk Liron had promised him.

Once they'd left, Caleb closed the door. When he turned around, he seemed more like himself. He clutched her to him once more. "Sela," he whispered against her hair. His voice shook, and his throat jerked as he swallowed. "I love you."

"Oh, Caleb. I love you too."

She drew back to see his face, and her hand brushed his arm.

He winced.

"You're injured!" she exclaimed. Had he really tangled with a boar? He could have been killed.

"The wounds are superficial." Still, he allowed her to guide him to the table, removing his waistcoat and shirt upon her request.

"Caleb!" She gasped as she cleaned the dust and blood from his upper arm and probed the wound. It revealed a deep graze rather than the gored flesh she'd anticipated. "This is no boar injury. 'Tis a pistol wound."

A pistol wound that almost perfectly matches mine.

"And this here." She touched the thin slice atop his shoulder. "'Tis the mark of a knife."

He met her eyes. "Aye."

"With whom did you spar?"

"I only did to him what he would have eventually done to us."

She sucked in a breath. "Tucker?"

Caleb's eyes flashed, but he shook his head.

"Uriah?" She sank into the chair opposite him. "Did you—"

"Aye. I killed him." His voice was exultant. "You are free of him, Sela. Forever."

Her head swam with nauseous images. The man who'd tormented her was dead. He would never come after her—or Liri—again. She should be rejoicing with Caleb. She should feel free. Why, then, did she only feel her and Caleb's shackles tighten?

"'Tis a shock, I know," he was saying, "but Smith's death is the Carver's will. I am certain of it."

She stared at him.

He leaned forward and claimed her mouth with a possessiveness she'd never felt from him. He kissed her hungrily, drawing her to her feet and continuing until they both gasped for air. Heedless of his injuries, Caleb ran his hands down either side of her spine. His fingers were firmer than the ribbing of her stays, closing her in like a vise.

She winced. "Caleb, you're hurting me."

At once, his grip relented. "I'm sorry. I didn't realize." He kissed her again.

Sela tried to remind herself that this was Caleb, not Uriah. But it was hard, when both of them would leave her with bruises.

When he finally lifted his head, she saw that his eyes were nearly black, with hardly a hint of blue touching them. Yet, he appeared exhilarated. "Are you not ready to leave all of this behind now, Sela? To become who we were born to be?"

"What do you mean?"

"The Carver always intended you to be mine. I knew it from the first moment I saw you aboard the *Deliverance*. We belong together."

She lifted her hands to his face, feeling the traces of stubble on his jaw and chin, willing it to anchor her to the present as her mind whirled like a spinning top. "Aye, Caleb. I believe so."

He pulled her close, and she felt the throb of his heartbeat against her chest. A wide, almost maniacal smile upended the corners of his mouth. She had seen it before.

On the clifftop, when he had nearly killed Tucker.

Her stomach squeezed. "I would bond with you in truth, Caleb. I admit, I have yearned to for many sevendays now."

He lowered his mouth to hers.

"But not like this," she whispered against his lips.

He stilled, and his grip on her waist loosened. "Like what?"

She stepped away from him, her eyes filling with tears. "I do not know you."

Caleb eyed the bodice of her dress with a grimace, as if only just realizing he'd smeared her favorite gown with his blood. "True, I hardly resemble my usual self." He indicated the pile of torn, bloodied, dusty clothes atop the table. "It can be rectified."

"'Tis more than the clothes." She pressed her palm against his bare chest, over his heart. "You know 'tis something deeper. Do you not feel it?"

"I feel only relief." His face hardened. "Do you not?"

"Aye, but—"

"Is it Ross, then, that ails you?"

She stared at him, her mouth agape. The jealousy in his eyes was unmistakable. "*Ross*?"

"Smith hinted you and he spent the night together."

Her lips turned down in disgust. "Do you know me so little that you would accuse me of such?"

He scowled and planted a hand against the table but did not answer.

"I was Uriah's *captive*. Ross asked for me in order to set me free. 'Twas a necessary subterfuge. He never touched me. *Never*."

Caleb remained silent.

"What do you fear for more, Caleb? My heart, or my soul?"

"Your *soul*?"

"Once upon a time, you would not touch me because you believed me soulless. Now, you consider me heartless, or at least liable to entrust my heart to another. What is it you *really* fear?"

He blinked, as if he'd never considered the question.

"It seems to me that the Carver's will is all too often determined by the interests of the men who say they serve him. What of truth? What of righteousness? What of the precepts you have lived your entire life by?"

His body grew rigid. He reached out and grasped her wrist. "Say what you're thinking, Sela."

"Did you kill Uriah for *my* sake, Caleb? Or did you kill him for yours?"

His eyes blazed. The fingers around her wrist all but branded her skin. "I killed him so we'd be free." He stepped closer. "Free to love each other as the Carver intended. So that you might look at me and no longer see the man who hurt you."

She softened, hearing the sudden brokenness in his voice. "You are nothing like him. You were *never* like him."

Letting her go, he spun away.

The old vulnerability flared to life, nudging them over the precipice from which no one—perhaps not even Magnus—could rescue them. "Is it love you feel for me, Caleb? Or only the relief that you are finally in possession of something you once believed you couldn't have?"

At once, Sela regretted the question, because her meaning was clear. It would be plainer than daylight to him. She had never once looked at Caleb and seen Uriah. Neither had she ever known Caleb to be a possessive man. Now, though, with his eyes nearly black, and full of bloodlust?

The fire in him had now extinguished, replaced by a deep coldness. A hard shell she could not penetrate. Any chance she might have had for reaching him appeared lost.

Since he would not face her, she spoke to his back. "We *are* free, Caleb. Did you not say it yourself? Uriah could not steal what he was never able to possess. But if you let him—if you continue down this path—a far greater treasure will be lost to me forever."

"And what is that?" he asked without turning. His voice betrayed sudden weariness.

"*You.*"

With tears streaming down her face fiercely enough to carve permanent trails across her cheeks, Sela flung open the door and ran from him.

Chapter Seventeen

ot tears blinded Sela. She heard Caleb calling her name, but he must have been wearier than he admitted, for she quickly outpaced him. Caleb might have caught up, but she was fresh and he was tired.

She was also driven by a nameless fear.

For all the months she'd known him, Caleb seemed strong, almost immutable. When she was weak, he became her strength. When she shook with fear, he gave her his courage. However, the man she'd spoken with moments ago resembled Tucker—or even Uriah—more than the Caleb she'd pledged her life to.

The sun had set, and Sela all but ran through Belladonna. She feared the curfew but thanked the Carver for the blessed darkness, which concealed her tears. Curious glances followed her from behind the dimly glowing windows of the settlement houses. Only when she reached the base of the hill that marked the ascent to the white house did she slow her steps, and then only because her legs trembled with fatigue.

Gathering her skirts, she began to climb, feeling as if the hill had tripled in size since the last time she'd summited it. Was she that weak? The lingering effects of the seasoning rippled through her legs, turning once-strong muscles to jelly. Her stays dug into her ribs as she dragged in one breath, then another. She passed the jacaranda tree, remembering how Thaddeus had carried her up the hill because she'd turned her ankle.

How she wished for his assistance now!

How she wanted Caleb! But not Caleb, the gleeful murderer.

She wanted Caleb as he had once been.

By the time Sela crested the hill, her head was spinning and her skin felt flushed. She stumbled onto the porch steps and fell against the door. It swung open, and a woman appeared. Roux danced around her heels, losing himself in the folds of Sela's gown.

"Sela?" Briella gasped her alarm and Sela sank to the deck. The older woman came with her, supporting Sela's waist as Tucker had done when she collapsed on the clifftop. The world lurched and teetered on the edge of a similar precipice. Roux yelped.

Footsteps clattered on the deck, and Liron's worried face appeared. "Were you attacked? Where is Caleb?"

"'Tis the seasoning," murmured Briella. "She has never fully recovered."

Liron caught her up in his arms. In her delirium, Sela recalled the way Caleb always held her. *Oh Carver of Souls, what more will you whittle from me?*

It was her last thought before her head lolled against her brother's chest.

Caleb's limbs ached, and his voice had grown hoarse by the time he passed the fort. Straining his eyes through the gloom, he caught a glimpse of his bondmate. She had reached the base of the hill.

Of course she would go to her siblings...and to the Remenant.

Though it might wound his pride, he would go after her. She deserved an apology. Not for killing Smith, but for suggesting she harbored feelings for Ross. He knew the strength of her love for him, even when they were far apart. She would always be his.

"What do you fear for more, Caleb? My heart, or my soul?"

Once, he had feared her love for the Carver might have faded. Once, he had feared for her soul, though his own soul teetered on tenuous footing of late.

She was right, of course. Many sevendays had passed since he'd thought of her soul. With Ross's return to Belladonna, Caleb had been ravaged by jealousy. Hatred too, if Caleb were honest, since it was because of Ross that Sela had finally given in to Smith.

The rumbling of hooves reached Caleb as he neared the base of the hill. He turned to see a dozen men on horseback, several of them bearing torches. The foremost, dressed in a white coat that gleamed in the torchlight, dismounted before they'd fully come to a halt, striding over to him with his jaw set.

"Tucker," Caleb ground out, spying the man's face. "'Tis not a good time."

His brother shrugged. "I have orders to take you to Lord Auberon."

"Whatever for?"

"He wishes to speak with you."

Caleb looked over his shoulder, back up the hill. "There is another matter I must attend to."

"'Twill surely keep, brother."

"And if it cannot?"

"Did you kill Uriah for my sake, Caleb? Or did you kill him for yours?" The memory of Sela's tear-streaked face returned to him like a blow. What else did she want from him? Still, he should go to her *now*, and make amends quickly.

"Do not let the sun go down on your anger," the priests always warned.

He grimaced. The sun had already set.

"You cannot disobey this summons, Caleb."

He sighed. At least Sela was safe among family and friends. They would look after her until he came for her.

One of Tucker's men found Caleb a horse and he mounted, his whole body throbbing. Had he been summoned to answer for his murder of Smith? It was hardly murder, he reasoned. The fight had been fair, practically a duel, but for the absence of witnesses.

Apart from his knife, which bore no identifying features or marks, he had left no trace of himself at the scene.

When they reached the fort, the riders clattered through the open gate, which quickly closed behind them. Caleb tugged at his shirt collar, though it was comfortably loose. He dismounted along with the others, but Tucker alone escorted him to Lord Auberon's quarters. His brother did not speak. Perhaps he remembered the last time they had met, when Caleb nearly killed him.

Lord Auberon was waiting for them. For once, he appeared without his gold-trimmed coat, which lay slung across the wooden shoulders of his chair. His torso was clad only in waistcoat and shirtsleeves—the only time he had appeared so informal, besides Caleb's flogging. Did Azazel's stifling humidity bother the elder more than he let on?

After closing the door, Tucker stood next to it, leaning against the wall with what Caleb knew was feigned nonchalance. What had Tucker so unsettled?

Lord Auberon leaned back in his chair. "I see you've been in a brawl, Caleb."

"'Tis settled, my lord."

"Settled?"

Caleb decided on brazen honesty. After all, the soldiers would likely find the body come morning. "Uriah Smith is dead."

Tucker gasped.

Wheat-colored eyebrows ascended considerable heights on Lord Auberon's unwrinkled forehead. "You *killed* him?"

Lord Auberon might execute him for admitting as such, but if Caleb guessed correctly, the elder had no fondness for the pirate. Smith was a rival, not his friend.

"Aye," Caleb said.

Slowly, the elder smiled. "Then you have done me a great favor."

"'Tis rumored you and he are allies, my lord."

"That is true." Lord Auberon grimaced. "Though 'twas an alliance forged out of mutual necessity, not shared ideology. An unhappy Binding, you might say. I am glad to be rid of it."

Caleb said naught.

Rising gracefully, Lord Auberon pushed back his chair. A thick curtain had been erected several yards behind his desk, and the elder slipped past it. He returned carrying a heavy chest.

Caleb recognized it instantly. The coins of the soulless. Memories of his past life came flooding back to him, both bitter and sweet.

"'Tis my place to seek the Carver," Lord Auberon said, setting the chest atop his desk. He gestured with a gloved hand to the curtained section from whence he'd come. "When matters of state permit."

For what purpose did Lord Auberon explain himself? Caleb kept his branded hands behind his back, though every limb screamed weariness. He longed to collapse into a chair.

Lord Auberon settled comfortably into his again. "I have had naught but time to contemplate my past actions, Caleb. It has been some sevendays since I realized I was harsh on you. Much too harsh."

Caleb blinked.

"For that reason, I have summoned you here. You see, my son, 'tis believed that the lot—that is, the soul mark—is permanent. But others, men of good stock and breeding, have found themselves in your position over the years. Wrongfully or mistakenly branded, either for sins not their own or sins that are...well, somewhat understandable."

Caleb fought to keep his balance. *My son*? *Wrongfully branded*? *Understandable sins*? "My lord, what do you suggest?"

"You are an uncommon man, and I was wrong to punish you as I did. Would you accept my humble plea for your forgiveness?"

"Of c-course," Caleb stammered, though inwardly he reeled, flipping back through his memories. Lord Auberon had *personally* flogged and branded him for admitting to saving the life of a branded woman. Tucker, though, had betrayed Caleb. Smith had stolen and abused Sela. On those matters, at least, Lord Auberon was innocent.

"There is a way back," Lord Auberon continued, "a way to return to the path of the soul-bearing, to the Pure. 'Tis not often spoken of, since it requires certain sacrifices."

Behind Caleb, Tucker shifted. Lord Auberon's gaze moved to him, narrowed, then returned to Caleb.

"What way, my lord?"

"The mark itself is easily taken care of, my son. There are chemicals that will fade the stain, or others that, although they cause a slight disfigurement, will mask it entirely. In the meantime, gloves conceal the affliction." He tapped his own gloved hand against his knee. "After all, the Righteous never remove their gloves in public."

Caleb suppressed a growing excitement. If a way back existed to the path of the Righteous, and if he and Sela—even Liri—could access such a thing, they might be able to escape Azazel forever. No wonder Tucker fidgeted. "What of the Carver's judgment?"

"The Carver understands our failings, my son."

"The Righteous say that the soul mark is permanent."

With a look that communicated infinite patience, Lord Auberon removed his gloves and set them on the table. He extended his hands, palms up.

Caleb leaned closer and inhaled sharply.

In the center of each of the elder's palms was a cross, no more than two thin white lines, faded nearly beyond recognition. If not for his close scrutiny and the light of the lantern atop Lord Auberon's desk, Caleb might never have seen them.

He reared back. "You bear the soul marks?"

Lord Auberon replaced his gloves. "Aye, 'twas a long time ago. A minor indiscretion in my youth. A thoughtless deed, the gravity of which was vastly overestimated. 'Tis of no consequence now."

When he did not elaborate, Caleb frowned. "The elders were merciful."

Lord Auberon swallowed. "Of sorts."

"What of righteousness, my lord? What of purity? You speak of an alliance with Uriah Smith."

Lord Auberon offered a fatherly smile. "We have both entertained unholy alliances in recent months, my son. Myself with Uriah Smith, and you with..." His words trailed away.

With Sela, Caleb finished silently. "Sela is my bondmate." He knotted his hands together in front of him, exposing the tattooed band.

"Aye, my son." Lord Auberon studied the band. "She is a remarkable woman. However, a choice lies before you."

Tucker coughed.

Caleb glanced at him and realized his brother had intended to draw Caleb's attention. His expression looked apologetic. Caleb grimaced. For what would his brother apologize? That his reckoning at the clifftop had been cut short?

Caleb turned back to Lord Auberon. "What do you propose, my lord?" Whatever he demanded, Caleb and Sela could accomplish it together. If it meant they could both return to the Old Town, to their families—

"This way is open only to those who were once one of the Righteous."

The color drained from Caleb's face.

Lord Auberon came around the desk. He patted the wooden chest once, then placed a gloved hand on Caleb's shoulder. "None need know what has happened here, Caleb. Back in the Old Town, the intrigues of Azazel are spoken of little and understood even less. You have, as yet, no children." He raised an eyebrow. "Is Sela with child?"

He swallowed. "Nay."

"Good. Set your bondmate aside permanently, and you will be welcomed back into our order, my son. It need not be a callous parting. Sela will be well provided for when you return to the Old Town. In return, I will give you everything you ever dreamed of. You will reclaim your title, your position, your wealth, and even your betrothal. Or another one of your choosing, with a beautiful woman of good character. One of the Pure, of course. You will take your place among your family and among our order. Everything that was taken from you will be returned threefold."

Lord Auberon's hand squeezed, and Caleb knew. It was not Tucker's reckoning he faced.

It was his own.

Liron stepped into the deeply shadowed room as Liri rose from her position beside the bed. "She sleeps?" He looked past his twin sister to where a figure lay beneath the covers, a puddle of red fur at her feet.

"Aye, like the dead," Liri replied. She took his elbow and steered him away. "She has been in and out of consciousness since she arrived. Her fever grows ever hotter. Is there any news of Caleb?"

"Jax rode to the cabin but found it empty. The men are searching for him."

"There was blood on her dress, Liron. Might the soldiers have taken Caleb by force?"

"I fear he already had some kind of altercation with them." He bit his lip, then told his sister of Caleb's arrival at the cabin, disheveled and blood-stained. He had not believed his brother-in-law's hasty admission, but neither had he thought Sela in danger. "Caleb would never harm her."

"I know," Liri replied softly. "But there is no doubt that the bond between them has been sorely tested of late."

Liron wished, not for the first time, that he could hunt down the wild men of the island—namely, Smith. That devil had damaged both of his sisters, and Sela seemed beyond repair. They needed Liron close, though, and for that reason alone he remained nearby.

The inaction chafed him.

"I will stay with her," he said at last.

Liri was gazing at Sela. "She gave herself up for us, you know. For Cadence, back home, and for me, on that jetty. I fear I will never be able to repay the debt." She choked back a sob. "Or that, sick as she is, she will not live to redeem it. I have never seen her so ill."

Liron gathered his sister into his arms and let her weep against his shoulder. "She will live, Liri. On that point, Magnus was certain. This is not the end."

He hugged her closer and quietly repeated it to himself like a mantra.

"She will live."

As if Lord Auberon sensed Caleb's shock, his next words came out a gentle purr. Tucker led Caleb to a stool and guided him onto it.

"Sela is tainted," Janus said. "You are Pure. It has always been so. From the very moment you saw her, you knew her to be such."

The space inside Caleb hollowed further, until he ached.

Lord Auberon zealously continued with his chisel. "You are young. Newly twenty-four, if my memory serves me. 'Tis not unheard of for a man to lose his head over a woman. But even the most foolish passions evaporate with time. What seems like agony now will not pain you forever."

Did Lord Auberon truly believe this? That Caleb was merely infatuated with Sela? She was a woman of strength and grace, beauty and compassion. Impulsive, but exceedingly loyal. Though he had at first been arrested by her unique eyes and fiery manner, he had since been held captive by her sweet interior. It was no trial for him to remain in her keeping.

"You must see, my son, that this woman has driven a wedge between you and your beloved brother. Between you and the Righteous. Worst of all, between you and the Carver."

Caleb considered the allegation. *Tucker's* wrongdoing had driven the wedge between them—not only because of his treatment of Sela, but also because of how he'd behaved toward Liri. As for the Righteous, they had cast Caleb out into the darkness without compunction.

But the Carver?

That accusation lingered. Ever since Caleb met Sela, he'd been unable to think clearly. Unable to enjoy the close bond he'd once shared with the Carver of his soul. Because of Sela, he had believed his soul in jeopardy. Was it in jeopardy still?

He remembered long days among the other acolytes, poring over ancient texts that revealed new insights into the Carver's nature. Hours of invigorating discussions with his mentors. Long runs in the fields outside the Old Town, feeling the freshness of the breeze upon his face and the caress of his Maker in his loosened hair. Communing with the Carver of Souls, by whose breath he was given life.

Aye, Lord Auberon's offer was not without appeal. Caleb could not pretend he did not often yearn to return to such a life. Not just the life of the Righteous, but the life of a soul untroubled by restive waters.

But in all of his dreams of returning to the Old Town, Sela had been standing beside him.

His muscles cramped, and he shifted on the stool. Lord Auberon had fallen quiet and was watching him. Tucker stood just behind the elder, wearing an expression Caleb could not decipher.

Suddenly, Caleb understood. The choice he faced was Tucker's own, made so many years ago. Would Caleb also exchange love and honor for the hope of deliverance? Would he let the woman he loved endure loneliness, shame, and scorn while his own name remained unsullied?

He looked down at his tattooed band. Like the soul mark, it was not easily concealed or erased. He flinched at the remembered pain during the ritual, rendered naught as soon as he beheld Sela in the gown he'd purchased. He remembered the love in her eyes as she pledged herself to him. What she had done on the jetty for Tucker, Liri, and her children, she had also done for *him*. That he might escape with his life.

Sela was his portion of mercy, given to him when he'd been consumed by his hunger for recognition, power, and prestige. His throat clenched. Aye, and his hunger for revenge.

"I do not know you," she'd said.

Sela was wrong. She *did* know him—better than anyone. In that moment, she'd seen him truly.

I am a fraud.

The elder drew close. "Azazel is a place of great darkness," Lord Auberon whispered into his ear. "'Tis no surprise that it has poisoned your soul, my son. But you have only to take the remedy."

Caleb looked past the elder to Tucker. An odd compassion had overtaken his brother's face, as if he sympathized with Caleb's struggle.

Caleb stood, shaking off Lord Auberon's hand. "There is great darkness on Azazel, aye. But the greater darkness, my lord, is the one you brought with you in your heart. From that darkness, no one can be cleansed, except by the Carver's hand."

Tucker's lips whitened.

The elder reared back. "*What did you say?*" he hissed.

Caleb straightened. "You are no mediator between me and the Carver, my lord, that you can determine the fate of my soul. 'Tis not for you to decide, and all the more since your sleeve is as sullied as mine. To remain in your employ would be apprenticing myself to Death." He glanced at Tucker. "I do not know who you serve, my lord, but 'tis not the Carver I once knew."

"Treason! Blasphemy!" Lord Auberon flung open the door and screeched for his guards.

"Caleb—" Tucker began.

What he planned to say was interrupted by Lord Auberon's return. "It seems that I was right about you, after all, Caleb Alexander." Hard, gray eyes raked him like a shovel through ashes. "'Twas your brother who showed promise, not you. I was right to send for him."

"*You* wrote the letter saying I was ill?"

"Aye."

Tucker took a step back, casting his face into shadow.

"I also wrote the letter to your parents suggesting a hasty betrothal might be in order. One of my better decisions concerning you, for all that you threw my efforts back in my face."

Boots pounded across the floor. Rough, white-gloved hands grabbed Caleb's arms with bruising strength. The muzzle of a gun pressed into his lower back. Amidst the scuffle, Caleb noticed that Lord Auberon's fine coat had slid from its high-backed perch to the dusty floor. When he discovered it, the man would be livid.

"Remove this man from my presence," Lord Auberon spat.

Tucker made no protest when the guards dragged Caleb from the room. Apparently, his brother was determined to remain a coward.

As Caleb was led out into the darkness, he was filled to overflowing with a sudden, crushing relief. His association with Lord Auberon was over. He would return to Sela. This time, however, he would be the man she needed. A life with her, saturated with the Carver's love, was the only one he wanted.

But wait! The guards did not take him to the gates. Instead, they were hauling him to the place where he'd once been tied to a post, flogged, and branded. Did Lord Auberon intend further retribution?

Caleb had thought to choose life. But now, it appeared that life would be denied him.

By the time the soldiers finished with him, it was near midnight. They had beat him with their fists, though Caleb felt the bite of the whip on several occasions.

Laughing, they untied him from the post. Caleb recognized a couple of his assailants as being on the receiving end of Lord Auberon's punishments in the past, following Caleb's reports.

Was this why they delighted in striking him?

Two men dragged him outside the fort, dumped him in the mud, and departed.

Groaning in agony, Caleb rolled onto his back, only to hiss as his raw wounds encountered earth. Every limb in his body screamed, and his head throbbed where they'd kicked him. His ribs burned. He was pretty sure the soldiers' blows had cracked some of them.

The night was pitch black. The moon had set, and he could not see his hands in front of his face. Not even the torches of the night watch were visible from his low vantage point.

Caleb had no idea how long he lay there, dragging in one ragged breath after another. Was this how Sela had felt in the desert? Not even a snake stirred nearby.

He was utterly alone.

A shuffling of footsteps sounded near his ear and he turned his head. A bright light flooded his eyes. He blinked. Somebody knelt beside his head—a man of considerable height, by the looks of his shadowed outline.

Water trickled against Caleb's lips, and he drank gratefully. "Thaddeus?" he ventured.

"Nay," came the deep reply. "But 'tis a friend."

It was not Liron or any of the others. The man helped Caleb raise his head and maneuver him into a sitting position. He suppressed a guttural scream and squeezed his eyes shut at the lantern's blinding glow. When he finally gained his feet with the man's help, Caleb lurched dizzily, but the arm beneath his shoulders remained strong.

He had only gone a few steps when he stumbled, and his knees gave out. The man turned and grabbed him, supporting his weight. When Caleb's legs gave out altogether, he simply lifted Caleb over his shoulder, grunting with the effort.

Caleb's head spun. What kind of man could carry someone of his height and breadth with such ease? Thaddeus could not have managed it. Yet this man, who was tall but slim in build, bore up well under Caleb's weight. He even stooped and picked up the lantern in his free hand. Shadows crawled over Caleb's vision as he passed out.

When he came to, the lantern was gone. He heard a rustle beside him, and he felt rather than saw the man crouch over him.

Caleb groaned. "Where am I? What time is it?" Sela would be devastated that he'd not come after her.

"We are in a cave near the sea, Caleb. 'Tis dawn."

How did the man know his name? "I can't see anything." Indeed, it was darker than ever. Darker than the midnight sky when he'd been thrown outside the fort. How far inside this cave did he lie?

The man spoke again. "The first rays of dawn greet us as I speak."

"And your lantern?"

"'Tis beside me."

Caleb sucked in a sharp, painful breath. The darkness did not come from the outside. Nay, it came from within. The cave in which he found himself bore not even the faintest hint of light.

He was blind.

Chapter Eighteen

"Who are you?" Fear blanketed Caleb's senses. *I am blind,* he repeated over and over. *I am blind.* Had the blow to the back of his head stolen his sight permanently?

"Do you not recognize my voice?" came the mild reply.

Caleb stilled, concentrating, while the man hummed a tune. "My head aches," he said at last. "I'm afraid I don't know you, sir."

"I am Magnus."

Magnus? Caleb had met the man several times. There was no way the supposed prince could have borne Caleb's weight, let alone dragged him from the fort to a sea cave. Not with his hitched shoulder.

Yet, he had.

"I am blind, sir," Caleb admitted. "You could be Lord Auberon, for all I know."

Magnus chuckled. "For a scholar, you are remarkably inattentive."

Caleb froze. "You know of me?"

"Aye, my son."

Lord Auberon had used this same endearment, an affection offered as readily as it was withdrawn. But from the prince—if a prince he truly was—it felt different. Magnus spoke to him as if he had known him for years.

As if Caleb were a friend.

"Why did you help me?" He struggled to a sitting position, then frowned. He patted his ribs, then ran his hands along the rest of his body. Nothing but a lingering stiffness remained of the beating he'd endured. The prince's medicine?

Yet, his blindness persisted. "I don't understand, Magnus. Last night...your shoulder..."

He heard a smile in the man's voice. "'Tis an affliction I gladly bore for Liron's sake...as I bore it for yours."

"You have the king's medicines. Why would you not ease your own burden? Your shoulder must pain you greatly."

"I will bear a greater burden yet," Magnus replied soberly, as if grieved by his words. "My father, the king, is aware of the depravity of Azazel. He will not let its evil fester forever. There must be a reckoning."

The king? A reckoning? If that were true, then Magnus should get as far away from Azazel as he could. He was unbranded and could leave without being detained. Why would he risk his life by lingering on the island?

"Do you have a medicine that will give me back my sight?"

Inwardly, Caleb chided himself. He had not even thanked the man for his help. When he bit his lip and thanked him, Magnus moved closer. Warmth radiated onto Caleb's skin. Was the sun shining into the cave?

"Aye, Caleb," Magnus replied. "I do have medicine."

He stilled, waiting. A breeze tousled the hair on his forehead but nothing happened. "I am still in darkness."

"Aye."

He remembered his parting words to Lord Auberon. Something had come over him as he spoke, a zeal he usually felt while on his knees before the Carver. *I do not know who you serve, but 'tis not the Carver I once knew.*

What had possessed him to speak thus? The elder might have killed him. But for Magnus, he probably would have.

"Even if you could see, my son, you would still be blind to the light."

Caleb turned sightless eyes in his direction, disoriented by the complete darkness. Sleep never felt this black. "What light?" He realized, belatedly, that he had long since dropped the *sir*.

"Did you not see it last night?"

He had, of course, seen the lantern. It shone as brightly as Sela had described. However, he had put it down to his injuries and aching head. "Aye, I saw it."

"Then you know who I am."

"Are you truly the son of the king?"

The man remained silent.

"The king is said to be a representative of the Carver," Caleb pressed. "Do you come on His behalf?"

"Why do you say that, my son?"

"Your medicines. I've never seen the like."

"Is that all you seek from me? Healing?"

Caleb hesitated. Was this his chance? "Nay," he said finally. "If you are truly the prince, the Carver's servant, I would ask you—" He paused and thought of Lord Auberon's offer. His greatest desire. "I would ask you how to return to the life of the Pure."

"For yourself, or for your bondmate?"

"For us both."

"Stretch out your hand," Magnus said, and Caleb obeyed. The man's thumb pressed against his palm, tracing the burnt ridges of the soul stain. "Do you believe yourself deserving of this mark?"

Unbidden, an image rose in Caleb's mind of his knife planted in Smith's chest. Frustrated, he shrugged it away. "Since I was a boy, I've lived my life to please the Carver."

"In all?"

"In all."

"From heart to fingertips?" Magnus probed. "With every corner and recess of your mind?"

What a strange question. "I have always strived to do so." No matter that his attempts to live such a life proved futile after coming to Azazel. As Lord Auberon had warned him, there was something about the mud that clung to one's boots. And his mind? His mind was a rather dangerous battlefield of late.

"Then you believed yourself one of the Pure."

"Aye. Well, nay. Oh, I don't know."

At one time, he might have answered in the affirmative. Over the past year, though, he had proven to himself that, given the opportunity, he could submerge himself in hatred, vengeance, and jealousy as easily as he could in grace and compassion.

"'Tis Azazel," Caleb said, hoping Magnus would understand the nature of his predicament and absolve him of wrongdoing. "'Tis this place that corrupts."

"This island was good before the people came."

"I speak not of the island itself, but of those who live here. How can one be set apart in such a place? How can one remain Pure? 'Tis as difficult as cleaning a glass with a filthy rag. Or scrubbing the body with mud instead of water."

Magnus's voice was gentle. "What good is a pure body, Caleb, without a pure mind? A soul swept free of every cobweb, but rotting from within?"

Did the prince know how much his words contradicted Lord Auberon's? "A pure mind? A rotting soul? What are you suggesting?"

"I offer no condemnation, young man, only conviction. The Righteous spend their lives whitewashing the outsides of their souls. However, they pay little attention to the ugliness within. To many, the tree of their labors appears whole and healthy. But on the inside, 'tis rotting from its heartwood."

Caleb had said something similar to Lord Auberon once. But to accuse *him*, Caleb Alexander, of such hypocrisy, when he'd ever served the Carver with love and fervor? "Then what you see in my soul is ugly?"

"From all you've glimpsed of it recently, would you deem it beautiful?"

"*Recently*?"

Magnus waited.

How was it possible to feel the man's scrutiny while blind? Caleb thought of Smith and his bloody end. Was Magnus in possession of some kind of prophetic foresight?

Caleb mentally relived the past year. He recalled the way he'd treated Sela aboard the *Deliverance* and during the first few months on Azazel. Unwilling to touch her, even believing she'd sold herself, pressing his coins into her hand as if he could keep her from such weakness. Hesitating to save her life even when she lay dying.

He'd not only held her at a distance, but he'd kept the rest of the branded at a distance, as well. Thaddeus and Briella Gaskell. Noemia, Jax, Esther, Ross...even Liri.

Because of his blindness, Caleb had failed to acknowledge the extent of Tucker's hostility toward Sela. If he had, he, her bond-mate, would have been at her side, instead of a coward who fled.

A myriad of other images pressed against his mind. When he'd first returned to Azazel, he loved Sela well in the beginning, but since? He'd grown distant, angry, and jealous. How could he have thought to keep his emotions from her?

He recalled Magnus, who shook his bare hand at their very first meeting. Who'd been there for Sela in her hour of greatest need—twice—and now for him. Who gave of himself at every opportunity. Who sailed into a nightmare to which he was neither obligated nor conscripted.

If any man was Pure, it was Magnus.

"Nay," Caleb said when he understood the extent of the blindness Magnus had referred to. "'Tis not beautiful." His shoulders slumped, and his chin fell forward. "I have failed Sela. I am also a murderer, the same as she."

"Stretch out your hand, my son."

"How can the Carver forgive me for taking a man's life?" Caleb asked bitterly. "'Twas murder, I know. I was consumed by my anger, but there is no excuse. I thought it would bring Sela back to me."

"Give me your hand."

Caleb obeyed. Though he could see nothing, he felt the prince's smooth palm against his marked one.

"The Carver forgives you, my son," Magnus said, his voice solemn and ringing with royal authority. "These things are counted against you no more."

Warmth had entered his voice, and it settled on Caleb like the sun shining directly onto his soul. This felt even better than when he'd first realized the truth of the Carver's love for him, as real and tangible as the lines of his palm. A weight he'd not known he carried slipped from his shoulders.

"Drink this." Magnus held the rim of a glass to Caleb's lips.

He drank deeply. The liquid tasted both bitter and sweet, like orange juice mixed with rind. When Magnus withdrew the glass, Caleb could see light glancing into the cavern. Streaks of orange and purple lit up the upturned bowl of the sky, turning the surface of the water into a rainbow of color. It was more vivid than any sunrise he remembered.

Caleb stared at the prince in wonder. He was, of course, the same bearded man who he'd first met at the house of Thaddeus, though he seemed more real than he once had. Joy suffused Magnus's rugged features, and gratitude swelled within Caleb. For the first time, he understood the zeal that had driven Liron to track down the prince.

Magnus possessed authority and nobility that, unlike Lord Auberon, was tempered by wisdom and kindness. Caleb no longer doubted Magnus was the prince Liron had declared him to be.

"For what purpose was I blinded?" Caleb asked, though he had a feeling he already knew the answer.

Magnus smiled. "So that in the absence of your own eyes, my dear son, you might learn to see with the Carver's."

Tucker's ascent of the staircase was flavored with regret. He owed his presence in this house to two strange miracles. The first, that Lord Auberon did not know of his defection, and the second, that upon finding Tucker on his doorstep, Thaddeus Gaskell had not picked him up and tossed him down the hill.

After dismissing the guards who might have beaten Caleb to death, Tucker had made his way outside the fort, only to find that his brother was gone. Relief swept through him. If Caleb was well enough to walk away, he had likely gone in search of help. As soon as dawn lightened the horizon, Tucker had ridden to the cabin but found it vacant. Remembering the white house, which had once sheltered both Sela and Caleb, he swung his horse's head in that direction.

Thaddeus had opened the door even before he'd knocked. A large and imposing man, Tucker remembered him from some of the meetings he had presided over. The settlement men and women looked up to and feared him, though he seemed a just man, albeit one with a violent past.

If Lord Auberon glimpsed Tucker seeking admittance to this house, he would likely demote him. Thaddeus was a close friend of the imposter-prince, Magnus—the very man who had eluded and divided Lord Auberon's soldiers with his ideas about the Carver's mercy. The man who claimed to be the heir of Lord Auberon's own sovereign, not that the connection had been bandied about.

"I'm looking for my brother, Caleb," Tucker had said before Thaddeus could shut the door. "And Sela."

"Caleb is not here," Thaddeus replied, "but Sela lies upstairs. She is very ill."

"Ill?"

"The seasoning," the man explained.

Tucker recalled the graves he'd seen when he'd arrived on Azazel. Many, Lord Auberon had said, did not survive their first year on the island.

"You must be Tucker. We have met once before, on the jetty."

He felt sure the man would slam the door in his face, but to Tucker's surprise, he opened it wider, ushering him inside.

"The morning is uncommonly bright," Thaddeus said when Tucker hesitated. "'Tis easy to spy a man on this hill, especially from the fort."

Tucker hastened inside, astonished that Thaddeus would express concern for his hide.

"Sela is upstairs," Thaddeus said. A blond woman appeared carrying a pot of tepid water, and Tucker's heart skipped a beat. "Liri will show you the way."

"Tucker!" she exclaimed.

He took the pot from her, his gloved fingers brushing against her bare ones. She turned slowly, leading the way up the staircase.

He followed her, admiring the graceful arch of her arm as her hand glided up the banister railing.

A bead of sweat that had naught to do with the heavy pot he carried trickled down between his shoulder blades. Smith's death meant Liri was truly free. That meant naught, of course. Unless Tucker left Lord Auberon's employ, his and Liri's paths would always diverge.

She led him into a darkened room, where a woman lay abed, the covers drawn up to her waist. Dark hair fanned over her pillow, refusing to curl even on her sweat-dampened brow.

Sela.

Liri retrieved the pot of water from Tucker's hands, set it on the bedside table, and plunged a rag within. Wringing the cloth out, she set about dabbing Sela's face.

"Where's Caleb?" Tucker ventured. It appeared Liri was not going to speak first, or even look at him.

"I could ask you the same question."

Sela stirred, and Liri bent over her, murmuring something reassuring.

"Did he come here last night?"

"Last night?" She straightened. "Have you seen him?"

"Aye, Lord Auberon summoned him to the fort."

Her eyes narrowed. "To discuss his future amongst the *Righteous*?"

Tucker nodded. "Caleb told Lord Auberon he wanted no future but the one he has with your sister. He refused to put her aside."

"How did Lord Auberon respond to that?"

"He had Caleb beaten and thrown from the fort for some insolent words my brother thought to offer him before he departed."

He would have let the soldiers kill him if I hadn't intervened. He said naught of that to Liri.

Liri's lip trembled. "We've not seen him. None of the men have found him."

"He wasn't outside the fort when I searched for him last night, or this morning. He will be fine, Liri." He reached for her hand, then thought better of it. "Caleb is strong." *Aye, stronger than you, Tucker.*

Judging by the look on Liri's face, she thought the same.

"I would speak to Sela."

Liri's head came up. "She is in and out of consciousness. She will not likely hear you."

"Please. I won't take more than a few minutes."

He understood her hesitation. The last time they'd left him alone with Sela, grievous misfortune had befallen her.

Liron appeared at the doorway. "Let him talk to her, Liri. I'll stand guard." Though his eyes were hard, Liron gave Tucker a nod.

Despair settled into the empty places inside Tucker. Liri's siblings loved Caleb, but they would never do more than tolerate Tucker.

He looks like his brother, they probably thought, *but he is nothing like him.*

They were right.

When they had both left, or at least retreated out of his sight, Tucker settled on the side of the bed. Not for the first time, he saw the beauty his brother admired. With Sela's eyes closed, he saw elegance in the strong set of her shoulders, the delicate hollow of her throat, and the determined tilt to her chin. She was stubborn, aye. But no more stubborn than Caleb.

Or Tucker.

Though she slept, he began to speak.

"You know, Sela, when I first met you, I hated you." He watched the slow rise and fall of her chest. Dauncy as she was, she might die. The knowledge would have warmed him a month ago, but something had changed.

He had changed.

"From birth, my brother was destined for greatness," Tucker went on. "A fine mind, a zealous heart, a sharp eye. He never once strayed from the path...not like me. While I was seducing your elder sister, he was poring over scrolls. He ignored the giggles and eyelash flutters of the women who looked his way. I always thought the woman he'd eventually bond with would be a gentle soul, working together with him, making him shine."

He took a deep breath and continued. "I came to Azazel expecting to find him as I find you now—sick and near death. But his actual fate seemed worse to me than death. He'd been demoted from his position. Branded. Mocked by the very men he'd once commanded. I believed 'twas all because of you."

A lump formed in his throat, large and immovable. He tried his best to speak around it. "I left you at that jetty not only because it gave me Liri, but also because I was jealous of you for taking Caleb from me. I could have fought—and died—at your side. I could have called Caleb. I could have let him go after you. But I wanted my brother back. I wanted him to have his life back. That was worth"—he nearly choked—"'twas worth your life, in my estimation.

"Then on that clifftop, when I thought 'twas all over, you came. You stood in front of me, shielding me from your bondmate. Protecting me, even though I'd failed to protect you. Protecting me from the very brother I'd given you up to save."

He bowed his head. "The worst part is, I don't know if I would make the same choice again. I have not loved you as a brother-in-law should, and I know my weaknesses well enough to realize I may fail you a second time. But 'tis some time since I realized that to truly love Caleb, I must also love you. For you are part of his flesh and joined to his soul. If you should die, my brother would live, but he would never again be the same man."

Carefully removing his glove, he reached out and took her bare hand. "You make him shine, Sela. And for that, I hope I could find the courage to stand in your place. For that, I would lend you my strength—my very lifeblood—if 'twould allow you to live."

Her slender fingers were cold in his, and she did not stir. Alarm flitted through him. He jumped to his feet, sending the chair flying.

Liron came running, followed by Liri. Had they heard him? He had intended to speak no louder than a whisper. "Her breathing is shallow," he told Liron, quickly replacing his glove as Liri hastened to the bed. "And she is very cold. 'Tis more than a simple fever. You must send for a doctor at once."

"There is no doctor for the branded," Liri said.

Tucker frowned. She was right. "This man, Magnus. Has he not brought medicines from the Old Town? If no one else will come, then send for him."

The twins exchanged a glance, then Liron turned and ran from the room.

"I will go for Caleb," Tucker said.

Liri looked up and met his eyes, and something inexplicable passed between them. Urgency and fear, but something else as well.

There was no time to unravel it further. "I will find him, Liri. I promise."

Caleb spent what felt like hours with Magnus, until his soul was full to brimming. For every question he asked, Magnus gave an answer. He knew the Book of Souls like none other. Had he really spent so much time among the priesthood and the Righteous? He, the prince and heir of Eremia? Why had Caleb never seen Magnus in the seminaries of the Old Town?

Caleb said his farewells reluctantly. He left the sea cave to walk along the beach, relishing the playful dance of light on the curling waves. *I will return to Sela.* He would beg her forgiveness. In his care, she would never again feel unloved.

The sound of hooves greeted him as he left the beach. He looked up, startled to see Tucker.

His brother reigned in his horse but did not dismount. He extended a gloved hand. "Caleb," he said breathlessly, "you must come with me."

A little of his old self reared its ugly head, and Caleb frowned. As the Carver had forgiven him, so he would eventually have to forgive his brother. *Later,* he decided. "For what purpose should

I ride with you? Have you come with another *offer* from Lord Auberon?"

Tucker tossed his head impatiently, but his eyes, when they settled on Caleb, were full of fear. "'Tis Sela."

Alarm rammed Caleb's stomach. "Sela?" Accepting his brother's hand, he swung up behind him.

"Aye. She is dying."

Chapter Nineteen

To Caleb's astonishment, Tucker not only accompanied him into the house, but he also followed him upstairs. The household had erupted into chaos. Briella contained the children in the living room with Jax's help, but when Caleb passed them, their faces were streaked with tears.

Liri and Noemia sat at Sela's bedside, while Roux lay curled at her feet, whimpering. When she saw Caleb, Liri's eyes turned glassy. She yielded her place on the mattress. Tucker remained in the doorway, watching them.

Caleb gripped Sela's hand, his fingers tightening. She was so cold. Tucker had mentioned a fever, but her forehead contained not even a hint of warmth. He moved deeper onto the bed, lifting her head and shoulders, and easing himself behind her. He tucked her back against his chest and dragged the covers over them both. Wrapping his arms around her, he willed his body heat to leach into her.

Roux padded over to them. He laid his head on what looked like the outline of Sela's knee.

"How long has she been ill?" Caleb asked in a hoarse voice.

"She arrived last night and collapsed into Briella's arms. At first, we thought 'twas merely a relapse of the seasoning, but she has gone so quickly downhill."

Liri touched his arm. "Do not blame yourself, Caleb. She has been much stronger of late. None of us could have predicted—"

"I should have been here." Guilt stabbed at him. "I knew she reached you safely, but I had no idea she was dauncy. Then Lord Auberon—"

"Tucker told us about the summons." Liri glanced at the doorway, where his brother leaned. "It could not be ignored."

"Still, I should have—"

"Liron and Thaddeus have gone looking for the prince," his usually timid sister-in-law interrupted.

"I was just with him." Caleb raised his head and found Noemia's sightless eyes on him. "Magnus carried me from the fort. I was blinded—in more ways than one—but he restored my sight with one of his medicines."

Tucker exclaimed softly, while Liri's eyes widened. Only Noemia appeared serene.

"Magnus will come," Caleb insisted. "I am sure of it."

Just then, Liron appeared in the doorway. Tucker vanished from sight, and Noemia slipped out, leaving Caleb alone with Sela and her siblings. Liron was breathing hard, but it was his stricken look that froze Caleb.

"Prince Magnus?" Liri asked her brother.

"He's gone."

"What do you mean, *gone*?"

"The rumor is that Magnus has ventured alone into the heart of Azazel. To do what, I do not know."

"That journey could take days," Liri said despairingly. "Sela doesn't have that long."

"Thaddeus has gone after him. He will do whatever he can to find him and bring him back. There is naught else to do now but wait."

Barely an hour had passed since Caleb sat in the sun-soaked cave with Magnus, learning all he could. Barely three hours since he'd regained his sight. He had witnessed Magnus's mercy and compassion firsthand. Somehow, the prince had known to come to his aid. Would he not now come to Sela's?

"Caleb?"

Sela stirred in his arms. Caleb shifted her so that her head fell against his upper arm. In the moment she opened her eyes, he forgot Liri and Liron were in the room.

Several men had attempted to possess the unique beauty of this woman, but she looked at *him* with love so tender and sweet that he bid himself to never forget it again. "I have been blind, my love. So blind."

She reached out and touched his face. "About Ross?"

"About everything. Forgive me."

"Aye," she whispered, "I already have."

"I met with Prince Magnus. Through him, I made my peace with the Carver. And I...I understand now. There is so much to tell you."

"'Tis Briella who belongs with Ross. Though he does not yet know that he loves her."

Did she still think Caleb doubted her regard for him? "That may be, but 'tis of no consequence to me, Sela. You were right about Uriah. When I shot him, 'twas myself who was mortally wounded along with him."

A quickly indrawn breath told him that Sela's siblings were still in the room, but he paid them no heed. "I should have been there for you that day, when he took you. Even more than that, I should have been there for you during all the days that followed. I was so foolish, my love. You were the one robbed, not I."

She traced the strands that had escaped his queue. "I should never have shut you out the way I did."

"I missed you."

"And I you." Her eyes misted. "But...what if I cannot stay?"

"The prince will come, my love."

"I fear 'tis too late."

Caleb was dimly aware that his bondmate was weakening. He tugged her closer, as if he might preserve her life by the sheer strength of his body. When he glanced at the twins, they were weeping, and he fought tears of his own.

Was it because of him that she'd given up hope? "Do not fear, Sela."

She raised her hand to his face, and he felt the brush of her mark against his cheek. "But the soul stain—"

"The prince promised to put all to rights, did he not? Even now, Magnus makes a way for us to return to the path of the Pure."

She frowned. "But Lord Auberon—"

"Lord Auberon has naught to do with it."

She settled back against him, clearly relaxing.

Caleb studied the face of the woman in his arms. Through her trials, the Carver had fashioned her into a new woman. Fiery, but not blinded by anger. Lion-hearted, but not reckless. Passionate, but not easily waylaid. The terrible things she'd endured had not shattered her, only refined her.

And...he loved her. He loved her even more than the day he'd first carried her home as his bondmate.

Her hand slid to his neck. "What are you thinking?"

"I'm thinking that I like holding you like this."

She smiled at him, touched her fingers to his face, and then went limp.

Caleb gasped and shook her gently. Then with a sigh of relief, he realized she had merely fallen asleep. He raised his head and looked at Liron. "The prince will come."

Liron did not answer, but doubt flickered in his eyes.

Tucker paused with his hand on the door knob, gathering himself into a semblance of order and dignity. He had answered Lord Auberon's latest summons with a growing unease. So far, he had evaded the spies sent to follow him, though their increase in number of late indicated that Lord Auberon feared Tucker's defection.

And for good reason.

The would-be prince, Magnus, had disappeared into the heart of Azazel, but his ideas were spreading. Fearing that Azazel's inhabitants—both soulless and soul-bearing—would turn from him in favor of the prince, and that the Righteous would learn of his failure to keep the island in good order, Lord Auberon had sent soldiers after the man.

So far, Magnus had eluded capture, but he could not hide for long. Azazel was, after all, hardly a large island.

Tucker felt a stab of pain. Sela was still very ill. Caleb hadn't left the white house in days. On the one occasion Tucker had visited, his brother sat beside Sela, looking as if he'd been carved from wood or stone. His jaw was set, and his white skin nearly matched the pallor of the woman on the bed.

Should Sela die, Caleb would surely die with her.

Then there was Liri. The determination of the lot was final, absolute. Regardless of Uriah's death, Tucker would never be able to have the only woman he wanted, not unless he joined her in exile.

If he did, what would become of him? What would become of their son?

Suppressing a sigh, he twisted the door knob and pushed against the heavy wood. His mentor was alone in his quarters, poring over a document with a zeal that would likely injure his eyes should his candle burn low.

"Tucker," the elder said gruffly, "take a seat."

Tucker claimed the chair that sat before the desk, waiting for Lord Auberon to finish. His attention slid to the closed chest perched on the elder's desk. Liri's coin had been in there once, although their son had been wearing it when Liron discovered the boy at the port of Consuela. If his and Liri's places had been exchanged, it might have been Tucker's coin—Tucker's soul—that Lord Auberon hoarded like other men collected knives or guns.

'Twas not the Carver's will, he reassured himself.

'Tis not the Carver's will that any *should be condemned,* a voice returned from nowhere. He jolted upright in his chair, staring at Lord Auberon.

The elder had not spoken. He wasn't even looking at Tucker, preoccupied as he was with his document. By the time Lord Auberon raised his head, Tucker had scraped together a semblance of composure.

"It seems our good Captain Smith is truly dead. He has not been seen for a sevenday now. Thankfully, many of his men have agreed to remain in our employ."

Tucker winced at the *our*.

"'Tis this Magnus who truly concerns me. With Smith gone, the men of Azazel will look to form new alliances. They will be searching for someone to lead them. A figurehead will do as well as any other man. 'Twill be of no consequence to them when he proves himself a fraud."

"And if he isn't?"

Lord Auberon's brows rose, sharper than the dagger Tucker kept in his boot. "What did you say?"

"What if Magnus truly is the king's heir?"

"You have never struck me as naïve, my son." The twin daggers drew closer together. "For what reason would the *real* prince of Eremia—if he lives—conceal his true identity by masquerading as a commoner?"

"Are you not trying to kill him?" The words escaped Tucker before he could reel them in. He mentally kicked himself.

Lord Auberon's gray eyes turned flinty, and Tucker tried not to recoil from the spark. "The true heir of the king has naught to fear from *me*," the elder said through gritted teeth, "nor from any of the Righteous."

Tucker agreed, though he would never voice it out loud, that Magnus had naught to fear. Not if he was truly the king's son. At a word from the prince and a flash of the heir's medallion, he could have a fleet of ships at his disposal.

"I do not know who you serve, but 'tis not the Carver I once knew."

Caleb's words reverberated in his mind. Did Tucker serve the wrong master also? Janus Auberon was powerful—not only on Azazel, but also back in Eremia, where his authority was second only to the high priest's. Tucker had seen what Lord Auberon had done to Caleb. If Tucker defected, Lord Auberon might harm Liri.

He might hurt Tucker's children.

"A minor indiscretion in my youth."

Tucker shivered and returned his attention to his mentor, whose fire had diminished. The simmering coals were now banked behind a pleasant expression that betrayed very little, both of the man himself and of what cruelties he was capable.

Aye, Magnus had naught to fear, but Tucker Alexander had plenty to fear for himself. So for now, he would stay. As he watched his mentor, he could not help uttering a tiny, inaudible prayer.

Please, Carver of Souls. If You can hear me, save Liri and our little ones.

Save my son.

When Sela opened her eyes, she didn't see Caleb. Instead, she saw an open field dotted with meadow flowers. Warmth suffused her skin, and she felt velvety grass beneath her bare feet. She wriggled her toes. She had been cold—so cold—but now, she was pleasantly warm.

The next thing she noticed was the absence of the stifling humidity. She could breathe easily again, and there was no longer a painful rattling in her chest.

"'Tis beautiful, is it not?"

She turned. Magnus sat beside her, not in his workworn clothes, but wearing courtly attire, like a prince of the realm might wear. They shone whiter—if possible—than the robes and military dress of the Righteous. The edge of a gold medallion glinted beneath the lapels of his coat.

She laughed. "You are dressed even more beautifully than this meadow, my lord prince, and you expect me to gaze at the flowers? Is this how you used to look?"

"Aye, before I came to Azazel."

Sela glanced down and realized her own gown was as white as his clothes—whiter than the gown she'd worn the day of her Binding. It felt lighter than the wings of a butterfly and smoother than the freshly baked seal on one of Noemia's meringues. She ran her hands down the skirt. Even spider silk was not so exquisite.

"If you appeared in such finery," she remarked, "even Lord Auberon would kiss the dust at your feet."

"'Tis not for man's praise that I came to Azazel, my daughter." He turned something over in his hand, maneuvering it deftly between his long fingers.

When she looked closer, she spied the glint of a coin. "What is that, my lord?"

Magnus held the coin up to the light. "Do you not know?"

Ah, but she did. After all, she had seen it many times before. Around the neck of Liri's son, Liron. Uriah too. Even Tucker Alexander wore one.

A sign of deliverance—or condemnation, depending on which side of the lot you stood. "You said you came to Azazel to put all to rights."

"Aye, for the branded and the unbranded alike." Magnus clenched the coin in his large fist. "For you to be truly free, I must fulfill the demands of the lot. Once and for all. Or Death will be the only king of this island."

"But—"

"Do you know where you are, Sela?"

The meadow melted away, and she saw her room in Thaddeus's house. Caleb knelt beside the bed, his shoulders bowed low with grief, sharp agony twisting his handsome features. He was clutching a limp, pale hand.

Just as she'd known the coin in Magnus's hand, Sela knew the body lying motionless on the bed was her own. So little breath remained—so little life. Weakened by the seasoning, she would not last much longer.

She looked at Magnus. His tears mirrored her own. "Why do you cry, my lord?"

"Because what you see there was never meant to be. You are a daughter to me, just as Caleb is like a son. And because..." He faced her, a hitch in his voice betraying the strength of his emotions. "Because I know what is coming."

"What is coming?"

"You will know soon enough. One day, Sela, we will meet again in this meadow. Caleb too. But the Carver tells me 'tis not your time. Not yet. Do you trust me, my daughter?"

The light dimmed, and his clothes regained their normal Azazelian hue. He extended his gloveless hand to her.

For a long moment, she stared at it, wondering that he, a prince and a stranger, could value her—a lowly subject of a cursed island—as he did.

Trust? She remembered his words to her in the desert.

"This is not the end."

She did not want to leave the warmth and peace of the meadow. However, she somehow knew she would not be leaving Magnus. She saw the love in his eyes—the Carver's love—and for the first time in her life, she craved it more than air.

She reached out and grasped his hand.

Against all odds, Sela hung on.

Another day dawned, the sky sucked clean of all color. A storm was coming in the next day or so. Caleb kept his vigil at Sela's bedside, along with Sela's siblings, who did what they could to help Sela cling to life.

But she was slipping away, a little more each day.

What could have possibly delayed the prince? Magnus had known Sela was in trouble before. Why not now? This was hardly the time to tour Azazel's wilderness regions.

Caleb's conversation with Magnus, the day he'd disappeared, replayed constantly in his head. "Lord Auberon could do you great harm," he'd warned Magnus, fearful for the prince's safety in light of what he knew of Lord Auberon's jealousy. In hindsight, was that the reason Magnus had fled?

Magnus had not even flinched at Caleb's warning.

"Why are you not afraid, my lord? Lord Auberon is powerful, and even greater powers stand behind him."

"Fear is the ancient enemy of love, my son. If I am seized by fear, how can I love? How can I trust? Fear makes me think of my own will. Love makes me think of others. And, most of all, of the Carver."

"Auberon's men will be everywhere, looking for you. Have you no concern for your own life, my lord?"

"Did I not instruct you to gaze with heavenly eyes, Caleb?"

"Aye, you did."

"What do you see? Which is the greater prize? A man's body, or his soul?"

"His soul, of course."

"Which is the greater foe? The man who merely works as Death's servant by hastening another's earthly end, or Death itself?"

Caleb frowned. "Death, I think. But the lot! Can you not simply abolish it, my lord?"

"Abolish it?" Magnus's stare grew intense. "Nay. The lot was established to pay the blood price for mankind's sins. 'Tis because of man's evil that its true purpose was distorted and corrupted. Never was it intended that one man pawn his soul for the sake of another. To grant the absolution you and so many others seek, Caleb, the lot must be fulfilled, not abolished. The blood debt must be paid."

"I don't understand."

"You will," Magnus had gently replied.

Below them, footsteps pounded across the porch of the white house. Liron, who sat opposite Caleb, glanced up. Voices rose, and the door to the bedroom was flung open. Liri hurtled inside and stopped in the middle of the room.

"What is it?" Liron asked, standing.

Liri exhaled sharply. "I cannot explain. You must come and see for yourself."

The others were waiting for them on the hill outside the white house. Ross stood beside Briella, holding Tempe, while she rocked and crooned to Thomas. Caleb spotted Noemia, standing guard over Liri's three children like a mother hen, and Jax, his mouth open wide. All eyes were riveted on the grassy expanse beyond the gardens Caleb had tended in the first days following his branding.

Anxiety tugging on his heartstrings—for he had no wish to leave Sela for long—Caleb followed their gazes.

Magnus stood there, his tall frame outlined by the lightening sky, his hands hanging loosely at his sides. Gathered on the hillside behind him stood a hundred or more people—men, women, and children—looking as if they had materialized from the fog.

Caleb stared. Could these be the captives from Uriah's hideout under the mountain? Perhaps those taken in the recent assault on Belladonna, the people Lord Auberon and his soldiers had long given up for dead?

Aye, they must be. Haggard and weary-faced, they looked more like ghosts than flesh-and-blood humans. They were real, though, as real as Thaddeus, who stood at Magnus's right hand, taller and straighter than Caleb had ever seen him.

Liri exclaimed and ran to Magnus. Caleb wanted to go to him too, but his legs felt as if they were made of heavy metal. After a soft exchange with Liri, the prince walked forward, sorrow in his eyes. Yet, more than sorrow, anger resided in the set of his jaw, and fire appeared in his roving gaze as he looked toward the fort.

Something stirred in Caleb's brain. *Sela. The medicine.*

At the moment he regained command over his body, Caleb heard the whinnying of horses, and he looked farther down the hill. A hiss escaped his lips. Fifty soldiers or more were headed their way, with a red-coated officer at their head. They galloped up the hill and surrounded Magnus in a half-circle, flintlocks and swords drawn.

Auberon's men.

"You there, Magnus," said an officer Caleb didn't recognize. "You must come with us."

Nay, a voice cried within Caleb, but once again, he couldn't move. He watched numbly as Magnus nodded. He mounted a riderless horse and rode away with the soldiers, his face devoid of expression.

He was going to Lord Auberon. How could he not be afraid?

Liri appeared beside Caleb, her face buoyant. "Caleb," she whispered. "We must return to Sela. Quickly."

Nay, they must go after Magnus. "The prince has the medicine."

"He gave it to me," Liri replied. "Just before they took him away."

Caleb stared at his sister-in-law, barely comprehending the small bottle she dangled before his eyes. Magnus had given them the medicine? Sela would live?

He did it. He came back!

Caleb looked after the party of soldiers heading for the fort, and his heart tore in two. The prince was at Lord Auberon's mercy, but Sela was near death. What should he do? How could he choose?

"Caleb," Liri repeated, more urgently. "We must hurry."

There was no choice. Feeling like the worst kind of traitor, Caleb took the bottle from Liri and hurried back to Sela.

Chapter Twenty

The blazing colors crackling in the sunset reminded Liri of fire. She thought of a blacksmith's hammer beating against molten metal. The sun began its descent beneath the lip of the horizon and she felt a sharp hiss, as if its bronzed mass had plunged into the ocean's cool trough, though the sun set behind the mountains. Like steam vapors, clouds drifted up and away, trailing after the vivid ribbons of butter-yellow, crimson-red, and lavender.

Liri sank her feet into the sand, relishing the feeling of freedom. With Uriah gone, her nightmares had diminished. She no longer glanced over her shoulder every moment. Even the children no longer asked after him. Aye, she was free. Free as the bird that now glided above her, his expansive wings expertly finding the currents that kept him aloft with so little effort.

Perhaps one day she could live so easily.

"Liri?"

She turned and saw Tucker walking along the beach. Although she expected him after receiving his cryptic note earlier, she felt a prickle of disquiet. Nay, a shiver, kin more to pleasure than pain. Twilight had approached while she'd lost herself in the sunset's dying hues. When he reached her, he took her hand and drew her away from the beach and into a grove of trees.

"I didn't know if you would come."

"How could I not?" Even after everything he'd done, her love for him had not faded. All through the long years with Uriah, she had thought only of Tucker, though she hated herself for it. For she had known that, soul-stained as she was, she could never be his.

Tucker's expression admitted a hint of emotion. "Your sister. She lives?"

Liri nodded. "The prince's medicine worked. She's weak, but she's going to pull through."

"And Caleb?"

"He is content." *Mostly.*

With Sela out of danger, they all worried about the prince. They had heard nothing since his arrest that morning. Would Tucker know more?

Wondering at Tucker's inquiring after Sela's health ahead of his brother's, she gazed up at his shadowed face. "For what did you summon me, Tucker? 'Tis risky, meeting like this."

He nodded and drew her deeper into the grove. "Aye, 'tis risky. Lord Auberon has had me followed constantly for the past two sevendays."

"Followed?" Alarmed, she stepped back.

"The man doesn't know I'm here. I lost him before I left the fort. But 'tis not long before he grows suspicious, if he isn't already." He swallowed and stared at his feet. "Lord Auberon will probably send me back to the Old Town soon. This will likely be the last time I will see you. You see, I came to say goodbye."

Tears came, but she blinked them away, glad for the semi-darkness that veiled them. "What of our children?"

"I will never abandon you *or* them, Liri. You have my word. I will send funds and letters through Thaddeus or Caleb as often as I can. I would take Liron with me as my ward, but"—he met her eyes—"he belongs with his mother."

"What about the soul mark?"

He nodded. "Aye. You will need to find a way to mark him, so the soldiers do not realize he is unbranded."

Tucker took her hands in his gloved ones. He stood with his back to the light straining through the trees, so she saw only the silhouette of his tall, broad frame as he peered down at her. The sun's dying light turned his copper hair to gold. He had, she realized dimly, their daughter's smile. Or rather, their daughter had *his* smile.

When he spoke, his voice was barely above a whisper. "I am not like my brother, Liri, but I want to be. If I could escape Lord Auberon without hurting you in the process—"

"Escape, Tucker?"

"Aye. While Auberon lives, I will never be free."

She understood. Just as Uriah had been her jailer, Lord Auberon was Tucker's. The man she loved had ever been torn between two worlds, a prisoner of his life as much as she was a prisoner of hers.

"Caleb and Sela—"

"We are not Caleb and Sela, are we?" His hands curled around her middle. "'Tis because of Caleb's defection that Lord Auberon watches me with eagle eyes. He will not lose two acolytes to the wilds of Azazel. And if he discovers the truth about us..."

She understood what tortured him. If he chose her, it would likely mean his death. If not hers, as well. And the children...

"I love you, Liri." He cradled her cheek with the tenderness of the Tucker of old. "There will never be any woman for me but you. I swear it."

"You cannot promise me—"

"Aye," he replied firmly, "I promise."

The affection in his pale blue eyes moved Liri to folly. She drew closer to him, entwining her hands around his back. "I love you, Tucker. I will never love another like I love you."

In a gesture as natural as breathing, he bent his head and kissed her. Though she should have pushed him away, she surrendered. How long had it been since they had last stood like this? Six, seven years?

The lonely expanse of time dissolved like salt in a vast array of glittering water. She was eighteen years old again, locked with Tucker in a desperate embrace, fearing the approaching lot.

As the eldest of their respective families, it had been foolish to spend time together, and more foolish still to fall in love. However, they had been children when they met, and barely adults when they were parted.

A month before their coming-of-age ceremony, fear had produced an unexpected passion, which they quickly regretted in the light of day. All the more when they learned she would not make the journey to Azazel alone.

That same despair clouded with desire surrounded them now, sounding warning bells in Liri's mind, but it was Tucker who pulled back. "I will not dishonor you, my love. I will not make the same mistake a second time."

"Nor I," she whispered. Inwardly, though, she craved the resoluteness she heard in his words.

"Lieutenant Commander!" A strident voice from deep within the trees tore apart the illusion of their private sanctuary. The heavy boots that neared might have belonged to giants. "Lieutenant Commander, stay where you are!"

An odd warning, but fear flashed across Tucker's face. "*Go*, Liri. Go now, before they see you."

"I will not leave you, Tucker. Not like this."

He leaned down and kissed her again, though the pressure of his lips seared more than soothed. "If they see you with me, you're as good as dead. You cannot ask me to watch you suffer thus."

She stilled. Was this perhaps her own reckoning? He bade her, once again, to flee like a coward, when they bore nothing but regret for the last time they'd fled. Perhaps it was time to face their enemies as boldly as Caleb and Sela had.

"Lieutenant Commander Alexander! Stop there, I say!"

"Think of our children, Liri."

Her insides softened to butter and her knees wobbled. She knew he was right.

Liri turned and ran just as something in the bushes crashed behind Tucker. She did not stop to look back, not even when he yelled.

Had Tucker's men seen them embrace? Would he be punished for meeting her? Tears turned the dirt on her face to muddy rivulets, but she kept up her pace until she was sure nobody had followed her. She was nearly to the base of the hill when she finally turned and gazed back at the fort. Only the torches burning in the watchtowers were visible.

You fool, Liri, she reprimanded herself. *How could you have wanted to stay with him? He betrayed Caleb and Sela.*

He betrayed you.

Halfway up the hill, at the base of the old jacaranda, she sank to her knees, sobbing like a child. "Tucker," she whispered brokenly. "*Tucker.*" All her self-castigation faded into nothingness.

For once again, he was lost to her.

"Allow me to ensure I have heard you correctly."

Seated behind his desk, Janus gazed at the man who sat serenely across from him, his hands folded in his lap. Even if he believed the man's preposterous claims, Janus would have known their falseness the moment he glimpsed the callused hands. For, unbranded as the man seemed to be, no prince of Eremia had such workworn palms. He was clearly a commoner, albeit with more than the usual share of political and religious aspirations.

"You declare you are the prince of Eremia, the heir of the king himself, come to Azazel for a...special purpose?"

Magnus remained silent.

"Am I correct?"

"'Tis as you say."

Janus clenched his hands into gloved fists beneath his desk, ignoring the man's glaring omission of the customary honorific *my lord.* "For what purpose have you remained in disguise all this time?"

"To free the captives."

"The captives? Do you mean the soulless?" Lord Auberon frowned, tapping his finger on the underside of the heavy desk. The face of Noemia flashed into his mind. "There has been no word—indeed, no order *at all* concerning the soulless—from the king."

"He wrote to you, and to your predecessors, that you should expect my arrival."

"I have viewed no such missive."

Again, the man gave no answer. For a commoner, he had an almost aristocratic bearing, evident more in the lines of his long body than in the harsh, weatherworn angles of his bearded face. One of his shoulders was hitched higher than the other. It was well-known that the prince had suffered an unfortunate accident as a youth, but what if this man feigned the injury?

"'Tis said you give the king's medicines to people who would never be able to afford them otherwise. To the *soulless*." Janus spat the word.

Magnus remained still, not even twitching.

"You restored a soul-stained woman near death."

Janus's muscles would not do their duty and stay calm as Magnus's had, and his jaw clenched. Sela Alexander was the woman in question. Hearing that she still lived, Janus had flown into a private rage. It would have been more than convenient for him if she had died of her illness.

Caleb might have finally seen the error of his ways.

"Do you deny the king's medicines are capable of such extraordinary results?"

"'Tis *my* interrogation, not yours." Janus bristled. "Perhaps the woman recovered on her own."

Behind him, Janus's officers shuffled their feet.

"My lord, there is no doubt that she was almost gone," whispered the usually timid Captain Foster. "And there are other accounts—"

Janus's neck snapped around like a whip. "Silence!"

Foster slunk back into the shadows.

"If you were of royal blood," Janus continued, "I would have recognized you."

"Truly, Lord Auberon, I never knew you."

"Then we have not met."

"As you say."

"If I understand you correctly, Magnus," Janus went on, "you wish an exchange. What among my possessions interests you?"

"The chest," Magnus replied.

They both turned to look at the heavy wooden chest that sat to Janus's right, padlocked and well-guarded day and night by his most competent guards. Not the real Chest of Souls, of course. That one was carefully concealed in a larger chest behind the curtain. This one was a decoy, a fake, with the slightest veneer of coins strewn atop a wooden insert.

However, it had clearly fooled Magnus.

Janus could afford to give up this empty chest, though he would need to feign reluctance in order for his capitulation to appear genuine. "You are in search of riches, then?"

"Nay. Souls."

"'Tis a costly thing you seek, this chest."

"Aye," Magnus replied. "Particularly the authentic one that resides in your quarters."

Janus nearly fell off his chair. Was there a spy among his guards? There must be, though they couldn't have known of the decoy. Not even Tucker knew. He forced a pretended calm. "What would you give me in exchange?"

"Anything you ask."

Janus rose. The scuff of his boots along the floorboards betrayed a mind troubled and distracted, which was rare. "*Anything*? Who are you to promise such a thing? You have not yet proven your identity. Of what value to me is a commoner?"

In answer, Magnus reached beneath his collar and pulled a heavy chain over his head. A round medallion hung from the chain, more finely wrought than anything Janus had seen outside of the king's most treasured possessions.

Magnus reached across the table and placed the medallion in Janus's outstretched palm.

By its weight, Janus knew it to be made of solid gold. The silver filigree bordering the center design—a depiction of the Soul Stars, carved in their ghostly splendor—was so exquisite it might have been divinely crafted.

"This proves naught," he scoffed, though inwardly, his stomach churned. He dismissed his men and sank into his chair.

"Do you not recognize the heir's medallion, Lord Auberon?"

"Aye, I do, though you might have torn it from the true prince's dead body."

Magnus's gaze was steady. "Even if I had, 'twould suit your purposes, would it not?"

"My purposes?" Janus echoed.

"You would return this to the king with the news that his heir is dead. 'Twould be well-received by those next in line to the throne."

Janus blinked. "Without this medallion, you have no claim to the kingship of Eremia."

"I know."

"It has been twenty years since you—that is, the *prince*—was seen in the Old Town. No one will recognize you, should you try to stake your claim."

"I am well aware of this, Lord Auberon."

"Then you would trade your—I mean, the *prince's*—birthright, his title, and his chance to rule...for what? A collection of coins?"

"For the souls of the lost." Magnus's eyes betrayed a depth Janus had not seen before. "For *all* the lost."

"I do not understand."

"In exchange for this medallion, Lord Auberon, the lot must end. Aye, and the second lot along with it. All on Azazel—all throughout Eremia—will be regarded as free men and women."

"I hardly possess such power."

"Are you not the treasurer of the Righteous?" Magnus indicated the chest. "Were you not one of those who indicated his support for the lot to remain?"

How could this imposter know of such a thing? His vote, cast in a secret meeting of elders, priests, and soldiers, had been part of a secret ballot. Janus shook his head. "No medallion is worth such an exchange."

"Is not your rule tenuous of late, Lord Auberon?" Magnus's intense gaze had him—*him,* an elder of the Righteous—wanting to squirm. "'Tis rumored you call for even more reinforcements from the Old Town to suppress rebellion."

Janus hardly needed the reminder. "Why, you dare to—"

"Give me what I ask for, and I will give you what you seek."

"I seek only the Carver's will."

Magnus said naught, but his gaze raked the coat Janus wore. The fine fabric, which had been pristine when he first arrived on Azazel, was beginning to show the filth of the place. Did Magnus know that, of late, Janus had been forced to be more politician than elder? Even if Magnus did, he could tell no one. He was completely at Janus's mercy.

Whatever happened next, the king would not need to know.

The door opened just then, and tainted, smoky night air rushed in. Janus rose to bark at the men who dared disturb them, but they continued on their course. Tucker Alexander entered, dragged between two officers, his face battered and purpling. The soldiers deposited him in an ungainly heap beside Magnus's chair.

"What is the meaning of this?" Janus barked.

"My lord," said the first officer—a tall, wiry fellow, and one of the spies he'd ordered to watch his acolyte. "You said we should come to you immediately if something was amiss."

Must this Magnus, this imposter, witness every one of my failures?

"What is amiss, man? Speak quickly."

"Elias and I followed Lieutenant Commander Alexander as you ordered, my lord. Just now, we found him."

"Well done," Janus returned in a biting tone, "since he wasn't exactly missing. What was he doing when you found him?"

The man drew himself up. "Alexander snuck off all secret-like, my lord. Thought he'd ditched us, but he hadn't. We caught up with him near the shore, not far from here, and saw him through the trees, clear as day. All jeddarty-jiddarty…with a woman."

The two officers who'd arrested Tucker exchanged verbal reports like blows, heedless of the gaps in their story and Lord Auberon's rising temper.

"We called out for Alexander to stay where he was."

Never mind that a competent spy would never cry out a warning, though Tucker was glad their clumsiness had allowed Liri to get away.

"The woman escaped before we could see much of her, my lord. It was already dark by then."

Five seconds after it was clear as day, apparently.

"When we tried to apprehend him, he attacked us."

More truthfully, they had attacked *him*, the bigger of the two men smacking him to the ground so hard it knocked the breath from him. If not for a tree root tangling around his ankle, Tucker might have recovered in time to get away. The soldiers had delighted in his downfall, binding his wrists tightly with rope and dragging him through the undergrowth like a common criminal.

While the two officers blundered their way through their report, Tucker chanced a look at Magnus. This was the man whose medicines had saved Sela's life, and the lives of many others. Who had journeyed alone into the heart of Azazel and returned with the captives Lord Auberon had forsaken. Tucker had barely exchanged three words with him, but he had heard the man's alien ideas from the settlement men and women.

"If wrong is done to you, count the offense as naught, and the Carver will count your own offenses as naught. For to forgive is the true mark of the Righteous."

If Magnus knew the nature of the man who stood on the other side of the desk, he might not be so generous with his pardons. Not only toward Lord Auberon, but toward Tucker himself.

If he knew what I've done...

Tucker eyed the chest that straddled the desk, feeling the weight of the coin at his neck like a blacksmith's anvil. If things had been different, it would have been *his* name trapped within. Aye, even without the lot's determination, he deserved such a fate.

Magnus met his gaze, and Tucker was surprised by the compassion flickering within the gray depths. No stranger looked thus at another. Disheveled as Tucker was, he could not put it down to deference to his rank. His fine coat was torn and glutted with mud.

The ramblings of the two officers came to an abrupt end, and Tucker glanced up to find Lord Auberon's eyes on him. Gray, aye, but sharper than a knife, and viselike in their grip.

"Is what these men say true, Tucker?" The question was strained, forced through a sieve of rigid calm.

He could deny it. The officers were blundering fools, anxious to please and obviously incompetent. Though he had to admit, they had been skilled enough to track him. Clearly, he'd been blinded by his thoughts of Liri.

Tucker didn't answer, his gaze drawn to Magnus. How many times had he shirked the Carver's commands? How many times had he denied the truth to protect himself?

Liri's words bounced around his skull, taunting him.

"The greatest shadow over us is the shadow you yourself cast. While you live a lie, you will never know contentment."

For nearly seven years, Tucker had lived a lie. He had run whenever his freedom was threatened. In contrast, Sela—a woman he'd despised from the beginning—had known what it was to stand her ground. To have courage. She had stood by Liri...and Caleb...and him. Even after everything she'd lost, she had begged Caleb for his brother's life.

Magnus's eyes seemed to demand the truth. By the look of him, the would-be prince already knew what Tucker would do.

He dropped his eyes from Magnus's and said nothing.

Lord Auberon uttered a disgusted sound and dismissed the officers, whose stares at Tucker held a mix of derision and glee. Had they rejoiced thus when Caleb was brought low?

Unlike Caleb, Tucker deserved this fate. He had deserved it from the beginning.

"Tucker Alexander," Lord Auberon began wearily, "I did not believe you capable of such iniquity. A kept woman. You are no better than your brother."

"Caleb is three times the man I am," Tucker replied stiffly.

"If that is true," replied the elder, who seemed to forget that Magnus was still in the room, "then 'twould only be fair if you received triple his punishment."

A cold fist clamped Tucker's windpipe.

"Will you not plead for your life, Tucker? For that is what will be demanded from you. Perhaps if you give me the name of the woman?"

"Nay."

Lord Auberon's head jerked up in surprise. His eyes narrowed. "'Tis only her name that I require, naught else."

"I will not betray her."

"'Tis betrayal or death, Tucker. Choose, and choose wisely."

"Lord Auberon."

Tucker glanced at Magnus.

The imposter-prince rose to his feet. "Earlier, we spoke of an exchange."

"Aye," said Lord Auberon warily.

"I meant what I said. I will give you what I promised"—he tilted his head, conveying a hidden meaning Tucker could not grasp—"in return for the agreed-upon price. You may do as you wish, and I will not challenge you. But there is one more thing."

Lord Auberon waited.

"You must spare this young man. I will remain here to settle his debts."

Something new gleamed in the elder's eyes, and Tucker felt sick at the sight of it. Whatever it was, Lord Auberon believed himself in possession of a victory.

"*All* his debts, Magnus? No matter the final tally?"

"All." Magnus's attention remained on the elder. "No matter the cost."

What could this man do to discharge his debts, if Tucker's trespass could be termed thus? Whatever Magnus offered was obviously valuable to Lord Auberon. Did the man have resources at his disposal—a deep purse, perhaps, that did not match his common look?

After an agonizing pause, Lord Auberon turned to Tucker. "'Tis your lucky day, boy. You will remain as you are, whole and unmarked. I suggest you make good use of your freedom and never show your face to me again."

Stunned by the elder's words, Tucker backed away. Lord Auberon called for his guards and barked his orders for Tucker's banishment from the fort.

As he was driven from the room, Tucker caught Magnus's eye.

The soft gray gaze showed considerable strength, not brittle or hard like Lord Auberon's, but nonetheless firm, as befitting a man of deep conviction. His eyes brimmed with compassion, but the sadness there surprised Tucker.

But for what? That his supposed coffers would be further depleted for Tucker's sake?

He dragged his gaze away. When Magnus concluded whatever business he had with Lord Auberon and departed the fort, Tucker would find him and offer his gratitude. He could repay him from his own family's coffers.

As the soldiers dragged him into the night, a prickling unease gnawed at Tucker's stomach. After what Lord Auberon had done to Caleb for simply touching a branded woman, why had he capitulated so easily to the sparing of Tucker?

After all, he had not only seduced a woman outside of the Binding, but he had also fathered two children with her. Not that Lord Auberon knew about the latter.

The sun had set completely, leaving faint smudges in its wake. Tucker hauled in a deep breath. He didn't mind the soldiers' bruising grip on his arms or the harsh bite of the rope against his wrists.

He was going to be free. He laughed at how easily it had happened. This very night, he would catch up Anwen and Liron in his arms and hold them close.

Tucker paused. Liri's words followed him from the fort and into the suffocating humidity.

"A father knows the true value of sacrifice."

Chapter Twenty-One

Caleb was shocked to find his brother standing outside the cabin after nightfall, well after curfew. He was further stunned when Sela encouraged him not only to let Tucker in, but to allow him to remain the night.

"Have you forgotten what he did to us the last time we trusted him?" Caleb pulled her into their bedroom, leaving Tucker standing in the center of their living room, looking forlorn. He glanced past her shoulder, determined not to let his brother out of his sight this time. He wished they had remained at the white house, but he had wanted to be home.

"Nay," Sela replied. "But even should he prove our enemy, he needs our help."

"You believe his dismal tale about being banished by Lord Auberon?"

"Did Liri not admit she met him by the shore tonight?"

Aye, she had, and rather sheepishly.

At first, Caleb feared his brother had sought to dishonor her again, but Liri reassured them that Tucker intended her no harm. Instead, he had helped her escape from the guards, who came to arrest him.

"Sela, my love. Tucker cannot be trusted."

"Perhaps not, but he is your brother, Caleb. And this is his hour of need."

Caleb scowled.

Sela slipped out of his embrace, wrapped her dressing gown tightly around her middle, and entered the living room. Tucker turned to watch her, and Caleb could discern no animosity in his gaze.

"I am sorry to disturb you so late," Tucker ventured, his usual suave, cocky manner nowhere in sight.

"'Tis no matter, Tucker. We had only just gone to bed." Sela's voice was gentle.

"I stopped at the white house to see the children, else I would have been here earlier."

"Did Thaddeus not offer you—"

"Aye, he did, but I thought it best not to trespass upon his hospitality."

"Yet, you presume to trespass upon ours," Caleb muttered from the doorway.

Tucker's face flamed. "Are we not still brothers, Caleb?"

Caleb grimaced. Aye, Tucker had come to see Sela while she was ailing, and Liri said he'd enquired of her health afterward. This brother of his seemed different tonight—more subdued.

But how could Caleb know for sure if Tucker had truly changed?

Leave the business of his soul to Me, a voice replied. *You have only to love him as you once did.*

Caleb closed his mouth on another bitter retort, gritting his teeth.

Sela spoke for him. "You are welcome here, Tucker. We also have your coat to return to you."

Tucker blanched. "'Twould seem I no longer have need of it, but thank you."

"Then you require fresh clothes," she replied, not missing a beat. She measured him with her eyes. "Caleb is about your size." She turned to look at her bondmate, raising an eyebrow in silent question.

Caleb gave a tight nod, consenting to the use of his wardrobe to clothe his prodigal brother.

"Thank you, Sela. You are very kind."

Too kind, Caleb mused, wondering that Tucker had twice now thanked her. His brother's gaze followed Sela as she returned to the bedroom for the promised clothes. Disliking the way he watched her, and almost preferring the old hatred to this new vulnerability, Caleb approached Tucker with folded arms. "If this is some ploy of Auberon's, I swear you'll live to regret it."

Tucker's face lost several shades of color, but not, Caleb thought, because of any underlying guilt. "'Tis no ploy." He kneaded his gloveless hands together, and a flash of his palms revealed that he remained unbranded. "Caleb, I came here to—"

"Put another log on the fire before you retire, would you?" Caleb turned, unwilling to hear any more of Tucker's confessions, not when Sela still woke in the nights writhing in the sheets.

Though admitting defeat was out of character for his brother, Tucker nodded. "Aye, I will."

Long after they had gone to bed, Caleb remained awake, sitting in a chair near the open bedroom door with his flintlock across his knees. His brother's footsteps had faded within five minutes of saying goodnight, but Caleb knew better than to trust his senses.

For what reason had Lord Auberon let his brother go unpunished? Though his clothes were torn and disheveled and his face bruised, there were no other marks on him. Nothing that would indicate he'd incurred the displeasure of the Righteous.

At least there had been no news of Magnus. Surely that was a good thing. Had the prince somehow convinced Lord Auberon of his claim to the throne?

Sela slept on, only awakening once with a soft cry. Caleb was there to comfort her, stroking her hair in the way she liked. She quickly drifted back to sleep. He ached to hold her, to curl his body around hers and join her in blissful slumber, but he could hardly do so with Tucker present.

He had to keep her safe.

An hour before dawn, Caleb padded out into the living room on bare feet. He was surprised to find his brother fully dressed in the clothes Sela had given him, lying on his back beside the fireplace, his arms curled beneath his head.

He sat up when Caleb entered. Unbound copper locks tangled around a face far too pale to be his brother's. The spaces beneath both eyes looked sunken, as if he had slept as little as Caleb had. The bruising on the left side of his face reminded Caleb of Beck's port-wine birthmark.

"I heard Sela's cry in the night," Tucker said, rising to his feet. "Is she well?"

"As well as can be expected," Caleb replied stiffly. In truth, she was doing far better than that, but it would not hurt Tucker to stew in his guilt a little longer.

Driven by a strange compulsion, or perhaps the pity he might feel for a wounded animal, Caleb joined his brother at the hearth. Tucker stood there, seemingly ignorant of the dust and ash that coated his clothing. Why had he claimed the floor instead of the spare room, or even the couch?

"She is a remarkable woman. To have endured what she has and remain unsullied..." Tucker's words trailed off.

The hard shell protecting Caleb's heart developed a tiny, hairline fracture. "Then you finally see her worth." He studied his brother. "The beauty of the woman within."

"I admit I could not see it. Not at first." Tucker sighed. "I blamed her for everything that happened to you. And the soul marks? I could see naught but that she was a murderer. But now—"

A pounding at the door interrupted Tucker, to Caleb's dismay. He found himself wanting to hear the entirety of his brother's confession. He glanced at Tucker, hoping he would continue, but the knocking began again in earnest.

Sela entered the living room in her dressing gown.

Unease filtered through his regret. Going to the window, Caleb checked for miscreants and soldiers before opening the door.

Ross Bryant staggered across the threshold. Behind him, his horse was tethered to the rail and caked with foamy mud, as if he'd ridden from the other side of Belladonna.

If Ross was surprised to see Tucker, he didn't show it. "Have you not heard, Alexanders?"

"Heard what?" Caleb studied the faintly lightening sky behind him. "'Tis not even dawn."

"The king—" Ross dragged in a ragged breath, then waved behind him. "Oh, 'tis easier if you come and see for yourselves."

The *boom* of a distant cannon punctuated the end of his sentence. Caleb, Tucker, and Sela hastened onto the porch, following Ross's pointing finger. Above the crown of trees that separated them from Belladonna's shoreline, Caleb glimpsed dozens of white blotches, flickering—nay, billowing—in the early morning breeze.

Ships, dozens of them—perhaps even hundreds. A whole fleet of warships anchored in the bay. They must have arrived during the night.

Tucker swore, and Sela gasped. "What are they?" she asked.

"The king has come to Azazel," Ross said between pants. "'Tis the entire fleet. The war with the mainland is over, they say—won by Eremia a sevenday past. Now, the king turns his fury on Azazel. He must know Lord Auberon has the prince in custody."

Caleb fought for balance. So much for the rumors that the king was ill and likely to die any day. "Then he comes for vengeance."

"Aye," said Ross. "For our reckoning."

Sela's heart clogged her throat while she dressed and then accompanied Caleb and the other men to the settlement. Though still dark, that breathless space between night and day where farmhands stirred and fishermen readied their boats, the streets were packed with people.

They had all heard of the king's arrival. The *king*, who had never been to Azazel, had suddenly appeared on their doorstep with the full weight of his army behind him. What would he think of Lord Auberon's management of Azazel? Of the lingering effects of Uriah Smith's reign of terror?

Many from the other settlements of Azazel had been drawn to Belladonna, driven by fear of Uriah's men. Their clandestine employment by Lord Auberon had awarded the pirates a license for cruelties the soldiers could not legally enact.

Belladonna's population had nearly doubled since Uriah's attack. The people brimmed with discontent. There had been more brawls, more riots.

And now, with the king's arrival?

Azazel's main settlement was a powder keg waiting to explode.

As they neared the cluster of taverns—where Ross said the people were gathering—Caleb drew Sela against him. "Stay close to me, my love." He eyed her with concern. "You're still not back to full—"

"I'm not going anywhere," she assured him. "And I feel fine."

It was true. The prince's medicine had returned Sela to nearly perfect health. If the king truly had suffered from an illness these past few years—the excuse quoted by his advisors for his frequent absences—why could he not take his own medicine? Did it not work on him?

The royal family was rumored to have gifts that ordinary people did not possess—healing and prophecy and the like. But perhaps, as with Magnus's shoulder injury, the medicines did not work so well on them.

As if by previous agreement, Tucker moved to protect Sela's other side. Ross disappeared into the crowd, muttering something about the white house. Despite the urgency of the situation, Sela smiled. No doubt Ross went in search of Briella. The closeness of the two of late had not escaped her.

"I saw the prince last night," Tucker said over her head to Caleb. "He was speaking with Lord Auberon."

"You *saw* him?"

"Aye." Tucker chewed on something weighty. Regret? Whatever troubled him, he clearly wished to keep it to himself.

Caleb pulled Sela so tightly against his side that she could feel the hard outline of his hip. "Do you believe he really is the prince, Tuck?"

Tucker nodded. "Aye, I do."

"Ah, but what can come of it now? If the king is here, he will have all of our heads. Azazel has caused him much trouble of late. He may wish to wipe us all out and start afresh."

Tucker swallowed. "I overheard Magnus tell Lord Auberon that he intends to make an exchange."

"What kind of exchange?"

"I did not hear the rest." The guilty look on Tucker's face remained in place.

A whisper of anticipation rippled through the crowd. Sela stood on tiptoes to see over the shoulder of the tall man in front of her. Caleb's hands came around her waist, and he moved to her back.

At the center of the crowd, a contingent of black-coated soldiers gathered, all heavily armed with swords and flintlocks, some of them holding torches. Within their circle stood three men—Lord Auberon, Magnus, and an older man Sela did not recognize.

The older man was tall like Magnus, but stocky, and his hair and beard were completely white. His queue was clubbed at his nape with a black ribbon. With such hair, he would have no need of a wig. A gold circlet atop his head glinted in the torchlight. Its brightness made a mockery of the gold stitching embroidering the edges of Lord Auberon's white coat, which had almost faded to brown.

The king? Had he come ashore alone, or were some of the soldiers in the circle his own men? Were the king's cannons even now trained on their location?

"Your Majesty." Lord Auberon bowed low to the king—so low that the lapels of his coat nearly brushed the muddy ground. "I must admit, I am surprised to see you here. There have been so many rumors—"

"Of my imminent death?" the king finished, raising a white brow. "Of my long illness? Lies, all lies. The work of several treacherous advisors I left to govern Eremia in my stead during my temporary absence."

Sela blinked. The king had been absent from the Old Town? Whatever for?

"As you can see," the king continued, "I am very much alive. Not to mention in perfect health."

"Very good, Majesty. I am beyond pleased. 'Tis good to see you in the flesh, though I assure you, I have everything well in hand, as always." Lord Auberon indicated the chains around Magnus's wrists.

The prince, so far, had not uttered a single word, and the king's gaze did not rest on him for longer than a moment.

"You do?" The king's dark eyes flicked to the elder of the Righteous. "Lord Auberon, I have heard many reports about this island you were appointed to govern. Some have even reached my ears on the high seas. Reports of riots, rebellion, murder, rape, pillaging."

Lord Auberon brushed something from his sleeve—an imaginary fleck of mud, Sela surmised. "The tyranny of the soulless, my king. Too long, they have had the run of this foul place, their evil unchecked and unchallenged by my predecessors. I assure you—in fact, I swear it on my own life—that this island will not be so wild once I am finished with it."

The king stared, unflinching.

Even though she knew the look was directed at the elder and not at her, beads of sweat rolled down Sela's spine.

"The Old Town has received your request for reinforcements," the king said. "I have a fleet of warships at my back. Tell me, Lord Auberon. What would you do with the evil that brews on this island?"

Sela's throat tightened at the king's words.

Lord Auberon's eyes gleamed. "Your Majesty, I am entirely devoted to your cause. Give me the use of your warships, and I will ensure talk of this island's transgressions never reaches your ears again. I will rid Azazel of its taint and cleanse it of its soul-deep wickedness. Say the word, Majesty, and I will be your sword, the keen edge of your justice wielded against all who deserve such judgment."

Murmurs of dismay rippled through the crowd.

"You would bring me the heads of the rebels?" the king asked. "The hands and feet of all those responsible for the recent madness?"

The elder's gaze swept the watching crowd and somehow, inexplicably, found Caleb and Tucker. "Aye, Majesty." His eyes snapped back to the king. "All of them." He pointed at Magnus. "Beginning with this upstart and imposter."

There was a long silence. The murmurs of the watching crowd slowly died away.

The king finally spoke. "And what, Lord Auberon, of the evil that brews within your own order?"

Thunder rumbled in the distance.

"Majesty?" Lord Auberon's perfect forehead wrinkled. "If you are speaking of the Alexander brothers, then rest assured that—"

"I hear rumors of my own," the king interrupted. "Of a representative of the Righteous who enacts justice without mercy. Who compromises with his enemies. Who scratches out his own sins while underlining the sins of others. Who, in his attempt to make others pay for their crimes, blots his own ledger with the red ink of innocent blood."

A film of sweat appeared on Lord Auberon's face. "Your Majesty, I assure you—"

"On my way here, I heard talk of an elder of the Righteous holding court in my stead. Now that I've arrived, I see only one man on this island who deserves to stand among the ranks of the Righteous. Only one man is deserving of their unblemished mantle."

The elder brightened. "Your Majesty." He looked halfway to congratulating himself.

"This man." The king pointed at Magnus. "He is the only one who deserves to live. He is the only one whose soul is not irreparably stained by all that has transpired on this island of late."

"B-but Your *Majesty,* this man is a fraud!"

The king's lips tightened into thin white lines. "You dare call my son a fraud?"

"Your *son?*" Lord Auberon's mouth fell open. "It cannot be true."

"Release him," the king ordered, "or I'll cut off your head and use it to adorn one of those stakes lining the shore."

A few black-coated soldiers stepped closer to the king, their swords drawn. Sela could see that their expressions were grim, their faces lined from hardship. These were faces of men who had seen battle, who had faced one bloody campaign on the mainland and would consider this petty skirmish mere child's play.

"M-m-majesty," Lord Auberon blubbered.

"Father," Magnus interrupted. He turned to the king. "I have already made an agreement with Lord Auberon. For all their sakes."

The king looked at Magnus, and his face softened. Was it Sela's imagination, or did his expression boast a hint of pride? "You are going through with it, then? As we discussed?"

"I gave you my word. There is no going back now."

The king swallowed, his throat cording. "Justice must be served in full. Hand yourself over to this man, and he will make you pay for everything. For all of them."

"I know, Father."

The king's proud shoulders drooped. "You gave him your medallion?"

"Aye, 'tis in his possession. You know what to do with it, of course."

The king nodded.

With one final look at his father, Magnus turned to Lord Auberon. "I am ready to fulfill my side of the bargain."

Lord Auberon snuck a glance at the king. "You cannot think I would—"

"My father will not interfere. Exact your punishment, Lord Auberon, and then we will have our duel. The Carver will determine who wins—and who dies."

Punishment? Duel? Sela clung to Caleb's arm, and he gripped her waist in return. On her other side, Tucker looked wan beneath his bruises.

The king turned his face away.

A smile stole over Lord Auberon's lips. "So be it."

Chapter Twenty-Two

One moment, Magnus was standing next to his father. The next, Lord Auberon's men dragged him away.

The crowd revolted, but not in defense of Magnus. Shoving against the soldiers, they went after the king, whose words had denounced them. However, the king's men formed a protective barrier too solid to infiltrate.

Lord Auberon remained behind to address the crowd. "This man, who you called the lost prince of Eremia, drives a hard bargain. Yet, generous soul that I am, I have agreed to his request and the terms of his surrender."

Two soldiers came forward bearing a heavy chest between them. Without ceremony, they upended it in the mud. Gold coins spilled from the chest until a mound of several hundred formed a gleaming pool.

What is this? Sela wondered. Magnus's ransom? Some kind of blood debt? Caleb had spoken of such things, but she did not have his knowledge of the laws of the Righteous.

"'Tis yours, people of Azazel," Lord Auberon announced, sneering at his subjects. "Do with it as you wish."

The people surged forward, trampling each other in their haste to reach what they must believe was some lost pirate treasure. A moment later, a man held up his lantern and squinted at the inscription written on one of the coins.

His eyes widened. "'Tis the coins of the soulless!"

At that, excitement swelled in the crowd. Many pressed close, shouting their names so they might find their own coins. Sela, Caleb, and Tucker were driven backward, struggling to stay upright amidst exclamations of glee or disappointment.

"Here 'tis! Constance, I see here! 'Tis my name!"

"Would ye read this for me, sir? I recognize the shape of my name, but I never learned the letters."

"Has anyone seen Samuel Clark?"

"Don't push! Wait yer turn!"

Amidst the fray, Liron found them. Caleb gripped his arm. "Where are the others?"

"Somewhere here. The men, that is. The women and children are back at the house." Liron glanced at Sela. "I lost sight of Thaddeus and the others while I was looking for you."

"Perhaps we could—"

Liron shook his head, and the light in Caleb's eyes faded. Liron kept his face angled away from any who might recognize him. "There are too many soldiers, brother. Every guard on the island is here, along with Smith's men. Nay, I'm afraid we can do nothing. From here on, everything depends on Magnus and the king."

Abruptly, the furor died down, leaving the area where Lord Auberon's chest had been upended looking as if it had been traversed by a mob of wild boar. Not a single coin remained on the ground, though many of the rightful owners would be dead. It was doubtful all had found their coins. Some seemed to be hoarding handfuls, carrying on a furtive black-market trade beneath the noses of the soldiers.

Sela scowled. Would they now sell what had been given freely?

Lord Auberon and the king waited, neither of them speaking. After half an hour, the soldiers returned, escorting a dripping-wet Magnus.

"Keelhauled," said Caleb, his voice hollow. "By all that is holy, they keelhauled him. Look away, Sela."

She couldn't. Her heart broke in two at the transformation.

The prince was covered in blood and mud, his clothes naught but shaky ribbons suspended from his tall frame. Beneath the rough weave of his shirt, more wounds oozed and bled. His misshapen shoulder appeared even more prominent than usual—or perhaps the joint had been newly dislocated. Blood streamed from his nose, his mouth, and his ears, and his hair hung in matted hanks. He was almost unrecognizable.

Beside Sela, Tucker shrank back. A woman clucked her tongue sympathetically, while in the arms of her neighbor, a baby wailed. An elderly man looked at his feet.

A single tear slid from the eye of the king. He did not open his mouth, though, or utter a single command. He did not raise his voice to summon the fleet of warships that lay beyond in Belladonna's bay.

Even though he could.

Lord Auberon mounted a white horse and drew his reins tight, forcing the beast to lift its drooping head. "Now, people of Azazel, we will proceed with the chief business of the morning." He snapped his fingers, and several guards surrounded the elder.

"Nay," Sela whispered as they drove the prince along the street in a southward direction. Where were they heading?

The crowd parted, and Magnus passed so close that she could have reached out and touched him. One of the soldiers struck his lower back with the pommel of his sword. "You move slower than an old man."

Thrown off-balance, Magnus stumbled and fell to his knees in the dirt.

Tearing herself from Caleb's hold, Sela rushed to the prince. She reached for Magnus's hands and looked up into his dirty, blood-streaked face.

Her breath left her with force enough to bend her double. Magnus had not only been keelhauled, though that would have been punishment enough. He had also been branded—not just on his hands, but also on both cheeks. The blood sheeting down his face had concealed the extent of his torture.

The degree of his shame.

Uriah had borne those very same marks, and he deserved each one. But this was *Magnus.* The man who had saved Sela's life, not once, but twice. The man who had loved her like a daughter.

Lord Auberon had stripped him of his soul.

A figure crouched beside her, his sun-browned hand outstretched. "You must fight this," Caleb said to the prince, his voice low and urgent. "'Tis your right—nay, your duty—to fight, my lord prince."

As if they reclined together in the sun, Magnus smiled, though his lips were raw and blistered. "And my joy to surrender, my son."

"You cannot let them do this to you."

"This was my choice, my son." Magnus did not take Caleb's hand. "In truth." The prince turned to Sela. "Remember what I said, my daughter. This is not the end."

Lord Auberon's voice sounded above them just as rough hands grabbed Sela, dragging her upright and pulling her away from Magnus.

"What is this? The soulless cavorting with the soulless in the mud?"

Caleb's fist connected with the jaw of the man who held Sela. He swiftly returned the favor. Caleb ducked, and the swing missed. The man raised his hand to strike a second time, but this time, Tucker intervened. He grabbed the man's arm and twisted hard.

The soldier screamed and let her go.

"Get behind us," Tucker urged. He propelled her backward into Liron's chest and stepped to Caleb's side.

At the same time, the truth of Magnus's branding was spreading through the crowd like a fever. Lord Auberon smiled as if he understood the reason for the sudden restlessness.

After Magnus had returned with Uriah's captives, there had been whispers that the prince would deliver them from the oppression of the Old Town, and even more so, from the tyranny of the Righteous and the priesthood. Perhaps, they speculated, the prince would even end the lots, allowing them to live their lives in peace and to keep their children. Some of them, Sela knew, were only drawn to Magnus for his medicines. Others were intrigued by his ideas or attracted to the controversy they engendered. Many, it seemed, cared for naught but their own freedom.

With a swiftness that astonished her, the tide of the crowd's opinion turned against Magnus. Branded and soulless as he now was, how could he uproot the very system that had condemned him? To them, it was the equivalent of asking directions from a blind woman.

Ignoring Caleb and Tucker, who both looked stricken, the procession moved past them, Magnus at its center. The people watched him, some stony-faced, some bereft, and others jeering. Fists clenched coins that, moments ago, had been so precious to them. Some even threw their coins at Magnus himself, their aim perfected by their proximity, the quickening of the crowd making them brazen. The prince flinched but kept his course. His strides were weakening.

Sela forced her way to Caleb's side. "Can we not do something? He is innocent! Lord Auberon cannot just—"

"Aye," replied her bondmate, "he can. If the king allows this, we cannot hope to stop it."

Helpless to do anything else, Sela and the others followed the soldiers. The sun edged closer to the lip of the horizon, bathing the eastern sky in pastel shades of pink and blush red.

Lord Auberon led the procession to the clifftop at the southern arm of the bay. With whips and jeers, his men drove Magnus up the steep incline. The king followed behind on foot, accompanied by his own contingent of soldiers. Lightning flashed in the distance.

By the time the crowd reached the part of the cliff where the crumbling outpost stood, Magnus looked unsteady. The soldiers surrounded the protruding lip of the cliff in a dense half-circle, three or even four men deep in places. In the center, Lord Auberon dismounted and faced the shackled prince.

Caleb pushed through the crowd, pausing when they reached the wall of soldiers. Breathless, Sela followed in his wake, Tucker and Liron right behind her. The guards formed a barrier between them and the trade winds that whipped at Lord Auberon and Magnus.

The sun nudged higher, streaking the sky with vivid arteries of gold amongst the thinner veins of red. Lord Auberon removed his coat and handed it to a nearby officer, while another soldier unchained Magnus.

This is not an execution. 'Tis a duel. Hope bubbled in Sela's stomach, and she remembered Magnus's words. *This is not the end.* Magnus had a chance.

Carefully, Lord Auberon rolled up his shirtsleeves, brushing another speck of dust from the hem of his waistcoat with a dainty gesture. He withdrew two ornate pistols from the velvet-lined wooden box a soldier offered him.

"I am a fair man, Magnus," the elder announced in a loud voice. He flicked a brief, nervous look at the king, as if he feared that the crowned sovereign of Eremia would intervene. "As we agreed, if you win this duel, you will go free. None shall challenge you again. But if you lose?" His eyes strayed to the edge of the cliff.

Sela gulped. They were going to fight each other to the death? She remembered the jagged rocks below, sharp enough to impale a man. The tide that would carry his lifeblood out to sea and back again in gentle, rhythmic mockery. The cliffs, devoid of handholds and treacherously slick from premature seasonal rains. The loose stones on the edge—

"Magnus will be a good fighter," Caleb whispered into her ear. "I have seen him in the fields. He is strong—and fast."

The ghostly figure who stood before them now appeared only a shadow of the man Caleb described. His shoulder looked dislocated, and the other arm hung at an unnatural angle. He had likely expended half his blood on the way up the mountain. From all Sela knew of keelhauling, it was a miracle Magnus had survived thus far.

"I don't understand why Lord Auberon would challenge the prince," Tucker said. "Surely the king would—"

"The root of Auberon's power is threatened," Caleb replied. "The very foundations of the Righteous have been challenged. 'Tis for the future of his order, and his own future, that Lord Auberon fights."

"'Tis hardly a fair fight," Sela said, and she looked at Magnus.

The elder of the Righteous was circling the prince. Magnus turned in a smaller arc, his frame tall and erect despite his injuries. Lord Auberon tossed him a pistol, and Magnus caught it with his good arm. The deft way he handled the weapon suggested that he knew how to use it.

"Here are the rules." Lord Auberon paused. Then he grinned. "There are none. On the count of three, we will discharge our weapons. If either of us misses, we must reload and shoot again. And so on and so forth, until a winner becomes apparent."

"Something's wrong," mused Liron. "I'm guessing Magnus's pistol is not loaded. Otherwise, Lord Auberon would not chance an injury."

Caleb and Tucker nodded in grim unison.

Sela gripped Caleb's arm, fearful he might rush the soldiers, but he pulled her against him, as if he knew it was folly. Her heart hammered in her chest.

Magnus was the prince. The son of the king, and a true son of the Carver. This would not end in death.

It couldn't.

Lord Auberon's chosen soldier began counting, and the men faced off. They did not go back-to-back, according to the rules of most duels. Their weapons were not even holstered.

On the third count, Sela's breath caught.

The elder raised his flintlock and fired. His movements were quick and precise. Clearly, he had been well-trained. Sela's eyes followed the shot's path to Magnus. She expected him to jerk out of the way as he discharged his own weapon.

He did nothing. The lead ball smashed into his chest, and Magnus stumbled backward. The grooves on his forehead deepened, and he expelled a gasp of pain.

Sela sucked in a breath. Was it a mortal wound?

"Fight back," Caleb ground out between clenched teeth. "Load the pistol and fight back."

Magnus raised his pistol arm, and for an instant, Sela's hopes rose. Lord Auberon was furiously reloading his weapon. Magnus, if he were truly armed, temporarily had the advantage.

The wind buffeted the lank strands of hair around Magnus's battered face and the painful angles of his body, but he remained standing. The sun had forced its way above the horizon and now bathed the crowd in pure gold, illuminating the cracks in the outpost behind them.

Instead of firing, Magnus tossed the pistol at the elder's feet.

Lord Auberon's mouth curled into a wolfish snarl. He raised his loaded pistol.

"*Nay*," Caleb gasped.

Sela braced herself for the shot. She felt Caleb's arm turn to steel.

But the shot never fired.

Magnus swayed, and Sela remembered how strong the trade winds were at the edge of the cliff. Did he remember too? He was close, precariously close to the edge, just as she had been the day she stood on the precipice. Lord Auberon had backed him into the farthest corner, as if he hoped Magnus would lose his balance and tumble over the cliff.

Lord Auberon's face swelled to a bloated, mottled red that matched the sunrise. With a roar, he tossed the pistol aside, reached into his boot, and drew a long, jagged knife.

Caleb tensed against Sela, and she knew he was remembering Uriah.

It did not take a seasoned soldier to determine that Lord Auberon's approach was foolish. Magnus could sidestep, and the elder would plummet to his death. Or deflect the blow and twist Lord Auberon around, using the man's weight and momentum against him, tossing him over the edge.

However, the prince did naught as Lord Auberon ran at him, nor did he make any attempt to block the blow.

"Move!" Caleb urged. "*Now!*"

The prince remained.

The blade sank into Magnus's chest almost to its hilt, and Lord Auberon's eyes gleamed with feral satisfaction. Sela heard herself cry out, and Caleb's guttural moan, and Liron's agonized yell. As if he feared what she might do, Tucker grabbed her arm and held on.

At the cliff edge, Lord Auberon said something Sela could not make out. His mouth curled upward, and she guessed it was some kind of jibe. A final insult.

Magnus looked past the elder at his father, but the wind tore the words he uttered from his lips, rendering him silent. His gaze moved to the crowd, the love in his eyes obvious. Did Sela only imagine it, or did the prince's eyes rest on her, Caleb, Tucker, and Liron for a moment?

He was still looking at them when Lord Auberon withdrew his knife and nudged the prince's body over the edge of the cliff.

It was finished. Janus bared his teeth in a savage snarl and surprised himself with an animalistic grunt. The whole thing had been too easy. So easy that he could have laughed.

Then he did laugh. Chuckles rolled from his chest like peals of thunder.

He turned to face the crowd, which stood in various shades of shock, delight, and outrage. The foremost of the watchers snared his attention.

Noemia.

The woman stood alone, her figure framed by two burly, black-coated guards. Her blind eyes seemed riveted on him, though none stood at her side to explain the scene. But nay. She looked not at Janus, but instead gazed beyond him to the cliff, where the would-be prince had taken his final tumble. Tears tracked silently down her proud face.

His heart twisted. She cried for *him*? For this imposter, Magnus?

She was a weak and foolish woman. She should be glad for him, her eldest son. For Janus. For this was his greatest triumph.

Turning away, he looked over the edge of the cliff, watching the frothy rocks below, waiting for Magnus's battered body to surface. After today, there was no telling what greatness awaited him. He'd challenged the prince and won. Why could he not challenge the king too?

The other elders would see the wisdom of making him their leader. So would the soldiers. Who else was more deserving than he?

Samael of Azazel was no more. He had died with Magnus Theodorus. Janus Auberon had taken his place.

After today, no one would ever again stand in his way.

Caleb sank to his knees beside Sela, his eyes wide with shock. Sela's veins surged with a mix of fury and indignation, and she forgot the futility of charging the soldiers.

Wrenching her arm from Tucker's grasp, she bounded forward, shoving at shoulders and backs in a bid to force her way through the wide trench of black-coated, white-fisted resistance.

Tucker came after her. He grabbed her around her middle, lifted her off her feet, and carried her back to Caleb through the heaving crowd.

"Let me go!" she shouted, shoving at his chest. "Let me go!"

He swore and hefted her higher, so she was nearly slung over his shoulder.

From that vantage point, she glimpsed what happened next. Lord Auberon leaned over the edge, gloating. The risen sun turned his queue to a river of molten gold. He scuffed the edge of the cliff with his heavy boot.

However, in his hubris, he had clearly forgotten the trade winds and the loose stones. As she watched, he faltered. His right boot skidded away from his left, and his arms pinwheeled as he fought to keep his balance.

He yelled, an exclamation that the mischievous trade winds snatched away, like a red fox stealing a white glove to dunk it in the surf. The soles of his boots gave way, yielding to steeper planes where they had no purchase.

As the crowd watched with equal parts of terror and awe, Janus Auberon, esteemed elder of the Righteous, leader and lost son of Azazel, disappeared from sight over the edge of the cliff.

Chapter Twenty-Three

The sun rose and set, and Magnus did not surface. Caleb and the others had watched from the clifftop for hours, while the king's men ran out longboats to search for his body. Caleb, Liron, and Ross had picked their way across the treacherous rocks to see if either Magnus or Lord Auberon had survived and hauled themselves from the water.

Lord Auberon's officers had rallied their men, who searched with equal diligence, if not enthusiasm. The elder of the Righteous was not well-loved, not even amongst his own kind.

Wearily, Caleb climbed the clifftop path a second time to where he had left Sela and the other women. Tucker and Thaddeus had stayed with them, keeping a lookout in case the prince appeared somewhere down below. Both men appeared as dejected as Caleb felt.

Briella peered over the cliff, while Liri stood huddled beside Noemia. The women bore signs of fresh grief, though Caleb knew that Noemia, Lord Auberon's mother, bore a double portion.

He took her arm, but she reached for his hands. Her fingertips probed the ridges of his brands. "Caleb," she whispered, "have you found them? Has the king—"

"Nay, Noemia. I am sorry." He squeezed her hands and wondered, not for the first time, how she knew him without the benefit of sight, while her own children knew her not at all. "'Tis nearly night, so the men have called off the search till morning."

The crowds had dissipated. Either stunned by what they'd witnessed—or perhaps daunted by the sight of the king's fleet in Belladonna's bay—there had been no more violence from them.

A single tear slipped down Noemia's cheek, and Caleb's heart cracked. This woman loved her son far better than Caleb loved his brother, even though Janus Auberon had done her great wrong. He'd kept his distance, when he might have provided for her.

Caleb put his arms around Noemia and let her sob against him. With a cringe of self-reproach, he remembered how months ago he had recoiled at Noemia touching his face. *How the Carver has changed me!*

Magnus had changed him. Caleb was no longer the same man, puffed up with self-righteousness. He was no longer chained to one particular tree, one single piece of truth, while the rest of the forest was uprooted and burned around him.

The prince had unshackled him from his pride. He had freed Sela from her fear and shame, and Liri, Thaddeus, and Briella from their guilt.

A wave of sadness flooded Caleb. Now, Magnus was dead.

No man could have survived such a fall, even if Magnus might have lived with the bullet and knife wounds in his chest. As for Lord Auberon? The elder was in peak physical condition, but the soldiers had seen him enter the water. Like Magnus, he had not resurfaced.

Both men must be lying in murky, underwater tombs.

What would the king do now? Would he have their heads, as he had threatened? An entire navy's worth of ships waited in the bay, their deadly cannons trained on Azazel's largest settlement, waiting.

Waiting for what?

"He is the only one of you who deserves to live."

Would the king let them live if his only son lay dead on the bottom of Belladonna's bay? If he chose to spare the people, would Lord Auberon's men hunt them down in their leader's absence?

"I had hoped," Noemia murmured against the lapels of Caleb's coat, "that the prince..." She faltered, then continued. "That Prince Magnus might bring my son home to me. But now..." She did not finish her sentence.

Caleb felt Noemia's hopelessness. He saw the same in the lines of Briella's face as she trudged away from the cliff edge. Without Magnus's medicine, she faced her own death.

Caleb saw it in the thirsty look Thaddeus sent toward the horizon, as if he knew it was not long before they would all crumble to pieces. Thaddeus's fragile strength had held the Remenant together, had built a place of refuge and safety—crumbling and peeling as it was—for those who did not want to live and die as Azazel bade them.

But Magnus had united them. Magnus had brought them all back to life.

Magnus had been their friend.

The prince's sacrifice had been in vain. The king, if he spared the people of Azazel, would go back to the Old Town. In time, the Old Town would send another elder to oppress them in Janus's place. The lots would remain. The blood debt would continue to be unfulfilled.

In a matter of months, everything would return to the way it had been.

As Noemia released Caleb, he saw Sela coming toward him. Roux followed at her heels, with Tucker and Thaddeus close behind.

Sela fell heavily into Caleb's arms. Roux sat at their feet, his pointed nose twitching like a dog's, his ears downcast. Over Sela's head, Caleb exchanged a look with Tucker. "Thank you," he mouthed. His brother had gone after Sela, when Caleb had been crippled with shock.

Tucker nodded. Caleb wondered at the guilt on his brother's face, for he did not think Tucker had truly known Magnus. Had Tucker finally realized what he had done to Liri and to Sela?

It was not until they returned to the cabin—the others to the white house—that Tucker sought him out. Caleb was grooming his horse, but the anguish on Tucker's face as he appeared in the doorway made him pause mid-brush. Carefully, he laid aside the curry comb and left the animal in the stall. In twenty-four years, he had never seen his older brother in such a state. Caleb might be the more level-headed brother, but Tucker was rarely ruffled by anything.

"What is it?" Caleb asked, leaning against the wooden frame of the stall for support, for the heart in his chest felt too heavy to bear.

Something between a choke and a sob issued from Tucker's throat. "'Twas for me that he made the exchange."

"For *you*? Who? I don't understand you, Tuck."

"The prince. He was there when Lord Auberon's spies dragged me in. They were talking about some kind of deal. I don't know the details, but Lord Auberon knew I'd been with Liri. By the Carver, Caleb, he probably knew about our children too. I...I refused to confess. Lord Auberon threatened me with death. He wanted me to betray Liri, but I thought of you and Sela, and I couldn't do it."

Caleb schooled his features into a blank expression. "Go on."

Tucker waded through the rest of the story. "And then, Magnus offered Lord Auberon some kind of exchange. Through it, he said, my debts would be settled. My *debts*, as if he knew about my past. At the time, I didn't think much of it. I swore to myself that I'd repay him for buying me a pardon. Money is no object for our family, and Father's business has been doing well of late. But now that I think back—"

A tear tumbled down Tucker's cheek. He looked so wretched that Caleb's heart turned over.

Tucker choked back another sob. "He told Lord Auberon that he would settle *all* of my debts. No matter the cost. And today, I realized that he didn't mean money. It had naught to do with riches. He meant his *life*, Caleb. He must have offered to take my place. You are all mourning his loss, wondering why he didn't fight back. But *I* know why. 'Twas because of *me*."

The sob became a gasp of pain. "I deserved my fate. But he never once deserved his."

Like a pair of deflated bellows, the fight went out of Tucker. He sank to his knees, heedless of the soiled straw. Caleb, gripping his brother's arms, went down with him. What had happened to this man, who had once been so fastidious with his appearance?

"I am nothing like you, Caleb. I am a thief and a liar." Tucker raised his face, a fistful of snarled copper hair tumbling over his pale, blue eyes. "I'm a coward and a murderer. That day I left Sela on the jetty, I might as well have killed her. I might as well have killed *you*."

Forgive him, Caleb. The voice in his head sounded remarkably like Magnus's.

How can you ask this of me? If you only knew...

But Magnus did know, Caleb realized. Somehow, he had always known.

Forgiveness is the true mark of the Righteous, came the gentle reply. *Have you not known that all along, my son?*

The inner nudge became an outright shove. After the mercy the Carver had extended to Caleb, how could he withhold it from Tucker?

"*They could never suffer enough to satisfy me,*" he had once assured Sela, speaking of Tucker and Uriah. As Caleb stared at his brother, he knew he'd spoken truly. His desire for retribution would never be satisfied. It had not perished with Uriah's death. And it would not die with Tucker.

"The prince knew what he was doing," Caleb said at last, returning to Tucker's earlier comment regarding Magnus's fate, since he did not know how he could manage the last.

"*This is not the end,*" Magnus had told Sela after Caleb urged him to fight. Sela had repeated it to him on their return to the cabin, though the words were accompanied by a dejected expression.

"Perhaps," Tucker replied, "but I fear he died for naught."

Was this the end? All at once, Caleb's own words swirled through his mind.

"*The lot was a divine agreement between our ancestors and the Carver. It was established and written into law by the sacrifice of innocent blood. Only by innocent blood can it be undone. The innocent party must be of royal blood.*"

Magnus had been innocent, aye, and he was of royal blood. He'd sacrificed himself. But what of death? If the king could do nothing, what hope did they have?

At the devastation in Tucker's eyes, Caleb finally found his courage. "On one count, at least, you are wrong, Tuck."

His brother looked up.

"You say I am nothing like you. That's not true. I am everything like you. Even before I killed Smith, I murdered him a thousand different ways in my mind. 'Tis only been recently, after Magnus restored my sight—"

Caleb halted, noticing Tucker's surprise. "We have a lot to discuss, I think. But I see things differently now. The entire world has changed. *I'm* changed. I've been studying the same page my whole life, and 'tis almost as if…as if it finally makes sense."

Tucker shook his head. "Your sleeve is not so sullied as mine. You said so yourself."

"Aye, I said that once, before I knew the extent of my own befoulment. But does not the lot teach us, Tuck, that 'tis the smallest of marks that deems us impure?" He flattened his palm, noting the scarred ridges of the cross that had once filled him with so much shame. In reality, the soul mark had first brought him to Magnus. Magnus, who had shown him the true meaning of sacrifice.

Aye, he *could* love his enemy. Why? Because Magnus had died for his.

Tucker's eyes widened in sudden understanding.

Caleb released a breath and said, "I forgive you, Tuck. For everything. Should you ask it of Sela, I have no doubt she will do the same." Still in a half-crouch, he extended his hand for his brother to rise.

"Do you truly know your own mind in this, Caleb?"

"Aye, I do. Wholeheartedly."

Tucker hesitated.

"We are brothers, are we not?" Caleb grinned. "We go down together, and we rise together." He thought of Liron, and the open acceptance the man had offered him. Soon, he hoped Liron would offer it to Tucker, as well. "My brother."

In that moment, Caleb knew Tucker had accepted his offer of forgiveness. Though he wore no gloves, Tucker placed his hand in Caleb's. The two brothers rose to their feet, neither minding that they smelled of manure and hay.

Tucker's eyes brimmed with emotion. "I have something for you. Something I should have returned to you a long time ago." He shoved his hand into his pocket and drew out a small object. It flashed in the light of the lantern. He pressed it carefully into Caleb's hand.

"My ring," Caleb murmured, tracing the cold metal.

"Lord Auberon gave it to me when I hoped to bring you back into the ranks of the Righteous."

Caleb smiled. He knew just what to do with it. Slipping it onto his finger for the time being, he embraced his brother.

The ease of old, the brotherly bond they'd once enjoyed, would return in increments, Caleb reminded himself as they returned to the cabin. *This is not the end of the story,* Magnus would say. The climax was not the conclusion.

The next morning, Caleb received a note from Thaddeus. Two corpses had washed ashore on the small beach near the white house. One was Lord Auberon's, punctured and battered, but recognizable.

The other body belonged to Magnus.

Sela was singing. Caleb could hear it from outside the room where she and the other women tended Magnus's body. A low, soft tune, more a lament than anything else, but the voice was hers. It washed over him with such beauty that it made him shiver.

He stood there for what felt like hours, listening to her song, wondering how in the depths of sorrow, Sela had finally found her voice again. The night before, Caleb had held her close while she drenched his shirt with her weeping. Then Roux joined her in a mournful howl, bringing Tucker running from the other room.

Caleb had done some weeping of his own in the horse stall, where he could lose himself in his grief. Sela had found him there, and for a long while, she'd held *him*.

For somewhere along the way, Magnus had become a brother to them. A friend.

A father.

The appearance of the bodies had obliterated any hope of their revival. Caleb attempted to shield the women from the sight, bloated with sea water and glutted with sand and blood. In the end, though, only the children were kept from the grisly scene.

But Magnus had been their friend, and young as they were, the children mourned too.

The soldiers had reclaimed the body of Lord Auberon and taken it away to be buried. Surprisingly, they allowed Magnus's body to remain with the Remenant, and so had the king. Had he allowed it because of the prince's brands, his soulless shame? Was the king even now preparing his vengeance?

The men had carried Magnus's body to the house, and now the women were at work, painstakingly washing and preparing it for burial. Tomorrow, he would be laid in the ground.

At the confirmation of her son's death, Noemia, burdened with sorrow, had drawn Jax close and kissed the young man's forehead. Caleb understood. She would resolve to follow the Carver, come what may. No matter the loss of her child, she would always be a mother.

The lament paused, and the door clicked open. Caleb straightened, hoping to slip away before he was caught listening, but the sight of Sela stilled him.

She closed the door behind her. "Were you listening?"

"How could I not?"

"It seemed something I could do to...to honor the prince."

"I have never heard anything more beautiful," he replied. "Where did you learn it?"

"'Tis one of Liri's old compositions," she said, "though the tune is of my own making."

Caleb nodded. It was the tune that haunted him. The words had been muffled through the door. He couldn't hide his surprise at her skill and his admiration at her humility. She was truly—

"Caleb." Noemia stood behind him. "I am sorry to disturb you, but I heard that the soldiers have buried my son. Down at the cemetery, near the docks. I wondered if you might escort me there so I can say my farewells."

His stomach tightened. He did not begrudge the dear woman her final goodbyes—the Carver knew she needed the closure—but Belladonna had grown restless since the deaths of Magnus and Lord Auberon. The officers had a tenuous hold on the situation for now, but it would take very little to rouse the settlement to violence. In addition, the king's fleet still waited in the bay. He had no wish to put Noemia in danger.

Sela squeezed his arm. When he glanced at her, she gave a small nod. His tension dissipated. He would trust her judgment.

"Of course," he agreed. "Though, we should be on our way. 'Tis afternoon, and I believe another storm approaches."

Noemia nodded. "Let me get my shawl."

"I'll come with you," Sela said when Noemia left.

Caleb tamped down a flicker of unease. He prayed the settlement would remain subdued, but he hated to leave the safety of the others. Even the cabin felt more isolated of late. However, if the king chose to punish them, there was no place they could hide. They were already soulless and exiled.

"There is naught to fear," Sela said, taking his arm. "Come on."

Not for the first time, Caleb hoped she was right.

A party of five made their way down to the cemetery, since Tucker and Liri had decided to come along. Caleb and Sela escorted Noemia between them, Caleb keeping his free hand close to his flintlock. Tucker, who seemed as tense as he was, did the same, his eyes constantly scanning their surroundings.

The settlement did naught but go about its usual business, even under the shadow of the king's wrath. By the time they reached the cemetery, Caleb had relaxed.

Perhaps Sela was right. There was naught to fear.

They paused beneath the hanging tree. A briny breeze stirred the corpses hanging in the branches, left there from a lynching three months prior.

Sela shivered, and Caleb remembered she had come ashore on Azazel nearly a year ago, at night. Were these bodies the first thing she'd seen? Not for the first time, he wished he had been there with her.

"'Tis a place of death." She rubbed her hands together and looked around. Then, her eyes alighted on a freshly dug grave not ten yards from the trunk of the tree. As if she too had seen it, Noemia accompanied them to the base of the mound, where a simple headstone marked Lord Auberon's final resting place. Sela read the inscription aloud.

Here lies Lord Samael Janus Auberon
Elder of the Righteous and Administrator of Azazel
We commend his soul to the Carver.

A pitiful eulogy for any man, but even more so for a man who had likely imagined his funeral to be a momentous occasion attended by thousands. It would not be long before gangs desecrated the gravestone or unearthed his body, for any officer who died on Azazel was never properly mourned or entombed. At times, the settlement men made effigies of the most-hated soldiers, parading their burning corpses through the streets before impaling their remains on stakes.

And Lord Auberon had been more hated than most.

Caleb slid his arm around the weeping Noemia's shoulders, and Sela hugged her waist. The woman had exchanged her usual garish colors for a gown of deepest gray, likely the darkest she owned.

No one spoke. They stood quietly while Noemia mourned the grave she would never see, for the son she had not known.

Caleb also grieved for his former mentor, wondering if he might have said or done anything to convince the elder of his error. In the end, though, Lord Auberon had faced Magnus himself.

He had chosen his fate.

"Caleb." Tucker's voice broke into his thoughts. "Do you smell smoke?"

Caleb looked up, sniffed, and frowned. Aye, there was smoke aplenty. What was burning? Leaving Noemia with Sela and Liri, he jogged the short distance to Tucker's side.

"Look!" Tucker pointed. "The ships!"

Caleb followed his brother's arm to the docks beyond, where flames licked at the gray curtain of an overcast sky. It wasn't the king's fleet. Those ships were anchored farther out in the bay.

Nay, these were the ships of Azazel's officers and merchants, which lay clustered around the docks. A schooner was alight, and as they watched, more ships fell prey to the fire. Screams reached them from across the water. There would likely be only skeleton crews manning the ships. If they were forced overboard, not all would be able to swim.

Caleb turned to find the women watching the scene. "Tucker and I must help," he told Sela. "Go back to the settlement and stay together until I come for you."

"I can help too." Sela gripped his arm.

Caleb shook his head. "'Tis too dangerous."

"People are diving overboard," she insisted. "I can swim. I can help them."

"You're afraid of the water." Though they were wasting time and he hated to remind her of her fear, he needed to make sure she was safe.

"I *am* afraid," Sela admitted, "but I will not let it defeat me." She held his gaze.

Caleb understood. He too needed to conquer his fear—his fear of losing her again.

"I'll stay with Noemia," Liri said quickly. "I'll keep her safe."

Caleb hesitated, then nodded. When Liri and Noemia turned back toward Belladonna, Sela raced alongside Caleb, joining Tucker as they headed for the docks. She kept up with them well enough, though her violet gown and slippers on the jetty's loose, wooden planks were no match for breeches and boots.

Even so, Sela did not complain as they entered the teeming, panicked mass of people. She ran directly into the screams, smoke, and flames from which others fled. Three of the largest vessels were beyond saving, their sails, masts, and rigging fully alight, and the decks an inferno of creaking, crackling timber. The crews who had abandoned their ships floated in the water around the blaze, some of them wailing for help.

Tucker helped a man drag a sodden, wriggling form onto the jetty, while Caleb shucked his boots and coat and prepared to enter the water. "Stay here," he said when he saw Sela eyeing her hem. She looked ready to rip the gown in half to enter the water after him. "There will be wounded to tend to."

She hesitated. Then she nodded, crouching beside the man Tucker had helped.

Caleb dived over the side of the jetty. He surfaced quickly, thankful that part of his training had included learning to swim. In his peripheral vision, he saw his brother, sans boots, follow him into the bay.

Caleb launched into a flurry of quick strokes and reached the first ailing marine within seconds. The man was barely afloat, no thanks in part to the heavy black coat he wore. He probably hadn't thought to kick off his boots when he entered the water.

"Hold on," Caleb yelled, and the marine's eyes widened. Fortunately, he didn't panic.

Treading water, Caleb directed the man to drag off his coat and then float on his back. Clenching a fistful of the marine's shirt, he tugged him toward the jetty. By the time he reached it, Tucker was there with his own drenched rat. Sela and several others leaned over to haul the man to safety.

Caleb glanced around and gaped. The king's soldiers! They too were hauling drowning sailors into their longboats, and even diving into the water. After everything Azazel had done to his only child, was the king still such an advocate for mercy?

Caleb intercepted Sela's gaze before returning to the sea. Time was of the essence, for even the strongest swimmers could not last forever, and his own strength would give out soon enough. He hoped they'd had the sense to grab something to keep them afloat before they left the ship.

The next marine was less calm. He thrashed in the water like a flailing infant, despite clinging to a large, empty barrel and in no imminent danger of drowning. He refused to take off his coat, eyeing Caleb's hands with distaste.

"Don't you touch me," he snarled. "Do you think I cannot see that you are branded?"

Never mind that they were both condemned men in the eyes of the king. "'Tis a matter of life and death," Caleb said between strokes. "Let me help you. I can tug you to safety, as I did your friend."

"Pah!" came the reply.

Caleb left him, knowing there were others in need of saving.

Half an hour later, he pulled himself and the last sailor from the water. The marine he'd rescued sobbed his thanks between kisses to the wooden planks. The man who'd refused Caleb's help was being hauled to safety by two of the king's soldiers. He seemed frail.

"Caleb!" Sela fell to her knees in front of him and tucked a blanket around his shoulders. "You're soaked through."

He pulled her against him, grinning when his slick hair dampened her cheek. "So are you."

Tucker appeared as sopping wet as Caleb and no less tired. But his eyes were alight. "'Tis not only these ships that burn, brother. The fort is also on fire."

"The fort?" Caleb pulled Sela to her feet, handed her the blanket, and strode down the jetty toward the beach, until the fort came into view. The others followed more slowly. Sure enough, thick plumes of smoke rose from the wooden structure, and Caleb registered the acrid tang of gunpowder. Gunshots and screams echoed across the water like splintered glass.

His heart faltered. "Belladonna is under attack."

"Aye," said a familiar voice behind him. "I thought I'd come back for a visit."

Tucker cursed, and Sela yelped.

Caleb felt the blood drain from his face. *It cannot be.*
He whirled.
Uriah Smith.

Chapter Twenty-Four

"**I** killed you," Caleb exclaimed in shock. "You were dead."

Smith smiled, the twin depressions in his cheeks making a mockery of Caleb's words. "In the future, you might want to stay until I am *truly* dead."

Caleb *had* returned to the site of the murder, only to find Smith's body gone. He had concluded that Smith's men—or Lord Auberon's—had found him, since the men had been working together.

Had Magnus known the pirate lived, when Caleb confessed to Smith's murder? If so, why had the prince not warned him?

In his periphery, Caleb saw Tucker standing beside Sela, who stood rigid with fear. Six or seven yards separated Caleb from them, twice the distance from him to Smith. This time, Caleb stood between the pirate and the people he loved most.

Smith looked at Sela. "You look beautiful, my dear. Far more beautiful than when you were in my possession. Perhaps I should steal you a second time."

"You will never touch her again." Caleb groped at his belt, only to realize that his pistol and sword were next to his boots. He had removed them before diving into the bay.

Caleb cursed his folly. He did not even have his knife.

Smith laughed. "Your passion is admirable, boy, but rather misguided. Here on Azazel, men have learned to bond with plain women. Perhaps you'd do best to follow their example." His gaze flicked to Tucker. "You and your brother both."

"How are you alive? I stabbed you in the chest."

"Aye, you did," Smith admitted. "If I hadn't been carrying a ledger from Auberon within my coat pockets, which bore the brunt of your attack, you *would* have killed me." His expression soured. "My fate remained uncertain for a long while, even after my men came for me. Your knife is sharp, Alexander." He drew a blade from within the folds of his coat.

Caleb recognized it as his own knife. "Your business is with me." He did not look at Sela. "You will leave my bondmate and my brother alone."

"Perhaps," Smith replied slyly. "'Twould depend on your reflexes, would it not?"

Caleb thought of Magnus. "'Tis not too late to turn from this life of evil, Uriah. Have you not heard of the prince?"

"What has he to do with anything?"

"He has to do with *everything*." Caleb swallowed his fear. "You have a soul. You always have. Do not place it in jeopardy by taking from others to suit yourself."

"Oh? What have I to fear? You and your brother? Neither of you are armed."

"The Carver will repay. He will repay you for every deed you ever performed, for good or ill. Unless you seek His forgiveness."

"Spare me the sermon, Alexander." The pirate's eyes turned hard. "'Tis the last-ditch effort of a man fighting for his life. You would do better to beg for *your* soul."

"I have no fear for my soul, Uriah." At least, not any more than he had before he was branded.

"Even if I kill you now?"

Caleb widened his stance and lifted his shoulders. "Even if you kill me now." He heard Sela's gasp and a brief scuffle. He guessed she'd tried to come to his aid, only to be restrained by Tucker. He mentally thanked his brother for his intervention. "Your reign of terror is over."

"Nay, 'tis only beginning." With the hand that held his flintlock, Uriah gestured toward Belladonna. "The fort burns, and the soldiers will burn with it. When that is done, we will wage war on the king's ships. Azazel will be a nation and power in its own right, if 'tis the last thing I do."

The pirate was completely mad! What hope had Smith to overcome the might of Eremia—which had already defeated the mainland countries—with barely a few hundred men? And with many of Azazel's ships now burned to splinters? With rebellion brewing, it was more likely that the king's cannons would pummel Belladonna until not a thing, living or inanimate, remained.

Rain began to fall, and thunder grumbled in the distance. Caleb felt Smith's rising uneasiness. The storms in this part of the world came on suddenly, so swiftly that while working in the fields Caleb had frequently been soaked through as he ran for cover.

A hot rain would descend, thick and sticky, sizzling against the steaming earth, draining away from sight before he could blink five times in succession. The storm that came now clearly intended to linger. The rain swelled to an all-out deluge, and soon the pirate was drenched.

Uriah stiffened. He lost his smile, and his mouth turned down. The twin dimples vanished, and his flintlock hung limply at his side.

"'Tis finished, Uriah," Caleb said. "With the king here, your rule of this island is at an end."

The pirate turned to face him. "If 'tis true, Alexander, then I will take you with me." He raised his flintlock.

Caleb prepared to dive to the side, but Uriah's arm swerved to the right. Caleb spun in time to see Tucker knock Sela to the jetty. He covered her with his body and twisted in midair, so that he bore the brunt of the fall. They fell close to the edge, rolled, and disappeared over the side with a splash.

Uriah growled, cursed, and holstered his double-barreled pistol. The powder must be too wet to fire a second time. He glanced at the sky, muttered, and spun in a tight pirouette before hightailing it down the jetty toward Belladonna.

Coward. Caleb ran to the edge of the jetty and dropped to his knees. Just as he was preparing to enter the water after his bond-mate and brother, Tucker stood in the shallows, a dripping Sela in his arms. Both appeared uninjured.

"Go after him, Caleb," Tucker said. "I'll stay with Sela. He must not escape this time."

Avoiding Sela's eyes, Caleb paused briefly to collect his boots and sword—the flintlock was probably useless—before sprinting down the jetty in search of Uriah.

Aye, this time he would not escape.

Tucker lifted Sela onto the jetty and hauled himself after her with a grunt of pain.

Sela gasped at the red seeping through his shirt. "Tucker! You've been shot!" Half of his upper back was also wet with blood, centered around a gaping wound below his shoulder.

Sela clamped down on her fear for Caleb's safety and focused on Tucker. Caleb would want her to see to his brother before coming after him. Kneeling, she eased Tucker onto his side, probing the wound with careful fingers. Bloodied water—or watery blood—puddled around them. The rain had eased, but only slightly.

Tucker swore beneath his breath and jerked away from her. "Easy, Sela. 'Tis no more than a flesh wound."

"Keep still." Retrieving Caleb's waistcoat from where he'd partially undressed, she pressed it tightly against the wound.

Tucker expelled another curse, chewing his lip. His face contorted with agony.

"I thought you sons of the Righteous were raised with only praises on your lips."

A grim smile appeared on his pale face. "And I thought Caleb had finally found a woman with a tongue as sweet as his own."

Aye, sarcasm would keep Tucker conscious. Other things must be said, however, should his wound prove mortal. Maintaining pressure on the site, she peered into his eyes. "You took this bullet for me. Why, Tucker? 'Tis not so long since you wanted me dead."

"I never wanted you dead," he replied between gasps. Icy blue eyes met hers and flickered before closing. "But I did wish you gone."

"Then why did you save me? Because of your brother?"

"Magnus." His face scrunched, then he opened his eyes, revealing a softer blue, like the freshly laundered sky after a storm. "'Twas the prince who showed me a better way." He reached out, gripped her hand that rested against his upper arm, and let his head fall against her knees. He squeezed her fingers. "Forgive me—for everything."

His warm blood slipped against her palm. He held her hand without comment, not flinching when her soul mark scraped against his bare skin. She saw Caleb in his face, as she once had, but Caleb as he had been before Magnus, utterly lost and writhing in torment.

Could she reach out her hand, as Magnus had done to her? Could she do so even when the sight of Uriah had resurrected the demons of her past?

Aye, I can. "I forgive you," she whispered, "my brother."

The lines in Tucker's face eased. "I should never have left you alone."

"I was never alone, Tucker."

"How so? 'Twas I who stole Caleb from you, when you needed him the most."

"Don't give yourself so much credit. Had you not taken Caleb from me, I might never have met the Carver...and discovered the strength I found at the end of my own."

"Your strength?" Tucker squeezed her hand again.

"Nay. *His.*"

Pain ripped through his injured shoulder, shortening and shallowing every breath, but Tucker kept his attention fixed on Sela. "The Carver?"

Sela nodded.

Tucker gritted his teeth. He understood both more and less about the Carver of Souls with every passing day, but one thing was clear. Sela had forgiven him. He stared into the violet eyes Smith had sought to possess, and at last, he knew the truth.

Uriah would never possess *her*. Not even if he captured her again. What she had within was not for any man to acquire, not even Caleb. She belonged—heart, mind, and soul—to the Carver. Everything else was a temporary loan.

"Thank you," Sela said, her soft voice so at odds with the pressure of her hand on his back, "for saving me."

"Had you been a man, Sela might not have stood at this clifftop and decided to end her life."

Caleb's words. Ah, but the debt was now repaid. Nay...forgiven.

"You're welcome." Tucker grinned. "Perhaps you might consider easing up on that wound as a sign of your gratitude."

"Not if you want to live."

Oh, but he did. He wanted to watch his brother's children—Sela's children—come into the world and grow to adulthood. He wanted to take Liri in his arms and plant kisses all over her face. He wanted to hold his children—even little Sela, who had wormed her way into his heart of late—and read them stories of the Carver that he and Caleb had first heard when they were boys. He wanted to be the man he had always hoped he would be.

Not just like Caleb...but like Magnus. And even like the king.

"A father knows the true value of sacrifice."

He wanted to live a life worthy of the man who had sacrificed royal blood for his sake. Sela's expression seemed to indicate that he, for now at least, still had the choice.

"I would lend you my strength, Tucker—my very lifeblood—if 'twould allow you to live."

Despite the agony of his shoulder, he raised his head. Had she really—

"Aye. I heard you on my deathbed. As I recall, you swore to love me as a brother. And there was something about me making Caleb shine?"

If doing so did not lance his body with daggers of pain, he would have indulged in a belly laugh. As it was, he settled on a chuckle. Aye, he could imagine loving her as a brother, the same love Caleb had demonstrated toward Liri from the beginning.

He patted her hand. "All right, then, *sister*. I will live."

Smoke from the burning fort seared Caleb's nostrils as he tracked Uriah. Thunder growled, but a flash of light to his left alerted him that the storm was nearly overhead. Water streamed over his hair and slid beneath his collar. Fighting to keep his breath, he gripped the hilt of his sword with grim determination, mastering the rage that sought to make him its servant.

Carver, help me.

He caught up with the pirate in the cemetery, beneath the hanging tree. He wondered if Uriah Smith was as weary as he was. When the pirate glanced fearfully at the sky, Caleb understood.

Uriah's head jerked around as Caleb approached, as if he'd forgotten he was being pursued. He held his sword in one hand and Caleb's knife in the other, but he looked, as Beck might have said, as limpsey as a cotton fish. The man who had terrorized the inhabitants of Azazel for years had been rendered mute by something as commonplace as a tropical storm.

Perhaps it was more than that, Caleb pondered. Sela had said that Uriah feared the Carver's judgment. "Smith."

The pirate shook himself and glared at Caleb.

"As I said," Caleb went on, "'tis not too late to cast yourself on the Carver's mercy."

The arm holding the sword stiffened. "Speaking as one of the Righteous, Alexander?"

"Nay. As one who was once as lost as you."

The dimpled smile returned. "Save your proselytizing, boy. I do not fear your Carver."

"Do you think that what you've done will go unanswered?" Caleb thought of Sela but kept his anger corralled. "The Carver will see to it that justice is served."

So would the king, presumably before the day ended.

"To your great pleasure, I imagine." Uriah tried for a nonchalant posture, but the furtive glances he continued to steal at the sky ruined the effect. "Yet, you spoke of mercy."

"Aye," Caleb said, remembering Magnus. "There is mercy, should you seek it with all your heart."

"Therein lies the problem," Uriah replied with a lazy grin. "I have no heart."

Without warning, he leaped forward, slashing at Caleb with his sword, who brought his own blade up just in time. Uriah danced away, then came at him again, remarkably agile for such a brawny man.

Caleb parried the blow and stepped to the side, delivering several of his own strikes.

The pirate easily blocked his strokes and smiled through their crossed blades. "You know, you are the last man I expected to try for my soul." He shoved away and attacked again, wielding his blade with such force that Caleb's weary arms throbbed.

"'Tis not I who tries for it." Caleb ducked to avoid a swing at his head. "'Tis the Carver."

"Well, since you seem to be on such good terms with Him"—Caleb narrowly avoided a thrust to his heart by leaping back—"you can tell Him that I have no interest in whatever He's offering."

Uriah swept his knife in a shallow arc, aiming for his torso.

Caleb jerked away, but the blade caught him near his left elbow. Blood slicked down to his palm, joining the rivulets of water from his clothes. He hissed and scuttled backward, shifting his sword to his right hand. Tamping down a surge of fear, he wished Tucker had come after him. He could have used his brother's blade.

The pirate's twin dimples deepened as Uriah came after him again. The ring of steel as Caleb met the pirate's sword was surpassed by the rumble of thunder overhead. However, something had lit Uriah's eyes, and he seemed to have momentarily forgotten the storm.

Blow after blow rained down, which Caleb met with his non-dominant arm, until at last, Uriah pushed past his defenses. As their blades skidded and shrieked against each other, the pirate shoved against Caleb's shoulder, kicking out his feet at the same time.

Caleb sprawled in the mud. Barely five yards from Lord Auberon's grave, he wondered dimly, *Will I share the fate of my former mentor?*

Uriah swung his sword in a downward sweep, a move clearly intended to cleave Caleb's skull in two. With both hands, Caleb lifted his blade at the last moment, meeting Uriah's sword mere inches from his face. Lightning flashed above the pirate's head, lending him a terrifying halo.

"Well fought, Alexander." Uriah's mouth twisted in faux pity. "But now, you die."

Carver of Souls, Caleb thought desperately. *Is this it?* His arms and shoulders burned, his elbow throbbed, and his breath came in sharp bursts. With both hands raised above his head, blood trickled down his forearm, dripping onto his face. In the distance, someone cried his name, but they were too far away to be of any use.

Carver, if this is truly my end, let Sela be safe in Your keeping.

His arms gave out.

A woman screamed, followed by the loudest gunshot his ears had ever registered. Light exploded overhead, intense enough to blind him. He heard a creaking, groaning, splintering noise, like a ship being torn apart in slow motion. Then a mighty crash, as if the earth had opened up to receive him into its muddy embrace.

Uriah crumpled as if he possessed no more substance than a vapor.

And darkness overtook Caleb.

Having left a stranger to keep the pressure on Tucker's wound, Sela came into sight of the hanging tree a split second before lightning struck it. Uriah crouched over Caleb, who lay on the ground, holding the pirate's sword at bay. Blood streamed down his arm.

Sela screamed, hoping to startle Uriah, just as lightning and thunder worked their fury. She dropped to the ground and covered her ears, watching helplessly as the strike hit the uppermost branches of the tree and raced down toward the earth.

An enormous branch broke away from the tree with a resounding *crack* and plummeted to the ground. Uriah broke its fall with a voiceless cry, collapsing on top of Caleb.

Sela broke into a run, chastising herself for not having come sooner. The tree groaned and shuddered. How extensive was its damage? She had seen trees scarred by lightning before, the bark peeled away in one long strip like the mulesing of a lamb.

Those trees usually remained standing. However, trees struck in their heartwood—the dense inner core where the hardest timber was found—did not fare as well. By the looks of the orange tongues licking their way through the trunk, it would not be long before the entire hanging tree collapsed.

Sela remembered the soldier's description her first night on the island. *"Rottin' from the inside, just like the soul of Azazel itself. An' like t' topple at any time, crushin' some poor soul on its way down."*

She shivered. The soldier's prediction sounded uncanny in hindsight.

Sela reached the men and stopped short. It was no use trying to save Uriah. A splinter the width of her arm protruded from the pirate's back. The rest of the branch that had felled him lay to the side, next to Uriah's sword and Caleb's knife.

Bile rose in her throat, and she choked down a sob. Had the pirate crushed Caleb? She sank to her knees, shoving at Uriah in an attempt to roll him off her bondmate. Finally, on the third try, he shifted, coming to rest on his back beside his sword.

Caleb lay unmoving, his face splattered with blood, and his partially unbuttoned shirt torn and muddied. A cry ripped from her chest. She crouched over him, reaching for his pulse with trembling fingers.

She heaved a sigh of relief when she felt his steady heartbeat. "Thank you, Carver."

He appeared uninjured, except for a slash near his elbow. However, she had no idea if he bore interior wounds or some kind of head injury.

"Caleb, my love," she whispered, cradling his face. "*Caleb.*"

When louder attempts at his name failed to rouse him, she glanced up at the tree. Several limbs swayed precariously, and the fire within the trunk had intensified. She had to move him *now*. She looked around. Surely, too much fallen debris lay about to drag him to safety. What if he was impaled by a tree branch as Uriah had been?

"Caleb, can you hear me? Wake up! I cannot move you alone." He was a fully grown man, and a tall, muscular one at that. He likely outweighed her by forty pounds. "Carver," she breathed. She thought of Magnus, who had saved her with a maimed shoulder. "Please help me."

There was nothing for it. Splinters or nay, she would have to drag him herself.

Hauling in a breath, she pulled Caleb to a sitting position by his wrists, which took more effort than she'd realized. She then maneuvered herself behind him, so that her chest faced his back. Hooking her arms beneath his armpits, she clambered to her feet.

How could she manage it? She had never lifted more than a quarter of Caleb's weight. Why had the Carver chosen her for this, a woman who had nearly died from the seasoning?

"Carver," she murmured again, "please lend me Your strength."

Grunting, she began dragging Caleb away from Uriah and the hanging tree, careful to avoid the fallen debris. She had moved him two yards before she had to stop to catch her breath. Her bondmate's hair had long since escaped its queue, and the long, wet strands trailed down his neck.

Behind her, the tree crackled. Above her, a small branch smacked against a lower one and tumbled to the ground not five yards away. No doubt larger ones would soon follow.

She had to get them out of there.

Sela bent over and grabbed for a better hold. She blinked in surprise when sudden energy lanced through her veins, more potent than any burst of adrenaline. In that moment, her limbs seemed to be made of iron. They moved two more yards, then five. Finally, she reached a safe distance from the tree. She sank to the ground, still holding Caleb.

Just then, the air filled with a cracking of timbers, like a thousand snapping bones. She watched, sitting on the ground with Caleb's head in her lap, as the tree collapsed in a fiery inferno, obscuring Uriah's body. The remaining dead branches burned with a vengeance, cremating everything in their path.

Everything Uriah had feared had come to pass, but not in the way he had expected.

"Sela?" Caleb stirred and opened his eyes.

Sela looked down. The rain had washed the blood from his face, and color had come back into his cheeks as blood returned to its proper places on the inside. "Lie still, my love. I don't know if your head was injured."

He did not lie still. He sat up, taking in first her, then the distance between them and the burning tree. "My head truly must have been injured, since it appears I navigated a substantial stretch of terrain without any recollection of doing so." He glimpsed the bloody, muddy streaks on the bodice of her dress, and his eyes widened. "Did you...did you save me?"

Sela nodded. "There was no time to wait. Uriah is dead. The tree was going to come down any moment."

"You saved my life," Caleb said in wonder, "though I have no idea how you accomplished the feat. I am no featherweight." Rain began to fall earnestly, and a large drop splashed off the end of his nose.

"'Twas not all me, Caleb. I asked the Carver for help, and He answered me." She reached for his hand. "I didn't see your sword," she added, "else I would have grabbed it for you."

"'Twould seem I no longer have need of it." Caleb was still looking at the burning tree. "Vengeance was the Carver's all along, for both Uriah Smith and Lord Auberon now lie beneath that tree, and not through any action of ours." He turned back to his bondmate.

Sela met his deep blue eyes just as he pulled her into his arms. He kissed her with a passion that never ceased to surprise her, scholar that he was. This kiss, though, surpassed all of the others and filled her to brimming with a stirring awareness of his love for her. If they survived this day, there was a great deal of unfinished business to attend to.

A throat cleared itself above them. Caleb broke off the kiss to peer up at his brother, who was studying the patch of ground beside them. "You've been shot." He set Sela aside and studied the bloody bandage encircling Tucker's shoulder.

"So Sela cleverly observed, brother. The bleeding has stopped, no thanks to your bondmate's rough doctoring. 'Twould seem it hit nothing important."

"You saved her life." Caleb glanced between them, his sharp gaze assessing the mirth in Tucker's eyes, though his face was still creased in pain. "And you've made amends," he added, looking to Sela, as if for confirmation.

She nodded, and Tucker grinned. "I take great pleasure in the fact that she now owes me."

"As I owe you, Tuck. Twice over."

Sela stared at Caleb. *Twice* over?

Her bondmate smiled. "Did you think I could not work out 'twas you, Tuck, who prevented the soldiers from killing me the night I was beaten? I knew someone had called them away."

Tucker dipped his head, his cheeks flaming. When he spoke, it was to answer Caleb, but his eyes flicked between them both. "Aye, I saved you, Caleb, just as I saved Sela. Just as Sela sacrificed herself for Cadence, and you for her, and her for Liri and both of us. Liri once told me there is no great love without great sacrifice. 'Tis true, you know. 'Twas for the love of a brother that I came to Azazel, hoping to reclaim what we once had without the interference of outsiders. But 'twas for the love of a brother—because I watched Magnus give his very life for a traitor—that I found the strength to give it up."

Caleb gasped.

Sela looked up, but her bondmate's gaze was not focused on Tucker.

The king stood on the other side of the cemetery, a hundred black-coated, white-fisted soldiers at his back.

The king muttered an order and waved his hand. The soldiers filtered through the gravestones toward them and the hanging tree that lay fallen behind them.

Caleb braced himself, squeezing Sela's hand tightly, but the soldiers didn't pause. They marched past them and on to the settlement beyond. To quell the pirates' rebellion once and for all?

The king came forward. Four soldiers followed at his back, carrying something large and rectangular. The king appeared just as he had the morning of Magnus's death, with his white queue trailing solemnly down his back. However, his eyes were underscored by dark shadows. Instead of his customary military dress, he wore ornate white robes, decorated with gold and scarlet trim.

"Caleb and Sela Alexander, Tucker Alexander," he said, nodding.

Caleb wondered how he knew their names. The king held something in his hand that glinted. When Caleb looked closely, he realized it was Magnus's medallion—the one Magnus said he'd given to Lord Auberon.

"Your Majesty," said Sela. The three of them bowed as low as they could—an easy feat for Caleb and Sela, who were already on the ground.

"You know where my son lies?" the king asked.

"Aye, Your Majesty," said Caleb. He recognized the object the guards carried as a stretcher. "He is being tended in the house of Thaddeus Gaskell, a prominent figure in Belladonna. The house lies beyond the fort."

"Will you take me to him?"

"Of course, Your Majesty."

The three of them led the way through the settlement, bloodied and soaked to the skin. The king's men were putting an end to the pirates. Passing shouts revealed that the sudden disappearance of Uriah Smith had thrown the renegades into disarray. Many of the settlement men, surprisingly, had gone over to the soldiers.

Caleb steered Sela, Tucker, the king, and his men clear of the few knots of fighting that remained. They collected Liri and Noemia on the way. They had taken shelter in a friend's house and were blessedly unharmed. When she sighted the king, Liri's lips parted. She clasped Tucker's good arm tightly, while Noemia—who, as usual, seemed to see better than any of them—gave a slight smile.

Fortunately, Thaddeus's house was still standing. The fort, however, with the exception of a few outbuildings, had burned to the ground, the pirates finishing what they'd started months before. Jutting out from the foggy hillside, the white house looked like a tomb, dark and uninviting.

Along the way, others joined the procession, but the party that reached the white house and ascended the stairs numbered only Caleb, Sela, Tucker, Liri, the king, and his men.

Liri tried to tend to Tucker's gunshot wound, but he shook his head. "Not yet."

Liri drew back, understanding in her eyes. Magnus had sacrificed himself for all of them, but the trade had been made for Tucker's life, especially. He would not leave the king's presence now.

It was nearing sunset when Caleb led the way into the room where the prince had been laid, awaiting his burial on the morrow. It was empty, Briella and Noemia and the others likely being forced to abandon their vigil in light of the attack.

Caleb grimaced at the battered state of Magnus's body, though the women had done an admirable job hiding the extent of his wounds. Magnus's bearded, branded face appeared noble even in death, showing an uncommon strength despite the disfigurement.

A tear slipped down Caleb's cheek. The king would see this. He would know. And when his grief turned to rage, what then? He had every right to destroy them all.

It was for Tucker that the prince had given his life, handing Lord Auberon his head on a silver platter. Why had Magnus not fought harder? Why had he not tried to reason with the elder, or others who might listen better? The prince had many friends on Azazel, even among Auberon's men. With the king's arrival, Magnus had no need to prove he was the prince.

A father knew his own son.

"Forgive us, Your Majesty," Caleb whispered. The king had not taken the empty chair beside the bed, but remained standing. "Death was a terrible waste of your son's life."

Caleb did not wish his brother condemned. He was forever grateful to Magnus for all he'd done. Not only for Tucker, but for little Sela and the twins. And for Caleb himself.

But at what cost?

The king motioned to his guards. Though they must have nearly fainted at the smell, they lifted the prince's body onto the stretcher. Slowly, reverently, they bore Magnus's corpse from the room.

Caleb looked to the king, who nodded. "Come with us, Caleb Alexander. All of you who are willing, come down to the beach below this house."

Taking Sela's cold hand in his, Caleb followed the funeral procession from the room. The king led the way down the stairs, walking just behind his son's body. The flash of his palms revealed smooth, unmarked skin—as unmarked as Caleb's had once been. A gold ring with silver filigree adorned the king's right index finger.

Caleb knew the pattern was a duplicate of the one on Magnus's medallion. When Magnus became king—if he had become king—he would have been given his father's ring. The final seal of his reign.

Tucker strode behind with Liri, the weight on his shoulders clearly deepening with every step. Caleb was dimly aware that Thaddeus and Liron had joined them, along with Noemia, Ross,

Briella, and Jax. A trustworthy woman from the settlement remained behind to watch the children.

A few soldiers followed, as well.

When they reached the beach, the king motioned for his men to set down the stretcher. He knelt beside Magnus, his magnificent robes pooling atop the sand. To Caleb's astonishment, as well as the rest of the watchers, the king reached out and took his son's lifeless hand. Unmarked skin brushed against the burned ridges of Magnus's soul mark.

What was he waiting for? Why the beach and not the cemetery? Waves pounded the shore, frothing and curling before receding. Caleb dimly recalled that he'd nearly drowned at this beach, after being caught in the deceptively calm current.

With great daring, Caleb approached and knelt in front of Magnus and the king. "Do you have medicine for him, Your Majesty?" As soon as Caleb said it, he wanted to kick himself. Sickness was one thing, but death?

"These wounds are beyond my healers' medicines," replied the king.

Caleb's heart sank to his stomach. So, it was impossible.

The king looked up, and a tear glistened in his eye—a tear that, as he tilted his head back, slid down his cheek.

Tucker stepped forward and knelt beside Caleb. "Your Majesty, 'twas for me that your son lost his life."

"For *you*?" The king set down Magnus's hand and gazed at Tucker. "Nay, my son, he did not lose it. To lose something is to imply one has no control over the lost item. Magnus went into exile willingly. He knew that, should he come here, he might never return to the Old Town."

Caleb stared at the king. "Then why would he come?"

"Because 'twas what we agreed," replied the king. "Azazel has languished too long, Caleb Alexander, Tucker Alexander, here in the middle of the high seas." He gazed past Caleb to Sela and Liri. "Magnus and I agreed something needed to be done. The lot could not be ended without cost, without consequence. The shedding of innocent blood established it, and innocent blood must end it, lest every soul perish. With one lot, the world began. And by one final lot—one man casting his coin into an empty chest, knowing 'twould be his name that was selected—the whole business of unabsolved souls would be finished forever."

Liri dissolved into sobs.

Tucker frowned. "I don't understand."

The king drew a breath. "'Tis the custom of men and women to bind themselves to unholy things, my son. To enter into Bindings that weigh down the soul."

Caleb looked at Liri, who must be thinking of her Binding to Uriah.

"And to tie knots that ensure one will never be free," the king said.

Caleb thought of Janus Auberon, the Righteous, and the rules that made it impossible to truly live.

"Only by binding himself to all your fates," continued the king, "could Magnus undo all those ties, not to mention the knots your ancestors tied so tightly. Only by binding himself could he set you all free."

"But the cost," said Tucker, echoing Caleb's thoughts.

Taking Magnus's medallion, the king bent and placed it around his son's neck. "There is no great love without great sacrifice," he said. "Don't you know that already, Tucker Alexander?"

The king stood, and the four guards came forward, wordlessly taking up the stretcher again. Silently, they glided toward the waves. This time, the king walked at the front of the procession.

Were they going to bury him in the ocean? Caleb stumbled forward, Sela beside him.

The king paused in the shallows. The water coiling around Caleb's ankles felt pleasantly warm. It carried no danger, sheeting forward and withdrawing just as suddenly, swirling and foaming around them, then abruptly retreating to recoup its strength.

Clearing his throat, the king looked at the little group.

"Is there nothing you can do?" Sela asked in a broken voice.

The king's gaze focused on her. "What do you expect, my daughter?"

"'Tis said the king has healing hands," she replied, though her eyes didn't drop to Magnus's body. "That the touch of a royal can restore someone, even someone beyond saving."

Caleb glanced at her. Kind as the king seemed, even now he could have her head for impertinence. "Sela—"

"Nay, Caleb. She is right." The king looked at her as a large wave hurtled toward them. "These wounds are beyond my healers' medicines, true."

The wave loomed closer. As it advanced, the gentle motion of the ocean dropped to a sigh, as if the entirety of Azazel held its breath.

"But they are not beyond my touch."

Chapter Twenty-Five

"This is not the end."

Why did those words reverberate in her head? Sela could see the prince's mangled form. Lord Auberon's corpse was already decaying in the ground. All Azazel birthed would forever be subject to death. The sun rose, the sun set, and the fates of men were like lengths of string. Some shorter, others longer, some hopelessly entangled with others around them, but always they came to an end.

'Twas the nature of life. A mess of unholy Bindings.

"A Soul, once lost, is lost forever. A Soul mark, once given, cannot be ungiven, hence the X placed on the palm during the branding, barring the way back to the body forever."

Father Monroe's words. They had always held a crushing finality.

When the king finished speaking, a rogue wave smashed against them. The warm, salty air was suddenly replaced by a cool wall of blue.

Caleb disappeared, along with the king, Magnus, and the four guards holding the corners of the stretcher. Suddenly, Sela found herself being sucked toward the horizon, her feet and hands swept out from under her as she was tossed to and fro like one of Caleb's gloves. The hem of her gown pressed against her knees.

Come to Me, said a voice in her mind, rich and full.

Who are you?

Have you not heard My voice?

Aye, she had, though it had been so long since she'd truly listened. If she were Liri, it might have sounded like seminary bells, throaty and compelling, with an impossibly long echo. Warmth was there too, like she had heard in her father's voice, before Liri was taken.

The waves sloshed against her like brazen drunkards, assaulting her from every direction. If she didn't find air soon, she was going to drown. She thrashed her arms and legs, thinking of the mountain cavern and tumbling down the river. Her foot struck a sandbar, but the current dragged her past it before she could take hold.

Wait, said the voice.

Was this the Carver's voice, or Magnus's, or perhaps the serpentine voice that had sought her death in the desert, and again on the clifftop? How could she tell them apart, when both seemed to crave her end?

She needed to find the surface, but which way was up?

Then she saw the light. It pierced the water like a thousand silver daggers, illuminating shafts of varying thicknesses, where sediment drifted lazily with the current. The light knifed the dark, until the space around her felt as warm as before, warmer than any bath she had ever soaked in.

Though Sela had no more breath, she remained there for several long moments, suspended in the largest sunbeam, basking in the filtered warmth as if she were a bear emerging into the sunlight after a long winter. She stretched out her arms, and the light turned her fingertips to gold, banding her skin with bracelets of liquid honey.

Where are you, Carver of Souls?

I am here.

A hand gripped hers. Then with a strength she had never felt from any man, it pulled her upward. As her head broke the surface, she looked for her rescuer, but she found herself blinded by the light.

"I have you," came a voice Sela remembered as intuitively as Noemia read the landmarks of a hand. She was caught up in a man's arms, and though the current had surely pulled her to where it was too deep for him to stand, he carried her out of the waves. There was no hitch in his stride, though the waves pushed and pulled at him.

When they reached the shallows, he set her on her feet.

The sun was setting, but Sela could see Caleb standing there, his face wreathed in an enormous smile, the four guards—sans stretcher—and the king. The man who'd carried her from the waves—

"Magnus." She fell at his feet—his and his father's. "Your Highness!"

He was the same man he'd ever been, dressed in the same work-worn, homespun clothes. Not the courtly dress she'd seen in the meadow, with a silk shirt and a white waistcoat trimmed with silver and gold and winking gold buttons. His shirt was ragged, his face still branded, and his skin still marked by numerous scars.

However, resting against the lapels of his coat was his medallion. By the dying light of the sun, it seemed to burn orange, as if it had been freshly forged.

On the beach, a woman screamed. Another gasped. Sela turned to see that Briella had swooned and was leaning heavily on Liri. Both women were trembling.

Sela drew her gaze back to the prince. "You were dead." Her voice shook. She studied his lined, bearded face and gentle smile. "I sat beside you, keeping the vigil."

"I *was* dead, my daughter. But no longer."

"'Tis impossible."

"Aye," he replied. He glanced at his father, whose noble profile was illuminated by golden light, even though his robes were dripping wet. "But as you said, the king has healing hands."

The prince came out of the waves. He approached Noemia, who stood barefooted in the shallow surf, the water lapping against her gray gown. Wordlessly, she stretched out her hands to his face as she had once done with Caleb, tracing the outline of the prince's features, and his scars, which she touched reverently.

Uriah had received a similar wound and not died, so Sela drew close to study it. Had Magnus been protected by some kind of armor, as Uriah had?

Nay, the cut on Magnus's chest was jagged and deep, and it was on the left side, directly over his heart. Even without Caleb to say so, she knew it to be a mortal wound. Had she not known the truth of it as she helped the others prepare his body?

At last, Noemia took the revenant prince's hands in hers. "I know you," she whispered, then repeated, "I *know* you. You're the one we've been waiting for all these long years."

"Aye, daughter. The Carver bless you for it."

"I don't understand," Sela said. "We all watched you die. Are you a—"

"Nay, Sela. I am no ghost." Leaving Noemia, he drew close to Sela, taking her hands in his.

She felt their warmth and roughness, just as she had when he pulled her from the waves. She registered the twin soul marks, cruelly burnt into his skin. She looked up and saw the brands on his cheeks, the edges of the marks reaching into his beard. He was Magnus, down to the smiling gray eyes she remembered.

But Magnus is dead.

"Don't fear," he said, as if he read her heart as well as her mind. "Come with me to the others, and you will see the truth."

She did as he bade, since Briella had now recovered enough to return to the white house. Liri passed Sela her shawl. She accepted it with a grateful smile, for she was shivering violently.

Those who'd followed them down to the beach crowded around Magnus. Murmurs were followed by exclamations and shouts of joy. Tucker appeared to be the most deeply moved. His face was filled with shame as he knelt at the prince's feet.

Magnus took Tucker's bare hand and raised him to his feet. "Rise, my son. The time for guilt is ended."

"You sacrificed yourself in my place," Tucker whispered. "You, a prince...for one such as me. 'Tis a gift I can never repay."

Magnus smiled. "'Tis a gift, my son, and as such requires no repayment." He turned to look at his father, then pulled the chain of his medallion over his head. "My father and I are agreed. I will not return to the Old Town."

Beside his brother, Caleb appeared stricken. "But Your Highness, the—"

"'Tis Magnus, Caleb. Do not fear. We have already discussed it. A new lot demands a new token. This medallion"—he indicated it with a nod—"will be melted down and reforged. All those who have no coin of their own will have one. The king will grant any and all requests. Their name will be written on their coin, so all will know it belongs to them, and only them."

"A new coin?" Tucker said, fingering his. "For all?"

"Aye, for all," said Magnus. "'Twill forever be a sign of the king's pardon, no matter the crime nor its magnitude." He looked at his father, then back at the crowd. "Since I am now an exile along with you, we are going to need a place of our own. Azazel will not do for us forever. I will go ahead on my father's fastest ship. With his help, I will find just the one. We will begin a new colony—a new Azazel. Any who desire to leave this island, and who request a coin from the king, will be given passage on the king's ships to the new land."

There was a long pause.

"And the soul mark?" Sela ventured, knowing the others were thinking the same.

This time, the king spoke. "'Twill be no more. Never again shall it rob you of your souls, or your children's souls, or have power over any of you. Today, you are all free men and women. You are pardoned of your original sentences, absolved of your responsibility as children of the lot. You will never be slaves again—only subjects of the king of Eremia, and of Prince Magnus, my son. And then only if you choose to be."

Caleb stepped forward. "But Your Majesty, the ships in the bay. The fleet you brought with you from the mainland."

The king's eyes turned sober. "You want to know why I didn't follow through on my threats and annihilate you all."

Caleb nodded.

The king looked to Magnus, and the prince rubbed one of the brands on his cheek. "My father, the king of Eremia, is a representative of the Carver—both His justice and His mercy. 'Tis because the Carver hungers for justice that the king will not allow evil to go unpunished."

Sela thought of Uriah Smith, and all his wickedness.

Magnus glanced at Sela, and his gaze turned compassionate. "'Tis because He thirsts for mercy that He made a way for all to be made right, that He conceived this plan. My father and I serve the will of the Carver. His will is always that His children might have life, not death. Life to its fullest and its utmost."

He smiled. "For mercy always triumphs over judgment."

Chapter Twenty-Six

It was Thaddeus who suggested they have some sort of celebration. He grinned at Sela and uttered a sly comment that all the prospective guests were already present. They had only to bathe and change their clothes. Most wore the stains of the skirmishes in the settlement, whether by participating in the fighting, or through tending to the injured.

"Oh, aye!" Liri exchanged an excited glance with Liron.

Sela understood her sister's enthusiasm. After all, Liri hadn't been present at Sela's Binding, apart from their brief meeting in the kitchen, and Liron hadn't been there at all.

They commandeered every scrap of food in Noemia's kitchen for the celebration. Somebody brought out a fiddle, which was quickly joined by another. There was music and dancing, not only among the Remenant, but for everyone who came to celebrate Magnus's return—soldiers and nightwalkers and captives from under the mountain.

The king declined to dance, but Magnus tapped his foot to the lively rhythm. When the children gathered around and begged him to join the circle of dancers, he did so enthusiastically.

"Has food ever tasted so good?" Sela mused to Liron. He had claimed the first jig with her and now whirled her around the living room, which had been cleared of all furniture. "Noemia's cooking is even better than I remember."

Though her tone was jovial, her brother sobered. Pausing, he nodded over her shoulder, where Caleb was speaking with Ross Bryant. "I have never seen a man brought so low by grief, as Caleb was when you were ill." Liron spoke so only she could hear, his green eyes unusually intense. "He loves you very much, Sela."

"I know." She had seen it in his face. If not for Magnus and the king, what would have become of Caleb?

A tanned hand appeared on Liron's shoulder, and they turned to see Caleb. "May I cut in, brother?"

She smiled, understanding. What they'd been through had brought them together, binding Caleb to Liri and Liron as closely as it bound him to her. There was more in Caleb's tone than a simple request for a dance.

He was asking, retrospectively, for Liron's permission to bond with his sister.

"Of course, *brother*." Liron smirked, though his eyes were as serious as Caleb's. "She is all yours."

Then Sela found herself in Caleb's arms. He held her close—closer than the rules of propriety normally allowed—and glided with her across the floorboards. The musicians began a softer piece, slow and dreamlike, and they could speak as they danced.

"You look beautiful," Caleb said, casting his gaze over her gown.

What did her bondmate think of her boldness—that she'd worn the dress from their Binding? Despite a hasty round of ablutions, her hair smelled faintly of the sea. The expression in Caleb's eyes, though, was more than encouraging.

"'Tis an extraordinary dress."

"Aye, for an extraordinary woman."

"You truly intended it to be such a color?"

His eyes sharpened, and she knew he understood her question. Did he really see her as worthy of it? White was a color that belonged to the Righteous. Of course, the king had pardoned them, but she had to know if—

"Aye. 'Twas my only specification when I had the dress commissioned."

Relief pulsed through her as she saw his peace. She lifted her hands to his face, feeling his stubble, and remembered what Liron had told her about the events that transpired while she was ill. That Caleb had been taken to the fort, interrogated by Lord Auberon, beaten, and then rescued and healed by Magnus.

"But Lord Auberon...Liron said he offered you—"

"He offered me ashes, Sela," came Caleb's emphatic reply. "Though up until that moment, I was too blind to see it."

"When Caleb Alexander realizes the Carver loves him just as he is, without anything else—or anyone else—to recommend him, he will finally possess the heart to love you truly, my daughter."

Aye, he possessed the heart.

By the time the celebrations died down, it was early morning. Sela blushed when Caleb lifted her atop his horse and mounted behind her, holding her sidesaddle. Roux sat beside Liron, clearly unhappy to be left behind, wearing what could only be described as a pout.

"I'll see you tomorrow," Liri had whispered into Sela's ear, followed by an uncharacteristically bold wink. "Or next sevenday, perhaps, depending on how long you are detained."

"Liri!" she chided, scandalized.

Caleb had started the whole thing, though, by asking that they return alone to their cabin, and in all honesty, she wouldn't mind the privacy. She and her bondmate had a great deal of unfinished business to attend to.

Her older sister smiled, bouncing Sela's namesake on her hip, as if in gentle reminder that Sela's own offspring might soon be forthcoming.

Fortunately, the ride back to their cabin did not feel awkward. There was much to discuss with Caleb, and he with her. It was not every day, after all, that the king raised a dead man and then extended a royal pardon to the entire population of Azazel.

When Caleb set her down after carrying her inside, Sela looked around, noting the flowers stashed in vases everywhere she looked. The cabin was a veritable riot of color. "Your sister has been busy," Caleb remarked, grinning. "Or do you think 'tis Briella?"

"Perhaps they colluded in their mischief." Indeed, the air between the two women had been clearer of late.

As for the cabin, the bedroom was swept, and the quilt replaced with a colorful new creation. In her heart, Sela blessed the women of the Remenant. How had they had time for such things?

"A new beginning," Caleb said from behind her.

She turned, surprised to find him so close. "There has been so much pain." New lines creased his face, and she knew what her death would have cost him. Magnus had spared them all of that...and more.

"Pain is but temporary, Sela." Caleb came closer and slipped his hands around her waist. "And there is great joy at the end of it."

Almost his exact words after he'd endured the tattooing ritual in preparation for their Binding. Though now, after everything they'd gone through, the words held even greater meaning. "Joy, Caleb?"

"Aye, and I suspect 'tis of a heavenly kind we are yet to comprehend." He traced a strand of hair down the side of her face. "Though I can think of at least one earthly comparison."

Her cheeks heated. "Then I take it you wish to break the agreement we made when you proposed bonding in name only."

He gave a slow smile. "Aye. I wish to break it." His voice took on a solemncholy air. "If you wish it also."

Her knees nearly caved in at the tenderness in his eyes. She knew this man. He was compassionate and noble, gentle and kind. He would be nothing like Uriah. She might have to banish the pirate and his nightmares from her thoughts, and all the more in the beginning. However, with Caleb's help and the Carver's, along with this new, easy transparency between them, she could do it. Her mind would teach the truth to her body.

"Whomsoever the king chooses to pardon," Magnus had told them, "may never again be accused."

She would never again shut either of them out. Magnus had seen the darkness in her. He'd likely known about Joss Brigham, and Molly, and especially Elsie, and he had not turned away from her. The prince had seen the worst of her cracked heart and loved her all the better for her brokenness. Now, her bondmate would endeavor with all his heart—with a scholar's devotion and a warrior's fervor—to do the same.

"Aye, Caleb," she whispered. "I wish it."

When Caleb woke late the next morning, he and Sela were not alone. She lay in his arms, where she'd fallen asleep the night before, and he caught his breath at her loveliness. The tattooed band of her finger rested against his chest, a sign the Binding was now complete. Dark eyelashes, and hair so soft it was all he could do not to run his fingers through it, as he had the previous night. Skin so smooth—

Abruptly, sunlight caught the glint of red fur, and Caleb started. Sela remained asleep, murmuring and curling onto her side.

Roux sat at the foot of the bed, fully awake and grinning, as if he'd been privy to the happenings of the night before and was prepared to sell their secrets to the enemy.

"When did *you* get here?" Caleb muttered. He could not stay angry at the fox for long, since Roux wisely kept his mouth shut and let Sela sleep. "*How* you got here, I will not ask," he continued, slipping from the bed and dressing. The fox's steady attention unnerved him. "Yet, it becomes clear to me that there are holes in this cabin I did not know about. Are you any good at hunting rabbits, at least?"

Roux gave a wide yawn in reply.

"You're impossible," Caleb declared and headed for the living room. He had other business to attend to. For as he lay awake in the early dawn, something had occurred to him.

He had retrieved his excerpts and found one of the passages he sought, when he felt soft footfalls behind him. Slim hands slipped around his chest, beneath his arms. A silky head leaned against his back, warm lips pressing against the nape of his neck.

"Is it to be the scholar again today, my love?"

He smiled, turned, and pulled her into his lap. His heartbeat accelerated when he realized she wore only the quilt from their bed.

"'Tis always the scholar." He kissed her lips. "But I wanted to show you something."

She followed his pointing finger to the excerpt from the Book of Souls, one of the oldest among his collection. "My name."

He felt her surprise. "Aye, though 'tis a slightly different spelling. Liron told me yesterday that you were all given musical names by your parents. Yaron—*he will sing*. Ashira—*I will sing*. Liron—*my song*. Liri, Cadence, and Sela."

He leaned back, holding her close. "The author of these passages—a poet and songwriter—gives glory to the Carver through many trials. Some of his writings are laments for the distress in which he finds himself. Some are full of pleading for the Carver to intervene. In some of them, there is this word—*selah*—a word we do not quite understand. It has several possible renderings. For some, 'tis used to mean 'forever.' For others, it means 'stop and listen,' or a direction for musical instruments. It may also have been used to mark a kind of musical pause—where the listener stops to reflect on the meaning of the passage before the song begins once again."

Caleb smiled at her. "This is only the ramblings of a scholar, my love, and I know not what your parents intended, but perhaps there is some deeper meaning. Some rhyme or reason. Something that might explain the years following our first meeting. A brief cessation of the music, while you learned the truth about the words...and why you sang in the first place."

He saw she was deeply moved. "Now that you have found your voice, perhaps 'tis time for you to sing again, just as you sang for the prince."

"Perhaps," she murmured. Her lips brushed against his throat, and he nearly forgot the Book of Souls altogether. Then she raised her head and smiled at him. "But though I am no scholar, Caleb, there is one meaning I think I like above all the rest."

"And what is that?"

The warmth of her love filled the cabin. "Forever."

Caleb watched his bondmate from across the tavern, his hand ready beside his flintlock. When Sela and Briella had decided to make another attempt to rescue Esther—bearing news of the king's pardon and his offer of a coin to any who would come to him—Caleb had insisted on going along, as had Liron.

While his brother-in-law escorted the women, Caleb had arrived early and chosen a vantage point that gave him a wide-angle view of the tavern. It was early afternoon, but the establishment was already filling with customers, along with the sharp scent of male sweat mingled with the yeasty smell of alcohol and the lingering, acrid tang of tallow.

While Sela and Briella headed to the new owner of the rebuilt establishment—Murphy had apparently died in Smith's attack on Belladonna—Caleb remained in the corner. Liron prowled the opposite end. He would have rather not exposed the women to unnecessary danger, but Briella insisted that Esther would never leave without them.

Caleb studied his bondmate with more than a little admiration. Sela had changed since her illness and Magnus's death and resurrection. Her fire had returned, tempered with a new wisdom and maturity. She surprised him with her eagerness to learn all she could about the Carver and the Book of Souls.

He smiled. Sela was everything he had ever wanted in a bondmate.

A soft hand on his arm dragged him from his reverie. He looked down, expecting to see Sela, only to discover that one of the tavern women had snagged his sleeve.

"Sir," she whispered with surprising boldness for one so young, "I wonder if you—"

"I thank you, lady," Caleb replied, detaching her hand from his arm, "but I do not seek company. I came here to help a friend."

"Lady?" She frowned, her honey-colored curls dancing on either side of her pale forehead. She blushed.

Caleb guessed she was less comfortable with the art of seduction than most of the women present. He looked into her eyes and recognized her. "Miss Esther Gray, is it not?"

She drew back warily. "How do you know me, sir?"

"My name is Caleb Alexander. I am bondmate to your friend Sela. Do you not remember me?"

The unease seeped out of her. "You saved my life that night. You and Sela, the night of the attack on Belladonna. Aye, I remember you, Mister Alexander."

"Caleb," he corrected. Looking past Esther, he caught Sela's gaze and tilted his head in a wordless summons. She hurried to his side, Briella and Liron trailing in her wake.

A guilty look crossed Esther's pretty features when she glimpsed Sela. "I am sorry, I did not—"

"There is naught to apologize for." Sela gave Caleb a quick smile. "You are just the person we were looking for."

"Me?" Esther appeared faint.

"Aye," said Sela. "We want to bring you home."

"This *is* my home," Esther replied bleakly. "I have no other."

"You have a home with *us*." Sela's tone was the same she used when reading her nieces and nephew a bedtime story. "And a family, should you wish it."

Briella was more direct. "There is nothing for you here, Esther." She reached out for the woman's hands. "Only death."

Caleb's gut squeezed. Sela had told him Briella was dying, and he had grieved with his bondmate. More than anyone, Briella knew the cost of the life from which they sought to rescue Esther. Briella had not asked the king or the prince to rescue her from her fate. Why not?

Esther clearly knew the full extent of Briella's tale. Her face paled, and she swayed on her feet.

"What's this?" a shrill voice barked from behind them. "I thought I told you women to get out."

Caleb turned, and his eyebrows rose. The high-pitched voice belonged to a man. Tall and bowlegged, he looked far more disagreeable than his smooth-talking predecessor.

"Mister Vilfort." Sela faced the proprietor. "You told us Miss Gray was not here. Yet, here she is, and she seems unwell."

"'Tis none of your business, Mistress Alexander," the man snarled.

His tone attracted attention from the nearby tables. Men looked up from their drinks, drawn like moths to the controversy, eyes flickering with interest. Some of the women looked more uncertain.

"Miss Gray does what she likes and is paid well for her troubles," Vilfort said.

"Then am I to understand she may leave at any time?"

Vilfort bristled. "She owes a month's rent."

Caleb slipped his arm around Sela's waist. "We will settle her debts."

"There is the food and the new dresses to consider."

"We will pay you whatever you demand in exchange for releasing her from your service."

Caleb felt Sela's astonishment at his words, but he stood his ground. Never again would he allow a woman to be harmed—not on *his* watch.

"Who is she to you?" Vilfort glanced slyly at Sela, as if he sought to provoke her jealousy at Caleb's gallantry.

"She is my sister," Caleb replied without flinching. "Her employment here was a mistake." He narrowed his eyes. "Are we agreed, Mister Vilfort?"

The man hesitated, grinding corn-yellow teeth together, then finally nodded. "You may not be so hasty when you view the final sum, Mister Alexander."

"As I said, sir. 'Tis of no consequence." Not only his money would free Esther, but also Thaddeus's, and Briella's, and even Liron's. They had all pitched in to help the girl.

There was also the king's pardon, which would cost her nothing.

Turning away from Vilfort, Caleb looked at Esther. Tears tracked down her ashen cheeks, and she gave the slightest shake of her head. "'Tis far more than I deserve, Mister Caleb."

Caleb opened his mouth, but Liron stepped forward, his green eyes filled with compassion. He held out his hand. "Everyone deserves a second chance, Miss Esther."

Esther stared at Liron, then at his unbranded hand.

He held her gaze without wavering, and something imperceptible was exchanged, invisible to anyone who had never felt such a bond with another human being. It was just as Caleb had felt the first time he locked eyes with Sela.

"Only a *second* chance?" Esther's lips trembled like the sky before a 'sooner.

"Or a third." Liron smiled back. "Or a fourth, or even a fifth. 'Tis the Carver's will that mercy be poured out on everyone willing to receive such a bounty. 'Tis through the king's pardon that all our pasts count as naught."

With painful slowness, her hand inched toward his.

"Leave now," growled Vilfort, "and you can never return, Miss Gray."

The prison warden's warning seemed to decide her. She slipped her hand into Liron's. "Aye. I will never return."

Liron's smile wreathed his face, and he nodded at her approvingly.

Esther headed upstairs to gather her things, along with Sela and Briella, while Liron accompanied Caleb to the bar, where they settled Esther's debts.

Caleb was happy to see the end of Vilfort, as well as the stares of the men and women whose attention had never left them. Even the music had ground to a halt. "I take it," Caleb whispered to his brother-in-law as they left the tavern, "that since you laud the Carver's virtues so heartily, you now believe in Him."

Carrying Esther's small bag, Liron grinned. "'Twas Prince Magnus who introduced us, you know." His gaze slid to Esther.

Caleb chuckled and watched Sela, who was deep in conversation with Briella and Esther. As if she felt his attention, she looked up and smiled at him.

Caleb nearly stumbled over his own feet. For as long as he lived, he would never tire of that smile.

The celebrations lasted for at least a sevenday. As each day bled into the next—days at the white house, nights at the cabin—Caleb recalled nothing but that these were some of the happiest days of his life.

Even some of the soldiers rejoiced at the prince's return. Many others in the months to come, Caleb guessed, would claim the pardon that had been won by the son of the king. They would also receive coins bearing their names.

At the end of a sevenday like none Caleb had ever known, he and Sela returned to their cabin, Roux trotting up the steps behind them. Belladonna enjoyed an uneasy truce, particularly between the soldiers and the settlement inhabitants. It might not last long, but everyone appeared thankful for the respite.

Seized by a sudden spirit of mischief, Caleb swept Sela into his arms and carried her the remainder of the way. The fox danced around his heels with such persistence that Caleb wondered if Roux wished him to fall and break his neck. When they entered the living room and Caleb dropped onto one of the couches, Roux flounced away through the open door, presumably to stalk a rabbit.

If foxes could huff, he would have.

"I suppose you're partial to that unusual pet of yours," Caleb remarked as Sela snuggled against him.

"I suppose I am." She grinned up at him. "Oh, but you were speaking of Roux."

He playfully swatted her nose. "I hope your sister doesn't give Tucker so much cheek. My brother isn't half as understanding as I am."

She stuck out her tongue then began humming.

Caleb and Sela had witnessed at least two miracles the past sevenday that would shape their lives for years to come. First of all, Tucker asked Liri to bond with him, and she agreed. They were bound together by Prince Magnus himself. Sela and Briella stood at her side during the Binding ceremony, and Caleb and Liron stood at Tucker's side. Liron had given his approval with little resistance.

The eyes of both Meriweather siblings were far from dry when Tucker gave his new bondmate a token of his love for her. He gave it not to Liri, but to her youngest daughter. Little Sela would bear Tucker's original coin from that day forward, having been adopted by him, along with her twin siblings. Tucker looked at Liri, and then at the elder Sela, and Caleb knew that what Tucker did, he did for the love of both sisters.

From that day on, there would be two Sela Alexanders, and Tucker would love each of them as his own flesh and blood.

"Two brothers bonded to two sisters," Noemia announced with satisfaction, and Briella had expelled a small, happy sigh.

The second miracle was not so widely anticipated or expected.

Though it puzzled Caleb, Noemia had not asked Magnus or the king for her sight. "I see better now than I ever did before," she explained when Sela questioned her.

Caleb saw her contentment and let the matter lie.

Briella, though, was dying. Thaddeus finally brought her to the king and Magnus.

The look on Briella's face when she knelt before the two royals was one Caleb knew well. An expression borne of guilt and shame, and the knowledge that she was undeserving of the mercy she so craved.

Caleb had felt it in the cave when he had first known himself to be a murderer.

Sela, he knew, had felt it after killing Elsie Smith.

Magnus did not hesitate. With a brief glance at his father, he placed his hands on Briella's shoulders, gazing into her eyes with such warmth that something broke and re-formed within Caleb. He saw the man he should have been when he first met Thaddeus and Briella Gaskell.

"You are healed, my daughter. Be at peace."

Magnus had his father's power? Caleb recalled Sela's words. *"'Tis said the king has healing hands."*

And Magnus *would* be king. He already wore his father's band around one of his fingers.

Briella wept, and Ross moved forward to comfort her, looking at Magnus as if he too saw him with new eyes. That night, after Ross declared himself, they all celebrated a second Binding ceremony.

Noemia made no complaint about the extra cooking, nor did the wounded, who remained at the white house, protest at the opportunity to enjoy more music and dancing. Caleb nudged Sela to join the singers, but she hesitated, though he did not know what held her back. Liri and Liron sang freely in her absence.

Now, the long sevenday was over, and Caleb held Sela in the silence of their cabin. He fingered his coin and thought over everything he had learnt from Magnus. Not all in the Old Town would accept what the king had decreed—or what Magnus had done.

In time, the old regime would attempt to reassert itself. The order of the Righteous would try to regain control. Once the prince sent word for his people, one of the king's ships would take them to the colony. The idea of a new country, opposite to Azazel in every way, made Caleb breathless with anticipation.

In the meantime, Caleb and the others must spread the word of the king's pardon. Men like Foley could return to Azazel, and more people would come from the Old Town, weighed down with the knowledge of their own guilt. Caleb, Sela, and their friends would speak the truth to any who would listen.

Roux sauntered back into the cabin, flopped on his side, and shifted onto his back. He closed both eyes and fell asleep, with all four legs suspended in the air. He occasionally expelled the vulpine version of a snore.

Caleb grinned. "My love, your pet grows less graceful with each passing sevenday."

"Perhaps Roux watches you sleep and attempts to mimic it."

He feigned an indignant look. "If my repose were truly so barbaric, you would not stray so often to *my* side of the bed."

She laughed and planted a kiss on his cheek.

Caleb leaned back, retrieving something from his pocket. "I have something for you."

"A new spirit of humility?"

He chuckled. "Nay, sadly not." He reached for her hand, pressing the object into her palm. "My brother pledged you his allegiance recently. And I would pledge you mine, Sela."

She unfolded her fingers to reveal his signet ring, and her eyes widened. "You have already pledged me your allegiance." She brushed her thumb over his tattooed finger.

"Aye, I have. But Tucker has his token, and this is mine. I do not know if either of us will see our parents again, or if any Alexander will ever return to the Old Town, but this is my promise to you. I will stay here with you on Azazel for as long as is needed. By the Carver's grace, we will grow old together and raise children...and grandchildren, perhaps. Because of Magnus, we will no longer fear the lot."

Enclosing the ring in her palm, she drew closer, wrapping her arms around his waist. His heartbeat quickened, as it always did when she was near. For the moment, though, he was content simply to hold her.

She leaned her head against his chest. "I love you, Caleb."

How often during their first months on Azazel had he longed to hear her say those words—and been terrified to say them himself? When the pirate stole her, he had not known how to go on, with so much of their lives in ruins.

Magnus had brought them together, and the knots that the Carver tied, naught could undo. Not the soul mark, nor the seasoning, nor even the end of a man's natural life. They were bound to each other, but more than that, they were bound to the Carver.

For love—and the Carver's love above all else—was stronger than death.

Eyes closing, he tugged her close. "I love you too, Sela."

<h1 style="text-align:center">Epilogue</h1>

C aleb shivered in the twilight, wondering if Sela felt the cold. She stood beside him with her arms crossed, watching the horizon as if she was determined not to cry. His gaze swept the group of Azazelians, wrapped in shawls and greatcoats, shifting their weight uncertainly, all looking as sober-faced as his bondmate.

A fog rolled in from the water, gentle waves lapping at the large wooden posts that supported the docks. However, the sun that shone so warmly earlier in the day had hidden its face from them.

Eighteen months had passed since he and Sela had first set foot on Azazel. Magnus lived on the island for six months, even after the king sailed away on an unknown errand. Some of the ships remained in the bay, but most of Eremia's fleet had left with the king.

"Will the king not return to the Old Town to restore order?" Caleb asked the prince.

"Aye, eventually," Magnus replied. "But the people of the Old Town have relied on the lot for a long time. Like you, they wear their coins as badges of their deliverance. They will not take well to the lot's dissolution."

Through a ship from the Old Town, they learned that Lord Brigham, Joss's father, had usurped the throne in the king's absence. The report of Lord Auberon's death and Magnus's coming—and most of all, the king's pardon—spread quickly. It was not long before people began arriving on the island, anxious to meet the lost heir of Eremia who had defied the power of the soul mark and abolished the lots.

Among the new arrivals came friends and loved ones, some of them driven from the Old Town by Lord Brigham's cruelties, others because they wanted to see their families again. Still more came because they wished to be under the rule of the rightful king, though they risked disgrace and might never see their loved ones in the Old Town again.

The first of the voluntary exiles to arrive was Captain Hiram Foley. He came with his bondmate and children, and Caleb and Sela were moved to see them reconciled to each other.

Next came Teodoir Gaskell, whose reunion with Sela and her siblings, his own children, and his grandchildren was enough to make a grown man weep. Caleb saw much of Thaddeus in him, and Briella too, and he was glad Tempe and Thomas would know their grandfather.

At last came Sela's parents, Yaron and Ashira Meriweather, and Sela's youngest sister, Cadence, who was a miniature of Liri. Caleb wept, witnessing his bondmate's reunion with her family, and her family's embrace of Liri after so many years apart.

Caleb's gaze strayed to Liron, who stood on the other side of Sela. Liron's intended bondmate, like Caleb's parents, had not come to Azazel. His letters to her, like Tucker's to their parents, had gone unanswered.

Perhaps there was hope for Sela's brother, though. Caleb had watched a friendship grow between Liron and the former night-walker, Esther, who stood beside him in the twilight. Perhaps out of the ashes of their mutual tragedies something new and beautiful would bloom.

Magnus, who had been making his way along the line, appeared in front of Caleb. In his peripheral vision, Caleb saw Sela bite her lip. At her heels, Roux whined pitifully. Though he clearly disapproved of additions to their circle, in light of so many new arrivals on Azazel, the fox had liked the prince from the first.

Sela darted forward and hugged Magnus, and Caleb was surprised that he allowed it—welcomed it, even. Then Caleb remembered. Though he was the prince, he was also the same Magnus they had known. He made no attempt to disguise the brands on his cheeks and his hands, which startled the newcomers to Azazel. They had not expected such marks to be borne by a prince.

Because of Magnus, the brand had come, with time, to be seen not as a symbol of death but of deliverance, and it was now worn proudly by many. Some scratched the soul mark onto the doors of their houses or stitched it into their clothing. Others with unmarked palms chose to be willingly branded, though such an action was not necessary to receive the king's pardon.

On the most humid of nights, when Caleb and Sela were driven outside in search of the breeze, they lay on their backs looking up at the Soul Stars, marveling that the soul mark had been stitched in the very sky before the world began.

"You cannot leave us alone," Sela said when she finally released Magnus.

Caleb understood her fear. The war with the mainland countries was won. Lord Brigham—Caleb refused to call the usurper *king*—would eventually turn his eye to Azazel, and they would know more opposition than the handful of people who had shunned them thus far.

Why the king did not eradicate all his enemies was presently unknown. Caleb suspected it was so mercy could be enacted in full prior to the king's day of reckoning—for both the Old Town and Azazel.

"I will not leave you alone, my daughter. One day soon, I will come back for you, to bring you to a place across the sea."

"Can you not take us with you now?" she persisted. "We wouldn't mind being part of the search for a new island."

"Nay, Sela. You have business here. But do not fear. When I return, I will take you with me. All of you. On the king's fastest ship."

Sela bowed her head. Tears sparkled at the corners of her eyes.

"Do you remember the meadow, my daughter?"

"Aye." She had told Caleb about her dream.

"Do you remember how we sat together in that place, and the peace you felt? How Azazel felt so much less important in light of it?"

"I do." She scrubbed her eyes with her sleeve.

"Then know that we will be there together again, Sela. I promise. On that day, there will be no more tears, for I will have wiped away the last of them." He smiled at her, then at Caleb, before embracing them both. For once, he was dressed in his courtly clothes. Seeing them, Caleb wondered how he could have ever thought the man an imposter.

As Tucker and Liri offered their farewells with tears in their eyes, Caleb drew Sela close, wrapping his arms around her middle and tucking his chin in the soft valley formed by her neck and shoulder. She trembled and leaned back against him, but her chin was set, her violet eyes determined. They watched as Magnus moved toward the docks, turned, and smiled at them.

Night had nearly fallen by the time he boarded his small ship. The last glance of sunset turned the sails to molten gold. Wisps of soft pink and gray trailed the ship as it moved into the dusk, guided effortlessly by expert hands, though only Magnus was aboard.

"What colors do you see, Liri?" Tucker asked.

A smile brightened his sister-in-law's voice. "White," came her soft reply. "Snow white."

Liron reached out and took Esther's hand. Tucker clutched his youngest daughter to his side, while he held Anwen's hand with his free one. Thaddeus hugged Noemia, while the blind woman latched onto Jax's arm. She was dressed in another hideous gown, but Caleb knew she could see Magnus better than any of them.

Sela's eyes misted. The Remenant had become their family. They would need family in the years to come as alliances shifted and changed around them. More would come, and news of Magnus would spread even to the mainland countries.

Those who came to Azazel would no longer find a barren desert, but a land of life and color, overflowing with love and truth. A land where Magnus's subjects were waiting for the new home he would find for them.

Twisting in his arms, Sela looked up into Caleb's face. She touched her hand to his cheek and smiled through her tears. "What are you thinking, my Caleb?"

"I'm thinking that I miss your voice...my Sela."

A tiny line appeared between her eyebrows, but then she nodded. Turning back to face the horizon, she opened her mouth and voiced the song she had shown him the day they learned Magnus must leave them.

A shadow danced in the whispering dark,
A voice from the future, a travelling spark.
But I did not hear, I would not sing,
For I waited for the end of all things.

Celestial jewels winked in a darkening sky,
And wind sated sails with barely a sigh.
Death had no bite, but life bore a sting,
In that place, at the end of all things.

Earth held its breath beneath a shimmering mist,
Rain on the rooftops sizzled and hissed.
But I could not see, and no peace did it bring,
For I waited for the end of all things.

A light in the desert, and hope at long last!
Gray pealed the thunder with a glance from the past.
But shadows drowned dreams, and to naught could I cling,
There at the end of all things.

Night settled over the barren expanse,
And no lantern could halt its steady advance.
The loss of the chosen, the son of the King,
And we had come to the end of all things.

A song began rumbling deep in the earth,
Declaring lost souls at last could know their great worth.
And all lying in shadows sprang to new life,

As a new day proclaimed the end of our strife.

And as surely I know the sun sets in the west,
The true King of our hearts is never at rest.
For at the end of all things, this much is true:
That 'tis not the end, because the darkness is through.

Caleb let the haunting melody of his bondmate's song drift over him as Magnus's ship disappeared from sight. Instead of loss, gratitude enveloped him. *How can we thank you enough, Carver? We are alive. We are redeemed. We are free.*

His children—Sela's children—would not be born into bondage. Their firstborn child, if and when he or she appeared, would never endure the lot. Aye, they would face the wilderness of Azazel, but it was a wilderness that no longer wielded any power—a wilderness they could endure together, with Magnus's promised help.

When the time came, they would set sail on the king's fastest ship for a colony, a country of their own, which would receive them with joy.

"How will we know the way?" Sela mused. "Our new home might be very far from here."

"That's easy," Caleb said. He lifted his palm to expose the soul mark. "We have only to follow the stars."

"The high priest carries the blood of animals into the Most Holy Place as a sin offering, but the bodies are burned outside the camp. And so Jesus also suffered outside the city gate to make the people holy through his own blood. Let us, then, go to him outside the camp, bearing the disgrace he bore. For here we do not have an enduring city, but we are looking for the city that is to come."

- Hebrews 13:11-14 (NIV)

Author's Note

I first conceived The Soul Mark Duology as an allegory of the story of Jesus Christ and an artistic transformation of the journey to the Christian faith, in the tradition of C.S. Lewis's *The Chronicles of Narnia*. It is, I must emphasize, an imperfect rendering, and thus exhibits creative license with several things (including the interpretation of the word "selah," which has not been firmly established by Bible translators).

I often think of the good news of Jesus, which Christians call the "Gospel," as being much like a diamond. When my husband proposed to me in 2013 at a deliciously foggy mountaintop lookout on a cold autumn morning after ordering me awake at a ridiculous hour, I was thrilled (and, I admit, a little sleepy), but it was only later, when the sun came out, that I appreciated the exquisite diamond ring he'd selected so carefully.

My husband actually proposed to me twice (though that's another story). Oddly enough, it is that second time he asked me to marry him—the second time he presented me with my ring—that I remember the best. All these years of marriage later, I still turn it this way and that (I'm a bit of a fidgeter). Each time I do so, I spy a new side of the gem's façade, and my ring sparkles the way it did when I glimpsed it for the first (and second) time.

My journey to faith has been no different. When I first became a Christian, everything seemed new and beautiful. I beheld Jesus's teachings with awe and wonder. *Love your enemies.* What does that mean? How do I love my work colleague who is giving me a hard time? How do I love the friend who gossips about me behind my back?

But with the passing of years, some of these beautiful truths lose their newness. In the same way that it takes a visit to the jeweler to clean and service my ring, and to return it to its original beauty and freshness, it has taken many trips back to the essential truths of the Christian faith to help me truly understand the nature of the God I follow.

As many have commented, sometimes it takes a dose of pure fantasy to show us reality—to illuminate once again, as the famous song goes, the wonder of the cross. And so, as a writer of Christian fantasy, I embarked on a quest of literary *jamais vu*—not to make the strange familiar, as in the case of *déjà vu*, but to make the familiar strange.

In writing The Soul Mark Duology, my aim was not to duplicate the Gospel story exactly, but in the true spirit of allegory, to rekindle your curiosity about an event many of us only revisit with glazed eyes at Easter and Christmas. It is my goal to capture some of the emotions and central ideas contained in the Gospel accounts so that you may see them—and even feel them—as if you are beholding them for the first time.

I hope that in reading Caleb's, Sela's, Tucker's, and Liri's stories, you may revisit the Gospel story with the same wonder you might have felt when you first read (or watched) *The Lion, The Witch and the Wardrobe* as a child and wished you could meet Aslan the Lion. I hope these books make the familiar sparkle for you as they shine light on different truths. Most of all, I hope they inspire you to read the story of Jesus for yourself, in any of the four Gospels of Matthew, Mark, Luke, and John (I took John's eyewitness account in particular as my reference point in writing these books). And in all the places where my rendering fails, I humbly beg God's and your forgiveness, and ask for a hefty dose of grace to cover any blunders.

Carver of Souls is my fourth book (chronologically) to date, and with heavy content in places, it was undoubtedly the most difficult to write. If you have a history of trauma, dear reader, it might be a difficult read. With this in mind, I made a concerted effort not to depict or dwell on the details of Sela's trauma, but to focus on the aftermath—the shame, guilt, and fear that arise when people are wronged in such a horrific way. For many people, it is these things—the emotional and spiritual significance of the trauma—that cause the most long-lasting distress.

However, as a trained psychologist, I do not intend to minimize the magnitude of recovery that must occur following such an ordeal(s), nor do I undercut the value of therapy and/or faithful, supportive family members and friends to help survivors learn how to navigate their new normal. I believe our loving God graciously places psychologists, counsellors, pastors, and other professionals into this world to tend our emotional wounds in the same way he places doctors, nurses, and paramedics to tend our physical ones.

While we live on this side of Heaven, our wounds (whether they be physical, emotional, or spiritual) will never completely heal. However, I believe that God is close to the broken-hearted and crushed-in-spirit (Psalm 34:18) and that He binds up their wounds. One day He will, as Revelation 21:4 assures us, wipe every tear from our eyes.

We have this promise—which has sustained me through a long, dark valley of chronic illness—that all of our present sufferings will hardly compare with the glory that will be revealed in us (Romans 8:18). We will, as Prince Magnus assures Sela, one day return to the meadow, and the Carver of Souls will be both our father, brother, and our friend.

And that, my dear friends, is what I'm hanging out for.

Soli Deo Gloria,

Jasmine

Acknowledgments

I honestly cannot believe that this, my sixth book, is soon to be out in the wild. The last few years have been a rollercoaster ride that I wouldn't trade for anything, even a majority share in a mango farm (yes, really). I'm so thankful for the opportunity to share yet another adventure with you—and to conclude yet another series.

As always, the most heartfelt of thanks to my readers. Many of you have read every book I've published, and keenly await the next installment. I'm so blessed and encouraged by your faithful support, even when I put you through yet another cliffhanger where a main character is in mortal peril (I won't do it again...well, I'll TRY not to. I gave you back Roux. What more do you want from me?).

Special thank-yous go out to the usual gang: the team at Mountain Brook Ink/Mountain Brook Fire for all their efforts in bringing this story to print; Miblart for their amazing work on cover design; my cover reveal and street teams for everything they've done to help this duology find more human friends. Thank you!

To my family and friends: you all bless me so much. A special welcome to my new little niece Audrey Elizabeth, who's about to experience the wonder of fictional worlds with the help of her awesome Aunty Jas.

A special shout-out to my dear friends and fellow authors Misi Troutman and Cathy McCrumb, who are some of the most spectacular people on the planet. Misi's help was invaluable in working out some major plot points in this book, and Cathy is my go-to person for weeping over all things writing and editing. Thank you both for being the most wonderful, kind, and generous-hearted friends. Your reward, should you choose to claim it, is ONE get-a-character-out-of-trouble card, to be used in subsequent book drafts when a character or animal is in mortal peril. More of these cards may be awarded in exchange for particularly exceptional cat memes.

A penultimate thank-you to my most wonderful and faithful husband, Dave, who never seems to mind our funds being employed in the acquisition of more books, exotic teas, and random Amazon toys for our cat, Simba. You never seem to be dismayed that you married an author, even though we're a somewhat terrifying species with a great propensity to burst into tears at random moments, mostly due to fictional deaths that are entirely under our control.

Lastly, and most of all, thank you to God, my Carver of Souls, who loved my soul even when it wasn't pretty. Thank you for the ultimate sacrifice of Your Son, and for the great Love that searches us out and saves us, no matter the wilderness.

Soli Deo Gloria,
Jasmine

About the Author

Jasmine's writing dream began with the anthology of zoo animals she painstakingly wrote and illustrated at age five, to rather limited acclaim. Thankfully, her writing (but not her drawing) has improved since then. Jasmine began writing her first proper novel at age fourteen, which eventually became her debut fantasy series, The Darcentaria Duology, which was published in 2021.

Jasmine completed her Bachelor's in English Literature and Creative Writing in 2012. Also a qualified psychologist with undergraduate and postgraduate degrees in clinical psychology, Jasmine's dream is to write stories that weave together her love for Jesus, her passion for mental health, and her struggles with chronic illness.

When she isn't killing defenseless houseplants, Jasmine enjoys devouring books, dabbling in floristry, playing the piano, eating peanut butter out of the jar, and wishing it rained more often. Jasmine is married to David, and together they make their home a couple of hours' north of Sydney, Australia, where they live to satisfy the every whim of their ginger overlord cat, Simba.

You can stalk Jasmine on social media or visit her official website at www.jjfischer.com, where she's always open to swapping good memes, talking about chickens, or complaining about Luke Skywalker.

Find Jasmine Online:
Official author website: www.jjfischer.com
Facebook: www.facebook.com/jjfischerauthor
Instagram: www.instagram.com/jjfischerauthor
Pinterest: www.pinterest.com.au/jjfischerauthor
Goodreads: www.goodreads.com/author/show/20763565.J_J
_Fischer
Amazon: www.amazon.com/J-J-Fischer/e/B08P12SJ8W

Also By J. J. Fischer

The Soul Mark Duology
The Soul Mark
Carver of Souls

The Darcentaria Duology
The Sword in His Hand
The Secret of Fire

The Nightingale Trilogy
Calor
Lumen
Memoria